David Fennell was born and raised in Belfast. He left for London at the tender age of eighteen and jobbed as a chef, waiter and bartender for several years before starting a career as a writer in the software industry. He is now a full-time novelist. David is the author of the multi-award nominated Sleeper series and the popular Grace Archer crime series. His sixth novel, *A Violent Heart,* won the 2025 Capital Crime Thriller of the Year award.

ALL
Killers
ABOARD

DAVID FENNELL

ORION

First published in Great Britain in 2026 by Orion Fiction,
an imprint of The Orion Publishing Group Ltd.
Carmelite House, 50 Victoria Embankment
London EC4Y 0DZ

An Hachette UK Company

The authorised representative in the EEA is Hachette Ireland,
8 Castlecourt Centre, Dublin 15, D15 XTP3,
Ireland (email: info@hbgi.ie)

1 3 5 7 9 10 8 6 4 2

A CIP catalogue record for this book is
available from the British Library.

ISBN (Hardback) 9781 3987 2803 5
ISBN (Export Trade Paperback) 9781 3987 2804 2
ISBN (Ebook) 9781 3987 2806 6
ISBN (Audio) 9781 3987 2807 3

Typeset by Input Data Services Ltd, Bridgwater, Somerset

Printed in Great Britain by Clays Ltd, Elcograf, S.p.A.

MIX
Paper | Supporting
responsible forestry
FSC www.fsc.org
FSC® C104740

www.orionbooks.co.uk

For Holly and Chris, and the beginning of a new chapter
in your beautiful young lives.

Prologue

North Woods, Central Park, New York

'Reapply when you've got more kills under your belt,' he said, and shut the door.

Six months later, his words still sting.

I'm standing by the old Huddlestone Arch, caressing the rough stone surface with my fingertips, like some pilgrim in search of enlightenment. Huddlestone is a marvel of late 19th-century engineering, constructed of elephantine, uncut boulders. It was given that quaint, benevolent name because the ancient stones appear to be huddling together. It has an otherworldly vibe. There's no mortar or underpinning, just gravity and pressure supporting the traffic on the park drive bridge above. Impressive.

I slip my glove back on.

I had tried to kill someone here last month, but that didn't quite go as planned. He was some old fart who had pranged my car at Walmart and then successfully sued me, claiming it was all my fault.

Rage burnt inside me.

He'd pay for what he had done.

I stalked him for weeks, keeping notes on his routine. Rain, snow or sleet, he'd walk here every morning.

One day, I followed him, having worked myself into a frenzy the night before. Taking out my knife, I overtook him under the arch and swiftly went in for the kill, but he was not as frail or weak as I'd expected. He fought back and kicked my ass good and hard. He'd probably been in the military. On reflection, he looked the sort. For a moment, it seemed I was finished. It took everything I had, but I broke free and sprinted across the park. Luckily, the rabbi disguise held – fake beard, hat, the lot – and no one recognised me. I'm not Jewish, but *Mazel tov!* kept echoing in my head.

If I wanted any chance of getting through those doors, I'd need to step up my game.

I signed up for self-defence classes and studied the attack techniques. I also thought it best to take backup knives with me on all my murders. You can never be too careful.

I sense that my moment is coming and look at the old arch. It's like the eye of a great dragon, the lid shaped by boulders, the dark tunnel of the iris framing the milky pupil. And in that pupil, I see movement. My heart skips a beat at the sight of a jogger approaching from the other side. I watch with the stillness of a hawk, evaluating its prey. Gangly in stature, he has an awkward gait and seems not to be running but . . . cantering. I've witnessed some 'classic' running styles in my time, but this schmuck is going for gold. The way he runs, all effort and no grace, like a man trying to escape himself.

He comes to a stop inside the tunnel. I swear under my breath, thinking he's about to turn back, but then he crouches down and begins to tie his laces. Relief swamps me.

I'm dressed in dark clothing and a rolled-up, black knitted balaclava that sits on my head like a beanie hat. I seize the moment and step inside the tunnel's gloom. Reaching into my pocket, I feel the hard steel of the filleting knife. It's sharp and long enough to do the job. I roll down the balaclava. I had sewn buttons onto the front: two large red ones with eye holes and nine small ones fashioned into a twisted smile. Disguises are important. I learnt that lesson already.

He's standing now and doing lunges with his hands on his hips. A memory from high school triggers me. Wendy 'freaking' Greer watching her asshole boyfriend lunge his tree-trunk thighs in the dining hall, of all places! I feel my stomach clenching. I was friendless, a loner and heavier than most of my peers back then. Uber bitch Wendy had bullied me mercilessly and loved to remind everyone that I had much bigger tits than she could ever hope to have. News got out that it was my birthday. As I carried my lunch to the table, Wendy encouraged her friends to sing 'Happy Birthday'. I was confused, but thought maybe this was a turning point and they actually liked me. As the singing finished, everyone watched my face eagerly. 'We have gifts for you,' she told me, a snakish grin forming on her lips. 'Now!' she cried. From behind their backs, Wendy, her friends and her asshole boyfriend showered me with cruddy, old, thrift-store brassieres. They hung over my head, shoulders, and lunch tray. I couldn't move. The dining hall erupted. The mocking laughter shook me. I felt like Carrie White at prom night when the bucket of pigs' blood fell over her head. I wished I had kinetic powers to make those fuckers pay. The best I could do was vow to get my own back.

And boy, did I.

I saw Wendy walking home alone one evening after a fight with her boyfriend. I had no plan, just a burning desire for vengeance. I followed her into the shadows, and when she stopped at the kerb to wait for a Greyhound bus to whizz by, without much thought, I sprang forward and pushed her into its path. There had been a lot of blood. I bolted, heart pounding, terrified, but at the same time, energised. I lay awake that night thinking about what I'd done. Wendy's death had been over in seconds, but something inside me had shifted. I felt no remorse or regret, only a heightened rush of triumph like a kid coming off a rollercoaster grinning and holding the scream inside. The following morning, I woke with a spring in my step and spread a rumour about Wendy and her boyfriend fighting. Chinese whispers did the rest, and he's still doing time today. So tragic.

I'm closing in on the jogger and see him clearly through the eyelets, despite the gloom. He's slim, in his forties, with a receding hairline, and wearing earphones. He sees me approach and pauses, confusion clouding his face. Wasting no time, I take out the knife, rush forward and plunge it swiftly three times into his chest. His mouth forms an O shape. His knees buckle, and he falls to the ground. I crouch beside him, thank him and tell him his death was about to change my life forever. He can't hear me because of the earphones, so I give him a thumbs up. Water pools in his eyes. I pat his shoulder reassuringly before waving goodbye and hurrying down the tunnel.

I see two more runners approaching, so I speed up. I hear them commenting on my mask. Exiting the tunnel, I dash into the woods and escape without incident. Kill number two is a success.

Later, the papers reported that police were looking for a killer who wore a knitted mask with a face made from buttons. The media called him Buttonface.

I'm stoked.

I have a name.

A legend is born.

Chapter One

Thirteen years later.

Martha

His lips are moving, and words are coming out, but they are words that I do not want to hear.

Oliver Burgess is my literary agent. At thirty-four, five years older than me, he is heavier than when I last saw him and has dark rings under his eyes. As a new parent, he's had many sleepless nights. I'm sitting in his office on Soho's Greek Street for a meeting to discuss the feedback from publishers on the crime novel I wrote, a satirical femme fatale noir novel called *Vesper,* about a female serial killer who goes on a rampage against the men who screwed up her life. He submitted it six months ago, and I've hardly slept since then, convinced as I was that the big five would be fighting for it in a heated auction.

I was pitifully wrong.

Rising from the chair, I pace, my arms crossed and locked. I turn my gaze to the open plan office beyond Oliver's wall of glass. An exposed brick wall is dedicated to tastefully framed prints of *Sunday Times* bestselling book covers. Another features neat black-and-white portraits of the agency's authors, all with benign smiles. My eyes screech to a stop at one photo. My stomach tightens.

Poppy Posey!

Poppy and I had been friends. We were both signed with Burgess and Black on the same day, one year ago. There was a party here at the office, and a fanfare made for Oliver's two prodigies, the shining future of commercial fiction. Oliver had recently secured a seven-figure deal for Poppy's Romantasy trilogy. I was floored when I heard. In an already saturated market, does the world really need more Romantasy books? I texted her a massive congrats and lied about how happy I was for her. She replied TWENTY-FOUR HOURS LATER with 'Thanks, babe' and several emojis, including a book, a heart, seven dollar signs, two fairies, and three dragons. For a writer lauded as the future of commercial fiction, she communicates a lot with emojis. I prayed for her books to bomb. And then there's her Instagram page. It became, and still is, unbearable. How many #grateful, #happy, #excited posts accompanied by selfies of her filtered and infuriatingly pretty, smiling face can one feed take?

It's just so . . . vapid.

She even has her own hashtags: #PoppyWrites #PoseyBooks

Looking at her portrait across the office, I imagine myself, sharpie in hand, blacking out her teeth, crossing her eyes, and giving her a monobrow.

'Martha . . . Martha?'

Oliver's voice crashes through my broodings.

'Did you hear what I said?'

'Sorry, I was trying to process the news. It's hard . . . rejection is tough.' I take the seat opposite him.

He smiles warmly and kindly. 'It's not all bad.'

I like Oliver. He's a good egg, but I can't help but look at him through a veil of suspicion. Did you try hard enough? Were you too invested in Poppy's Romantasy to sell my femme fatale noir novel?

'I need a coffee. Can I get you something?' he asks, beckoning to his assistant JJ.

Slim, bearded and dressed in a creased, linen, short-sleeved shirt, JJ gets up from his immaculately tidy desk and sweeps into Oliver's office with long, thin legs and an imperious air like a strutting ostrich. For some unfathomable reason, JJ doesn't like me and takes great pride in demonstrating this. Insufferable prick. He loves Poppy, though, and can't get enough of her on Insta where he floods her posts with vomit-inducing praise and cringe hashtags such as #GoPoppy #TeamOliver #GirlBoss. She once told me he was a sycophantic lickspittle and that he was the closest thing she had to an online stalker. Harsh. I almost felt sorry for him.

'Can I get a coffee, JJ? My usual. Thanks,' says Oliver.

'Sure thing. Just to say, Jacqui's called four times while you've been . . .' He nods at me rather than saying my name.

Prick.

'Right. If she calls again, tell her I'll get right back to her.'

JJ turns to leave.

'Do you want anything, Martha?' says Oliver.

I'm about to decline the offer but change my mind. 'I'll have an iced, oat milk latte.'

JJ sighs and affects a bored expression. 'We don't have oat milk in our coffee machine,' he says. I already know this. 'It'll have to be cow's milk,' he adds.

I put my hand on my chest and give Oliver a sad look. 'Perhaps not then.'

'JJ, pop out to that cafe in Wardour Street and get Martha her latte. Actually, get two. I'll have one also.'

A tight smile flashes on JJ's face. 'Of course.'

'Make sure you get a paper straw. No plastic,' I add.

Eyes wide, JJ cocks his head, forces out a fake laugh and leaves.

'So, I was thinking we could try a different approach?' says Oliver.

'Could you please give me the feedback first?'

'From the publishers?'

'Yes! Just read it to me.'

Oliver scrunches his face. 'I'm not sure that's a good idea.'

My heart sinks. Did I write a turkey? I feel my ambitions as a published author crumbling to dust and scattering into oblivion. 'It would be good for me to know. I . . . I could learn from what they said.'

Oliver holds my gaze, tapping his fingers on his laptop. Shrugging, he says, 'OK.'

I sit back and take a breath.

Oliver opens his laptop. 'This is from Jemima Forbes: "No, thank you."'

I blink. Ouch. 'That's it?'

'Sorry.'

'Top feedback. Thank you, Jemima.'

'This is from Anthony Speers-Flannigan . . .'

'Who?'

'He's from a digital-first imprint.'

'I didn't know you were submitting it to ebook-only publishers?'

'I wasn't. Someone forwarded it to him without consulting me. I'm not impressed.'

I shake my head and sigh.

'Anthony said: "Great writing and a compelling story but needs to be more of a high-concept thriller."'

I roll my eyes.

'This is from Harriet Maybury: "Dear Oliver, thanks so much for sending this to me. I didn't have time to read it, so I gave it to my husband. As you know, he's a writer of horror fiction. He thought the writing accomplished, the characters well drawn, but couldn't see how it would work in the horror genre."'

'It's not a bollocking horror story, that's why!'

Oliver gives me a reassuring, apologetic look.

'It's all crap, I know. Let me read the others.'

'Don't . . . I've heard enough.'

Oliver's phone begins vibrating on his desk. He glances at it, his face tightening.

'Take the call if you need to,' I say.

'I'll call her back.'

Resting his elbows on the desk, he knits his fingers together. 'I've been thinking—'

'I've been thinking too . . . like maybe I should get a proper job.'

'How about we change *Vesper*?'

'Change it how?'

'OK, don't lose your shit with me, hear me out. As you know, I would never advise any of my writers to write for the market, but how about you reimagine Vesper as a kick-ass heroine in a faux, medieval world. A world a bit like ours but supernatural. Rather than a gun, give her a sword to fight demons, vampires, dragons, you choose. Basically, the same story, it's all there, but just in a different world.'

I want to scream. 'A fantasy world?'

He chews his lip. 'I suppose you could call it that.'

'And let me guess, maybe add some romance?'

'That would help sell the book.'

'Oliver, you're asking me to write for the market.'

'It's where the market's at right now . . . Poppy is riding on the crest of a wave.'

His phone is buzzing again.

'No. No. No. Oliver, I don't read Romantasy and wouldn't know where to start.'

He sighs. 'Let me take this call.'

JJ arrives with the coffees and sets them on Oliver's desk.

'Cheers, my good man,' I say.

JJ gives me a withering look. I smile back at him, pleased with my victory. So petty, I know. Oliver is talking to someone called Jacqui. I signal to him that I'm going to the toilet.

JJ is at his desk squirting a blob of £60 Loewe 'Tomato Leaves' hand sanitiser onto his palm. At a launch party, I once heard the out and proud OCD JJ tell everyone in earshot that his condition had left him 'poor as a church mouse'. I had suggested he buy sanitiser from the pound shop. He almost choked on his Prosecco and garbled out some long-winded bollocks about delicate skin that I lost interest in.

Returning five minutes later, I see JJ talking with Oliver in his office. With the lightest of fingers, I lift the bottle of sanitiser and slide it furtively into the pocket of my jeans.

I knock on Oliver's door. He looks up and beckons me inside.

JJ leaves without sparing me a glance.

'So, I have another proposition for you.'

'Oliver, I can't write Romantasy. It's just not my thing.'

'It's nothing like that. It's a job.'

My heart sinks. 'Oliver, just 'cause I said I should get a proper job, doesn't mean that I meant it. I'm a writer. I want to be published.'

'It's a writing job. I recently signed Jacqui DuLac, an American celebrity and former star of *Lady Detective*. Do you know her?'

I don't recognise her name, and shrug.

'Jacqui wants to write a crime novel, but I can tell you straight, she can't write for toffee. She needs a ghostwriter, and I think you'd be perfect.'

I wonder if I've fallen asleep on the bus home and this is a cruel dream.

'Martha?'

'A ghostwriter?'

'The pay is good.'

I perk up. I'm up to my eyes in student debt and have £25.62 in my Monzo account.

'Interested?'

'How much do I get paid?'

'After my cut, you'll get . . .' He types on his keyboard, '£22,000. Not bad, eh?'

I clear my throat. 'That's . . . erm . . . adequate.' Did I really just say adequate? It's not Poppy Posey numbers, but this is ghostwriting, and I am skint.

'Fab. There's more. To get started, you'll need to accompany her on the *Jewel of the Atlantic* cruise ship from Southampton to New York. It's the ship's final voyage and a special occasion to boot. Jacqui is a VIP guest. She'll be doing a retrospective and meeting fans, that sort of thing. A room will be sorted for you, and expenses will be covered, within reason, of course.'

I'm only half listening and feel a heaviness in my stomach. 'New York?' I mutter.

'Yep! Gotham itself. The city that never sleeps.'

I rub my arms.

'Martha?'

'I . . . I'm not sure.'

Oliver is frowning. 'You're not sure?'

I bite the skin of my thumb. Pull yourself together. It was a long time ago. You need this job. 'On a cruise ship?'

'Exciting, no?'

Doubt niggles at me. Aside from my reluctance to return to New York, this opportunity is too good to be true. 'What's the catch?'

A pause before he answers. 'So, you'll need to drop whatever it is you're doing and pack a case. The ship leaves first thing tomorrow morning.'

'Excuse me?!'

'Yeah . . . it's a little short notice.'

'Understatement of the year! Why are you asking me the day before?' But then it dawns on me. 'I'm not the first person you've asked, am I?'

He chuckles. 'You're smarter than I ever gave you credit for.'

'Charming.'

'The other candidate pulled out last minute. Artistic differences apparently. I'm bloody fuming!'

'I need more time to think this over.'

'This is your Charlie Bucket golden ticket opportunity. It'll get you on the circuit.'

My mind is racing.

'Martha, I need an answer.'

I feel a small fire igniting inside me. This could be the chance to exorcise some demons, and does it really matter that I'm second choice? Besides, what's the worst that could happen?

Chapter Two

Martha

Before I met with Oliver, Diane had phoned while I was on the bus travelling to Central London. I was nervous and didn't want to talk to her. I had meant to decline the call but my butter fingers tapped the Accept button instead. 'Shit,' I muttered.

'How'd it go?' she asked eagerly.

'I'm not seeing him until 4 p.m. I told you that already,' I replied sharply.

I heard her sighing. 'Are you sure you're doing the right thing?'

I felt a rush of petulance. 'That's rich, coming from you Diane.'

'Please don't call me that, dear.' Diane is my mother, by the way. I had stopped calling her Mum fourteen years ago when she kicked Dad out because 'she was bored and needed to move on with her life'. I've never forgiven her. My stomach churned at the memory. 'There's no money in books, darling,' she said.

'Oh, do remind me of that again, why don't you.' I could be pretty snarky sometimes.

'You need to look for a proper job.' Diane started talking rapidly. I closed my eyes and held the phone away from my face. I've heard it all before.

'Martha? . . . Are you there?' her tinny, distant voice called.

'I have to go.'

'Sven said Greggs are hiring . . .'

I felt my face flushing. Is that what my life had come to? All those years studying and honing my craft only to end up selling sausage rolls. I ended the call. My eyes watered, and I took a breath. Diane was six months into a new relationship with her tantric massage therapist, a Dane named Sven, who was twelve years younger than her and nine years older than me. The age gap had set the local gossips on fire. That wasn't the only thing on fire, judging by the screams from her bedroom. I shudder, pushing the memories from my head.

So, setting aside my lofty ambitions to be a novelist, I didn't need to think too hard about Oliver's offer with the all-expenses-paid cruise to New York. The destination was my biggest issue. I couldn't think about that, so I pushed it from my head and wrote a quick text to Dad telling him about my change of fortune. OK, it was a ghost writing job, but that's good, isn't it? I'm still a writer, and besides, doesn't one door open another? This is a dream opportunity. That's what Dad would say.

I return home with a bounce in my step. I'm eager to rub my good news in Diane and Sven's smug faces. Entering the house, it feels strangely quiet. I wonder if they are in the dining room, which was recently converted into Sven's tantric love 'clinic'. I listen, my stomach clenching as I wait for the sound of slapping flesh as if a couple of walruses are wrestling in an oily pit. To my relief, there's only silence. I find a note on the kitchen table beside a wad of tenners.

Sven and I have booked a last-minute naturist yoga retreat for three nights. Tried to tell you on the phone, but the line cut out. As usual! Love, Mum. PS. Some cash for you. PPS. Will send pics.

'Eww.'

Having the house to myself would normally make me happy, but I can't help feeling cheated from the victory of announcing my new writing job. I quickly text Diane with a simple request to not under any circumstances send me any pictures. I consider telling her my news, but that could wait until I was comfortably sipping a Negroni Sbagliato, midway across the Atlantic. The cash catches my eye. I hesitate, but guilt gets the better of me, and I drop a second text to Diane.

PS. Thanks for cash.

I begin to plan my evening. I have packing to do and research on Jacqui DuLac to start. It occurs to me I haven't used my passport in years and have no idea where it is. I feel a rush of fear and wonder if it's still valid. I spend over an hour in a state of panic, tearing my room apart, and eventually find it lying in a shoebox filled with stuff underneath my bed. The items in question are souvenirs, small things like ornaments, a fridge magnet, a roll-on deodorant, pens, and unopened sweet packets; I could go on. Reaching into my bag, I take out JJ's sanitiser bottle and place it inside the box.

I check the dates on my passport; two years remain. Relief washes over me despite cringing at the grim-faced, twenty-one-year-old me. I had a monobrow, frizzy hair, and an unsettling frown. They were unhappy times. I was friendless, lost, and heartbroken. I close the passport quickly and shove it into my backpack. There is too much to do.

I pack a case, stuffing inside whatever clean clothes I can find. At bedtime, I'm too wired with excitement, so I swallow two of Diane's melatonin before settling down in bed with my laptop to do some research. On YouTube, I find an episode of *Lady Detective,* the show Jacqui DuLac is most famous for, playing the lead, Detective Cassie Kowalski. The opening credits play. The theme tune is dramatic. A black-and-white spiral spins on the small screen, revealing a pistol being fired. The spiral disappears, and Jacqui is seen holding the gun. 'Starring Jacqui DuLac' appears in large, gold lettering. Cassie's hair is blonde and tousled. She has a serious, determined expression, and is undeniably beautiful. The next reel zooms in on Jacqui's long, tanned legs in white heels descending thick carpeted stairs. There are more short reels: Cassie grappling with a criminal, Cassie undercover as an air hostess, a hairdresser, then she's speeding in a car through some American city chasing bad guys. The credits come to a close, and my eyes grow heavy as the melatonin kicks in. I want to watch more, but sleep takes me.

It's the following day, and I'm sitting in the busy carriage of a bone rattler from London Waterloo to Southampton. Naturally, nothing is running on time. I'm supposed to meet Jacqui for check-in at 1 p.m. The train is thirty minutes behind. I don't have her number, so I texted Oliver to let her know that I'm late. I haven't heard back. Maybe he's in a meeting. Diane's cash won't get me far, so I had pleaded poverty to Oliver earlier this morning. He paid for my travel upfront. I cheekily asked for a sub, but he told me to get a grip, and besides, he added, all the food and drinks are free on the cruise. I'm pumped about that and anticipate eating and drinking myself all the way across the Atlantic. I've never been on a cruise and am excited, not just for the job, but also for the experience.

The train is full of chattering tourists, middle-aged and older Americans, and a ton of baggage clogging the aisles. I second glance a man around my age sitting alone in a window seat across the carriage. With unkempt, mousey-blond hair, tanned skin, and a loose-fitting, creased, white cotton shirt with rolled-up sleeves, he has a dirty, preppy-boy vibe that I'm totally here for. More importantly, he's reading a book, a rarity in the age of smartphones. As he turns the page, I see the cover: *In Cold Blood* by Truman Capote. A classic of true crime and a long-standing favourite of mine. I've read it five times. If he were sitting opposite, I might strike up a conversation, but he's not, so I pop in my earbuds and search for a crime podcast. I download the latest episode of *Bizarre Tales: Who Knew*? I've been waiting for this one. Settling back, I listen to the disquieting and fascinating tale of Sheila Morgan, wife of at least a dozen Death Row jailbirds, including serial murderers, cartel bosses, gang leaders, terrorists and cult leaders. She has also given birth to several of their children before the fathers' inevitable grim departure from this world. I'm gripped.

An hour has passed, and the train is approaching Southampton Central. It's 1.30 p.m. I cheekily edge my way ahead of the other passengers as it comes to a stop. I'm travelling light with my clothes, laptop and notebooks occupying space in my trolley case and backpack. On the platform, I navigate through the tourists and hustle my way to the taxi queue. Fifteen minutes crawl by before I'm en route to the cruise ship.

My phone rings. It's Oliver.

'Oli!' I say cheerily.

'Where the hell are you?' He sounds stressed.

'I'll be there shortly. The train was delayed.'

'Jacqui's waiting . . . she hates being kept waiting.'

'I shouted at the train driver to step on it. He wasn't having any of it.'

'You shouted at the train driver?' he replies, incredulously.

'It's a joke, Oli.'

'Hilarious. Don't give Jacqui any sass. Just apologise profusely and blame the trains.'

'It was the trains.'

He sighs heavily. 'She's at the Queen Elizabeth II terminal and is getting mobbed apparently. Just get there as quickly as you can.'

In the distance, I can see the terminal building dwarfed by the enormous, regal beauty of the *Jewel of the Atlantic* cruise ship.

'Wowzers!' I say.

'Can you see her?'

I feel my heart skipping. The bow is painted a crimson red and is shaped like a scythe designed to cut like butter through tricky waters. The ship is gleaming white, glittering in the bright sunshine and looming on top is the famous gold funnel with evenly patterned jewels of red, giving the impression of a tall, ruby-encrusted crown.

'It's beautiful.'

'Oh God, she's calling again. I need to take this.'

'I'm minutes away.'

'Rescue her and get her onboard . . .'

'OK.' I hear the uncertainty in my voice and begin to wonder if she's ever travelled before.

'Call me when she's happy.' He ends the call abruptly, leaving me to wonder what he means by 'when she's happy'.

The cab pulls up into a free space among a long line of taxis and coaches. There are hundreds of people. I feel a knot in my tummy and worry that finding Jacqui might be a challenge. I thank the driver, pay him and make my way through the horde of passengers pushing trolleys full of luggage. I'm struck by how similarly dressed they are. There are a lot of beige trousers, bright polo shirts and hats. Oh, and men wearing shorts with white socks and sandals. What's that about? I feel like I've stepped into another world. I scan for any sign of Jacqui, which is impossible because I'm not tall enough to see over the swarm of people. I walk towards the terminal entrance and notice a crowd gathered like bees around a honeypot. I move towards the perimeter and stand on my tiptoes but can't see beyond the rows of baseball caps.

'It's really her,' I hear one American man with a dry, throaty voice say. 'Dang it, I had such a boner for her back in the day.'

'I'd have a boner now, but those days are long behind me,' a second man replies.

'I have some gel for that.'

'Is it legal?'

'I hope not!'

The two men choke out laughter that causes them both to cough from rattling chests.

A voice comes over the Tannoy, asking all remaining passengers to check in. The crowd begins to disperse, and I see her. She's standing with her arms around two adoring female fans, both women in their fifties, leaning in for pictures being taken by their respective husbands. Jacqui is all smiles, perfect, white teeth behind pink, shiny lips and wide eyes that look like they've had some surgical assistance. I had read somewhere she was fifty-five, but that must have been an old article. She's at least sixty-five but admittedly looks incredible. Dressed in a stylish Gucci tracksuit, her shoulder-length blonde hair is topped with a wide-brimmed sun hat. A large pair of Gucci sunglasses hang off one hand with diamonds glittering from gold rings. She dazzles like the beam of a Super Trouper spotlight.

'Hey ladies, shall we get your dads in the picture?' she hollers, with a wry, flirtatious smile at the two men. The women laugh, and the two husbands, evidently bowled over by her glamour and attention, huddle in, stretching out their arms to take selfies. More passengers flock around her, taking snaps. To the delight of her admirers, Jacqui strikes several poses like a Hollywood star.

I hear the click of a petrol lighter and turn to see a tall, swarthy man with long, dark hair pulled into a ponytail. Dressed in a black suit and an AC/DC T-shirt, he has the look of a funeral director on his way to a heavy metal gig. Drawing on a cigarette, he exhales a plume of bitter, blue smoke that engulfs the people near him. Me included. I wrinkle my nose and step out of the haze.

'This is a final call for passengers boarding the *Jewel of the Atlantic*. Please proceed to check in,' the voice reminds us.

The crowd begins to disperse, people jostling and pushing each other to get to the ship. I try to squeeze through and get to Jacqui when some sweaty, unwashed idiot with a paunch and an undersized, faded Hawaiian shirt steamrolls through, knocking me, the smoking man, and one other person wearing a baseball cap together.

'Oi!' I say, but Hawaiian shirt ignores me.

'Asshole,' hisses the smoking man, extinguishing his cigarette with the sole of his black cowboy boot.

'Hey doll,' the Hawaiian shirt says to Jacqui.

She blinks, looks him up and down and takes a step back.

The smoking man has a fresh, unlit cigarette in his mouth and is patting his pockets for his lighter, which he can't seem to find.

I look back towards Jacqui. 'The name's Lamb, Terence Lamb,' the man says in a corny pastiche of Sean Connery's Bond. 'I'm in the Entertainment business, too.'

She regards him with a cautious smile. 'That's nice.'

'I'm on the cruise. Maybe we could have a drink sometime.'

'Will you excuse me; I need to make a call?'

'I do magic and tell jokes.'

Jacqui disappears behind sunglasses and takes out her phone. Terence Lamb turns and leaves, red-faced and flustered.

The smoking man is looking around him with a puzzled

expression. In his hand is a bright red button, the size of a fifty pence piece, which seems out of sync with his mortician-cum-ageing rocker vibe, but hey, each to their own.

Now that Jacqui is free, I hurry towards her and thrust out my hand. 'Jacqui, hi. It's Martha. Good to meet you.'

She turns to look my way. I can't see her eyes, but I can certainly see she's not smiling.

'You're who?' she asks, curtly.

'Martha.'

'Do you want a picture?'

'No, I'm here to help you write your book. I'm the ghostwriter.'

A cool breeze blows between us.

'A ghostwriter?'

'Yes, from the agency. Oliver—'

Her lips tighten. 'That son of a bitch!' She makes a call on her phone. After a moment, she shakes her head and hisses, 'Voicemail, always voicemail . . . Oliver, you've sent me another freaking ghostwriter. What the hell has got into you? It's an assistant I need, not a ghostwriter.' She ends the call.

I feel my muscles tighten. Assistant? I'm worried my dream job is slipping away. Her phone rings. I recognise the tune from the *Lady Detective* TV show.

'What the hell, Oliver?' she says. 'Yes . . . we had an agreement . . .' I look down at my phone, pretending not to listen.

'Hey, you.' I look up to see Jacqui glaring at me, sunglasses off. 'This is a private conversation!' She motions to a nearby trolley full of Louis Vuitton luggage. 'Stand over there.' I look at her, perplexed, and do what she asks, vexation igniting inside me. I can't hear what she's saying, but I can tell she's on fire.

The call ends, and she slips on her glasses. Her half-exposed expression tells me nothing. 'Bring the luggage,' she commands.

I look at the cases, five in total, stacked on top of each other on a lopsided trolley. I turn back to her, but she's gone, making her way to check in.

'I'm a writer!' I shout.

'Congratulations!' she retorts. 'You're also late, and check-in is closing.'

Chapter Three

Martha

I'm hot, sweaty and ruffled as I check in Jacqui's luggage and mine, while trying to get through to Oliver. He doesn't answer. I leave a message: 'We need to talk, Oliver!' A black cloud hangs over me as I head to the gangway, intent on speaking to Jacqui and staking my claim on the ghost writing position. Funny, yesterday I would probably have snapped up the assistant job to start chipping away at my debt, but I can't help feeling betrayed and lied to, and I am not prepared to give in lightly.

As I approach the entrance to the ship, I hear classical music. 'Hello!' comes a jolly American voice. 'Welcome to the *Jewel of the Atlantic*!' A crew member, dressed in a 1920s-style double-breasted white jacket with gold braid trim, sweeps his arm across the expansive, posh, and bustling Art Deco lobby. He has blond highlights in his neat side-parted hair. 'My name is Rudy Turner. I'm the Onboard Manager and Events Director. Any questions about what we have to offer, talk to me.' He waves a hand theatrically in the air. 'You'll see me around the ship a lot. You'll probably hear me first, though.' He winks and leans forward, 'Nice to see a younger face on the ship,' he whispers.

I smile. 'Thank you,' I say, marvelling at how good Americans are at customer service compared to us Brits, who are frankly, rubbish.

He nods at the oldies gathering in the lobby for welcome refreshments. 'God's waiting room takes to the high seas.' He laughs and snatches a flute of bubbles from the tray of a passing waiter and hands it to me. 'No warm Prosecco for you. I can tell you're a Champagne gal.'

'I bathe in it,' I say, taking a mouthful.

He snorts a laugh, 'Go have fun. See you soon.'

I thank him and make my way through the crowd, eyes searching for Jacqui. No sign of her. Sweeping down to the lobby is a wide staircase with a bronze and wrought iron balustrade, elegant with ornate curves, delicate patterns and geometric shapes. On the stairwell landing is a string quartet, the source of the music. Four young women dressed in evening wear. Very fancy. Behind the musicians, a gleaming, glass lift with a Bakelite arch floats silently upwards.

I recognise the music and tune in, trying to figure out what it is.

'Jeez, are they really playing that song?' I hear a woman say. 'Doesn't fill me with confidence. Are there still icebergs in the Atlantic?'

I almost spit out my Champagne. How did I not recognise the theme tune to the *Titanic* movie? I feel weirdly nostalgic because I loved that movie back in the day. Dad took me to the cinema to see the 3D re-release. It was 2012, the year of the London Olympics. I had never seen anything like it. I was transfixed and became obsessed with Rose and Jack, as well as everything about the ship. I smile at the memory, take out my phone and start texting.

Hey Dad. You'll never guess. There's a quartet playing the

Titanic *theme tune on the ship. Remember how we (well, me) loved it. Haha. M XX*

I try calling Oliver again and finally get through. My phone buzzes with a text message. That'll be from Dad's phone.

'Is she happy?' Oliver asks, without a greeting, an apology, or explanation.

I suppress the urge to vomit out expletives and compose myself. 'An assistant, Oliver!'

'You're not an assistant. You're more than that.'

I blink. 'More than that? Either I'm her ghostwriter or I'm not.'

'Listen—'

'You lied to me, Oliver.'

'It wasn't a lie.'

'Don't tell me, it was just you being economical with the truth.'

'The bottom line is you're hired as her ghostwriter. It's in the contract, so don't worry about that. It's just . . . you may have certain hurdles to jump.'

'Hurdles?'

'She's a celebrity. She's used to getting what she wants.'

The reality of my situation is starting to sink in.

'You'll be good for her.'

'In my assistant slash ghostwriter status?' I say, drily.

'All I ask is that you trust me.'

I sigh and shrug. What choice do I have? 'OK.'

'Great!'

The music changes to something more upbeat. I recognise the *Lady Detective* theme tune. The crowd begins to part in front of me, and I see Rudy holding a microphone, escorting Jacqui. Her hat and glasses are gone, and she's smiling sweetly at the adoring crowd, who start to clap.

'Jacqui's here. I should go.'

'You got this.'

Do I?

I end the call. Jacqui catches my eye. I smile as sincerely as I can and clap along with the others.

'TV royalty in the house!' yells Rudy. 'Star of *Return to Hollywood Wives, LA Dolls,* and *Lady Detective*. Ladies and gentlemen, I bring you the one, the only, Jacqui DuLac.' Rudy claps and the passengers join him with cheers. Jacqui smiles demurely and waves. 'Doesn't she look amazing, everyone?' Someone wolf whistles. Jacqui affects a coquettish pose, beams and blows a kiss. 'Jacqui will be on stage in the Silver Siren theatre this week with yours truly discussing her life and career.' More cheers and clapping. Rudy is on a roll: 'I hope Jacqui doesn't mind me mentioning this. We had a brief chat about a possible cameo in my production of *Murder She Didn't Write*.' He looks to her for confirmation. She doesn't return his gaze. Her wan smile says everything. Rudy forces an awkward laugh and addresses the crowd. 'In your rooms, you'll find a colour brochure containing full details of all our events.'

I feel a man edging in beside me, clapping enthusiastically. He's tall, in his sixties, dressed in a dapper tweed suit and has the smell of clove oil about him. 'Oh, I do love her!' he says, glancing my way.

'She's certainly popular.'

I stop clapping because my hands are beginning to hurt, plus she was rude to me.

'I feel you are perhaps a little too young to know who she is,' he says.

I detect a European accent laced within his North American enunciation.

'Oh, I know her all right. Not that well. But I know her.'

'Intriguing,' he replies, studying me with interest. His eyes seem locked on my mouth, which is unsettling. I close it, feeling self-conscious. He seems to have got the message.

'Oh, do excuse me,' he says. 'I have a dental background and sometimes can't stop myself from looking at people's teeth. Yours are . . . unique.'

I shift on my feet, uncomfortable with this stranger's focus on my teeth. And what the fuck does he mean by unique? I run my tongue around them in a panic, feeling for gaps and protrusions that I may have taken for granted.

'Bernard,' comes a woman's voice.

He winks at me and turns, 'Hallo, Wilma.'

I see him leaning down and air-kissing a dowdy, matronly woman wearing horn-rimmed glasses and an orange and brown dress. My eye catches the brooch pinned to her dress – a small, dark emblem shaped like a hood, the face inside split cleanly in two – one half a theatre mask with a faint smile, the other a cracked skull.

'I'm crossing off names, making sure everyone's onboard,' she says, glancing at a clipboard. 'Just a few more and I'll have everyone.'

She looks my way and extends a chubby hand. 'Any friend of Bernard's is a friend of mine. Wilma Franklin.'

I shake her hand, 'Martha . . . erm . . . Bernard and I are not friends.'

'Are you with the chorus, dear?' she asks, scanning a paper list on the clipboard. 'Don't see a Martha.'

'I was in the school choir. I can hold a note, but it takes a few drinks to bring out my inner rock bitch.'

Her face tightens. 'Sorry to trouble you,' she says, pulling her clipboard to her chest. 'Come, Bernard. Let's say hello to the others.'

Bernard grins at me. He has the strangest teeth. Small, like a baby's, as if they stopped growing when he was a toddler. He's staring at my mouth again, as if waiting for me to smile and give him the money shot. I look away and scan for Jacqui. Rudy is escorting her out of the lobby. My phone pings. It's a text from Oliver with Jacqui's mobile number. I add the number to my WhatsApp and compose a text.

Hi Jacqui. It's Martha, ghostwriter-slash-assistant . . .

I hesitate.

I understand now that there will be hurdles, but I'm smart enough to know that before Jacqui and I work together, boundaries need to be set. I delete slash-assistant and replace it with: *I'm looking forward to helping you write this novel. If you need anything, let me know* and press send.

Chapter Four

Martha

I eventually get my room key from customer services and leave the main reception area of the lobby, head to the lifts and press level six. I feel lightheaded from a second glass of bubbles and a lack of food. I had declined the canapés because they smelt a little too fishy for my tastes.

My room is one floor up from the lobby, so I exit at the next level. It takes several minutes to navigate passengers and luggage down a long corridor decorated in a black and yellow Art Deco style. Some couples are bickering about where their suite is and whether they are on the right floor or not. I spot my bags sitting at the doorway to a room and make a beeline towards them. Tapping the electronic key, I smile at the green light and enter.

The door closes behind me, and I take it all in. My heart skips. I grin and rest my hands on my hips. 'Sweet.'

It's compact with a double bed, a built-in wardrobe, a mirrored dressing table, and a small sofa. It's stylish, with the same Art Deco theme, bright, clean, and cheerful. Wow. Bijou but perfect. A thin, gold-coloured curtain at the opposite side of the room blows open with a cooling breeze. I walk towards it and peer outside. There's a small balcony with a table and chairs.

OK, there's a lifeboat hanging nearby half blocking the view, but I have a balcony! I punch my fists in the air and laugh. My phone pings. It's a message from Jacqui.

I'm in the Queen Suite on deck 11

I'm not sure what I'm supposed to say. I begin typing.

I'm on deck 6. *My room's small but nice.*

She's typing a response.

???

Charming.

Do you want me to come to your suite?

She replies, *Yes!* with an eye roll emoji.

My fingers pound the screen of my phone.

Fine. I'm on my way.

She reads the message and goes offline. I feel myself bristling.

I exit my lovely room with the dinky balcony and make my way back up the corridor to the lifts. My muscles are tense, and I'm breathing heavily through my nose. I sense people side-stepping out of my way as they clock my thunderous expression. I feel bad for them and annoyed with my quick temper, too. As for Jacqui's bloody attitude . . .

I press the button and call the lift, while taking three deep breaths. The doors part, I step inside without making eye contact with anyone, and press deck eleven. The lift makes a slow ascent.

I sense someone looking at me. Frowning, I turn to meet their gaze. To my surprise, it's the hot, wavy-haired reader from the train. Classic retro-style sunglasses hide his eyes.

'Hi,' he says. His accent is American, his voice warm and masculine.

'Hello,' I reply, composing myself and smiling. 'You were on the train.'

'So were you. I'm Zach.'

'Martha.'

He smiles.

His phone rings.

'Excuse me,' he says.

Great timing.

'I just checked in,' he says to the caller. 'Heading there now, then to the departure cocktail drinks . . . Yeah, 5 p.m. on the main deck . . .'

The lift stops at deck eleven, and the doors open. This is my stop. As I exit, I glance at Zach and take in his body. He's around 5'11 and satisfyingly athletic. I collide with someone entering the lift, and smell clove oil.

'Hallo Martha.'

I look up to see Bernard of the toddler teeth looking down at me. 'Oh hi . . . and sorry.' The doors are closing, and I clumsily dance my way around him to get out. 'And bye.'

'Nice to see you again,' he says.

The doors close. Glancing back, I catch Zach smiling at me. I feel a warm glow inside. I think I might just make an appearance at the same cocktail party. I feel instantly better and decide it's best I now approach Jacqui with kindness and understanding.

I arrive at her suite and politely knock on the door. A woman is walking down the corridor. It's hard to determine her age, but I reckon somewhere in the late sixties. She's had work. Her face has been stretched thinly over sharp cheekbones and a chin that reminds me of a throwing knife. Her lips are surprisingly thin, painted a pillar-box red; they resemble a wound from a surgeon's blade. But what is most remarkable about her is that she oozes wealth and privilege. She is head to toe in haute couture, dressed in a flowing black dress that could almost pass as a graduation gown. Her thin legs are fitted with navy Burlington patterned tights, and on her feet are lacquered red ankle boots with a metal stiletto heel, sharp spikes on the toe and a melded logo buckle. I can't take my eyes off them.

'They're Christian Louboutin,' she says, stopping beside me, stretching out a foot.

'They're quite something.'

The door swings open, and Jacqui appears. She looks at me before turning to the woman. Her face drops.

'Jacqui!' the woman says.

Jacqui's eyes widen, her hand flies to her chest. 'Cilla . . . my God!'

The woman called Cilla blinks and takes a step towards Jacqui. They tilt forward and air kiss, keeping their distance as if another pandemic has just been announced.

'It's been too long,' says Cilla. 'I had heard you were working on the ship. Room servicing, is it? Mine needs a good polish when you've finished up in there.'

I raise an eyebrow at what is clearly a first shot fired.

'It's such a shock to see you. I'd heard you were dead.' Jacqui takes her in. 'I see why people thought that.'

'You've filled out since I last saw you. It suits you.'

'Your doctors still hauling that old skin over those ancient bones?'

I am so here for this exchange right now and wish I had pop-corn.

Cilla takes a step back and smiles through clenched teeth. 'You've embraced your age at last. I remember when you used to tell everyone you were fifty-five. That old chestnut dragged on for a decade. At least.'

'I'll always be younger than you, dear. Fact. Tell me, is your surgeon still giving you a 2-for-1 deal on both your faces?'

'I could speak to him about a 2-for-1 deal on chin lifts, if you're interested.'

Jacqui fixes a cold smile at Cilla. 'What are you doing here? You're the last person I expected to see mixing with the hoi polloi on a cruise.'

'I'm here on business. My dead husband, may he rest in peace, owned the company that operates this ship. Naturally, it's mine now.'

'Another dead husband. Funny how your many marriages end in tragedy.'

Despite nothing moving on Cilla's botoxed and taut face, her lack of retort shows that Jacqui has hit a nerve. She turns to leave.

Jacqui gives her an icy glare before beckoning me inside. She slams the door behind me, muttering something indecipherable. There's a bottle of chardonnay sitting on a coffee table. She picks it up and pours herself a large glass, which she downs in one.

'An old friend of yours?' I ask.

Jacqui gives me a withering look. 'What do you think?'

I shrug and think I should write down their exchange. I could use it in a story. I take in her suite, which is like a large palatial apartment. It makes my room seem like the cabin boy's quarters. It has a dual aspect and two balconies, with a sweeping staircase leading up to the bedroom. 'Nice digs,' I say.

She narrows her eyes at me, 'Digs?'

I can see she's frazzled from her exchange with Cilla and say nothing, not wanting to fan the flames.

She pours herself a second glass of wine. 'I need help unpacking.'

I look behind me and around the room. There's no one else here. 'I'm sorry, are you talking to me?'

'There's only you in the room.' Jacqui's tone is harsh, sharpened with two large chardonnays.

Set expectations now and make your position clear.

'I'm a writer employed to help you write your book. I'm not an assistant.'

'It's the same job.'

'That's news to me.'

'It ain't news to me, sweetie. You don't like it, leave. The boat is still docked.'

'Fine. Good luck writing your book!'

Jacqui swirls the wine glass. 'You think I can't do it.'

'I think you could write a pretty decent shopping list.'

'Is that supposed to be funny?'

'Here's a truth: I don't know the first thing about acting. I wouldn't dream of auditioning for a part when I have no experience or talent. Therefore, what makes you think you can just suddenly pick up a pen and write a novel?'

'Anyone can write a book. It's not rocket science, honey.' She grins and locks her eyes with mine. If this were a Quentin Tarantino movie, we'd be unsheathing our Samurai swords. I'm not letting this pass. I go in for the kill. 'There are times when brutal honesty is the best policy, honey. My job is to help you because, according to Oliver, "Jacqui can't write for toffee!"'

She flinches. 'You're fired!'

'I quit!'

It's then that a bell rings and a voice comes over the Tannoy. 'Good evening, and welcome everyone to the *Jewel of the Atlantic*. This is your Captain, Dexter Perry, speaking. We are just about to bid farewell to Southampton and begin another epic journey across the Atlantic to New York City . . .'

'Fuck!' I mutter.

'Looks like you'll have to swim back to shore.'

I make my way to the door. 'For what it's worth, I do agree with you about one thing. Writing is not rocket science. Writing is so much more than that. Putting words to a page means excavating your heart and soul and using what you find to breathe life into your characters and story. I could have helped you do that.' I shake my head in disbelief and pull the door shut behind me. Swallowing, I feel a tear spill forward and make my way up the corridor. I wipe away the tear and pull out my phone. I need to text my dad.

Chapter Five

Martha

I decide not to go to the departure cocktail drinks. I'm too frazzled from the run-in with Jacqui and not in the right frame of mind to be flirty and jolly with Zach. As the ship sets sail, I enter my cabin and make a beeline for the balcony where I watch the port shrink as we cruise west across the sea.

I've been fired. I'm jobless and broke again.

Fuck!

I ought to talk to Oliver, but I need time to gather my thoughts. With nowhere else to go, I'm stuck on the ship. So, I might as well make the most of it.

I pop indoors and begin unpacking my case. With my thrift-store dresses, shirts, and blazer hanging up, I decide to get ready for the evening, regardless of my situation. First up, I need a hot shower. I kick off my boots, undress and slip under the steaming hot water. Taking full advantage of the fancy soap, shampoo and conditioners, I go to town. I'm feeling better already. Wrapped up in the ship's monogrammed fluffy white bathrobe, I blow-dry my hair in front of the vanity mirror and think of my brief encounter in the lift with Zach, and how he confidently just gave me his name. I decide I should track him down, have a few drinks and flirt outrageously with him.

At 7 p.m., I go to the bustling main deck, where the sun is beaming down, and perch myself under the shade of the bar. Laughter and chatter come from the pool where cocktail-sipping, ageing party animals sit with their feet dipped in the water. Passing by are dozens of crew, almost invisible, as they keep the wheels turning and the passengers smiling: hospitality and entertainment dressed in 1920s-style white shirts and cream trousers for the men, and stiff blouses with long dark skirts for the women. Among them are maintenance personnel dressed in brown fatigues, and patrolling duty officers dressed in white uniforms.

'What can I get you?' asks the bartender, an older gentleman with a warm smile and thick New York accent.

I take a moment to decide. 'I've never had one, and honestly don't know if I'll even like it, but I'll try a Negroni Sbagliato, please.'

'Coming right up.'

I scan the deck area and casually look towards the sun loungers. Playing it cool, I tell myself I'm not looking for Zach but of course I am. The sun deck is being cleared of loungers. They are being stacked, presumably to make room for the party later. Facing the bar at the opposite end of the deck is a round restaurant where people are eating an early dinner. On the floor above, there is a balcony with three sets of floor-to-ceiling windows through which I can see rows of bookshelves.

'Your Negroni Sbagliato,' says the bartender, handing me a tumbler of red liquid that looks like medicine. I thank him, hand over my ship pass and ask him to charge it to my room. I hope that Oliver will still cover my expenses. 'Is that a library?' I ask, pointing to the rear of the deck.

'It is. Bet you can't guess how many books it holds.'

'Challenge accepted.' It's too far away to make a sound assessment, and I really have no idea, but I take a wild stab. '1,200.'

'Higher.'

'2,200.'

He smiles. 'It has over 6,000 titles.'

'Wow. Are they teeny tiny books that only pixies can read?'

He laughs. 'No, they're regular sizes.'

'That's impressive.' I take a sip of my drink.

'It's a nice place to relax. Don't see much footfall on some trips; that's why they hire the place out. For parties, talks, that kind of thing. How's your cocktail?'

I take a second sip and try not to pull a face. I'm not certain I like it. 'Very nice,' I tell him.

'If you don't mind me saying, you don't seem so sure.'

'No, honestly, it's unusual . . . but, uhm, nice.'

'OK. Let me know if you need anything else.'

'Absolutely.'

I eat alone in the Seven Dials, the main restaurant, on deck seven, where the all-inclusive buffet is situated. It's a vast space full of light from the expansive windows, overlooking the pale wooden deck and the ocean beyond. The interior is decorated in the ship's trademark *'style moderne'* with chrome rails, black-and-gold wallpaper, and Bakelite galore. It's a glaring contrast to the clientele whose outfits are making my eyes water. I see long tie-dye skirts that have seen better days, comfy stretch slacks, Walmart jeans, every colour of the rainbow polo shirts, hats, caps, you name it. It's as if a crowd of brash tourists have just rolled onto the set of an Agatha Christie adaptation. I browse the impressive selection of food and fill my plate with roast chicken, mashed potatoes, and gravy. The sushi looks good, so I grab a side plate of that and a couple of sesame toasts that catch my eye. I launch myself at a free table out of the way by the window with a view of the distant sunset. It's beautiful. The waiter, a stiff in a crisp white shirt and black tie, takes my order for a glass of Rioja wine and glances at the picnic haul on my table.

'Shall I order drinks for your companions?' he asks.

I almost choke on a mouthful of potato and take a sip of water. 'Just me, thanks . . .' I focus in on his name badge, 'Doug.'

Doug raises a brow, nods and leaves to fetch my vino.

More passengers file inside and fill their boots in preparation for the welcome party at 9 p.m. I recognise a few faces from the lobby earlier, including Bernard the tooth fancier, and his friend Wilma, the squat clipboard lady who'd asked if I was part of her chorus. I lift my head and scan the restaurant for Zach but see no sign of him. My phone pings with a message. It's from Diane. A photo of her and Sven, semi-naked and grinning like mentalists: *Having the best time! Wish you were here*. Ugh. No thanks. Though I have some residual guilt about how I left things, so I text her back.

Glad you're having fun. I got a job. I'll be away for a week

I reread it and think it's too curt and formal. But then I remember how eternally irritated I am by Diane and send it anyway.

It's almost party time, which is a relief. I'm already bored with my own company and have finished my Rioja, which was delicious. I leave the restaurant and make my way outside. The sun has set, it's pleasantly warm, and the deck is lit with pretty fairy lights. There's a DJ near the bar playing pop music. Passengers stream in like ants from all four corners, helping themselves to drinks from the trays of passing service staff.

My phone rings.

It's Oliver.

'Hey, what's going on, Martha?'

Hello to you too. 'I've been fired. That's what's going on.'

'Wait. Jacqui said you quit.'

'She fired me. And then I quit.'

'Right. That makes complete sense,' he says, exasperation in his tone.

'It was too late to get off the ship. I'm stuck here now with no money—'

'Let me just stop you there. I will talk to Jacqui and fix this. I'll call you back in a few minutes.'

'Good luck with that,' I scoff.

He hangs up, and I grab a mojito from the tray of a passing waiter. *'Muchas gracias,'* I say cheerily, despite the waiter's unimpressed expression.

I take a large slug of the cocktail. It's a little sweet for me, but it's not unpleasant.

My phone rings with another call from Oliver.

'It's all fixed. You're no longer fired.'

I feel my heart bounce but can't keep the cynic in me from saying my piece. 'Good of her to come to her senses.'

'Apparently, she can't write for toffee.'

I feel myself cringe inside. 'Oh.'

'That was a fun conversation.'

'Sorry, Oliver.'

'Don't sweat it.'

'How did you get her to change her mind?'

'I pushed home the fact that the book is already way behind schedule and, according to her publishers, who I met with today, if they don't see an outline in the next five days, the deal is off. No deal equals no advance for Jacqui and no £22,000 for you.'

'Shit!'

'Exactly. Where are you now?'

'At the Welcome Party.'

'She's on her way there. Talk to her. Be nice. Make this work for all our sakes.'

I knock back the remainder of the mojito and feel myself getting jittery with the weight of the responsibility. We say our goodbyes, and I grab a second cocktail and scan for Jacqui, but there's no sign of her. Forty minutes pass before she arrives, which is supremely irritating. She's on the arm of Rudy, the Events Director, smiling at the modest round of applause she receives. A waiter carrying a tray with a single martini and offers it to Jacqui. She puts on a show of being surprised and delighted before taking the drink and toasting the crowd. They cheer. I'm overcome with nerves suddenly and don't know why. I've had enough Dutch courage. I make my way towards them, navigating through the throng. I see Jacqui and Rudy making their way to a roped-off seating area. Jacqui catches my eye. 'Martha!' she calls. At least she remembered my name.

'Hi. You made it,' I say, trying not to sound sarcastic.

'Didn't we meet earlier?' Rudy says, unhooking the rope.

'Yeah.'

'I greet everyone where possible. Don't recall all the faces, but I remember yours. Champagne bather, right?'

'The very one.'

'Martha works for me,' Jacqui says.

'Oh, she's the assistant,' Rudy says.

I laugh and try not to make it sound fake.

Jacqui arches a brow. Rudy chuckles, but I detect an uncertainty in his expression.

'You look . . . glamorous,' I say to Jacqui, who is splendidly dressed in heels, a sequinned jumpsuit and a multi coloured, glittering summer coat.

'Martha's helping me with a secret project I'm working on,' Jacqui says.

'A secret project?' says Rudy. 'Please tell me *Lady Detective* is coming back!'

Jacqui grimaces. 'Apparently it is. But not with me.'

'Get out of here! There can be no *Lady Detective* without Jacqui DuLac!'

Jacqui gazes down at her martini wistfully, stabbing the olive inside with the cocktail stick. She necks it in one. 'Cassie Kowalski will return, but not as we know her. She will be living in the present day and will be played by some lame bimbo with no talent.'

'Oh my!' Rudy says.

I bite into a wedge of lime and enjoy the sour taste.

Jacqui continues. 'I pushed for her return, making the case for an older Cassie, a divorced mom with two grown-up kids, and a career fighting crime in what is still a man's world. The same Cassie, just older, wiser . . .' I notice her steely expression falter momentarily and hold my gaze. Is she welling up? '. . . I reassembled the old team. My pals. The writers, production team, and cast members, those who are still alive, that is. They were all on board. We were on the verge of being greenlit until the studio decided that to move forward, we had to reset Cassie as a younger version in modern times. They fired me but kept my team. I was ghosted by them and the studio. Jettisoned from my ship like the corpse of a much-admired captain whose time was long over.' Jacqui shrugs and looks around for a passing waiter.

'Bastards!' says Rudy.

'That's the industry.'

I almost feel bad for her. That really sucks.

'Hey, did you give any thought about doing a cameo in my play?' Rudy asks.

Jacqui holds up her glass. 'Sweetie, my mind is on one thing. Another martini.'

Chapter Six

The Undertaker

In the sixty-three years of Ernest Ridgewell's eventful life, he had never once travelled outside of the United States. That didn't mean he had not travelled, per se. No, sir. He had hitch-hiked, taken the Greyhound, ridden the trains north, south, east and west of the good ol' USA. In truth, Ernest considered himself one of life's nomads. Not a 'drifter' as some had unkindly called him. Nope, he was a nomad, a roamer, a gypsy. He stood firm in the belief that he had Romany blood streaming through his veins. His skin was swarthy and weather-beaten, and his hair was dark and pulled back into a ponytail. His hairline was receding, and he had strands of silver that he did not like one bit. But that was ageing and there was not a goddamn thing he could do about that.

The evening was warm and calm. The ship radiated a warm, spherical glow, yet beyond it, the sky was an ominous black, and the sea a mottled, dark mirror. Ernest had the odd feeling that he was trapped on board a tiny ship, like an antique ornament, inside a bottle. Strangely, it gave him comfort.

Alone on the library balcony, he flicked the flame of a plastic lighter on and off, a nervous habit he had never grown out of.

It was a backup to his beloved petrol lighter he had owned for thirty years or more. That had gone missing right before he boarded the ship. Either he dropped it, or some schmuck had lifted it from his pocket.

His lungs ached for a hit of nicotine, but smoking was not allowed on the balcony. There was a single designated spot for smokers, located on the upper deck at the front of the ship. He looked hungrily in its direction. It was a trek, but he figured the walk would do him good before hitting the sack. On the deck below, there was a party for the regular passengers, but he paid it no heed. Behind him, inside the library, he could hear the idle chatter and laughter of his colleagues who were having their own private welcome party marking the 25th anniversary of The Midnight Chorus Society. Ernest returned to his musings. He was Romany Gypsy all right and darn sure of it, despite having no proof. It was just something he felt deep inside. Terence Lamb, also known as 'The Fool', suggested he had Mexican blood. Ernest had not been happy about that. No, by his very nature, he was a wanderer and needed to move from place to place. For that reason, Ernest was as sure as eggs is eggs that he was Romany.

'You should get your DNA checked,' a stranger in the bar of a backwater town had said to him once. 'You just spit some into a bottle and mail it off to Ancestors dot whoever . . . they run it through some sort of system, a database I think, and write back with a full report on your history. They might even find family members like you. Ain't that somethin'?'

Ernest had supped quietly on his beer. Yep, that is somethin' he'd thought, but 1. He did not much like the idea of surrendering his undocumented DNA to anyone 'cause Lord knows he'd left enough of it at dozens of spots across the United States. And 2. There was no one like Ernest Ridgewell. Family or no family, he weren't interested in meetin' them. Hell, no!

A woman's voice interrupted his thoughts, 'Ernest, we haven't had the opportunity to catch up yet.'

He turned to see Wilma Franklin step onto the balcony. Her hands are clutched together, resting on her abdomen as if she's about to burst into song.

'No ma'am.'

She stood beside him and looked at the thinning party below with interest. 'Bernard tells me your first ever flight went well.'

'I took a few Ambien and slept through the entire ordeal.'

She smiled. 'I'm so glad you came. It wouldn't have been the same without you.'

He supposed that was true. Ernest has been a member of the Society for twenty years now and was elevated to the board fifteen years ago.

'We need your expertise and experience,' Wilma had told him.

At the time, he had resisted his proposed appointment because that meant he would have responsibilities, and in his book, nomads don't have no responsibilities. But the fact was, Ernest was getting to an age, as Wilma often reminded him, and ageing imposed challenges to his traditional lifestyle. 'You're not a young man anymore, Ernest. It's time to rethink your customs.' He understood that and knew he had to slow down. And so reluctantly, with the guidance of Wilma and his old friend, Bernard, he based himself in a remote trailer park in Idaho, where he settled into a semi-nomadic life with choral responsibilities that he had come to embrace. To his surprise, he was moderately content. And now, here he was cruising across the Atlantic, having just left a foreign land that had both entranced and puzzled him.

'They sure do talk funny, in the old world,' Ernest said, with a grin. 'One young lady spoke to me like she was a sweep straight out of *Mary Poppins*.'

Wilma leant forward, 'Some I could just not understand at all,' she said with a girlish giggle.

'Bernard has travelled the world. He understood. I didn't have to say much.'

A moment of silence hung in the air between them, broken by Wilma. 'Will you come inside and join the party?'

Ernest shook his head. 'It's late and I'm beat, Wilma. I need me some sleep. Big day tomorrow.'

She reached across and squeezed his arm. 'Of course. You go get some shut-eye and I'll see you at breakfast.'

They said good night, and Ernest made his way inside, navigating the throng and avoiding eye contact. He badly wanted a cigarette and then his bed.

A firm hand gripped his arm. 'Señor Ernesto! Where you headed, amigo?'

Ernest felt the muscles in his back tighten. Failed comedian-cum-stage-magician, Terence Lamb, a thorn in his side and a skid mark on the shoe of the Society. He was drunk. When Terence had been on the liquor, there was no one more obnoxious. He began to talk in an exaggerated Mexican accent. '*Yo mi chicano.* Let this gringo get you a margarita.'

Ernest reached for his lighter, furtively sparked the flame and placed it over Lamb's fingers. The idiot cried out and snatched his hand away. 'What the fuck?!'

'Dip it in a margarita. Cool it down, amigo,' Ernest said in a mock Mexican accent.

Lamb glared at him.

Ernest bade him good night.

On the deck below, the passenger party was over. The waiting staff were collecting glasses and cleaning debris from the tables and floor. A few inebriated stragglers were trying to find their way to their rooms. Otherwise, the walk towards the front of the ship was pleasant, peaceful and uninterrupted. He climbed the steps to the upper deck. It was dark up there with no sign of anyone else. Perfect, he thought. Maybe I'll have two smokes. He took the packet from his jacket pocket, removed a cigarette and placed it between his lips. Ernest thumbed the fleet wheel, but it failed to spark. He tried a second time, then a third but still no flame. 'Goddamn piece of crap.'

The familiar clink of a petrol lighter opening startled him. The flame whooshed into life. Someone was standing directly in front of him, holding his missing lighter. Their head was covered in a thick woolly balaclava. Instead of eye holes, there were large red buttons. The mouth was a twisted grin fashioned from different coloured buttons. 'Hello, Ernest.'

Ernest frowned, 'Do I know you?'

The masked stranger tilted their head. Ernest felt a primal instinct kick in. Fight or flight. Before he could do anything, the masked figure swung at him. Ernest felt a blinding pain ring through his temple. His head spun, his knees wobbled. They struck again, this time with greater force. Ernest dropped to his knees, the cigarette tumbling to the ground in a shower of spit. He could smell the coppery scent of blood. It was warm and ran over his ear and down to his neck. He heard a clanging sound and, through blurred vision, thought he could make out what looked like a large meat mallet on the floor. He tried to speak but couldn't. He felt the stranger's hands pulling him up and pushing him backwards. A fury burnt inside him, fuelling his need to survive. Then they slammed him against the deck rail. Ernest looked below. His vision was blurred, but he knew that was quite a drop. 'Nooo!' He growled, his voice dry and harsh. It was not his time. He swung his hands and furiously clawed at the button face. He tried to pull at the mask, but could only get a purchase on a button, which he hoicked off. Ernest blinked, confusion overwhelming him. And then an arm hooked underneath his crotch and tossed him over the rail. Fight or flight. The latter, it seemed. The masked figure repeatedly lit the lighter on and off as Ernest flailed helplessly at the air and plummeted to the deck below. Pain seared through his body as he crashed to the hard surface, and then the lights went dark forevermore.

Chapter Seven

Martha

The woman's scream chilled me to the core.

I had walked to the front of the ship for a pre-bedtime stroll to clear my head after necking three glasses of complimentary champers before the party ended. Jacqui had wished everyone and their daughter, and granddaughters, good night, leaving the soirée a little worse for wear, escorted by her number 1 fan, Rudy, who had done his best to make her exit as dignified as possible.

The scream!

With Dutch courage in my veins, I run in its direction with the intent of rescuing a sister from who or what I had no idea. I see a woman, trembling and pointing to the deck above. I follow her gaze. It's dark up there, but I make out the silhouette of someone looking down. Whoever they are, they step back, melt into the shadows, and disappear.

The woman turns her attention to the floor. Someone is lying near her feet. As I hurry towards her, I see, and I understand. It's the twisted body of a man, dressed head to toe in a black suit. I recognise him. It's the smoking man from check-in. My throat dries. His eyes are wide and seem to be fixed on me, yet they are lifeless. I notice a deep, bloody gash on his temple. I'm about to dial 999 when I come to my senses and realise where I am. My stomach churns, and I flinch when the woman lets out a second, ear-splitting scream. Other passengers are rushing towards us. I'm trembling, yet I hurry to the woman and take her hand, which is soft, podgy and cool. I feel myself break into a sweat. 'Come with me,' I tell her in a calm but shaky voice. She doesn't resist, and we both step back, averting our eyes from the dead man.

'Oh my God!' I hear a man cry. 'Did he jump?'

'I think I'm going to puke,' a woman says.

'Please, get some help,' I cry.

Minutes later, crew members arrive and begin shepherding us away from the scene. A tall, broad man with cropped hair directs their efforts.

'How are you doing?' I ask the woman.

'I'm scared,' she replies.

'Don't be. I learnt this in therapy. Take a few breaths with me,' I tell her, holding her hands gently, breathing in slowly and exhaling. She follows my rhythm, her eyes fixed on mine. After three breaths, I smile at her and she smiles weakly back. She tells me her name is Patty Ortiz and she's from Illinois. I notice her wedding band. 'Are you travelling with your husband?'

She nods.

'Where is he?'

'Drunk and snoring.'

I see her sneak a glance at the body. 'Don't look,' I tell her gently.

'I saw what happened,' Patty says.

'What do you mean?'

She looks up at the upper deck where we had both seen the

shadowy figure. 'There was a struggle. He was pushed over the edge.' Her eyes glistened with tears.

'Excuse me, ladies,' comes a deep baritone voice.

I turn to see the broad crew member with cropped hair.

'I'm the ship's Head of Security. My name is Todd Atkins. A passenger mentioned you were at the scene before anyone else. Did either of you see what happened?'

'He was murdered!' Patty cries.

The expression on Todd's face turns grim. 'Ma'am, please, keep your voice down.'

I reason that Todd does not want to panic the other passengers and turn my gaze back to the scene. Two crew members are unfurling a fire blanket. Patty can't contain herself. 'There was a fight. Someone pushed him over.'

Todd frowns at Patty. 'How certain are you?'

She shrugs, unable to articulate 'He was . . . He was—'

'Ma'am, don't say anything more for the time being. I need you both to come with me and make a statement.' He looks behind him at two approaching crew members. 'Can we get some help here?' he calls, but his voice seems distant.

I can't stop staring at the body, his wild, dead eyes and the growing pool of blood. My stomach lurches once more, and I feel bile burn my throat. And then it comes: a tsunami of food and alcohol spills from my mouth and onto the deck floor. My head is spinning. I need to get away, so I turn, and I run to the edge of the deck.

With the remaining contents of my stomach barfed into the Atlantic, Patty and I are taken down to Todd's office in the depths of the ship for questioning. I sit on a bench in the corridor outside, drinking a bottle of water. I'm feeling a little better despite an emerging headache and being tired. It's fair to say today hasn't been a regular day. I've become the assistant to a

Hollywood diva, who fired me and subsequently rehired me. I then stumble onto a murder scene and chuck my guts up. Great start to the journey. It can only get better, I reassure myself.

Patty's first in with Todd, accompanied by her rotund bathrobe- and croc-wearing husband, who, judging by his bloodshot eyes and unkempt hair, has just been hauled from his bed. I can see them through the blinds. Patty is upset, crying. Her husband seems to be doing a lot of talking. Occasionally, I see Todd glance my way.

Thirty minutes pass before Patty and her husband leave. I wish her good night and tell her to take care, but she doesn't seem to hear me.

'Miss Hammond. You can come in now,' says Todd.

I enter.

It's a long, galley-style office with a desk that's too wide for the narrow space. The walls are adorned with plans of each deck. I notice a glass cabinet with a set of keys. One is labelled The Brig.

'Take a seat, Miss Hammond,' he says, adopting a formal air. Todd is a big man with colossal thighs and has to squeeze past his desk and into his chair.

'How are you feeling?'

My head is beginning to throb. I shrug.

He rests his massive arms on the desk and knits his fingers together. 'It would seem Mrs Ortiz has rethought her story.'

'Why?'

'She had a lot to drink and is now of the opinion that she might have imagined it.'

'Bullshit.'

'Excuse me?'

'I saw him too.'

Todd frowns. 'Who did you see?'

'The man on the upper deck.'

He sighs. 'Miss Hammond, how much did you have to drink this evening?'

I fold my arms. 'What has that got to do with anything?'

'I checked your bar receipts.'

I feel my stomach clenching.

'Mrs Ortiz had a lot to drink also.'

'Oh, so we're just two hysterical, drunk women. Is that what you're saying?'

'That's not at all what I'm saying.'

'I didn't have a lot to drink!' This is a lie, but I feel it's justified because he clearly doesn't believe either of us.

'Miss Hammond, I don't mean any disrespect. I just have to take yours and Mrs Ortiz's alcohol consumption into consideration when I file my report.'

I feel myself bristling. 'Patty saw everything.'

'Thank you, Miss Hammond. It's late. Please get some sleep. We'll talk again.'

Furious, I stand and try my best not to tremble.

'I'll see you out.'

Chapter Eight

Martha

I'm running up the corridor of the ship, glancing back at the masked man pursuing me. Dressed in running gear, my heart pounds as I sprint for my life. The lights are flashing, and my body is damp with sweat.

'Help me!' I cry, but all the doors remain shut, and no one comes.

'They're all dead and you will be too!' the killer cries.

The corridor feels never-ending and despite the distance between us, it feels like we're on a treadmill, yet still he is gaining on me. Ahead, I see an abandoned trolley of rotten, half-eaten food outside a room. As I pass it, I use all my strength to haul it across the corridor to block him. He skids to a stop to push it away, buying me a few precious moments. At last, the end of the corridor nears and I see the stairs. I leap at them, taking them two at a time until I reach the doorway to the main deck and burst outside. I scream for help, but no one is around. I realise it's not the main deck but the upper deck.

I hear his footfalls pound the stairs.

I have to get out of here but can see no exit. Just barriers all around. I run to one, and below, I see my fellow passengers partying at the main bar.

'Heeeelp me!' I cry, but they do not hear.

I feel an arm around my neck, squeezing the windpipe, blocking oxygen. He's dragging me to the other side of the deck. I try to fight but he is strong and I'm weakening. He lifts me onto the barrier.

'You could swim your way back to shore,' he says, but it's not a man's voice. It's Jacqui's.

She pushes me over. My hands flail at her, my fingers catch her mask. I pull it off, and as I fall, I look back to see Diane's face laughing at me.

I scream . . .

. . . And wake from the nightmare, my body coated in sweat. The room is fiercely bright. I raise my hand to stave off the glare from the balcony window. I sit up too quickly, head spinning. As my vision adjusts, I look through a gap in the curtains and see that the sky is a deep aqua blue, with the sun beaming. I take a moment to gather my thoughts and shake the dream from my head. The events of the night before return to me. The murder of the smoking man and the fact that Todd Atkins seems so keen to cover it up. Is he involved or is he trying to protect the company? I rub my arms and try to make sense of it all but can't. I need to structure my thoughts. I check my phone. No messages. The time is 6.22 a.m. I'm wide awake now and feel grubby. I take a long, hot shower and brush my teeth. These simple, familiar routines help me process my thoughts. I blow-dry my hair, get dressed, and ready for the day.

Something is burning inside me. Partly it's fear, because a killer is on the ship, but mostly I'm overcome with the need to find the truth. Head of Security Todd is eager to dismiss mine and Patty's stories. I feel a surge of anger at his implication that just because we delicate women had a little too much to drink our imaginations ran away with us.

My phone rings.

It's Jacqui. 'Shit!' I'd completely forgotten why I'm here. My job. My dream job! I consider ignoring the call but decide against it. Despite my new focus, I have responsibilities. I swipe and answer. 'Morning!' I say, forcing a fake cheeriness.

'Thank God you're awake!' she says, her voice croaky.

'Yeah, couldn't sleep—'

'I need drugs.'

What the hell? Are her assistants also drug dealers? 'I'm not sure I can help you there. I'm not a drug kinda gal.'

'Not those sort of drugs, goddamnit, it's my head!'

'Oh, sorry . . . I might have paracetamol.'

'Para what? No, I need Advel . . . Tylenol . . . aspirin.'

'It's just gone 7 a.m. I'm not sure the chemist will be open.'

'This is America, honey, we have drug stores, and they will be open.'

I want to remind her that we're on the Atlantic and it's day two; we're therefore probably closer to the UK than to America, but I hold my tongue. 'I'll see what I can do.'

'I want all three!' she bellows and hangs up.

I roll my eyes and search my toilet bag. I find four remaining paracetamol. I grab them and exit the cabin. I'll make a stop at 'the drug store', but for now, I have one location I need to get to fast.

I hurry up the corridor, passing pockets of people leaving their cabins and heading in the direction of the breakfast buffet. There's a cluster of hungry pensioners waiting impatiently for the lift. I take the stairs instead.

It's a beautiful, cool morning. The crew are setting up the sun loungers and a few brave souls are already swimming in the pool, which must be freezing at this time of day. I hurry to the stairwell leading up to the upper deck and notice a chain with a 'CLOSED' sign blocking access, along with a crew member standing guard. I wonder if the killer left any evidence behind. I stroll casually towards the guard, smile and say good morning. He wears a Security badge pinned to his shirt. His name is Tony Gomez. Job title: Security Deputy.

He returns the greeting minus the smile.

I shift on my feet. 'Could I get by, please?' You don't ask, you don't get.

'I'm afraid the deck is closed for the time being, ma'am.'

Shit.

'Is everything OK?' I ask cheekily.

'Everything is just fine.'

I nod a thanks, stroll casually away and perch myself on a nearby sun lounger. I pretend to scroll on my phone but keep a watchful eye on him. Almost fifteen minutes pass, and to my frustration, he hasn't moved. Time is running short, and I can practically feel Jacqui's irritation reach across the ship and jab me like a giant tentacle. I see two men descend the stairs from the upper deck. One is Head of Security, Todd Atkins, the other is an older man dressed in a bright white shirt with starred lapels. I assume he must be the captain. The guard unhooks the chain and lets them pass. The three men talk quietly for a moment before, to my surprise, leaving. The chain with the sign remains in place. I watch them disappear out of sight and make my way towards the stairs. When I'm sure no one is watching, I unhook the chain, reattach it and leg it up to the deck.

It's a functional space and seems little more than an elevated deck with uninterrupted 360-degree views. I feel my heart pounding as I make my way forward, retracing what I think are the murderer's steps. I scan the area but see nothing; there is no crime scene tape or evidence markers. I'm unsure whether cruise ships have police officers or not. Todd is Head of Security; Gomez is his deputy. Is that the extent of the policing on board? I peer over the balcony and look down. I see Todd and the captain below. Todd looks up, and I pull quickly away. Did he see me? I crouch and examine the wall of the balcony. It takes a few moments until I see it. Taking out my phone, I photograph the spray of blood. I think about the dead man. He was looking at me with those lifeless eyes, and on his temple was a large gash. He'd been struck by a weapon of some sort before being tossed over the balcony. I pocket my phone and hurry back to the stairs. My heart sinks when I see a grim-faced Todd making his way up.

Chapter Nine

Martha

I'm back in the depths of the ship, sitting in the hallway outside Todd Atkins's office. It has a stale coffee mixed with an unnatural air freshener smell about it. I perch on the world's least comfortable chair, the kind designed to punish anyone who sits on it. I have no signal or Wi-Fi on my phone. If Jacqui texts or calls, demanding to know where her drug store haul is, there's nothing I can do about it. She should really call room service. Inside, Todd's voice rumbles low, occasionally cut by the deputy's humourless bark. I can't make out the words, but I don't need to. The subject is me: Martha, idiot amateur, who wandered into a crime scene like it was a matinee show.

'Coffee?'

I look up.

A young woman holding a Styrofoam cup in each hand smiles at me. She has brown curls falling out of a bun and wears an oversized blazer. Her badge is crooked. I tilt my head to read her name: Janie Callaghan, Security Assistant.

'I, um . . . thought you might like one.' She holds it out like an offering.

I take it, the warmth seeping into my cold fingers. 'Thanks. You read minds?'

She laughs, a quick nervous flutter. 'Just faces. You looked like someone who needed coffee more than oxygen.'

'Accurate,' I admit, sipping. It's weak and has sugar. Not my beverage of choice, but I appreciate the gesture.

She leans against the wall, lowering her voice. 'Don't worry too much. Todd's fair. Gomez, though . . .' She trails off, chewing her lip. 'He doesn't do shades of grey.'

From inside, Gomez's voice spikes, sharp as a slap. Todd counters, steady but heavy.

I glance at Janie. She can't be more than twenty-two, fresh out of school, still wearing the shine of someone who thinks hard work will protect her.

'You like your job?'

'Yeah, I guess. It's my first trip. My mom says it'll build character.'

I give a dry laugh. 'Yeah, well, so does prison.'

Her eyes widen, then she laughs too, softer, conspiratorial.

Through the door, chairs scrape. Todd's baritone cuts off Gomez's growl. A moment later, the handle rattles.

'Guess you're up,' Janie whispers, squeezing my arm before she slips away, leaving me with the coffee, and a withering look from Gomez, who, I suspect, would like nothing better than to toss me overboard.

Todd's office is compact and windowless.

Last night I was a little worse for wear and in shock, too. The sight of the smoking man's twisted corpse still lurks at the front of my consciousness, but at least I'm feeling better than when I last sat in this seat. Todd eases his bulk into his chair. I notice a brown evidence bag on his desktop, with UPPER DECK and today's date written on it.

'You should get a larger office,' I tell him. 'Or a smaller desk.'

He ignores my comment.

'What's in the bag?' I ask.

His eyes fall to the evidence bag. Reaching for it, he opens a desk drawer, drops it inside and locks it.

Our eyes meet. He's found something, and he knows I can see straight through him.

'Is it a secret?'

'What were you doing on the upper deck?' he asks.

I ignore his question and nod at the wall. 'I was just looking at your key box. You have a brig.'

'And a morgue.'

'Are they both occupied?'

'The morgue has a guest.'

I'm suddenly fascinated that there's a morgue on this ship and want to know more, but I don't want to lose my thread. 'No killer locked up in the brig then?'

He regards me in silence.

I smile thinly at him.

'The upper deck was clearly off limits to passengers. What were you doing there?' he says.

'Probably the same as you. Looking for clues.'

He fixes me with an impatient, steely gaze. 'It was suicide, Miss Hammond.'

'Suicide?' I ask, incredulously.

'They are not uncommon on cruise ships.'

'Yet you have an evidence bag.'

'And what do you suppose might be in that evidence bag?'

'A murder weapon?'

'Or a suicide note?'

'Patty witnessed a murder.'

'What did she tell you? Her exact words, please.'

'She told me there had been a struggle between two men. One threw the dead guy over the balcony.'

He nods slowly as I speak, his gaze is unsettling, his eyes never leaving mine.

'What did you see?'

'I saw a dead man who had just fallen to his death—'

'Did you see him fall?'

'No.'

'Did you hear a struggle?'

'Well . . . no.'

'Did you see a struggle?'

'No, but—'

'Did you see this other man on the upper deck?'

I hesitate before answering. Todd is a pro, and I'm starting to feel out of my depth. 'It was dark. I—'

'You saw shadows.'

'Patty said she saw him.'

'Yes, you keep saying that, except Mrs Ortiz has decided that she may have been confused.'

'What changed her mind?'

'Her husband seems to think she has a fertile imagination. Mrs Ortiz agrees with him.'

I feel myself bristling. Mr Ortiz is clearly a gaslighting swine. 'Are you saying you believe Mr Ortiz over his wife?'

'You had a lot to drink yesterday, Miss Hammond.'

'You've seen my bar receipts. I remember.'

'I also spoke to staff at the reception and the welcome party.'

'Wow. You're really going out of your way to prove that Patty and I are wrong.'

He shrugs. 'I hope you have recovered?'

'Something I ate didn't agree with me.' Another lie.

He holds my gaze for a moment. 'I'm sorry to hear that. Would you like to file a complaint?'

'I'm better now.'

He nods.

I glance at the screen of my phone. 'Is that the time. My boss needs me. I should get going.'

'Of course.'

I stand.

'One last thing,' says Todd. 'Miss Hammond, this gentleman has taken his own life. That is the only logical explanation. I must therefore ask you to keep this, and Mrs Ortiz's wild theories, to yourself. Do not discuss them with anyone. Not even Mrs Ortiz. You can imagine that if this story gets around, it will upset many of our passengers and ruin the vacation they have spent a lot of money on.'

His warning is as subtle as being slapped on the face by a wet fish. This is not so much about whether there was a murder or not. This is about avoiding litigious passengers suing for compensation because the death of a fellow passenger has ruined their holiday. I fix a smile. 'I understand.'

'Thank you for your time. You have a good day now.'

Being a true crime obsessive, and having read enough detective novels to fast track me into the service, I know to find a killer you start by understanding the victim. Before I leave, I ask, 'What's the dead man's name?'

He arches a brow at me. 'I can't tell you that.'

I exit the office feeling a little shaken. Despite Todd's warning, I need to speak with Patty and find out why she has changed her mind. First things first, I need to report to Lady Detective HQ.

I make my way to the lifts and exit at the VIP deck. I spot Jacqui's 'arch-enemy', Cilla of the Christian Louboutin boots, talking privately with the captain. 'Good morning,' I say. Cilla is not impressed with the interruption and fires daggers at me, but the captain is courteous and replies with a good morning. Their eyes follow me as I walk by. When I'm safely out of earshot, they resume their conversation. I recall Cilla owns the cruise company and assume the captain is briefing her on what they're calling a 'suicide'.

I'm about to knock on the door to Jacqui's apartment, but I stop when I hear laughter. I put my ear to the door and listen.

'You're a riot!' I hear Jacqui cry. She seems to have made a miraculous recovery from her hangover.

The door swings open, and I almost tumble into Rudy. 'Found her!' he says.

'I bring drugs,' I say.

'Nice of you to finally show up,' says Jacqui. 'Thanks, but Rudy, my saviour, beat you to it.'

'Sorry, I got delayed.'

'I heard you'd been arrested.'

'What?! No, of course not.'

'Rudy saw you cuffed and escorted down to the brig against your will.' I spot her winking at him.

'Did you bust out or something? Are you on the run?' Rudy asks.

They both burst into fits of laughter.

'Very funny. I wasn't cuffed.'

'So, what happened?' Jacqui asks.

Todd's warning rings in my ears. 'I'd rather not say.'

'Have you been doing drugs?' she asks, her face serious.

'Let's have a party!' Rudy laughs.

'Of course not,' I say. 'I told you, I don't do drugs.'

'Then why were you arrested?'

'I wasn't arrested. I was questioned.'

'About what?'

'I'm not allowed to talk about it.'

'There was an accident last night,' Rudy says. 'Someone was hurt. We've all been briefed on it.' He gives me a furtive wink. 'I should get back to work. See you gals later.'

I mouth a thank-you to him as he leaves.

'We need to start work,' I hear Jacqui say.

'Let's get to it,' I reply.

Chapter Ten

Wilma

Ernest Ridgewell had been scheduled to assist Wilma and her husband Frank set up and man the reception desk for the Society's annual convention. But Ernest had not shown up, and Wilma found herself in a cockamamie flap as she hurried down the secluded corridor carrying another goddamn box of who knew what to the spot where the desk was situated. Fortunately, Wilma and Frank were both early risers, which bought her time to set everything up by herself, having dispatched Frank to find Ernest.

It was not unusual for Wilma and Frank to work out of hours, whether early in the morning or late into the night. They were the proud owners of the Franklin Guest House back home in Kennebunkport, Maine, where flexibility was essential to ensure that the needs of their customers were met, and the couple's personal and somewhat 'niche' pursuits were satisfied. Built as a private mansion for a former tea merchant in the 1890s, the bed and breakfast was tucked away in a quiet part of town and was open to anyone, especially those in need. Over the years, Wilma and Frank had positively impacted many lives, and to the locals, they were considered pillars of the community.

They had even set up a neighbourhood watch scheme, which had seen Kennebunkport become a safe and secure place, all thanks to the efforts of the Franklins.

But mainly Wilma.

Sitting alone at the reception desk at the entrance to the Hefferman conference centre, a private space away from the other passengers, she took a breath and smiled to reassure herself. With the blade of scissors, she sliced through the box's plastic tape, opened the flap and lifted out a stack of itineraries. She felt a swelling of pride for what was another of her outstanding achievements: the Society, which today entered its twenty-fifth year. 'The happiest of birthdays,' she said, quiet as a mouse. Letting out a giggle, Wilma slid her tortoise shell glasses up her nose, examined the itinerary and grinned. This was surely the greatest line-up of events and panels they had ever had. And the closing party was going to be the icing on the cake. Each year, Wilma organised the annual convention, and with the recent exponential rise in members and appreciators, this was to be the biggest celebration of the Society to date.

'I knocked on his door, but he didn't answer!'

Lost in her thoughts, Wilma jumped at the sound of Frank's voice. At eighty-three, he was seven years older than her, and she'd often forget how light on his feet he could be for a man of his advanced years. He could still pad down a dark alleyway, with the stealth of a panther stalking its prey despite his creaking knees and clicking hip. 'How hard did you knock?'

'I knocked hard, dear.'

'And you're sure it was the right room.'

'As sure as I'm standing right here.'

'Did you call him like I asked you?'

'I did . . .'

'And?'

'It went to his voicemail again.'

'Shoot!'

'But I heard his phone ringing.'

'In the room?'

'Yes, in the room.'

'I phoned again but no answer.'

Wilma chewed her lip. It was not like Ernest to be unresponsive. Sure, he was a loner who would take himself off for weeks on end to do what he needed to do. But when it came to his chorus responsibilities, he was committed to his duties. 'Help me get set up.' Wilma pointed to a brown cardboard box on the floor. 'The name badges need sorting.'

'But that's Ernest's job.'

Wilma felt her neck and face flushing. 'Darn it, Frank, Ernest has gone AWOL, and we are about to be set upon by one hundred and forty-eight guests, so will you quit your damn dawdling and get to helping me some.'

Wilma's sharp tone had kicked her husband into action. Frank began tearing open the box.

She paused at the sound of footsteps approaching. Urgent, and male, judging by the heavy tread. Two men dressed in white uniforms came into view. Wilma and Frank exchanged a nervous glance. One of the men was tall and broad with cropped hair. The second was smaller and looked Spanish. The tall one spoke. 'Good morning.'

Wilma returned the greeting, quickly placed the itineraries back in the box and rested her hands protectively on top, 'This is a private conference. It's an off-limits event even to members of the crew.'

'That I understand, ma'am. If I could introduce myself. My name is Todd Atkins. I'm the Head of Security onboard the ship. This is Deputy Gomez. Are you Wilma Franklin?'

Wilma felt a twist in her stomach. 'That is correct. What can I do for you, Mr Atkins?'

'Could we talk . . .' He glanced at Frank. '. . . in private?'

'We have fifteen minutes until registration, and there's only us to set up. Can it wait?'

'I'm afraid it cannot.'

Wilma's lips tightened. She was a stickler for timings and did not want to be late, no matter the reason. She felt like screaming at these two man-cows but that would not be dignified. Besides, he was Security, and she, for the sake of the Society, had to play by the rules of the ship. 'My husband and I have no secrets. We can talk here.'

'Let's take a room,' he said. Her fingers tightened on the open scissors when Atkins stepped around her desk and opened the door to one of the conference rooms. He nodded for them to enter.

Atkins closed the door behind him. The Deputy waited outside. Frank stood by the door, shifting nervously on his feet. Wilma felt a sharp pain in her hand and realised she was still squeezing the scissors. She relaxed and looked down to see a thin cut on her palm. An omen, she thought.

'Mr Ernest Ridgewell was travelling with you, I believe.'

Wilma blinked. 'Yes. That's correct.'

'How well do you know him?'

'Well enough. Has something happened?'

'I'm afraid that Mr Ridgewell has passed away.'

Wilma felt her eyes widening at this bombshell. 'But I only saw him last night.'

'How did he seem?'

'Fine. Tired from travelling, but otherwise he seemed himself.'

'Did he act like he was in any sort of trouble?'

'Trouble?' Wilma did not like the implication of the question.

'Any help you can give us would be greatly appreciated.'

'No, he was just Ernest.'

The door opened suddenly, and Priscilla Hefferman stepped inside with a thunderous expression. 'Mr Atkins, the captain would like to speak with you.'

Atkins as good as stood to attention, 'Ma'am. Good morning. I was following up—'

'The captain, Mr Atkins,' Priscilla said sharply.

'Yes, ma'am.' And with that, he said farewell and exited the conference room.

Wilma stared at Priscilla. 'What on earth is going on?'

'Ridgewell is dead is what's going on.'

'But how?'

'The idiot fell from the upper deck, apparently.'

'An accident?'

'No. Someone killed him.'

'Who?'

'That we need to find out. There's a witness who claims she saw him being tossed over the rail. For the sake of my company, we've managed to convince her otherwise, but we need to be mindful. Someone in the Society has crossed the line.'

Wilma felt her throat drying. How could this have happened? There had been one golden rule for every Midnight Chorus Society convention for the past twenty-five years: NO MURDERS DURING CONFERENCE. Until now, that rule had been sacred. If she were truly honest with herself, then Wilma would admit she was surprised it had not happened sooner, especially with a society whose members were made up of serial killers and their appreciators.

Chapter Eleven

Martha

Jacqui and I are making our way up the stairs to the main deck. She's setting her Apple Watch to capture her steps. Ten thousand is the goal. I estimate that it will take between forty minutes and one hour of power walking several times around the perimeter of the ship. Oh hurrah. Exercise is not my thing. But at least we're starting work. We move against a stream of people coming down the stairs, lanyards swinging from their necks. I catch a glimpse of a logo I vaguely recognise and wonder if there's some conference happening on board.

We exit onto the deck and shield our eyes from the mid-morning sun.

'Perfect!' Jacqui says, slipping on her Gucci sunglasses and smiling at the clear blue sky.

It occurs to me I don't have sun cream, which puts me into a panic. I make a mental note to buy some later. Jacqui is wearing her wide-brimmed sun hat. Her skin is clear, almost doll-like for a woman of her years. 'You have great skin,' I tell her.

She smiles at me, surprised at the compliment. 'Genetics. Plus, I stay out of the sun. Have done for thirty years. That's why I look so youthful.'

I bite my tongue. Perhaps some surgical assistance here and there, I think.

It's a buzz of activity outside. The sun loungers are occupied, the pool is a soup of middle-aged and elderly paddlers, with clusters of passengers standing around chatting and laughing. I feel a bite of paranoia and scan the faces, wondering if one of them is the killer. I tune into conversations as I pass, listening for any mention of last night's incident. But I hear nothing. I follow Jacqui to the rail at the edge of the deck. With one hand holding on to her hat, she leans against it and looks out to sea. After a moment, she says, 'It's glorious, isn't it?'

'Yes, it is.'

'We're almost following the same route as the *Titanic*.'

'I hope we make it to New York. I'm not quite ready to die yet.'

Jacqui chuckles. 'Me neither.'

We take in the view and the splendour of the cruiser slicing through the ocean. Looming above us, the ship's gold funnel catches the morning sun, its band of red gemstones gleaming like a crown studded with rubies. I have to admit it's quite something to lose yourself in.

'Have you been to New York?' Jacqui asks.

I blink at her and turn away. 'Once,' I say, my voice quiet.

'You know what they say about New York?'

I change the subject. 'I was a superfan of the movie . . . *Titanic*. I've lost count of how many times I've seen it.'

'My daughter was too.'

'Is she still a fan?'

Jacqui glances at her watch. 'Shall we get to walking and working?' she replies, ignoring my question.

'Yes, of course.'

We begin the marathon.

'So, tell me. Have you watched *Lady Detective*?'

'I was only hired two days back. Sorry. But I did see the opening titles on YouTube.'

'Right. We should fix that.'

'I did a bit of research online in the time I had.'

'What did you learn?'

'Well . . . it's a cop show from the nineties. It ran for four seasons—'

'Forget the technicalities. Tell me what you know or think you know about Cassie Kowalski.'

Recalling the show's trailer on YouTube and the Wikipedia entry, I begin to compose my thoughts. 'So, Cassie is the only female detective working in a male environment. That brings its challenges, although she does have some supportive male colleagues . . .' I glance at Jacqui to ensure she's not cringing before carrying on '. . . Cassie is beautiful, kick-ass and criminally underestimated by her boss, colleagues and the bad guys . . .' Aside from the beautiful part it feels I might be making this up. Still, perhaps I'm just super smart and was able to ascertain it all from the trailer alone. 'She's assigned cases that men cannot do. She goes undercover as an air hostess, a hairdresser, a nun.'

'Don't forget hooker.'

'I don't think we use that term anymore.'

Jacqui lets out a cackling laugh. 'Oh, please. Let's not go there.'

'I'm just saying it's offensive to those who work in the sex industry.'

'Oh, really? And they've told you this, have they?'

'We should be more aware of people's feelings.'

'Jeez, what is it with you Gen Z people?'

'I'm not Gen Z!' I say, my voice a little high.

'Well, you must be older, which means you're a millennial . . . that explains a few things.'

'Excuse me?'

I see her looking me up and down. My tomboyish outfit and DM boots.

'Are you a lesbian?'

'Why would you ask that?' I say exasperated.

She shrugs. 'It's OK if you are.'

'Just because I don't wear pretty frocks and paint my face, that makes me a lesbian? Very progressive thinking.'

She purses her lips. 'Are you binary, non-binary, tri-binary? I want you to know it's OK if you're any of those, and a lesbian too.'

I'm wound up now, and it's coming through in my voice. 'No, I'm not. I'm me, Martha. I like boys and I identify as she/her. And what's tri-binary?'

She slides her sunglasses down and peers at me over the rims. 'OK, OK. No need to lose your shit.'

Taking some deep breaths, I try to calm myself.

'I was just teasing you.' Jacqui says.

I don't look at her.

'What is tri-binary, anyway?' she asks.

'You tell me.'

'Maybe I made it up.'

I sigh.

'So, where were we? . . . Hookers.'

I roll my eyes.

'*Lady Detective* ran for four seasons with twenty-four episodes each. That was a tough schedule. You don't see that these days. You get a third of that if you're lucky. In each season, there was a bunch of different undercover careers for Cassie to investigate crimes. The premise was to find a killer, you start by understanding the victim. It worked. Viewers loved seeing Cassie take on a new role each week and solve a murder.'

We walk in silence for a moment, Jacqui smiling, lost in nostalgia, I imagine.

'We never repeated the same job, except for one exception. Can you guess what that was?' she says.

I don't need to guess. I know what she's going to say, but I'm stubborn and shake my head, 'No idea.'

'Have a guess,' she persists.

I shrug.

'Every season I was a hooker of some sort. You need to understand that those days were different. That's what . . . sex workers . . . were called. If you asked a hooker what she did for a living, she'd say, I'm a hooker. It's obviously not the case now. But back then, that's how it was.'

I want to remind her that this is not the nineties, but I bite my lip. I feel like an invisible wall has been erected between us, which is not good for our collaboration. 'I wasn't diminishing the show or you.'

'What do you think the fascination with the sex trade said about the show and the viewers?'

I picture a room full of overweight, smoking white male writers having a wankfest over the hot detective lady who went undercover as a hooker . . . sex worker . . . one week and a lusty librarian the following week, but I keep my thoughts to myself. 'People like sex and danger. Preferably in the same episode?'

'Cassie was important . . . important to me and so many women. Through your woke eyes, you see a woman created by a patriarchy of writers . . .' I avert my gaze. Did she read my mind? '. . . But what you fail to recognise is that I was the star of that show and I had those guys wrapped round my finger. I wanted to cover the sex trade in the show because it was a mirror of what was happening on the streets at the time. Our ratings increased, and some people came to understand what those women went through. I shaped Cassie and made her the heroine that people still love today. And that is why I want her back.'

I feel a sneaking admiration that I resent feeling.

We've reached the front of the ship where I saw the body last night. There are pockets of passengers and crew all around. I feel a knot in my stomach, so I slow my pace. Am I being watched? Did the killer see me last night? I freeze without realising it and look down at the spot where the body had lain. It's clean with no indication of bloodstains. I recall his face and dead eyes, but more importantly, the large wound on his temple. Someone had walloped him before tossing him over the balcony. I look up to where I saw the mysterious figure last night.

I wonder if he will kill again.

I don't doubt he will. There's danger on this ship. I feel isolated, far away from the safety of home and everything I know. A killer is among us. Somewhere, within the happy faces of the passengers and crew, is a murderer.

'Martha!'

Jacqui's voice shakes me from my thoughts. I see her way ahead, waving to me. 'Come on' she calls. 'Only 9300 steps to go before lunch.'

Chapter Twelve

Wilma

The Midnight Chorus Society. Twenty-five years old and still Wilma's proudest creation. Her personal body count might be her true legacy, but this was the one that would outlive her. She'd dreamt of a world where people like her and Frank could stop pretending, could turn their urges into craft. So she built it. A club for excellence, not chaos. An invitation-only refuge for those who valued precision over impulse, mentorship over mess. They came for safety, stayed for admiration, and found belonging. Five years in, the conferences began, killers flying in from every corner. She needed a name, a brand, something harmless, even charming. The Midnight Chorus Society sounded social, musical, almost sweet. Beneath it lay the truth: a choir of predators, the children of the night, making their own kind of music. Their logo was a hood-shaped emblem, the face inside split cleanly in two – half theatre mask, half skull. Elegant, polished, and unsettling, it was a perfect nod to the Society's performance of respectability, the choral façade that hid its true nature.

Before his untimely demise, Ernest Ridgewell had achieved a rare legendary status in his specialist field. His exploits were documented online; on websites, federal databases and he had been the subject of several true crime podcasts. A wanted man for almost thirty years yet no one knew his name. Vague, unverified sightings of a tall man with dark hair, wearing a black suit, had been recorded, but his identity had remained hidden. The press had called him 'The Undertaker'. It seemed a fitting characterisation, even though Ernest never buried his victims. There was never enough time for that. Instead, he ensured they were always laid out peacefully as if in a coffin and wearing their Sunday finest. It was both respectful and decent. Wilma had always admired that about him.

But since his Christ-effing death, she was mightily vexed at him for not being more careful.

'Darn it, Ernest you goddamn bog sucker!' she muttered under her breath.

Wilma made an announcement that due to unforeseen circumstances, Ernest's hotly anticipated panel *Coffins Not Included* was now cancelled. However, the queue remained firmly in place. They were not taking 'no' for an answer.

'But I saw him last night at the welcome party,' shrilled a bespectacled young man with buck teeth and a grey shirt buttoned up to the collar. Frank was manning the reception desk. 'Well, he ain't here, no more!' he said, sharply.

Wilma had insisted Ernest's murder remain under wraps for the duration of the voyage. Suspicion and paranoia were ingrained in the DNA of society members. If the news were to get out, speculation and gossip would spread like a forest fire in a blistering summer. The sacred rule of NO MURDERS DURING CONFERENCE had been broken. It was possible that Ernest's murder was a one-off; revenge from a resourceful relative of a victim who discovered The Undertaker's true identity. However, Wilma knew that was a foolish assumption. She was on a ship carrying approximately 1,300 passengers. Almost 10 per cent of those were made up of seasoned serial killers, wannabes and their fans. She had no doubt there would be more murders and therefore had to find the killer. Wilma was not prepared to risk her life and the society's long-standing impeccable reputation.

She stepped forward and addressed the throng. 'Once again, please accept our deepest apologies. We will compensate you with a partial refund, I promise. Now please, do come back at 11 a.m. when we will reopen the desk.'

She bit her tongue and listened patiently to their discontent before deciding that enough was enough. Frank was shuffling flyers and avoiding eye contact with the disgruntled customers. Leaning across, she said, 'I have to go, dear. The others are waiting.'

He glanced nervously at the crowd, which was thankfully dwindling. 'I'll join you in a moment.'

Wilma fixed a smile at the remaining attendees and hurried down the corridor to Conference Room 1, the empty event space where Ernest's cancelled event was to be held.

The board sat in the front row and looked up as she entered: Bernard Koch, the Dentist; Timothy Garland, the Reverend; and Terence Lamb, the Fool. Along with Wilma, Frank, and the deceased Ernest, they formed the ruling circle of the Midnight Chorus Society. Each was a seasoned killer, their pasts stacked with years and bodies in equal measure. Some began in vengeance, others by accident, but once the itch took hold, it never left. Murder rewired them. It quieted the noise. It was, in its own way, their form of peace.

'Thank you all for coming.'

'Is it true?' Bernard asked, his face pale.

'I'm sorry, Bernard. I know you and Ernest were old friends.'

'The Mexican finally croaked it then,' said Terence with a dark chuckle. 'Good riddance.'

At forty-three, Terence was the youngest member of the board. His stage career had been cut short seven years ago chiefly because he lacked talent. He could be funny, Wilma sometimes saw that in him, but it rarely translated to the stage, which caused him no end of bitterness. He never stopped believing in his magic, though, specifically the twisted, dark kind that he practised, such as sawing his victims in half – literally. Wilma was always happy to give credit where credit was due.

Bernard glared at him. 'Show some respect.'

'What respect did that schmuck ever show me?'

Wilma noticed Bernard's fists clenching. 'You had a run-in with him last night.'

'And?'

'And now he's dead!'

The Reverend Timothy watched on with an amused expression. 'If you don't mind me elucidating my opinion. We have all, at some stage during our tenure on the board, had a run-in with Ernest. That said, if anyone's guilty of his murder in this room, my money is on the Fool.'

'What the fuck, man!' said Terence.

A slight, balding man with large, round glasses and pale white skin, the good Reverend was the only British person on the board. He sometimes reminded her of a village pastor from an episode of *Downton Abbey* she had once watched. However, he was anything but a benevolent, clichéd pastor. His resume of assisted dying and presiding over the funerals of his victims had long impressed Wilma; so much so that she had personally sought him out to join the Society two years back. Yet there was something about him, something she couldn't quite put her finger on, that troubled her.

'Hear, hear,' Bernard replied.

Terence's face reddened. He grabbed his crotch, squeezed it and said, 'Suck my fat one, you kraut tooth jockey!'

In the blink of an eye, Bernard was on his feet, brandishing a shining scalpel, the blade pressed into Terence's pale throat.

'Cut me and you lose your balls, old man,' said Terence, who had his own weapon, a serrated knife, lodged between Bernard's legs.

Wilma stepped forward, her hands raised in an appeasing gesture. 'Please, Bernard, Terence, put those toys away. We should not be arguing like this.' Both men levelled their eyes at the other before withdrawing. 'And Terence, please don't be so crass.'

'It was just a joke, Wilma.'

Wilma shook her head and tried to gather her thoughts.

'I heard you two arguing in his cabin,' Timothy replied, looking at Bernard.

Wilma frowned. It was unlike the Reverend to stir the pot.

'What on earth are you implying?!' said Bernard.

'Everyone, please just calm down,' said Wilma.

'We were all at the party when Ernest died,' said Terence.

'How do you know that for sure?' Bernard asked. 'Do we know what exact time he was murdered? I suspect you do.'

'Enough!' cried Wilma, noting the clouds of suspicion darkening their faces. 'This is a time for calm, a time for us to figure out what steps to take next, not turn on each other,' she said.

The door opened, and Frank shuffled inside. 'That's the last of them good and gone.'

Wilma continued. 'We're a team and we have the society to think about. As board members, I need each of you to be vigilant. Someone murdered Ernest. Despite your individual views of him, he was one of us. The Society has been violated. Our most sacred rule has been broken. This cannot go unpunished.'

'How do you suggest we do that?' Terence asked.

'We hunt the perpetrator down, give them a taste of their own medicine and bury them at sea.'

Chapter Thirteen

Martha

I'm ravenous after the walk and shaky because I skipped breakfast and slept badly. The buffet is bustling with hungry passengers cooing over the hot and cold delights on offer. I nab myself a double cheeseburger, chips, and a thick wedge of delicious-looking double pepperoni pizza. I also pour a large Diet Coke from the dispenser. Best not to push the calories too high.

Jacqui raises her eyebrows at my tray of junk but says nothing, which seems a little out of character. Maybe she thinks we're making progress with our working relationship. I will remain the obedient employee, but for now, I'm still wary of her outdated ideas and diva-ish behaviour.

We pass a table with four American tourists who plead for her to sit with them. Jacqui puts on a faux show of protest before seating herself. 'If you insist,' she tells them, proudly setting her appetite-of-a-sparrow plate of salad and melon in front of her. 'This is my assistant, Martha.'

Vexation scratches at me, but I ignore it and say good morning. They smile warmly and return the greeting. There are two men I recognise from my arrival in Southampton when they admitted to each other about having 'a boner' for Jacqui 'back in the day'. Bob and Don are their names. Bob is thickset with a bushy moustache, and Don is thin and balding. The other two are a married couple called Larry and Debbie. Both are wearing matching pink Lacoste polo shirts.

'We've been married for thirty years,' Larry says, in an accent I think is Deep South American.

'We've been saving for a long time to make this trip, isn't that right, Larry?'

'It sure is.'

'We're both divorced,' Bob tells us. 'Our wives left us.' Both Bob and Don chuckle at this.

I lift my enormous burger and take a huge bite. It's meaty, cheesy, greasy and delicious.

'Oh, I'm sorry to hear that,' Jacqui says sympathetically.

'Now there's a story,' says Don.

'They're shacking up together,' Bob adds.

'Your wives?' I ask, quickly swallowing and covering my mouth.

'Yup. They married.'

Jacqui says: 'I thought Martha was a lesbian, but I was wrong. She's a millennial.'

I give her a tight smile and take a sip of Diet Coke.

'Are you coming to my talk tomorrow evening?' Jacqui asks the table.

'Larry and I will definitely be there. We're so looking forward to it, isn't that right Larry?'

'Wouldn't miss it.'

'We'll be in the front row if I can extract Bob from the bar.'

Everyone laughs. I take another bite of my burger and spot a familiar face entering the buffet room. It's Patty Ortiz. Accompanying her with a stern face is her husband. I watch them make their way to a table for two. Patty takes a seat, and her husband leaves for the buffet. I need to talk to her quickly while she's alone. I tell Jacqui I'll be back momentarily and excuse myself from the table. I notice Mr Ortiz circling the hot food bar, sizing up what he wants for lunch. I hurry across to Patty's table and sit opposite her.

'Hi.'

She jolts in fright. 'You made me jump.'

'How are you doing?'

She looks down and begins to fidget with her cutlery and napkin.

'Patty?'

She looks across the buffet in the direction of her husband. 'I'm not allowed to talk to anyone.'

'What? Why?' I look across and see her husband building a mountain of potatoes on his plate. 'You can talk to whoever you like. Don't let your husband or anyone else tell you what to do.'

She stiffens and starts to wring the napkin.

'Someone was murdered last night. You saw it happen. Remember?'

She shakes her head, 'I'm not sure what I saw.'

'We were both there. You saw the killer!' I say gently but firmly.

She looks across the diner, searching for her husband.

'I saw him too. Up on the balcony where the dead man had fallen from.'

She looks at me then, eyes wide and full of fear.

'What did Todd say to you?'

She shakes her head.

'Did he threaten you?'

'No! He was very sweet. They upgraded our room to a suite.'

'You mean he's bought your silence.' I see her husband making his way to the drinks machine. He'll be back any moment.

'Can you meet me later?'

'I'm not allowed anywhere without my husband.'

Jesus, 'Patty, it's like you're living in an episode of *The Handmaid's Tale.*'

'I don't know what that is.'

'Never mind.'

'I prayed for his soul. We both did.'

'Did you get his name?'

She hesitates before answering. 'My husband asked so that we could pray for him properly. Can't pray without a name.'

I perk up. 'What is it?'

'I'm not allowed to say.'

Shit!

I bless myself, then reach across and take Patty's hands. 'I need to pray, too, Patty.' I give her the most benevolent smile I can muster. I'm positively glowing holiness. 'Help me, Patty. Help me pray for that poor man who was taken from us too soon . . . Lord Jesus . . . erm . . . save us, and him . . . take his soul . . . and compel it into the light . . . The power of Christ compels you! Let the power of Christ—' I frown to myself. Did I just quote from *The Exorcist*? I shoot a glance at Patty. Her eyes are down; her head is dipped. Phew. I close my eyes and roll my head back and forth and wonder if I should speak in tongues. I have no idea what I'm doing.

I open my eyes.

Patty's mouth is hanging open. Have I blown it?

She smiles. 'I knew you were a Christian woman. Is Jesus your saviour?' she says.

'Hell yes! Praise him . . . praise Jesus, and Mary and God . . . and all of . . . the Apostles. Except for Judas. He was a tosser, obviously.'

A flicker of uncertainty appears briefly on Patty's face before she gently squeezes my hands and dips her head once more. 'Pray with me now, Martha. Lord Jesus, hear our prayer. We beseech you to find a place in heaven for the troubled soul that was Ernest Ridgewell. Please, Jesus, find him peace in your holy realm.'

Ernest Ridgewell. I have you.

I tell Patty my room number and tell her to come see me anytime if she thinks of anything else.

'Patty!'

I look up to see Mr Ortiz's grim face looking my way. Patty loosens her grip, and I stand. 'Just praying for lost souls, Mr Ortiz,' I say. I look at Patty, smile sympathetically and thank her.

Now that I have his name, I feel confident I have a sound lead. There's much to dig up. It's quite possible Ernest was just a random kill, but then again, it's equally likely he was targeted. Had the killer been following him? Could the victim be someone close to the killer? So many questions, but this is good because I'm ready to go full-on Nancy Drew to uncover who he is.

I return to the table and find my seat has been taken, and the remainder of my lunch too. Jacqui is holding court with Bob, Don, Debbie, Larry and four new faces. She's waxing lyrical to the court of eager listeners about her years as the star of *Lady Detective*. I listen for a moment and smile at her anecdote about a real-life experience foiling a bank robbery when the 'dim-witted' thief panicked and fled upon seeing Detective Cassie Kowalski enter the building. 'Stop or I'll shoot, goddamnit! I shouted, but the guy was gone in a cloud of dust. Dumbass. He could have been rich if he had a few more brain cells.' She has a natural charm and wit that has the table laughing out loud. I might have laughed too if last night's murder was not forefront in my mind. I need to find out more about Ernest Ridgewell.

I've no doubt Todd has ensured a wall of silence has been erected when it comes to questions about the victim. But I wonder if I can convince the one crew member on the ship with whom I have formed a bond to tell me what he knows about Ernest Ridgewell. I needed to find Rudy.

Chapter Fourteen

Martha

I told Jacqui I had an errand to run and that I would see her at 2 p.m. She pursed her lips and suggested 1 p.m. instead. 'We have a lot to cover in the remaining days,' she reminded me. The hands of the Art Deco-style analogue clock on the wall were at 12.30 p.m. exactly. That didn't give me a lot of time to scour the ship for Rudy, persuade him to reveal a nugget of ship's gossip about the dead man, never mind getting back for my next session with the Queen of 90s TV detectives. After some haggling, we agreed on 1.15 p.m. I could tell from Jacqui's cool gaze that she was unimpressed. She'd probably lose her shit later and fire me again. I couldn't think of that right now, so I made my apologies and hurried out of the restaurant.

Finding Rudy was easier than I anticipated. A crew member told me he was directing the rehearsals for the *Murder She Didn't Write* production. I took the lift down to the fifth floor and made my way to the theatre. A sign reading 'No Entry: Rehearsals in Progress' was fixed to the door.

There is no one around, so I gently push down the handle and let myself in. The seating area is dark. The stage, however, is lit by spotlights and is made up like a cottage-style living room.

I see Rudy dressed in what I can only describe as an homage to TV's fictional sleuth-cum-bestselling-author, Jessica Fletcher, wearing sensible shoes, cream slacks, and a pink shirt with a maroon sweater tied over his shoulders. Around his neck is a string of pearls, and on his head is a caramel-coloured wig, the hair short and softly permed. Next to him, with hands on his hips, is a round man dressed as a sheriff. There are four other cast members kitted out in dated eighties-style costumes. One wears heels, a big-haired wig, and a glamorous red dress with exaggerated shoulder pads. There's a second woman dressed in dowdy, plain clothes, perched meekly on a threadbare sofa. Standing by a fireplace with a cigar in his mouth is a man in an oversized, pinstripe suit and a bad grey wig. Finally, a vicar is holding a china cup and saucer, just as vicars do in all crime dramas. A classic line-up of suspects. I tiptoe cautiously down the stairs and take a seat in the shadows out of sight.

'OK people! One more time,' says Rudy. He closes his eyes and dips his head. I assume he's getting into character. His cast members side-glance him and wait. Rudy raises a thumb and lifts his head, opening his eyes wide. He turns his gaze to the woman in the red dress and cocks his head, theatrically. 'So, Monica, I bet this is the last place you expected to see me.'

With a flourish, the character called Monica turns to face Jessica, 'Whatever are you implying?'

'I'm implying you committed a second murder to cover up the first. Chad knew about your affair with . . .' Jessica lets the line hang for dramatic effect as she scans the faces of the cast, '. . . the vicar!'

The dowdy woman stands abruptly. 'Jeffrey, how could you?' she cries.

'Yes, Jeffrey, how could you?' Jessica adds.

Vicar Jeffrey reaches into his pocket and tries to pull something out. Whatever it is, it won't budge. His face reddens, and after a moment, he says, 'Can't . . . get . . . my gun out.'

I wonder if this is part of what is clearly a pastiche but decide it's not when an exasperated Rudy pulls off his wig and cries, 'Right, that's it. We're done for the day.'

The actor in the red dress drops to the sofa and pulls off his heels, 'My chuffing feet are killing me,' he says.

'Sorry, Rudy,' says the vicar, brandishing a pistol, which looks unsettlingly real. 'I'll do better tomorrow.'

'We'll get there,' says Rudy with a heavy sigh.

I'm conscious of the time and make my way down to the stage. 'Oh hi,' I say.

'You shouldn't be in here,' says Monica, frowning.

'You do realise I'm armed,' adds the vicar.

I raise my hands. 'You got me.'

'She's with me,' says Rudy.

'You guys were great,' I say. 'I was on the edge of my seat.'

Rudy gives me a wry smile as the other cast members leave. 'This production will be the death of me.' He sits on the sofa and sets the wig gently beside him like it's a pet guinea pig. 'So, what did you really think?'

I step up to the stage. 'Honestly, I didn't see that much. But I enjoyed the campy, comedy elements injected into the performances.'

He blanches. 'Oh God. That's the opposite of what I'm trying to do.'

Shit! 'Erm . . . sorry. I didn't see much, so don't take my word for it. What do I know?'

He lets out a roaring laugh, gives me a playful shove and says, 'I'm shittin' ya, bitch!'

'Haha! You got me there.' I'm relieved but also use this as

segue into why I'm here. 'Listen. You know that so-called accident from last night?'

'The one that no one's allowed to talk about?'

'Yeah, that one. I was there. I saw it.'

His eyes widen. 'You saw him fall?'

'No . . . not exactly . . . actually, not at all. I got there just after he hit the deck. But there was another woman there who saw it all.'

'She witnessed a suicide? The poor woman. How horrible.'

'It wasn't a suicide. It was a murder.'

'Don't be ridiculous.'

'It's true! She saw someone throw a man over the balcony.'

'I heard she'd been drinking.'

'She'd had a few, but I saw him too.'

'But you said you didn't see the victim fall.'

'I saw someone up on the balcony, after the event.'

'Who?'

I shrug. 'I don't know . . . it was dark.'

'How certain are you?'

'Certain.'

'And the other woman?'

'She definitely saw him.' I don't tell him that she has changed her story. I need him to be on my side and not have any more doubts.

'Does she know what he looked like?'

'It was too dark.'

My time is running short. I need to hurry. 'Could you do me a massive favour?'

'Depends on what it is.'

'The dead man's name is Ernest Ridgewell.'

He frowns and shakes his head at me. 'You're not supposed to know that.'

'Can you tell me anything about him?'

'Nada.'

'Please!'

'Why do you want to know about some dead stranger? What was he to you?'

'No one.'

'Then why ask?'

'Because someone killed him and Security don't want to do anything about it.'

'Death on a cruise is bad for business.'

'It's not right that the killer should be left to wander the ship. He might kill again.'

'I'm risking my job just having this conversation with you.'

'I won't say anything, I promise.'

'I can't help you, Martha. I'm sorry. I have to get back to work.' He gives me a theatrical bow and turns to exit stage left. Ever the thespian.

'Wait!' I call. An idea is forming in my head. 'What if I ask Jacqui to work on your stage production? If I do that, will you help me?'

Rudy slows to a stop and looks at me. I can see from his eyes that this suggestion has ignited something. I can't lose this moment. 'How about a crossover play – Jessica Fletcher and Detective Cassie Kowalski work together to solve the mystery? That would be amazing, no?'

'She'd never agree.'

'Yes, she would! She'd love to do it.' Bugger. I hope she will.

Rudy's face brightens, 'She said that?'

I feel a pang of anxiety. When did I become such an accomplished liar? 'We'll work it out.'

'I'll get you what you need if you make this happen.'

I swallow and wonder just what the hell I've let myself in for.

Chapter Fifteen

Wilma

Loath as she was to admit it, the members of the Midnight Chorus Society, Wilma thought, had become an uneven bunch. Once, it was an elite circle of true professionals. Now it was cluttered with beginners and hangers-on. The seasoned killers she respected. The fledglings she tolerated. But the oddballs, the voyeurs, the worshippers, she had little time for. They paid obscene fees through the Dark Web for the privilege of belonging, treating the Society like some exclusive fan club. She had watched it evolve over the years, mostly with pride and love, but sometimes with quiet disgust. She kept these thoughts to herself. What had begun as a sanctuary for the gifted had become a business. A profitable one, yes, but vulgar all the same. She blamed the Spider.

Wilma sat alone at a table for two in the diner, sipping a whiskey sour. She'd never usually drink alcohol during a workday, but after the morning she'd had, Wilma needed some good old American medicine.

She had been friends with Bernard Koch for more than thirty years. They had first met when he stayed at their guest house in Kennebunkport. To her surprise, she had warmed to him instantly. He had been polite and charming, yet there was something about his energy that ignited a spark in her. She had only ever experienced that from one other person: her husband, Frank, obviously. She would later discover that in Bernard, she had recognised a kindred spirit.

She recalled her first ever conversation with Bernard. He had told her he was travelling through Kennebunkport on business. When she asked what kind, he replied, 'I work with teeth.' She had assumed he was a dentist because he carried an old-fashioned doctor's bag. But he was no dentist, as his victims could attest – if they were still alive, that was. Bernard was a craftsman and a collector of precious things, which included the teeth of his dead. From the teeth, he would create jewellery and works of art that he would sell to specialist buyers and collectors. You could say he'd made a killing not just of the victims but their teeth too.

The lunchtime rush was easing; people were leaving the restaurant, much to Wilma's relief. Less chance of unwanted ears listening in on their conversation. Her phone said it was 10 after 2. Bernard was late, which was unusual for him. Wilma didn't mind. It gave her time to gather her thoughts, and besides, she wasn't hungry. Stress will do that to a gal.

He entered the diner at last, tall and elegant, dressed in grey tweeds, eyes searching for her. She brushed her fingers through her hair, pushing down stray strands before raising her hand. He saw her, waved and navigated his way through the dissipating diners.

'Wilma, I am so sorry. This business with Ernest . . . I am discombobulated.'

She gave him a sympathetic look. 'That's quite all right. I understand.'

'I've been walking around thinking who would do such a terrible thing.'

'That's what I intend to find out.'

'Poor, poor Ernest.'

Wilma sighed. 'I will miss him.'

'Me too.'

A waiter arrived at the table, a young man called Tyler, with tanned skin and alert eyes. Wilma ordered a second whiskey sour. Just one more to ease the burden. Bernard opted for a glass of riesling. She clocked his gaze lingering on the young man's smile. When he left, Bernard was frowning.

'Is everything OK?' she asked.

'Young people today . . . their teeth are just so unnatural. They remind me of those little hard chewing gums, all the same size, the same colour. I am an artist, Wilma, how can I be expected to create great art from chewing gum.'

'I can see that would be challenging,' she mused.

Wilma's realisation that she and Bernard were like-minded souls came two days into his first stay at the guest house. It was late at night. She and Frank were on a 'Neighbourhood Watch' patrol searching for a nasty vagrant who had eluded them for almost a week. The hunt was on, and Wilma couldn't wait to finish that darn son of a whore tomcat in the dungeon of their beautiful bed and breakfast. They had tracked him down just out of town and pursued him in the car with the lights out. When he suddenly disappeared from the side of the road, they hotfooted it in his direction, carrying knives and a rope under the light of the stars. They found him unconscious in a cornfield, and to their astonishment, Bernard was kneeling over him, pulling out the man's teeth. They had been friends ever since.

'Is Frank not joining us?' Bernard asked.

'He's taking over Ernest's duties for the time being.'

The waiter returned with the drinks.

'We should toast an old friend,' said Wilma.

'We should.'

They clinked glasses.

'The Undertaker,' said Bernard.

They sat in silence for a moment, savouring their drinks, before Bernard broke it. 'Have you ever wondered, Wilma, how you, I, our members became the people they are today?'

'It's something I think of from time to time. Nature or nurture, sometimes both, but it's not for me to go prying into other people's business. Especially Society members.'

'Yes, of course. Have I told you my story?'

'Only snippets.'

'I have only told one person. That was our dear friend, Ernest. But he is gone now, and I feel strangely alone now that no one knows my tale.'

'Tell me.'

He nodded and took a sip of wine. 'I was born an only child in Hamburg in 1950. We emigrated to Quebec in 1962. My father, by trade, was a dentist, but not a very accomplished one. My mother was a dental nurse. They set up a practice in the family home when I was five. It was the only surgery for miles and was very busy. In those days, dentistry was unsophisticated. There was not much in the way of pain relief.'

'I remember those times all too well,' said Wilma.

'Most days, I would hear people scream. The cries frightened me at first, but I became used to them. I was a curious child, some might say morbid. I wanted to see what was going on in the surgery. I had to. The screams began to excite me, you see. Eventually, I was able to sneak in . . .' Bernard smiled, lost in the memory. '. . . I couldn't believe my eyes. From that day forward, I would run home from school in the hope of secretly watching my parents' patients bleed and writhe in agony during my father's somewhat fat-fingered, clumsy procedures. There were a lot of teeth. I would collect any that were left behind. Some I still have today.'

'Souvenirs are important to people like us. Back home, we have a trophy cabinet that contains one thing from each of our victims. It's often a piece of jewellery, or something plain like a hair ribbon, a pen, a shoelace, or a wristwatch. They all mean something. My favourite is a glass eye. It catches the morning light beautifully.'

He smiled at her before continuing. 'My father's dentistry was part incompetence and part brutality. The latter was part of his nature. Mother and I knew this all too well. He would beat us. He broke our bones, blackened our eyes and fattened our lips.'

'Oh, I'm so sorry.'

He shrugged. 'That was our life.'

'You were just a child.'

'When I was sixteen, I killed him . . . pushed him down the stairs. He cracked his skull and died quickly, which was convenient. Mother was distraught. She still loved him. I did, too, in a way, but we were free of him at last. His death was recorded as an accident, and that was that.'

'Did you never think of becoming a dentist like your father?'

He chuckled. 'The worst thing was that I missed my father's performances in the surgery. Had he lived, I might have gone on to be a dentist. But he left us with nothing, and we became poor with barely enough money to eat, never mind to pay for college.'

'But look at you now. A legend in our lifetime.'

'You flatter me.'

'I speak only the truth. You're an artist and a good man, Bernard.'

He raised his glass and nodded his appreciation. 'I'm glad we are friends. Truly.'

'Me too.'

'So, we should talk about this situation we find ourselves in.'

'I'm so vexed about it. Aside from Frank, I trust you more than anyone, Bernard. You know that don't you?'

'Of course.'

'Ernest's murder changes everything. We have a traitor among us.'

'I agree.'

'Priscilla thinks she has it under control, but I'm not convinced. The Society is in danger. That means we are in danger.'

'Do you have an inkling of who the killer might be?'

'We have one hundred and forty-eight Society members onboard. It's a safe bet one of them killed Ernest.'

'What about the rest of the ship?'

'Fifteen hundred passengers and staff. None of them has a clue who they're travelling with. I'm certain.'

Bernard smiled. 'Imagine if they found out.'

'It would be murder.'

Bernard choked back a laugh and raised his glass. 'We can but dream.' He sipped his drink and asked: 'What do you suggest we do next?'

'With the exception of you, me, and Frank, no one in the Society, be they member or admirer, is above suspicion.'

'That's a lot of people.'

'Our lives depend on finding the murderer.'

Bernard leant back, eyes steady. 'Does that include the committee?'

'Everyone.'

'Terence is trouble,' Bernard said.

'I know you two don't get along.'

'I've never understood how he got his seat. Reckless then, worse now with the liquor.'

Wilma looked away. She didn't believe in regret. It was a waste of energy, but Bernard had a point. The Society was too precious for weakness. 'There was a time when Frank and I were so very fond of him,' she said. 'He'd visit us in Kennebunkport, do a little magic, tell stories, make us laugh. He had the charm for recruitment, the sort who could bring people in.'

Bernard frowned. 'He jumped the system.'

There were only two routes into the Society. The elite came through referral, vouched for by two established members. The rest earned their place through the formal recruitment process, a quiet, disciplined system that kept standards high. Then Terence had invented a third. Killer Pitch, he called it, an open-mic spectacle where fledgling killers stood before a panel of veterans and sold their worth like performers. He hosted it himself, preening on stage while they begged for approval. Over time, it had become vulgar, undignified, and to her irritation, wildly popular. For those reasons, Wilma had to end it.

Wilma nodded once. 'Because I let him.'

'What's done is done,' Bernard said. 'We must make do.'

'I'd like you to keep an eye on him.'

Bernard's mouth curved into a wolfish grin. 'I was hoping you'd say that.'

'I will watch over the Reverend and the Spider.'

'You think Priscilla could be responsible?'

'The Spider has the interests of her business to focus on. She will put it above the Society, which adds an extra element of danger. I need to keep her close.'

'I understand.'

'I also need you and Frank to watch the conference like the hawks you are. Be vigilant, look for anything suspicious or out of the ordinary and report it back to me. We must find the traitor before they kill again and expose us. If we don't, we're finished.'

Bernard smiled. 'I think, Wilma, in a different life, you might have made an excellent detective.'

Chapter Sixteen

Martha

I reach Jacqui's apartment on time by the skin of my teeth and plonk myself down on the sofa as she closes the door.

'Make yourself comfortable, why don't you.'

I ignore the snark in her tone. 'I was rushing and didn't want to be late.'

'You're sweating.'

From the bar, Jacqui grabs a bottle of water and a posh folded napkin, and hands them to me. I thank her, dab my face and take a swig.

'What was so important that you had to vanish suddenly only to race back here, as if your life depended on it?' she asks.

'Erm . . . nothing.'

I can see from her expression that she's unconvinced, but my mind is occupied with how to get her to star in Rudy's play. I shrug. 'Just an errand that's all.' I'm tempted to say what I do in my spare time is my business, but I don't want to 'release the Kraken'. I take another slug and look away. 'OK, shall we get to it.'

We take our seats at the dining table, which has a westerly aspect over one of Jacqui's balconies. She tells me there are two others. One in the guest room and one in her bedroom upstairs.

'Very bougie,' I say.

'It's a nice ship, but the theme is too fake for my tastes. I wouldn't expect anything less from Priscilla Hefferman.'

'How do you know her?'

'There's a story. She's from old money. The family fortune was lost by her corrupt father who went to prison for fraud, tax evasion, you name it. We met on a set. She was a bit-part actress at the time, trying to make it in Hollywood. "Actress" is maybe overstating it. Walking, talking mannequin is a better descriptor.' I laugh. 'She was engaged to Joe Wells. Joe owned the studio that produced *LA Dolls*, and later, *Lady Detective*. He and I were sleeping together during *LA Dolls*. I played mistress and super bitch, Sabrina Logan. Cilla had a minor part in the show.'

I'm intrigued by this ménage à trois, but more so by the 'mistress and super bitch'.

'Sabrina sounds like someone I'd like to know more about.'

'Some people said, unkindly, that Sabrina was a part that had been written with me in mind. Like her, I was ambitious, disrupted lives and slapped a lot of faces.' She smiles to herself.

'Did you really?'

'Slap a lot of faces?'

I nod.

'We all did. It was a thing back then.'

'Sounds fun,' I say, my thoughts drift to my imaginary hand slapping *my Romantasy nemesis, Poppy Posey's face*.

'I was also an on-and-off-screen mistress. You could say I was an exquisite example of life imitating art.'

'With Priscilla's fiancé?'

'Joe and I were pals and lovers. In today's language, they'd say we were "friends with benefits". Theirs was a loveless relationship and later a loveless marriage. But that was not unusual for Priscilla. She only ever married for money. Usually very old, rich men who were on the cusp of meeting their maker. Joe was the exception. He got out of that situation fast. Interestingly, he's the only one of her husbands who is still living.'

'Did you love him?'

'In a way. It was a fling that lasted a few years.'

'That must have reassured Priscilla,' I say, keeping my tone light.

'When she found out, she had me fired from *LA Dolls*. I don't blame her. I'd have done the same. But I left that show pregnant and nine months later gave birth to my beautiful daughter.'

'Every cloud.'

She turns her gaze to the balcony and the glittering blue ocean beyond. I notice a dip in her posture and a sadness in her expression, or is it regret? I can't tell.

'How old is she now?'

It takes her a moment to come out of her fugue and respond. 'We should get some more ideas down.'

'Yes, absolutely,' I reply, conscious that this is the second time Jacqui has avoided talking about her daughter. I wonder if they don't talk, and picture Jacqui as Faye Dunaway playing an unhinged Joan Crawford in *Mommie Dearest*.

'Where's your notepad?' Jacqui asks.

I grimace. In the hurry to get out of my room earlier, I forgot my bag. 'Sorry, I left it behind.'

Jacqui sighs, gets up from the table and returns moments later with a pen and a swish *Jewel of the Atlantic* notepad. 'Just try and be more professional.'

That stings. I take them from her. 'Thank you.'

My phone buzzes. I glance at it quickly and see a voice message from Diane. I'll listen later.

'OK. Where were we?' says Jacqui.

We spend the next three hours brainstorming ideas that neither of us can agree on. Jacqui can't seem to extract herself from the past. She wants a *Lady Detective* story set in the late 90s, five years after the final Cassie Kowalski aired, the opposite of what her ambitions for the TV show had been. Her goal is to sell a ton of books and become a *New York Times* and *Sunday Times* bestseller. I'm with her on aiming high, but I'm not convinced that Cassie Kowalski and that time period will be a draw for readers. If she wants a continuation of the show, which is rarely, if ever, aired, then the demographic will be fans of the show, such as the old folks on this ship, for instance. Is that enough to hit the bestseller list? Perhaps in the US, but not in the UK, where her celebrity listing might be 'D'. I'm utterly conflicted. I like to think I have a sound knowledge of publishing and books, but the reality is I'm just an unpublished writer, so what do I know? Jacqui could be right, and I could be wrong, but I'm going to follow what my gut is telling me. 'How about we do a reboot of Cassie?'

The faintest of creases appears on Jacqui's botoxed brow.

'We tell Oliver the book is based on the classic hit TV series, but we set it in the present day. This could broaden our audience. Picture young Cassie starting out as a detective – like the FBI's Clarice Starling in *The Silence of the Lambs* – dealing with contemporary crimes, and modern issues.'

'That book was published in the late 80s, so your argument is horseshit.'

'Hear me out . . . so . . . Cassie is dealing with misogyny – that shit never goes away. Maybe she's a single mum, she could be diverse, maybe she doesn't like men in that way and is exploring her sexuality. She could be gender-fluid.'

Jacqui's face reddens. She stands abruptly, her expression

thunderous. 'No! She's not gender-fluid. Nor is she a they/them or whatever else. God help us! She likes men. She's me. I am Cassie Kowalski!'

I recoil at her outburst.

Her jaw is set, and her nails furiously tap the tabletop. 'You need to come up with better ideas or else this is not going to work.'

'They were solid ideas.'

She curls her lips. 'The kind of solid that can only be flushed down a toilet.'

'I'm trying to make Cassie appeal to a wider demographic.'

'And who is this demographic? A generation of device-obsessed zombies who can only decide what to eat or wear, who to fuck, or who not to fuck from social media.'

I'm burning inside. This feels like I'm arguing with Diane.

'You should go. We're done for the day.'

I gather my notes.

I notice she's trembling. 'See yourself out.'

I'm angry, but I can't help feeling that something's not right. 'Jacqui—'

'Just go!' she says.

She doesn't look at me as I leave.

'See you tomorrow, same time?'

No response.

'Bye then.'

I close the door behind me, feeling a mix of frustration and disappointment. I really thought we were making progress. I can understand that Jacqui feels anchored to her character, I really can, but I'm spooked by her rising Richter scale of unconscious bias. Plus, any chance of getting her to be in Rudy's play now seems remote. I decide to go for a drink and do some thinking in the sunshine. Maybe I'll call Oliver and get his take.

The sun is beaming gloriously on the deck, and the bar is buzzing. I grab a table in the shade under a parasol and plop myself down. A waiter is nearby, delivering two delicious-looking cocktails that resemble vanilla milkshakes. I wave at him, give him that British 'if it's not too much trouble, could you serve me please' expression. He nods a confirmation, and I scroll through my contacts searching for Oliver's number.

The waiter arrives. 'What can I get you?'

I point towards the milkshakes. 'What are those?'

'Pina Colada. Our cocktail of the day. Freshly made and I can't recommend them highly enough.'

'You had me at Pina Colada.'

He smiles. 'Coming up.'

Taking out my phone, I remember Diane has left me a message. I listen.

Hi darling, it's me. Congratulations on the new job. So exciting! Sven thought it might be at Greggs, but I told him you'd gone away somewhere. Then he said it must be the Greggs training programme. Anyway, how wonderful! You must be thrilled. Call when you can, I'd love to hear all about it. Loads of love, Mum . . . well, Diane, as you prefer.

I roll my eyes and try not to get irritated at their obsession with me working at Greggs. I call Oliver. The phone rings for a few moments before he answers. 'Please tell me you haven't been fired again!'

I hesitate before answering, 'That remains to be seen.'

He sighs heavily. 'What's happened?'

I go through our entire conversation, including Jacqui's revelations about her affair, and my thoughts on rebooting Cassie Kowalski.

'I like that . . . I like that a lot. Resetting Cassie to the present day is much more commercial, but don't forget this is Jacqui's project. The reality is readers would not accept a straight white author whose main character is a person of colour, or a queer one. Also, Jacqui is correct when she said she is Cassie Kowalski. That's the book's USP.'

I feel better hearing this. 'Do you think you could talk to her?'

The waiter returns with two Pina Coladas. I cover the phone microphone. 'I only ordered one.'

He mouths 'cocktail hour' at me. I beam at him like I've won at bingo and give him a big thumbs up.

'I'll call her this evening and remind her that the deal is off if we don't get an outline in the next few days. What I need you to do is to start working on it with or without her. Can you do that?'

I feel a squeeze of pressure at this new responsibility and hesitate before answering. 'Sure, I can.' The Pina Colada glass is wonderfully cold. I take a large swig. It's thick, creamy and delicious like potent, coconut ice cream. I'm in heaven, aside from the brain freeze. 'So, what's the tea on Jacqui and Priscilla Hefferman?'

'They go way back. Jacqui and Priscilla were love rivals for the affections of Priscilla's husband. That didn't end well for anyone.'

'Jacqui did get a daughter out of it, who she clearly adores.'

'She didn't tell you?'

'Tell me what?'

'Billie was Jacqui's daughter's name. She passed away at the age of fifteen. From Leukaemia. Jacqui's never gotten over it.'

Shit! I feel an ache in my chest. Oliver is talking, but I've involuntarily zoned out. I can't help it.

'Martha, are you there?'

'Yeah, sorry . . . I didn't know.'

'She might have money. She may be hard work, but she's lost everything. Billie, Joe, her career and the TV reboot. This book deal is all she has now. Help her.'

'Yeah, of course.'

We say our goodbyes. I sit quietly thinking about Jacqui and what she must have gone through and is still going through. I pick up my phone and compose a text to Dad.

Hey, just checking in. Hope you're all right. M xxx

Chapter Seventeen

Martha

As well as my hangover, I'm feeling grubby after a morning of power walking in the sunshine with the unstoppable Madam DuLac, followed by the narrow window I had for my desperate lunchtime sprint around the ship searching for Rudy. I'm also feeling lightheaded from the Pina Coladas and need a refresh, so I head back to my room, which is immaculate thanks to the cabin steward. I get undressed, drop my clothes on the floor, and jump into the shower. The hot water feels glorious.

I think about Ernest Ridgewell's murder, and the cruise ship cover-up. Both have rattled me, and I'm fired up and eager to uncover the truth. Despite my latest run-in with Jacqui, my sleuthing has got me excited and distracted. Yet I need to prioritise the book outline and deliver it in the next few days. If I don't, the publishers will pull the plug on Jacqui, which means we both lose big time. But I just can't let this murder go. I know I can do both. I'm the queen of multitasking in my humble opinion. I have more hurdles to jump before Rudy will give me intel on the dead man. First up, I need to get back into Jacqui's good graces. I then must convince her to take a role in Rudy's play and investigate whatever information I receive from Rudy about the victim. His family and friends deserve the truth, and I can deliver it to them. I have my own personal reasons too, but that's a whole different story.

Reinvigorated from the shower, I turn off the water, grab a towel, and pat down my hair and dry my body. It occurs to me that I have no idea what I would do once I find the killer. Wrapping the towel around my head, I pull on the robe, enter the bedroom, sit on the bed, and imagine the scene. Wrestle them to the ground and call for help? Perform a citizens' arrest? Is that even possible at sea? I bite my thumb as the realisation that I have no plan sinks in. I can't do this alone. It would make sense to share everything I know with Todd from Security, but would he listen, and can he be trusted? This is dangerous. I need to tread carefully.

First things first. Extend an olive branch to Jacqui. I text her on WhatsApp.

Hey Jacqui. Are you hungry? Shall we get dinner? Martha

Moments later, she comes online, reads the message, and goes offline again. I wait a few more moments in case she's thinking about it, but I get nothing. I send a second text.

I'll be at the buffet around seven thirty if you want to join. Hope you're OK.

She doesn't read it and is clearly still upset. Perhaps it's best to let the dust settle. Maybe she'll show up anyway.

I get dressed and hear a knock on my door. Buttoning up my shirt, I check my reflection, fix my hair and open it. Standing in the corridor is the last person I expected to see. Patty Ortiz, oppressed wife and lover of all things Jesus, is wringing her hands, her face drawn as if she's aged a decade since we spoke earlier. 'Patty!' I say, feeling a pang of worry. Peering outside, I glance up and down the corridor. There's no one around. 'Come in.'

Patty tentatively steps into my room. 'I . . . I didn't know where else to go.'

'Is everything OK?'

She looks distractedly around my room. The cabin steward's magic has been undone by a grown-up millennial toddler. Strewn across the room are my dress, bra, pants, socks, boots, towels and robe. 'It's nice,' she says quietly, without much conviction.

'Can I get you something to drink?'

She shakes her head.

'You look like you have something on your mind.'

I don't want to push her, so I let the silence hang between us.

'I did see him.'

I feel my pulse race. 'The killer?'

'Yes . . . no, well not exactly.' That makes a lot of sense.

'Would you recognise him if you saw him again?'

'He was wearing a mask.'

'What kind of mask?'

'It covered his whole head.'

'Like a balaclava?'

She nods her head.

I hold my breath. Something dark triggers inside me.

'When I saw the two men fighting, I had no idea what would happen . . . or else I would never have filmed it.'

I feel my mouth open involuntarily. 'You filmed the murder?'

Tears fill her eyes. I put my arms around her and gently hug her. 'Why didn't you say anything last night?'

'At the time, I just didn't think. But I told Todd, this morning.'

'What did he say?'

'I showed him the video. He told me under no circumstances was I to mention it to anyone. He took my phone as evidence . . .'

I recall the evidence bag on Todd's desk. '. . . And then the next day they upgraded us and promised a refund and a free cruise next year.' She's trembling now. I pour her a glass of water and hand it to her. She gratefully takes a sip. 'I don't feel safe, and I don't think it's right that everything goes on as normal when there's a killer on board this ship.'

'I'm inclined to agree.'

She checks her wristwatch. 'I should go, or else there'll be hell to pay.' She shudders. 'I've had nightmares about that face. It was so sinister.'

'But he was wearing a balaclava.'

'Yes, but there were buttons sewn onto it to make up a face. Two red buttons for eyes and a twisted smile.'

And suddenly it feels like the walls are closing in around me. 'A button face mask?'

'Yes. It was horrible.'

It's like I've been sucker-punched. Patty is talking but I don't take anything in. And then she's gone and I stand there, speechless, holding my breath. I stumble into the bathroom and look at my reflection. I'm pale, sick-looking, my skin glistening with sweat. I splash cold water onto my face, walk like a zombie into the room and sit on the edge of the bed. I breathe in, out, in, out, and try to compose myself like my therapist had taught me. The mask flashes in my head, and I tremble. I take out my phone and start typing a text.

Daddy, if you're there, I need help. He's here. The man in the mask. The one who took you from me. He's here and I don't know what to do.

I press Send as hot tears stream down my face. How long has it been since I properly cried? I couldn't say.

A moment later, my phone pings. I swallow and read the message.

The number you are trying to contact is either out of service or disconnected. Please try again later.

I type another message and send it.

I miss you, Daddy. Love M XX

My phone pings once more.

The number you are trying to contact is either out of service or disconnected. Please try again later.

I curl over and let the tears flow.

But only for a short time.

The familiar chaos that I'd long ago learnt to control once again rages in my head. I could never talk about my dad. It's just too painful. Certainly not to Diane, whom I partly blame for his death. Had she not got bored, then maybe he'd still be alive.

I rub my arms and pace up and down my room. The mess of discarded clothing and towels bothers me. Swiftly, I begin to gather them up, placing my underwear in the wash basket, my boots in the wardrobe, where I also hang my dress. I spend time tightening the bed covers so that you could bounce a coin on top. I shake the pillows, fluff them, and gently place them at an angle at the head of the bed.

No more chaos.

I start to focus my thoughts.

When my father was murdered under Huddlestone Arch, an eyewitness saw someone wearing a balaclava with a face made from buttons hurry from the scene. I can't quite believe that masked killer is the same person who murdered Ernest Ridgewell. And here I am on a ship pursuing him. I don't believe in coincidences, but I do believe in destiny, and this was clearly meant to be.

Something in me has changed. A rage burns inside, one that I had long ago suppressed. My part-time search for justice for Ernest Ridgewell has taken on a darker tone.

It's now personal.

It's revenge.

I think about Jacqui and the loss of her daughter, Billie. Grief is something, probably the only thing, we have in common. It remains a constant in your life and never goes away. At first, it's unbearable, but you learn to live with it like an unwanted piece of furniture that you can't bear to part with. Other people's grief is so triggering. Oliver's reveal about Billie's passing has touched me deeply. I close my eyes and take a breath. I should have recognised the signs in Jacqui, the behaviours, the pain behind the eyes that no amount of make-up or smiling can conceal. I decide that when I'm with her, we focus on the book and not bring up her daughter or my dad, who was murdered in Central Park thirteen years ago by a mask-wearing psychopath.

The fire roars inside me.

The press had given him a name.

Buttonface.

That name has haunted me ever since.

Chapter Eighteen

Martha

I'm on a mission and going out as planned with the intention of sizing up my fellow passengers as possible suspects. I freshen up my face, apply some light make-up, and head out into the night with an unflinching determination to find the killer of my dad and Ernest Ridgewell.

I walk into the restaurant. It's noisy with chatter and the clinking of cutlery on china. Different scents greet me: garlic, rosemary, roasting meats, and melted cheese. My mouth waters. It takes me a few minutes to find a table which is inconveniently located on the far side of the diner, a distance away from the buffet. Beggars can't be choosers. I take a seat and scan the faces of my fellow diners until a waiter greets me. I order a large glass of Rioja and then head to the buffet to decide what I want to eat. Regardless of the glorious smells in the air, my anxiety about Buttonface, and Jacqui too for that matter, has squashed my appetite.

'Hi,' comes a voice.

I turn to see Zach, the hot guy from the train, smiling at me. He's been sunbathing, his skin is the colour of honey. Tasty, lickable honey. 'Oh hi!' What on earth has got into me, I think? Does danger bring out the desire in me?

'They do an awesome Caesar salad,' he says.

The server hands him his plate.

I glance at it. Spears of lettuce leaves and anchovies, dusted with Parmesan, and topped with succulent, breaded chicken. 'It looks delicious.' I feel my appetite returning.

'Same for me,' I tell the server.

'Dining alone?'

'Looks like it. I thought I might be eating with my boss, but we argued, and it became difficult.'

'I get it. Have you guys made up?'

I think about Jacqui losing it earlier. 'I don't know. I think she's going to fire me again. She does that a lot.'

'I'm sorry to hear that.'

'What will be will be.'

The server hands my salad across. I thank her.

'I think you should have dinner with me,' says Zach.

'I'd like that.'

He smiles, 'Let's grab a table.'

'Follow me.' I tell him.

I lead him to my table at the back and sip wine as he browses the wine list. The waiter stands idly by. I give him a polite smile, which he doesn't acknowledge. Rude.

Zach glances at my glass. 'What are you drinking?'

'Rioja.'

'How is it?'

'Very nice.'

Zach closes the menu. 'We'll have a bottle of the Rioja,' he says to the waiter.

For the next ninety minutes or so, we talk, laugh, and flirt. I should be watching the other passengers but Zach is charming and funny. I think he believes his flirting is subtle. It's really not, but I don't care. I'm enjoying the distraction of his attention, something I'm not used to getting from guys like him. He works on Wall Street, which he detests. He says he feels like Disney's Nemo in shark-infested waters. I find that sad, but also hot, and as I drink more, I think he's perfect boyfriend material. He wants to make something of his life, escape the shallowness of capitalism and move abroad to work as a volunteer helping in war-ravaged countries such as Ukraine or Palestine. I became instantly concerned about our imaginary future and that of our children.

'Hey, the restaurant's closing,' he says. 'Fancy a drink at the deck bar?'

I'm feeling drunk; two strong Pina Coladas and half a bottle of red wine will do that, but perhaps a nightcap might be nice. And so, we leave the Seven Dials restaurant and take an evening stroll to the bar. We hear pop music, a song I think is Britney Spears's 'Baby One More Time', horribly belted out by some bloke. The upper deck, where Ernest Ridgewell had taken flight, is a buzz of activity.

'It's karaoke,' says Zach.

'I love karaoke!'

'Stay there,' says Zach, grinning. 'I'll get us another bottle, and we can crash it.'

A moment of unease ripples through me. Someone was murdered there last night, and Zach is hurrying to the bar. A selfish part of me thinks, 'What the hell?' We're both having such a good time. Why spoil it? I make my way towards the steps, the same ones that were guarded this morning. There's a sign blocking the entrance.

ONLY MURDERING OF SONGS ALLOWED

PRIVATE PARTY

The irony, I think, as a cool ocean breeze causes my skin to erupt in goosebumps. I hear rapid footsteps and turn to see Zach holding up a Champagne bottle and two glasses. 'Veuve Clicquot. Thought I'd splash out.'

'That's so nice,' I say and point at the sign. 'It's a private party, though.'

'And we're very private people,' he responds in an impressive imitation of my English accent.

I laugh. He's such a flirt.

'Let's go,' he says, slipping past the sign and hurrying up the stairs.

It's crowded on the upper deck. Everyone has their backs to us. We edge our way round the perimeter and find a spot out of view. I do a quick count and estimate that there are around a hundred or more people. Deck chairs are laid out, and a makeshift stage has been erected containing a large TV screen with a karaoke machine attached. I recognise the man on stage belting out one of Britney's finest. It's Bernard the tooth fancier. I lean into Zach as he pours the Champagne.

'He was in the lift with us yesterday,' I say.

'Oh yeah. That old dude. Would not have pegged him as a Britney fan.'

'Takes all sorts.'

Zach has filled my glass up. We toast our good health, and he holds my gaze once more. 'Drink or it's bad luck.'

I take a sip. It's cold, delicious and tickles my throat.

Bernard finishes to a round of tepid applause. The man who bumped into me at the port on his way to speak to Jacqui appears on the stage. He's wearing shorts, a Hawaiian shirt and a red velvet dickie bow. Each to their own. He takes the microphone from Bernard.

'Thank you to our very own tooth snatcher, Bernard Koch . . . that's spelt K O C H . . . not . . . C O . . . well, you catch my drift.' Judging from the lack of laughter, no one does catch his drift.

'Honestly, Bernard dude, don't give up your day job . . . and stay away from my teeth!' He lets out an odd fake shriek.

This gets a small ripple of laughter.

'My name is Terence Lamb; most of you know me as Terence Lamb,' he says, looking to the audience with a gormless grin, waiting for a laugh, but once again, nothing. 'I'm your MC for the evening. If you'd like to come on up and sing your dark little heart out, then talk to yours truly. I'll add your name to the roster along with your song of choice and do my very best to accommodate you. Next up on stage is the Franklins. A big round of applause, ladies and gentlemen, please.'

I recognise Bernard's friend, Wilma, helping an older man onto the stage. Is that her husband? The audience applauds enthusiastically. They are clearly popular. With mics in their hands, Wilma gives a nod to Terence, the MC at the karaoke machine. A familiar fast bass starts to play. I start moving my hips to the beat. 'You're the One That I Want' from *Grease*. The audience cheers. Zach and I share a look of disbelief and start giggling. He almost chokes on his bubbles. To make it worse, the gender roles have been reversed. Wilma is singing John Travolta's part. Zach and I slide to the floor in a fit of laughter.

Several 'murdered' songs later, culminating in a surreal, squealing version of Björk's 'It's Oh So Quiet' sung by two women who look like grown-up versions of the Overlook Hotel twins. This had Zach and me howling. We're out of Champagne, and I am beyond 'merry'.

Terence is back on stage, addressing the audience. 'We have time for one more song. Any takers?'

I turn to Zach. 'The stage awaits me,' I say.

'Go for it,' he replies.

So, without much thought, I bolt across the deck, elbowing the creepy twins out of the way. I notice they're both wearing lanyards with *The Midnight Chorus Society* and a small logo I can't make out printed on the card. If these people were part of a chorus and I was at one of their gigs, I'd ask for my money back.

I jump onto the stage and grab Terence's mic, but he doesn't let go. I lean into it. 'I'd like to sing, please.'

Terence tugs the mic back. 'Sure thing, young lady. What's your name, and where do you come from?'

I pull the mic back. 'My name is Martha and I'm from London.'

The audience applauds.

'What's your song choice, Martha?' Terence asks.

I whisper it to him.

'Coming right up.'

I raise the mic with both hands and face the audience. 'I'm dedicating this song to two people. One is my dad who loved this band. The second is a man I'm looking for.'

Cheers from the audience.

'Not like that,' I say. 'He's a bad man.'

'You've come to the right place!' someone cries.

I laugh.

The electric guitar riff of Blondie's 'One Way or Another' kicks in. I feel buoyed, stoked as if a fire has been lit in my heart and is spreading across the stage. 'I will find you,' I say . . . before I launch into the vocals. I give it everything I can and dance across the stage like a possessed Debbie Harry. The audience is on their feet, clapping and singing along. They love me and I love them. I am drunk after all. This is for you, Dad. It's all for you. At the rear of the deck, I see Zach. He's looking at me and smiling. The song finishes, and the applause continues; I take a glorious bow, but inside, the experience has left me feeling raw. It has triggered me, and my heart feels shattered. I take a breath and force back tears of suppressed rage.

Chapter Nineteen

The Fool

He might be totally tanked but Terence Lamb still had a spring in his step as he exited the elevator on the fourth floor and made his way down the blurred, dimly lit corridor to his budget, windowless cabin. The karaoke evening – his baby and sole contribution to the conference – had been fucking five-star epic, bro!

'Go me!' he hollered, punching the air with his fists and kicking out a victorious leg. His flip-flop slipped from his foot and spun somewhere into the gloom. The absurdity of it made him chuckle. Never one to do things by halves – unless it was sawing a nubile female in half, that is – he kicked off his remaining flip-flop and at the top of his voice said, 'Take that one too, motherfucker!'

Behind him he heard a door opening and a woman's stern voice, 'Can you keep the damn racket down!'

He turned to look at the harpy who had the nerve to interrupt his fun. She was in her fifties; a heavy broad dressed in pink pyjamas that were a bit snug. He swayed on his feet, sniffed, raised a brow and gave her a small bow. 'Ma'am, I do beg your pardon.'

'You're drunk!'

His gaze lingered over her bosom. Despite her age and size, she was totally doable. 'And horny,' he said.

She gasped, her hand reaching for her neck.

Terence squeezed his crotch gently and leant forward. 'How'd ya like the gift of pearls for that lovely pink neck?'

She let out a shriek and disappeared, slamming the door behind her.

'I'm down the hall if you change your mind,' he called, crying with laughter.

Continuing to his room, Terence's thoughts returned to the karaoke. The vibe from the audience had been immense, particularly at the end when that chick from London stormed the stage. OK, she wasn't the best vocalist, but she delivered a standout performance that even he had to admit was freakin' awesome. He'd given her a double high five before slipping his arm tightly around her waist and asking the audience to 'Give it up for Martha.' And boy, did they. She must be new to the Society because he hadn't noticed her at the conference. He'd look out for her tomorrow and take her for a drink. Chicks love a free drink. She'd reminded him of Mandy . . . Mandy . . . he could never remember her surname. He'd met her in the bar of a small town he'd been passing through. She wasn't much to look at, but they got to talking and she invited him back to her place. She was drunk and fell asleep after downing a spiked beer. Terence got to work. From his car, he brought out his magician's tools, swiftly assembling the boxes: one over her torso, the second over her hips and legs. With his saw in hand, hey presto, Mandy, who had been one, became two. He smiled at the memory.

Blinking, he spotted his flip-flops. One lay on the floor upside down, while the other leant against the wall. Yawning, he used his foot to slide them across the floor to the entrance of his cabin. He rummaged in his pockets for the door key. After a moment of uncertainty and grumbling, he found it buried underneath an old handkerchief. Opening the door, he clumsily kicked his flip-flops inside. The tiny room was as dark as a cave. Terence switched on the lights and let the door close behind him. He smiled at the thought of the broad in the pink pyjama's hooters. He had to admit they had triggered something inside him. The thought of Martha also played on his mind. Something was stirring downstairs . . . something that needed attention. Terence undid his shorts, dropped them and perched on the edge of the bed. He thumbed the waistband of his Y Fronts in preparation for a few moments of 'self-abuse' but stopped when he noticed the letter.

It was lying on the floor beside one of his flip-flops, an envelope made of expensive-looking gold paper with his name written in what appeared to be skilled calligraphy. The room was so small that he was able to reach across and pick it up. The envelope was scented with a perfume he recognised but did not know the name of. Only one person he knew wore this fragrance. Ripping open the envelope, he took out the letter inside. It was written in the same beautiful script as his name had been.

Dear Terence,
In light of all the horrible things that have been happening, I have a secret I can no longer hide. Once again, you have worked your 'magic', and I have to tell you my true feelings. I might explode if I don't see you and know you feel the same as I do. Say nothing, to no one. If our paths cross, I shall pretend we are colleagues, and nothing more. Please do not think me cruel. In the meantime, I will

arrange a suitable time and location for us to meet privately.
With love.
PH x

'With love.' Terence scratched his balls and inhaled the letter's perfume. PH. Priscilla fucking Hefferman was juiced for him. Who knew? He certainly didn't but supposed it wasn't surprising. He may have a paunch, a receding hairline, and greasy skin, but he was a dude that women clearly still found attractive. Could they have a future together? It occurred to him that she did not have a great track record in relationships. It was rumoured that after watching a *Columbo* rerun where the killer stages a murder at the home of a businessman, an inspired Priscilla copied the scene and killed off her first douchebag husband. To her surprise, she had apparently enjoyed the experience. Unfortunately, his so-called fortune was barely enough to cover her annual shoe bill. And so began years of ruthless ambition as Priscilla extended her web, married, murdered, married and murdered again. Forever the grieving widow, Priscilla spent money faster than it could be printed. She was always looking for her next opportunity. Someone's gotta pay up for those Louboutins. But why was she interested in Terence? He had no money. No property. No nothing. Just his talent and animal magnetism. It could only be lust. He recalled the last time he'd seen her. It was a Society board meeting three months back when they met over dinner to discuss the final plans for the 25th Anniversary convention. Terence had drunk too much and afterwards made a move on her. He had thought her smoking hot for an old doll. The following day, the events of the evening were a blur, but Wilma told him: 'Priscilla was very flattered, Terence dear, but she's a grieving widow. Perhaps another time.'

Another time had clearly arrived.

Did the letter mean she was no longer grieving and was ready to receive his spicy baloney into her soft, warm love cave?

'Hell yeah! She's only human after all . . . and rich. Boy oh boy, is she rich.'

Terence yanked down his Ys, lay back, closed his eyes and held his baloney between his thumb and two fingers. On occasion, usually when he'd had a few, he would talk up his schlong to some bar babe in the expectation that she would jump into the sack and ride him into La La Land. But the reality was his baloney was more of a chipolata, and his drunken passes typically ended up with Terence alone in his pit, jacking himself off.

He thought about Priscilla, her bony body on top of his. As hard as he tried, he couldn't quite whip himself into a frenzy.

But the karaoke singer was still lurking in his head.

He willed her into the fantasy and kept Priscilla in play. The three of them together. A sandwich with Terence as the filling.

'Fuck yeah!'

It was working.

Thirty seconds . . . sixty seconds . . . his body trembled, his mouth opened involuntarily, and he let out a girlish moan.

His heart was pounding.

It was over.

Ninety seconds to bust out.

Was that a record?

Wiping his sticky hand on the bed, he thinks of Martha. She needs some special Terence attention. He had finished his duties at the conference and had a lot of spare time. Tomorrow, he'd track her down whether she liked it or not.

Chapter Twenty

Martha

I wake the following morning with a murderous headache. My tongue feels like it's velcroed to the top of my mouth, and my brain feels like microwaved scrambled eggs. Ugh. The curtains are tightly closed; the room is mercifully dark. I push myself slowly up and slide to the edge of the bed. I'm still dressed, boots and all. I think back to last night. Zach and I had ended up crashing a karaoke party, I had sung my heart out on stage and brought the house down. We were kicked out by that weird Wilma woman who shooed us away like naughty children. We had been drunk as lords as we bolted from the karaoke to the piano bar on the fifth floor, where Zach had to hold me back from the stage. I shake my head in embarrassment and recall that we consumed another bottle of Champagne. After that, everything is a blur.

Reaching for the water bottle on my bedside table, I greedily gulp down the entire contents in one go. I feel a protest spike in my head as the rehydration process begins. Ouch. I need to pee, so I shuffle like creeping death to the bathroom and lower myself gently onto the loo. I do my business and then run the shower. As the water heats up, I peel off my clothes and tumble into steaming rain.

Under the dim light of a bedside lamp, I slowly get dressed. I search for more water, but there's none. 'Shit!'

I pull the curtains open, flinch and stumble backwards onto the bed like Dracula recoiling from the deadly, blistering rays of the sun. As my eyes adjust, I search for my phone, which I find under the pillow. Just great. I wonder if my poor brain has been cooked by mobile radiation in my sleep.

I have three missed calls from Jacqui. The time is 9.34 a.m. I'm late for our next session. Bollocks! A memory flashes in my mind. I was here late last night alone on the bed, talking on the phone to someone. It was emotional. There were tears. But who was it? Zach? No. Diane? No, definitely not. I check my call log. Fuck! I made seven calls to Jacqui last night. A message pings on my phone. It's from Jacqui.

You're late!!!

Three exclamation marks. I'm in trouble but at least I'm not fired. I text back my apologies, tell her I slept in, and I'm on my way.

Crunching down on a breakfast of paracetamol, I grab two Americanos from the barista on the sun deck and get a wriggle on to Jacqui's suite. I'm nervous about seeing her. We didn't part on good terms yesterday and Lord knows what garbled nonsense I left on her voicemail.

I knock on the door.

Jacqui opens and regards me with a curious expression. Her eyes fall on the coffee. She grabs one. 'Thank God. I've ordered room service, but they haven't bothered bringing it.'

I enter the suite and give her a concerned look. 'How long ago did you order?'

'Fifteen minutes.'

'It's a trek from the kitchen. I'm sure it's on the way.'

'The same thing happened last night. No food arrived. I sat

here alone, miserable and hungry.' I want to remind her that I had invited her to eat, but I hold my tongue. 'It's Priscilla Hefferman's doing,' she says. 'It's her ship and she wants to make my life as miserable as hers.'

'Do you want me to go get you something?' I suddenly realise I have inadvertently allowed myself to become her actual assistant.

Jacqui takes a sip of coffee and ponders this momentarily. She's about to speak but stops when we hear a firm knock on the door. 'Could you get that?'

Obediently, I open the door. A waiter stands in the hallway with a trolley laden with food. 'Good morning. Room service,' he says.

'Come right in.'

He pushes the trolley inside.

Jacqui tips him a generous twenty, and he leaves.

The trolley is crammed with food: eggs, bacon, sausage, pancakes, toast, hash browns, beans, fruit, yoghurt, pastries. 'You must really be hungry,' I say, my tummy rumbling. I estimate it must be more than twelve hours since I had dinner with Zach.

'I called them and made it clear I was not happy about last night's fiasco. Anyway, this isn't for me. It's for you.'

'I'm touched, but that's a lot of food.'

'Honey, I've seen what you can put away. Sickening that you're not twice the size, but some people are just lucky that way.' Jacqui picks up a small plate and begins to help herself to melon slices and toast. 'Anyway, I assumed, as you were just out of bed, you had no time to eat and judging by the intoxicated voice messages you left me, you'd be craving carbs.'

I feel my face go hot. 'Oh God. What did I say?'

Jacqui cackles. 'She doesn't remember. That's priceless! Eat. Then let's get to work.'

I help myself to eggs, bacon, sausage, pancakes, and whatever else I can fit on my plate. Jacqui is at the table with the glorious view of the Atlantic. The sea is calm like a pond. I sit opposite her. She looks at me, a wicked smile forming on her lips. 'A little birdy who works on the ship, and whose name shall remain anonymous, told me something about Cilla Hefferman and her "oh so perfect" cruise line company.'

'Was it Rudy?'

Pinching her fingers, she makes a zipping gesture across her lips. 'I couldn't possibly say. Anyway, he told me that Cilla has employed dozens of undocumented immigrants with no working visas on the ship. She's paying them next to nothing. Slave labour.'

'That's appalling.'

'She always was stingy. In my experience, people who come from old money have the tightest purse strings! Rumour is she's being investigated. There might even be someone on this ship right now watching her. How exciting is that?'

'I suppose it is,' I say, and I mean it, but I have more important issues on my mind right now.

She's grazing her food. 'I was thinking over our conversation about reinventing Cassie . . .'

I arch my brows and nod at her. With a mouth full of pancake, sausage and bacon, it's the most I can do right now.

'The Lady Detective character should be put to bed. I get it that times have moved on. Cassie Kowalski, on the other hand, is still relevant.'

I chew and nod, intrigued to hear where she's going with this.

'I was thinking about my project to reboot the TV show. We were going to do the same 90s-style show, but with an older Cassie. I understand that elements of that cop drama are outdated. Case in point – Cassie undercover as a flight attendant, a hairdresser, or a sex worker, etc.'

I take a sip of my Americano and feel a small victory that Jacqui is no longer using the offensive *hooker* term.

'If the book were a pastiche, then things might be different. But I don't want it to be.' Unconsciously, she pushes a melon slice around the plate and pauses before continuing. 'For those reasons, I want us to write Cassie as a senior police officer, maybe a year or two from retirement. She's operating in a man's world, dealing with all the bullshit that comes with that. At home, she has a daughter in her mid-twenties, pregnant with her first child. The baby is born and brings joy to Cassie and her daughter. But that changes when Cassie's daughter is diagnosed with terminal cancer.'

I swallow my food and feel a swell of emotion. I place my knife and fork down. 'Jacqui, that's brilliant.'

'I want us to retain the heart of the show. Jacqui is still kick-ass at solving murders, but I want her vulnerable, like she's never been before. I also don't want a meditation on grief or anything like that. I want a celebration of life, and the embracing of new challenges after the shit that life throws at you.'

My eyes are watering, tears threaten to seep through, but I push them back.

'Are you crying?'

I shake my head and look away. Jacqui's intention to draw on real-life experience has floored me. Her daughter Billie's death, her long career screwed over by men and her ability to consistently pick herself up and carry on. Have I ever been able to do that? I'm not sure that I have. My dad was murdered by a psychopath in a mask. For years, his death directly determined the decisions I made about my education and the career I eventually wanted to pursue. And here I am sharing a cruise with his killer, trying my best with a dream job that I'm desperate not to lose, yet I feel I've been given a different purpose that I cannot turn away from.

Jacqui gets up from the table, grabs a clean napkin from the trolley and hands it to me.

Whether it's a combination of Jacqui's story or the raw emotion triggered by last night's karaoke, I don't know. The tears begin to spill, and I crumble. I wipe my face and nose with a napkin. Jacqui has an uncomfortable look about her that screams, 'Please stop!' It takes me a moment to compose myself.

'Is this about your father?' she asks.

Fuck! I bury my face in the napkin and feel my defensive walls going up. I blow my nose, leave the table and take another clean napkin from the trolley. 'Is what about my father?' Dumb question. I obviously spilt the beans.

'In your voicemail, you told me what happened to him in New York. You told me you know all about grief and that you understood what I was going through. You said we should use our shared experiences to write a story about Cassie. A story with a strong mystery that also focuses on her career and her home life too.' Jacqui stands, takes her plate and coffee to the trolley and piles them on top of the remaining food. 'Assume you're finished here,' she says, her eyebrows arched.

'Did I say anything else?'

'You did. There was a lot of crying. I had to switch it off in the end. I can't bear wet sobbing.'

I'm afraid to ask, but I need to know. 'What did I say?'

'Nothing major . . . only that your dad's murderer is onboard the ship and has killed someone . . .'

'Oh.'

Jacqui takes her seat back at the table, folds her arms and

looks at me. 'Please tell me that was a poor attempt at humour.'

I could apologise and say it was a drunken, irrational prank, but what would be the point? She'd lose trust in me and probably fire me again. I think about my dad. Honesty is always best, he would say.

I take a breath.

My throat feels tight, the air thick in my chest.

'We were in New York,' I tell her. 'Dad was on business. He brought me along because I'd never been, and he thought I could use the break. One morning I woke when I heard him moving around. He was going out for a run. I remember him lacing his trainers, humming a tune. He was wearing his headphones listening to Blondie, his favourite band.'

I swallow.

'He kissed the top of my head, whispered goodbye. As he was leaving, I noticed his one of his laces was loose. I called after him, but he didn't hear me. I drifted back to sleep and woke up a few hours later. I waited and waited. I thought maybe he'd been called into the office. That happened sometimes. Hours passed, and he still hadn't come back. I saw the news. A man stabbed in Central Park. I thought it couldn't be him.' I pause. 'And then came the knock on the door.'

Jacqui says nothing. Just listens.

'Two officers. They didn't say much. They didn't need to tell me. I knew. I screamed . . . I couldn't help myself. He was gone. I was alone and so far from everything I knew.'

I stare down at the napkin twisted in my hand.

Jacqui reaches across the table, rests her hand on mine. 'People always say time heals. It doesn't. It just teaches you how to fake being OK. You go back to work, you laugh at jokes, you stop crying in supermarkets. It's all a performance.'

I force a small laugh that sounds wrong. 'I still text him sometimes. Stupid, I know. But it helps. It's like he's still somewhere, still hearing me.'

'That's not stupid,' she says quietly.

I nod, blinking hard. 'The thing is, the man who killed him is here too. So maybe time's finally giving me something back.'

'That could make a good episode of *Lady Detective*.'

'I suppose it could.'

Jacqui looks at me thoughtfully. I squirm. This is unfamiliar territory.

'Just you and your mom now?'

I nod.

'You guys close?'

'No.'

'Why?'

'It's her fault my dad is dead.'

Jacqui's expression tightens, but she doesn't push it. I don't want to talk about Diane. My head is already full.

A wild idea forms in my head. It's so ridiculous, I surprise myself when the words tumble from my mouth. 'You could help me find him.'

She tilts her head at me. 'We have an outline to finish, and a book to write.'

The more I think about it, the more the idea grows on me. 'But you have all that experience as a TV Detective. You must have spent time with real-life cops. How many crime scripts have you read? Four seasons each with twenty-four episodes. That's ninety-six episodes in total.'

'At least. You missed out the holiday specials.'

'I rest my case.'

She shakes her head. 'I don't know.'

'We could make a proposal for a second book based on the experience.'

Her eyes flash. She's thinking. I don't want to push her so I say: 'Let's do some work and we can talk some more later.'

We spend the next four hours mapping out a storyline and characters before Jacqui orders in lunch and insists we watch an episode of *Lady Detective* on her laptop. She chooses an episode called *The Murder Swing* with Cassie Kowalski going undercover as a newly employed circus trapeze artist to solve the mystery of her predecessor's death. I can't help but snigger as the leggy detective clashes with the strong man, bitter clowns, a bearded lady (I kid you not), and a bullying ringmaster. I'm partly wondering who wrote this shit, but I'm also glued to Cassie's constant jeopardy and impressive trapeze skills.

'It's not supposed to be funny,' Jacqui says with an edge to her voice.

'I know, but the characters are coked up on cliché.'

Jacqui gives me the side eye.

'I'm really enjoying it. You're great and I'm loving your work on the swing . . . the murder swing, that is.'

A half-smile appears on her lips. 'There was little in the way of health and safety back then.'

'Did you do all your own stunts?'

'Pretty much all of them.'

'Wow.'

'This episode was Billie's favourite. She would watch it over and over.'

I'm suddenly overcome with guilt and rest my hand on Jacqui's, but she snatches it away. We sit in silence for a moment before I decide to jump the next hurdle. 'Hey, I was talking to Rudy. He was wondering if you'd be interested in a part in his play.'

'What, no! Are you kidding me?'

'Imagine we have you playing Cassie. What a kick in that ass that will be to those "treacherous sons of bitches" that pushed you from your own project.'

She's deep in thought, looking beyond me as she taps a finger on the tabletop.

'You'd pack in the house. Could be good PR for Cassie and the book.'

I see a light in Jacqui's eyes. 'I like that idea.'

'Shall I tell him you're in?'

She nods. 'Just a cameo. No more.'

'Perfect.'

'And about Buttonface, I will help you . . .' She raises a finger. 'Only so that I can keep an eye on you.'

I raise three fingers in a *Hunger Games* silent salute.

Jacqui frowns at me. 'I have a FaceTime call with Oliver at 5 p.m. I'd like you to be present for that.'

'Sure.'

We finish for the day. I know she feels the same as I do, that we have turned a corner in our working relationship. I'm excited about the book. What we've come up with has far exceeded my expectations. I'm also excited about teaming up with her to do some real-life investigating. The icing on the cake is that Jacqui has agreed to appear in Rudy's play. I take out my phone and text him the good news.

Jacqui's in. She'll do the play. Fewer lines the better. Now I need you to uphold your end of the bargain.

It takes a moment for the ellipsis to appear with his response.

I can't believe you did it! That's incredible!!!

No mention of our bargain. I feel a knot in my stomach, but a moment later the ellipsis reappears.

He was travelling with a group called the Midnight Chorus Society. That's all I know.

Chapter Twenty-One

Martha

The Midnight Chorus Society. Wilma and Bernard's names spring to mind. I sang at their karaoke party. But who are they? Their name suggests they could be a choir. But are they? Not one single person at that event could sing. I have no idea what kind of organisation they might be, so I'm on my way to find out. I leg it down the sweeping staircase with the plush black-and-gold carpet to the fifth-floor lobby. Below, I see the sleek, gleaming lift bursting with passengers, some squashed against the glass walls. The doors slide closed, and it rises slowly, faltering momentarily before hauling itself upwards once more. I wonder just how reliable it is as I turn at the landing where the string quartet had played when we boarded two days earlier.

Arriving in the lobby, I head straight to reception, passing a Bakelite sign with elegant writing and an arrow pointing towards the 'Department Stores'. I navigate clusters of passengers with branded shopping bags, milling around, chatting with other passengers. Two bearded men with conference lanyards linger at the edge of the lobby, talking in low voices. They're watching a woman half their age drift past. Something in me tightens, a prickle of warning. I stop, meet their eyes. They look away. I shake my head and keep moving.

The reception desk has two agents. One is thankfully free; the other is talking to a tall man wearing a white, short-sleeved shirt, carrying a Bible that he places on the desk. I wonder if he's a Mormon. He turns to look at me, and stares in a disquieting way that makes me quickly focus my attention on the second receptionist, a young man with gopher-like features and spray-tanned skin. I give him my warmest smile.

'Hi there.'

'One moment,' he replies, nimble fingers dancing like ballerinas across a keyboard.

'Take your time,' I say casually, despite not meaning it.

Finishing on the computer, he picks up the phone and quickly dials a three-digit number. 'Betty, hi, it's Kelvin . . . yeah, it's busy . . . I've been rushed off my feet all day . . . I know, super crazy, right . . . hey, just to update you, Mrs Draper from room 4.102 is still agitated . . . piece of work is one way to describe her. OK, great. Thanks, Betty. Bye.'

Kelvin turns to me with a thin, officious smile. 'How can I help you, ma'am?'

'I'm looking for the Midnight Chorus Society. I'd like to know where I can find them?'

'The who?'

'The Midnight Chorus Society. They're travelling on the ship.'

'I don't recognise the name.'

I wave a finger at his computer. 'Maybe you could have a look.'

An insincere expression flits across his face as his fingers tap the keys. After a moment, he arches his brows and exits whatever screen he had just been on. 'I'm sorry, but I can't give you that information.'

'What do you mean?'

'Is there anything else I can help you with?'

'You found something, didn't you?'

His phone rings. 'Ma'am, if there's nothing else I can help you with, I'll take this call.'

'What are you not telling me?'

'Ma'am, there's nothing to report. Have a nice day,' he says, and picks up the phone.

Bollocks.

'Hey,' comes a voice.

I look across to see the Mormon smiling at me. 'You were the girl who sang at the karaoke last night.' He has a soft American accent, from somewhere in the South, I think.

I blink. 'You were there?'

'I was. You were something else, if you don't mind me saying.'

I shrug. 'Thank you, I had a few too many—'

'I overheard you asking the gentleman about the Midnight Chorus Society,' he says.

He has my interest. 'You heard correctly.'

'You're here for the convention?'

'Erm . . . obviously,' I say, perking up.

Leaning across, he whispers conspiratorially, 'Me too.' He raises his arm. Wrapped around his wrist like a friendship bracelet is the slim red rope of a lanyard with a printed card attached. It has an emblem of a half theatre mask, half skull wearing a hood. Where have I seen that before? There's a name.

VICTOR FRYER

The Midnight Chorus Society

25th Anniversary Convention

I almost hear Hallelujah sung from the Heavens.

'You must be Victor,' I say.

'In the flesh.'

'Nice to meet you, Victor. I'm Martha.'

'The pleasure is all mine.'

We shake. His hand is callused and rough.

'Are you going there now?' I ask.

'I've just left. I'm going back to my room. Do you want to come with me?'

I choke out a cough and laugh nervously.

'I'm sorry . . . I don't mean it in that way.'

I'm a little creeped out, but he could be my way into the chorus. 'I'm busy right now, Victor, thank you . . . but I'm so glad to have met you. I haven't been to the convention yet. There was a mix-up with my luggage, which I still don't have.'

'I thought I hadn't seen that sweet face today.'

'Haha . . . that's, erm, nice. Could you please direct me to where it's being held?'

He grins a disquieting smile that gives his face a deranged expression. I notice his canines are unusually pointy. Leaning towards me once more, he whispers. 'Sure thing, Martha.' He nods to the passengers in the lobby. 'We gotta keep this a secret, right?'

I lean back. 'Right.'

'Take the elevator to level 2. Exit and you'll see directions for the casino on your right. Cut through the casino and follow the signs to the Hefferman Conference Rooms. Keep walking until you see the tall red curtains. Go through them and continue until you reach a desk. It will be manned by either Wilma or Frank.'

Like a jigsaw, some pieces slot into place. I recall where I've seen the Society's emblem. Wilma wore it as a brooch when I first met her. 'Thank you, Victor.'

'You're very welcome. You have a good day now.'

As Victor leaves, I notice he has left his Bible on the reception desk. I'm about to call after him when I hesitate. A plan forms in my head. This old book could be useful.

Following Victor's directions, I make my way down to level 2 and navigate my way through a busy, colourful casino of musical slot machines, spinning roulette wheels, and poker games. I notice Bob and Don sitting at a card table with a group of other players. Bob catches my eye.

'Hey Martha!'

I feel suddenly conspicuous, but I smile, wave, and hurry on. Exiting the casino, I enter a quiet corridor. The noise from the casino diminishes the deeper I go. Gripping the Bible like a talisman, I slow my pace as I come to a crossroads. Where do I go? If I had a coin, I'd flip it, but who has actual coins these days? A sliver of light slices through the darkness in the corridor to my left. I see two shapes emerge from behind a curtain. Bingo! The red curtain. Why is it so dark down here? Do the electrics not work? I feel an attack of nerves and almost turn back, but I've been seen by the two people making their way towards me. I recognise them. It's the creepy 'Shining' twins from last night's karaoke. Their eyes are wide and fixed on me like I'm their prey. They close in on me, and in this dim light, I can see they're much older than their babydoll dresses would suggest. They circle me. 'What are you doing here?' one of them asks in a breathy whisper.

'I'm here for the convention.'

'Your name's Martha,' the other says.

I laugh nervously. 'You remember.'

The scent they wear is smoky and clings like incense: altars and ashes, prayer turned into warning.

In unison, they chant my name, and then they begin to sing:

Pretty stranger, don't be late,
The chorus sings, it seals your fate.
Candles burn and shadows grow,
Inside's a truth you shouldn't know.

The hairs on my neck rise. I push through them and hurry towards the curtain in the wake of their weird girly giggles and horrible perfume. Turning back, I'm relieved to see they've gone. What the hell was that about? I tug at the curtain, searching for the gap. It's plush, heavy, old, and oddly out of place, as if it belongs to an old theatre, rather than a cruise ship. I find the split, open it a fraction and peek inside. There are two large double doors with traffic coming and going. I see a tall roll-up banner, the hooded emblem looming large – half theatre mask, half skull. Beneath it, in bold gold letters, the words **Welcome to the Midnight Chorus Society 25th Anniversary Conference**. Above the doors is an elaborate blue plaque that says: THE PRISCILLA HEFFERMAN CONFERENCE CENTRE. I see various people I half recognise wearing lanyards similar to the one Victor was wearing. I walk through the doors and instantly spot the check-in desk, which is manned by a spectacled, grey-haired elderly gentleman. Or it would be manned if he wasn't sleeping. I recognise him as the same man who sang 'You're the One That I Want' with Wilma at the karaoke. I take a breath, slip inside, and make my way to the desk.

'Hello.' I say to him. Frank Franklin is the name on his badge.

He blinks his eyes and, for a moment, looks confused.

'Can you help me?' I ask.

He looks up at me, squinting.

'Help you?'

'Is this the Midnight Chorus Society?'

With a trembling hand, he pushes his glasses up his nose and takes stock of me. 'You should be wearing your name badge, young lady. That's the rules.' His voice is dry and gritty like a phonograph with a worn needle.

'I lost it.'

He frowns. 'You lost it?!'

'A gust of wind blew it overboard.'

'Did it now . . . I suppose you'll be wanting a replacement.'

'Yes, please.'

'Well, the printer's not working, so I can't use that. I'll hand-write it for you. What's your name?'

'Mar—'

I pause.

I don't want to use my own name. I'm about to take a pass that I have not paid for. That could land me in trouble.

He looks up at me with an expectant expression, 'Mar?'

'Marsha!'

He frowns momentarily. 'Second name?'

'Kowalski.'

'How do you spell that?'

I spell it out for him. He takes forever to write it in a wobbly scrawl. 'Try not to lose this one, y'hear?' he says, sliding it across.

'I won't.' I hold out the Bible. 'Oh, I'm returning this.'

He frowns and takes it from me, but it slips from his shaking hands and falls open on his desktop. I stifle a gasp. The pages inside have been carved out. Inside is a jagged, dirty knife with a crucifix-shaped hilt, and an old pewter hip flask with dried flakes of red around the lid.

'That belongs to Victor. He'd misplace his head if it wasn't screwed on.'

Stepping back, I thank him, turn and make my way out of there fast, wondering what the hell is a Mormon doing with a knife concealed in a Bible and just what kind of convention is this?

Chapter Twenty-Two

Martha

The lifts are busy, so I climb the stairs two at a time, rushing back to my room, alarm bells ringing in my head. I have so many questions. Where to begin? Let's start with the Midnight Chorus Society. Who are they? What kind of choral group has creepy, intimidating, unhinged twins and a faux-bible-carrying-knife-wielding Mormon? Who is he, and could he be Buttonface? Victor Fryer is wiry, tall, and certainly looks strong enough to toss a grown man over a guardrail. My heart pounds as I clear the stairs and scramble down the corridor to my room. I glance behind me, half expecting to see him, or the freaky sisters for that matter, appear out of nowhere and curse me with more unhinged chanting and dancing, but thankfully, there's no one.

I fumble for my key, unlock the door and tumble inside. Double locking the door, I take a breath and give myself a moment before sitting on the bed and opening my laptop.

I google Victor Fryer.

The Wi-Fi is painfully slow, taking several minutes to load. Pages of results appear, with different Victor Fryers interspersed among Air Fryer product links and recipes. *Not helpful*. I settle back nervously and sift through the horribly slow links. Twenty minutes pass, with multiple searches, but I find nothing, so I throw in the towel and bite my lip before googling the Midnight Chorus Society. The search results display pages of links to choral societies across the globe, none of which are the one I'm looking for. *Thanks, Google.* I wade through them anyway, looking at pictures and videos in the vain hope of finding a familiar face, maybe Wilma or Frank, but there's nothing.

I google both of their names together.

This time I get a positive result.

There is one listing at the top of the page that takes me to the Franklin Guest House. I click on the link. The page slowly loads and displays a picture of a quaint Victorian mansion house, with a block of on-screen text:

Welcome to the Franklin Guest House, here in the heart of Kennebunkport, where you will find a lovely home from home and some good old-fashioned, cosy Maine hospitality courtesy of Wilma and Frank Franklin.

Aside from a booking form, that's all there is. Neither Wilma nor Frank have Instagram or Facebook accounts, which is not surprising for that generation, I suppose. Strangely, neither does their guest house. You would think that to attract business, they would at least feature on one social media platform.

My phone pings with a text message from Jacqui.

Have you made any progress? Don't forget our conference call with Oliver at 5.

J

Yikes! It's almost four. Time has flown by, and I've done none of the work I promised I'd do. I push aside any thoughts of Wilma, Frank and Victor and pull together this morning's notes, which in truth only covers the first few chapters. I work for the next sixty minutes at light speed, typing them up on my laptop and putting them into some semblance of order. With five minutes to spare, I save the file, close the computer and run to Jacqui's suite, taking the stairs two at a time. I'm sweaty and out of breath again by the time I'm knocking on her door.

It swings open.

Jacqui is holding a martini and is dressed in a breezy, aquamarine kaftan with pink and turquoise patterns. 'You're on time. That's a first.'

I fake a smile and step inside.

'Do you want a drink?' she asks.

'I need a night off,' I tell her.

'Bravo, you,' she says, a slur in her voice.

'How many of those have you had?'

'Not enough,' she says with an edge to her voice.

Something has rattled her. I wonder what it could be.

We take our seats at the table in front of Jacqui's laptop just as Oliver's call comes through. Jacqui answers, and Oliver's smiling face fills the screen. 'Hey! How's my favourite crime writing duo?'

Jacqui raises her glass, 'Peachy.'

'Doing good,' I say, positively.

'How's the cruise going?'

Jacqui takes a swig of her martini and shrugs.

'That good, huh?' says Oliver.

Jacqui smiles, but it's more of a grimace. 'Aside from the fact that a former associate, Cilla Ryder, is onboard, it's fine.'

'Who is she?' Oliver asks.

'A whor—'

'She's the CEO of the company that runs the *Jewel of the Atlantic*,' I interrupt.

'Oh, you mean Priscilla.'

Jacqui scoffs. 'She's an unwelcome distraction,' she says.

Oliver's eyes dart suspiciously from Jacqui to me and back to Jacqui. 'A distraction?'

'Nothing I can't handle,' says Jacqui, swirling the remainder of her cocktail.

'We're making good progress,' I say. 'Shall I take you through where we are at?'

'Let's hear it.'

Opening up my laptop, I give him a summary of what Jacqui and I agreed this morning. Despite not having a complete second act and a denouement, I wing it and make something up. 'And so, Cassie solves the murders, while being a doting grandmother and a devoted mum to her sick daughter.' Oliver is nodding his head. 'It's still a work in progress, but we're on it, aren't we?' I say, looking at Jacqui.

She holds my gaze momentarily with the trace of a smile. 'We're on it.'

'Great!' says Oliver. 'About this "distraction", on a scale of one to ten, how would you rate the impact it could have on the completion date of the outline?'

Jacqui sighs and folds her arms.

'Oliver, trust me. It won't impact the outline. I promise,' I say quickly before Jacqui puts her foot in it.

He's looking at us, uncertain. 'OK . . . that's good to hear. I'm happy with the direction you're taking, so keep going.'

The meeting ends with an exchange of niceties and good wishes. Relieved the meeting's over, I close my laptop. 'Did something happen with you and Priscilla today?'

Jacqui stands. 'I need a coffee and some air,' she says. 'Let's go for a walk.'

We head to the coffee bar on the main deck, where a handful of people sit around reading novels or doom-scrolling on their phones. I order two Americanos as Jacqui sits at an empty table, sunglasses on, her kaftan billowing in the ocean breeze. With the coffees in hand, I take the seat opposite her. Jacqui is quiet, watching the dark, choppy waters of the Atlantic.

'What happened today?' I ask.

It takes a moment for her to respond. 'I let her get under my skin is what happened.'

'Priscilla?'

'Who else?!' Slipping the lid off her disposable cup, she takes a sip and winces. 'Should have stuck to the martinis.'

'Please tell me you slapped her face.'

She snorts. 'I remember slapping that face when it was flesh and bone. Now it's just sculpted Tupperware.'

'Do you think she peels it off at night like the lid of a kitchen storage container?'

'No question. And she presses the edges down every morning to seal it closed.'

I laugh, and Jacqui laughs with me. In moments, we are giggling uncontrollably. People peer over their books and devices with curious expressions. A moment of silence passes, broken by Jacqui. 'Billie would be around your age now.'

'Have you been thinking about her?'

'A day doesn't go by that I don't think about my daughter. I hate life without her, but I carry on because that is what she wanted me to do. She knew she would die, despite my insistence . . . my lies . . . that the doctors could cure her.' Jacqui's voice cracks. 'She could sense it coming. She said to me that I had to rebuild my career and become like the amazing Cassie Kowalski once more.' Jacqui looks at the ornate gold rings on her fingers and fiddles with them. 'When she was small, she really believed she was watching her mom chase and catch criminals. She was so sweet, so selfless, so innocent. Nothing like me.'

'She must have loved you a lot.'

'Yeah, she did.'

I take a sip of my coffee. It's bitter and more like liquid ash. 'This coffee really is disgusting.'

'I bumped into Cilla today. There was a rare moment of civility between us, until she asked after Billie.'

'Didn't she know?'

'Of course she knew. She was just being a bitch. She can stick the knife into me, I can deal with that, but disrespecting my daughter is overstepping the line.'

'What did you do?'

'Nothing.'

'Oh . . .'

Jacqui shakes her head and takes off her sunglasses. Her eyes are glistening. 'I did nothing. What would be the point? I just walked away from her. Let's change the subject. Tell me about your day and skip the bullshit about working on the outline. Oliver may have bought it. I didn't.'

'I did work on the outline!'

'Is that before or after you went looking for the Midnight Chorus Society?'

I shift uncomfortably in my seat. 'You've been talking to Rudy.'

'It doesn't take much to get the truth from him.'

'For you, perhaps.'

'So come on, Nancy Drew, we're in this together, remember? What did you uncover?'

Sighing, I tell her everything about meeting Victor Fryer, his Bible, the twins, and the strangely private convention that no one, not even certain members of the crew, knows much about.

'Interesting,' says Jacqui. 'And you think this Victor could be Buttonface?'

'Honestly, I don't know, but he's my prime suspect for now.'

'This sounds dangerous,' says Jacqui. 'I hope you're not thinking of confronting him.'

I fold my arms. 'Of course not. But I will attend the convention.'

'Please could you finish the outline before he stabs you dead?'

'I'll work on it tonight. I promise.'

'You spoken to your mom yet?'

'She's left a few messages.'

'Have you called her back?'

'No.'

Jacqui nods, quiet for a moment. 'Listen, I don't know what your mom and dad were going through, but relationships are never easy. You should call her.'

I say nothing and glance at a grim-looking seagull glaring at me from the next table. It lets out a rasping kee-arh.

'Grief's messy. It makes you angry—'

'I'm not angry.'

'Silence doesn't heal anything.'

I fold my arms.

'Call her,' Jacqui says, standing. 'Even if it's awkward. Especially if it is.'

When she's gone, I sit there staring at my phone, the gull's cry cutting through the quiet she's left behind.

Chapter Twenty-Three

Wilma

Wilma stood in a crowded elevator inching its way to the eighth floor. To her irritation, it stopped at every level, slowed further by the heavyset passengers pressing in around her. She scanned the faces. There was no one she knew. Just holidaymakers in loud shirts and sunburnt skin, chatting about buffets and trivia nights. Ordinary people, dull and oblivious. They should take the stairs, she thought. Might do their waistlines some good.

She had just left the conference in Frank and Bernard's capable hands . . . correction, 'semi-capable' hands. Frank, the poor dear, was really getting on. His Parkinson's was worsening, and she feared the events over the past few days had taken their toll. Bernard, on the other hand, was physically capable, but he was easily distracted by a toothy smile, regardless of who it belonged to. She needed to manage them both. She also needed to manage the other key player in the Society's committee. Their patron, Priscilla 'The Spider' Hefferman.

As a result of yesterday afternoon's private meeting with Bernard, Wilma had decided to stay close to the Spider during this crisis. The Midnight Chorus's sacred code had been broken. Goddamnit! Oh Lord, she hated profanity, but this situation had sure messed with her marbles. A murder had been committed. And it was not just any murder; the victim was one of their own. A traitor had upset the darn applecart and was now hiding among them in plain sight. With Frank and Bernard by her side, she would root out this shit-eating, little ass punk and make him pay. Wilma was on the warpath. But – and this was a big but – to complicate matters, she had to tread carefully with Priscilla. The Society was, at most, a side hustle for her. For Wilma, it was everything.

The elevator pings. The fifth floor. Only three more to go. The doors yawn open, and no one gets in or out. Wilma bristles. She could have climbed the stairs quicker if it weren't for her varicose veins. The doors close slowly. The ascent begins once more.

Priscilla was ruthless. She was also volatile, unpredictable and as cold as the string of rich dead husbands that she had buried over the years. Wilma had known her for twenty-five years and had no doubt she would throw them all under the bus, or in this instance, the cruise ship, if there was any more trouble. What were they even doing here in the middle of the Atlantic Ocean, away from the safer, remote locations of previous conventions? Darn it! Why had she agreed to hold the convention on this ship?

Eventually, the elevator reached the eighth floor. Wilma made a swift exit as the doors opened, and a swarm of rude people pushed their way inside.

They must find the killer quickly. Wilma was convinced he would not stop at Ernest. She knew it took a killer to understand another's instincts. They had to find him before he killed again. The first place to start was Ernest's room, where Priscilla was waiting.

She hurried down the long corridor as fast as her little legs, and varicose veins for that matter, would allow. She heard a door opening, halted, took out her cell phone and placed it to her ear as if she were on a call. 'That's quite correct, dear,' she said, in a sing-song voice to no one.

A couple were exiting a room. They were smartly dressed as if they were going to dinner. They smiled at Wilma as they passed. She smiled back and faked a laugh as if the pretend person had just told her a joke on the other end of the line. She waited until the couple was far enough away before lightly tapping Ernest's door with the five coded knocks she and Priscilla had agreed on that morning. She waited a moment before the knock was returned, and Wilma, rolling her eyes, repeated the sequence of five.

The door cracked open. Priscilla's large, unblinking, mascaraed eye peered out at her.

'Are you going to let me in?'

'Were you followed?'

'No. I was not followed!'

The door swung open. 'Get inside, quick!'

'For Pete's sake, calm down, Priscilla. This is not the Cold War.'

'Calm down?! Do you know what I'm risking by being here with you?'

'We're both risking a lot if we don't work together.'

'Some of us have more to lose than others.'

'We're in this together, dear. Don't forget that,' Wilma said.

'Are we?'

Wilma bristled. Did Priscilla think she was behind the murder? 'One of us goes down, we all go down.'

The air crackled between them.

Priscilla broke the tension. 'What have you and the others discovered so far?'

'Nothing yet.'

'Nothing?!'

'Frank and Bernard are on the case—'

'Trembles and the Tooth Fairy! Oh, for Christ's sake, Wilma, is that the best you have?'

Wilma felt her face flushing. 'I'll ask you to please not refer to Frank as "Trembles", thank you very much.'

'Fucking fuck! We are well and truly screwed.'

Wilma flinched at Priscilla's vulgar language. She looked around the modest room. It was much smaller than hers, with no windows or a balcony. There was a trace of nicotine in the air, from Ernest's clothes she assumed, some of which lay strewn across the bed.

'According to my Head of Security, whoever killed the Undertaker was wearing a mask.'

'What kind of mask?'

'A balaclava with buttons for a face. Do I need to say any more?'

Wilma felt her blood run cold. She had not heard much about him for a long time. 'I thought he was dead.'

'NEWSFLASH, WILMA! HE'S ALIVE AND ONBOARD MY SHIP.'

Wilma steadied herself. 'This is not good.'

'Understatement! Did he have beef with Ernest?'

'None that I'm aware of.'

'It's my guess they had some history. We might find a clue in this room. I've already searched the drawers. You check his clothes.'

'What are we looking for?' Wilma asked.

'Something that might lead us to finding out who murdered the son of a bitch.'

Wilma felt her hackles rise but held her tongue at Priscilla's disrespect for Ernest. But she knew better than to stir up this angry arachnid. She needed Priscilla onside.

Wilma picked the clothes from the bed and began to search through the pockets. She found loose change, dollars, cigarette packets, but nothing else. She could see nothing in the clothes hanging in the wardrobe. She checked inside his socks, shoes and sneakers. Nothing. 'Has this room been cleaned since we lost Ernest?'

'No. Atkins wants it left as is for the cops when we dock in New York.'

'I thought you had thrown him off the scent?'

'Warned him off more like, but he won't listen to reason. Too moral for his own good. What a loser! We may have to dispose of him before we dock. He has a severe and convenient allergy to shellfish. I have a few drops of a concoction I created that I can add to his coffee when the time is right.'

'Good.' Wilma entered the bathroom. A towel hung over the shower, and a toothbrush, hairbrush, and shaving blade were lined up next to each other. Nothing out of place here. There was a small bin underneath the sink. Wilma crouched down and opened it. Inside were crumpled old tissues and waxy cotton buds. Something red and round caught her eye. She fished it out. It was a button, approximately 3cm in diameter, the type commonly found on a coat. Ernest only wore black, so it could not be his. She turned it over and held her breath. Two eyes and a twisted smile had been daubed on the face.

'What's that?' said Priscilla.

Wilma handed it across.

Priscilla took it and frowned as best she could, considering the amount of work her face had been subjected to. 'His calling card,' she said. 'Subtle.'

'He may not stop at Ernest.'

The Spider cocked her head at Wilma. 'He's a serial killer!'

Wilma bristled but ignored Priscilla's sarcasm. 'We need extra security at the convention.'

'Ya think?'

Wilma bunched her hands into fists. She hated profanity, she truly did, but what a Christ shitting crisis this was turning out to be!

Chapter Twenty-Four

Martha

Jacqui's words keep looping in my head. My relationship with Diane is fractured, but maybe I'm the problem. It's easier to blame her than admit I shut her out first. Every time she calls, I find an excuse not to answer. Every message goes into the archive of things I don't want to feel.

It's just past midnight. I'm in my bathrobe, sitting on the bed with cold pizza, my laptop, and a mess of notes. I'm wired on caffeine, trying to keep my promise to Jacqui and Oliver. Between work, the Diane stuff, and the thought of Buttonface and Victor Fryer still out there, my head feels like a war zone.

But I'm being paid to write, which is what I've always wanted. And Jacqui likes my ideas – most of them anyway – which is the next best thing to writing something of my own. I take a breath, shove the noise aside, and force myself to focus.

One slice of congealed, double pepperoni remains in the greasy box. I decide to take a five-minute break and eat it as I ponder what I should do tomorrow while Jacqui spends her day at the spa.

A knock on the door startles me.

Who could that be at this time of night? I think of the twins, or even Victor. Maybe he got a tip-off that I'd dropped his Bible at the convention desk, and he was popping by to tell me all about the Church of Jesus Christ of Latter-day Saints before plunging his dirty knife into my neck.

I tiptoe across the room and peer through the peephole.

My heart skips.

It's Zach.

I open the door. 'Hi.'

'Hey.'

His shirt is half unbuttoned and dishevelled, he's wearing sunglasses and carrying a bottle of half-empty vodka. He peers at me over his shades. I catch a sadness in his eyes.

'Everything OK?'

He sways and shrugs. 'Can we talk?'

Today is a day for encountering drunk people. 'Sure. Do you want to come in?'

'Only, if that's OK.'

I step aside. 'How did you know where my room is?'

He smiles at me. 'You don't remember me helping you back here last night after our final bottle of Champagne?'

'Oh, right. Slipped my mind.'

'Can I get you anything?' I gesture to the complimentary bottles of water. 'Fizzy or still.'

He taps the bottle. 'I have vodka, thank you,' he slurs.

'I can see that. How much have you drunk?'

He shrugs once more. 'Too much.'

'Let's get some air,' I tell him, leading him out to the balcony.

'If you don't mind, I'd rather talk here, in private.'

'Oh, sounds serious.' I gesture to the small sofa. 'Take a pew.' I'd apologise for the mess on my bed, but I'm not sure he'd notice.

He chuckles. '"Take a pew."'

'British for sit down. A pew is a—'

'A church bench.'

'That's right.'

'But this is a couch.'

'We're a strange bunch of people.'

'I like that about you.'

He sits on the sofa, nurses the bottle, and says nothing for a while. Leaning forward, Zach rests his elbows on his knees, and stares blankly at the carpet. The bottle tips over. I reach across and take it gently from him before it spills.

'What's up?' I ask.

'Last night when you told me about your dad and what happened to him . . . I . . .'

I feel myself shrinking inside. I clearly told not only Jacqui, but Zach too. I've always been so private about my dad. I still miss him so much and can't bear to talk about him, yet apparently not anymore. All it takes is shit-faced Martha to start blabbing. My mind turns to Dad lying all alone in that tunnel in Central Park. I shudder.

'. . . I was really touched by your story. You see . . . I can relate. The same thing happened to me when I was a kid.'

I blink, not quite believing what he's just told me. I don't know what to say.

He rubs his thighs. 'I'm fine, y'know . . . it's just your story triggered some old memories, that's all.'

He's clearly not fine. I sit beside him and take his hand. 'Zach, I'm so sorry.'

'It was my mom. She had some issues with alcohol. My dad was an abusive asshole to her. Physically and mentally. They would fight. It would get messy. I spent a lot of time in foster care. Mom ended up going off the rails. She left the state, is what I was told. Time went by with no word from her. I made my foster parents go to the police. It was then that Mom became a missing person, until one day, they found her.'

A tide of sorrow rises and engulfs me to the point of breathlessness. I gently squeeze his hand. He leans into me and silently weeps. 'You never had closure,' I say.

Sitting back, he wipes his eyes with the back of his hands. 'Neither did you. Your dad's killer was never found. That's tough.'

He lets go of my hand. I fold my arms.

'My mom's disappearance has shaped my life, you might say.'

'She'd be so proud of you.'

'I don't know about that.'

'Of course she would.'

'I went off the rails myself . . . never quite got back on.'

'But you're a different person now. Successful. Kind. Handsome.'

'Could I get some water, please?' he asks.

'Sure.' I stand and grab the water bottle from the bedside table. The glasses are unclean, so I take one to the bathroom and rinse it under the tap. Returning a moment later, Zach is lying down and quietly snoring. I watch him for a moment and feel a twist in my stomach. I've never met anyone who has had the same trauma, and I'm not sure how I feel about it. As much as I like Zach, I don't want to dredge up those old feelings. But I also feel an empathy that I have never felt with anyone other than people I've read about or seen on the news. He's hurting and is vulnerable. For that reason, I don't want to disturb him or ask him to leave.

Gently, I remove his sunglasses, untie his laces and slide off his trainers. There's a spare blanket in the wardrobe that I drape over him. It's getting late but I don't feel tired. I brush my teeth, clear the bed, bin the pizza and slip into bed. I look across at him sleeping peacefully. Switching off the lights, I grab my laptop and, under the glow of the screen, continue working on the outline.

Chapter Twenty-Five

Wilma

The conference centre keys jangled in Wilma's hand as she hurried through the casino, her lips pursed in judgement at the grim-faced losers who had clearly been up all night gambling and drinking. It was a shame she was at sea. If this were a casino on dry land, Wilma had no doubt she and Frank would be sitting outside in their van, waiting to befriend and drug one of these hapless fools before taking them home to the Kennebunkport guest house for a spot of torture and death in the dungeon. The thought gave her a thrill and a bounce in her step.

She glanced behind her, looking for a sign of Frank, but the poor dear was slow, and she had no time to wait. Last night, before bedtime, she had WhatsApped the committee and called an early morning crisis meeting. Before leaving the US, she had insisted they all install the WhatsApp messaging service on their cell phones. She had never heard of the app until the Reverend suggested they use it as a precaution during their travels. Their exchanges would be encrypted and therefore inaccessible to the authorities, the Reverend informed her. Encrypted or not, Wilma didn't trust technology, yet it seemed this app might be a useful tool. So, she agreed with the caveat that no one in the

WhatsApp group should mention any potentially incriminating detail about the conference or each other.

'All hail our esteemed mighty leader!' came a slurred voice.

Wilma felt her stomach clench and slid her eyes in the voice's direction. Terence was sitting nearby at a craps table with two older men whom she didn't recognise.

'Come and join us!' said Terence, waving a half-empty beer glass.

He was wearing the same Hawaiian shirt and shorts that he had worn for the past two days. Gritting her teeth, she made her way to the table, 'Good morning, Terence . . .' she laughed nervously and glanced at the two men. One was heavy with a bushy moustache, and the other was thin and balding.

'Bob, Don, meet Wilma,' said Terence.

'Nice to meet you, Wilma,' said the heavy one.

'They're police officers,' said Terence with a wink.

'Retired,' added the thin one.

Wilma blinked and held her breath.

'Do you play?' asked the heavy man.

'I beg your pardon?'

'Craps . . . do you play craps?'

'Oh, no. I never gamble.'

'That's too bad,' he said. 'We're bleeding your boyfriend dry.'

'He's not my . . .' Wilma smiled thinly and shook her head. That wasn't polite, and she would not dignify it with a response. She met Terence's gaze. His eyes were glazed and bloodshot. He winked at her, a second time. She frowned and nodded at the Exit doors. He arched his brows and shrugged. This was becoming tiresome. 'Terence, could we have a quick private word?'

'Sure, if you buy me a beer, sweetcakes.'

Wilma felt herself flushing with humiliation and anger.

Terence waved at a passing waitress. Wilma tugged his arm

and pulled him out of earshot of the two men. He reeked of beer and stale body odour. 'What the hell are you playing at?' she hissed. 'Cops, of all people!'

'They're nice guys.'

'You're putting us at risk!'

'It's all good, Wilma. They know nothing about us. Trust me!'

Wilma closed her eyes momentarily and tried to calm herself. 'We have a meeting. Right now!' she said.

'Now? But—'

'We talked about it on our WhatsApp group last night.'

'Whassap?'

'Oh, for heaven's sake!' she said, her voice rising.

Bob and Don looked up from the craps table with curious expressions. Wilma shrank from their view behind Terence. 'Pull yourself together, for the sake of the Society.'

He saluted her, 'Yes, ma'am. I can do that.'

She noticed the Gentlemen's restroom near the exit. 'Come with me,' she said, leading him towards it. 'Go inside, get cleaned up and meet me and the others in the office at the rear of the conference centre.'

'At the rear of the conference centre,' he slurred.

'It's important, Terence,' she said, squeezing his bicep, or lack thereof.

'Ouch,' he said, pulling it away. 'OK, OK.'

'It's the office where we store the materials.'

'Materials!' he said, turning and entering the restroom. 'Five minutes . . .' The bathroom door shut behind him.

Wilma sighed heavily and hurried out of the casino with no confidence that he would show up.

Bernard and the Reverend were waiting at the entrance draped by the old theatrical curtain that Priscilla had shipped from Paris. It was over one hundred years old and had hung for many years in the famous Théâtre du Grand-Guignol during the 1920s, the Spider had informed them. It was tradition for Wilma to oversee conference décor, but for the 25th anniversary, Priscilla had insisted on inserting her own ideas above Wilma's. Wilma had objected to the French curtain, saying it was a little grand and ostentatious, but the Spider would not back down. 'The Parisian theatre had been dedicated to horror productions. It was perfect for their needs,' the Spider had told them. Everyone agreed and Wilma quietly fumed. The Midnight Chorus Society was her baby. She might be the Director, but Priscilla was their patron, and without her money, the Society would not function. This gave the Spider a lot of power that Wilma deeply resented.

'Morning,' said Wilma, 'Sorry I'm late. I had to help Frank get ready.'

'Is he joining us?' asked Bernard.

'He'll be along soon,' she replied, slipping through the curtain and unlocking the entrance with the brass key. She led them to the private office at the rear of the conference centre. There were eighteen keys, all different sizes, attached to a brass ring, and she couldn't remember which one fitted the lock on the office door. She tried three that didn't work. Fumbling through the metal keys, she tried two more, but neither would turn the lock. She could feel a sweat break out on her skin.

A hand brushed past her and pushed down on the door handle.

The door opened.

'That wasn't too hard, was it?' said the Reverend.

Wilma felt her face flushing and wanted to scream. For an unkind moment, she pictured the Reverend chained up, naked and bloody, in her dungeon. The thought calmed her.

'Après vous,' said the Reverend, gesturing to the open door.

She flashed him a half-smile, stepped inside, and switched

on the light. There was a desk with a chair, a whiteboard, and several boxes of conference materials, including the convention itinerary, booklets profiling the speakers, and guest photographs to sign and sell. There was also a box of flyers publicising the Franklin Guest House with special rates for Society members. Wilma liked making money for the Society and her bed and breakfast. She might not be quick off the mark with keys, but she was a discerning businesswoman and knew how to turn a profit.

'Ahoy, sailors!'

Wilma flinched and turned to see Terence. His face and hair were wet, and he looked brighter than he did five minutes ago. 'Don't panic. I'm here to sort out all our problems,' he said, rubbing his hands together.

Frank was behind him, shuffling forward, a pained expression on his creased face.

'Shut the door, please, dear,' Wilma told Frank.

They leant against the wall, a motley crew of seasoned serial killers, their eyes trained on Wilma. The Reverend, whom she didn't like or trust, folded his arms and looked bored. Terence had one foot on the ground, the other pressed against the wall. His hands were in the pockets of his shorts, and he was fumbling . . . oh no, she looked away. Her beloved Frank blinked at her. He was holding his left arm with his right hand, a habit he had developed to stop it from shaking. Sweet Bernard smiled affably at her. He was a good friend, but in truth, not a reliable one. He was so easily distracted by a winning smile. He had already put himself and the Society at risk twice on this god darn ship. Of late, she wondered if his marbles were slipping away as swiftly as Frank's.

'Let's begin,' she said. 'Frank, dear, the whiteboard.'

He gave her a puzzled look. It took a few seconds to register before he raised a finger. 'I remember!'

Earlier that morning she had told him her plan for the meeting and what she expected from him. *Oh Lord*. Frank shuffled across the office to the whiteboard, picked up a black marker, and began to draw.

'Are you going to tell us what this is about?' asked the Reverend.

Wilma cleared her throat. 'I'm coming to that.'

She glanced at Frank, relieved to see he had actually remembered what she had asked him to do. 'As you know, the Spider and I have been looking into who murdered Ernest.'

Their gaze was focused on the whiteboard. Despite Frank's shaking hand, he was doing a grand job.

'What the hell, man?' laughed Terence. 'Don't give up your day job.'

Frank set down his marker. He had drawn a picture of Buttonface. It was childish but there was no mistaking who it was.

'What does this mean, Wilma?' Bernard asked.

'Let me hazard a guess,' said Terence. 'Buttonface killed the Undertaker?'

'We believe so,' she replied. 'A witness saw him.'

'Do we know if he's attending the conference?' the Reverend asked.

Wilma let out a heavy sigh. 'He could be. We don't know.'

'He could be anyone,' said Bernard.

Terence chuckled. 'This is awesome. He could even be one of us.'

'That's right,' said Wilma. 'No one is above suspicion.'

'For the record. It ain't me. I'd put my money on the tooth fairy if I were you.'

'We all know you're good at losing money,' said Bernard.

Terence flipped the bird at Bernard. 'Fuck you, Grandpa!'

Bernard's hand flew into his jacket pocket. Wilma knew he was reaching for his scalpel.

'Enough!' said Wilma. 'Can we please try to work together?'

'Is that a realistic ask if one of us is Buttonface?' asked the Reverend.

'What choice do we have?' said Bernard.

Silence settled. They watched each other like strangers.

'Why would he kill Ernest?' Bernard broke the quiet.

'I think we'd all like to know that,' said Wilma.

'And will he kill again?'

Terence laughed. 'He's one of the most successful serial killers in American history. What do you think?'

'I'm certain he will,' said Wilma. 'The question is, have any of you met him?'

They exchanged uneasy looks, then shook their heads.

'He's a private individual,' said Bernard. 'No one's ever seen his face, I think.'

'Wait,' said Terence. 'How do we even know he's a he?'

Wilma frowned. 'We don't.'

'I think he's a man,' said Bernard.

'Could be Wilma,' said Terence, smirking.

Wilma rolled her eyes.

'Didn't he apply to join the Society once?' said Bernard.

Wilma blinked. 'Excuse me?'

'Yes. Ten years ago, maybe more. Ernest mentioned it once.'

Wilma's pulse quickened. 'Why was I not told?'

'I don't know,' said Terence. 'The Undertaker handled applications.'

'He didn't tell me!' Her voice rose in pitch. 'What happened to the application?'

'Ernest took that to the grave,' said Bernard.

'To the morgue, you mean,' said Terence. 'He's not buried yet.'

Wilma turned to him. 'You were also in recruitment. Did you know?'

Terence swayed, squinting. 'I talked to a lot of people. Don't recall him.'

She looked at her husband. 'Frank?'

His eyes widened, he shook his head.

They kept no records. That was the rule.

Now there was no way to know what had passed between Ernest and Buttonface.

Wilma exhaled. 'We're in trouble.'

Chapter Twenty-Six

Martha

My eyes flicker open to the sound of a light tapping on my room door. The curtains are parted, the room is bright, and the balcony door is ajar. It's morning, and the balmy, salty perfume of the ocean swirls delicately under my nose. I'm half in, half out of the sheets. Stretching, I push myself up, feeling warm and mellow. I yawn and remember Zach stayed the night. I look at the sofa, but he's not there, and the blanket has been neatly folded.

The person at the door knocks harder this time. I jump out of bed, pull on the robe, and open the door.

'Good morning, ma'am. Room service,' says a smiling Rudy, holding up a tray of food with one hand. I notice a single rose inserted into a small vase.

'Rudy,' I say confused. 'But I didn't order anything.'

He frowns. Using his free hand, he retrieves a piece of paper from his trouser pocket and reads it. 'You are Martha Hammond?'

'Obviously'

'A gift from another passenger.'

'Oh . . . from who?'

'I am not privy to that information, but perhaps you could find out on the card.'

'The card?'

He lowers the tray. I see a small, white envelope with my name on it.

I take the tray from him. 'Thank you. Come in.'

Rudy steps inside and closes the door behind him. 'Late night?' His eyes skim the cluttered room.

'I worked late,' I say. 'You're the Events Director and a waiter now?'

He smirks. 'One of the stewards said he was delivering here. I told him I'd take it. Said you were a friend. Figured I'd save him the trip.'

'That's thoughtful.'

'If Priscilla Hefferman had her way, I'd be running this ship single-handed. She likes people to "go beyond their job spec".'

'I bet she doesn't reward them for it.'

'You got that right. She ain't big on dipping those manicured nails into that overflowing purse of hers.'

'She probably thinks fair pay is a socialist conspiracy.'

Rudy laughs. 'Hey, I wanted to thank you for getting Jacqui involved in my play.'

'You're welcome.'

'It'll be fun.'

'Yeah.'

'How'd you get on with the Midnight Chorus crowd?'

'God, they're weird. I did a bit of snooping. There's this guy – Victor – who carries a Bible with a knife hidden inside. What is that about?'

Rudy shudders. 'Creepy. No idea. That conference is private. Crew aren't allowed anywhere near the Hefferman Centre. For the best, if you ask me.'

'That doesn't strike you as unusual?'

He shrugs. 'It happens. Big money, secret clubs. Best not to ask questions.' He checks his watch. 'Anyway, I've got a pool aerobics class to run.'

'Rather you than me.'

He grins. 'Enjoy your breakfast.'

I open the envelope and read the note inside.

I'm sorry, but I had to bail early. Something came up with work.

Thank you for listening.

Enjoy breakfast.

Z x

P.S. Be my date for the Masquerade Ball?

Yikes! Be my date. Of course, I will. I'm a little giddy, which is something I have not felt since my last crush two years ago. Seems like a lifetime.

I pour myself a coffee and dive into the food: pancakes, bacon, sausage, and eggs. It's very American but delicious, just like my new cruise-ship crush. I wonder about his job. I don't know much about what he does, other than that he works in Finance. Those industry wheels never stop turning, I suppose. My phone pings with a text from Jacqui.

Got the outline proposal. I'll try to get to it between health and beauty torture. J.

I had worked on the outline proposal until 2 a.m., when I emailed it to Jacqui. It was in her hands now and I have no doubt there will be further discussions and disagreements to be had.

I think about the day ahead. Jacqui is at the spa this morning; in the afternoon, she's at the hairdressers. It's her interview on stage this evening, so she's got to look and feel her best.

I should continue working on the outline for the novel, but my head is elsewhere, partly on Zach's revelation and partly on the Midnight Chorus Society. I still don't know who or what they are, and my curiosity is getting the better of me. Despite the alarm bells ringing in my head, I decide I should go back to the convention and investigate further. What's the worst that can happen? I get spotted by Wilma and she turfs me out? Big deal.

From the bedside table, I pick up the convention badge I received yesterday and roll it over my fingers. This is my ticket to ride. Is it enough to buy me time before someone spots me as a conference crasher? It would make sense to go incognito to get the most out of this mission. As reluctant as I am to steal again, it's time to use my seasoned klepto skills and find a disguise.

I leave the room with an empty tote bag. Each level on the ship has at least two laundromats. After visiting four, I've acquired a plaid shirt and a faded MAGA cap (Made in China, no less). Walking through the deck area, I deftly snatch a pair of black-rimmed glasses from the table of a lady who had just gone for a dip.

I'm in the lift descending to the second floor, wearing the plaid shirt, which is too big for me but perfect for the look I'm going for – frumpy, unsophisticated, shortsighted, redneck. The polar opposite of me, obviously. I tuck my hair inside the baseball cap and slip on the glasses. The lenses are strong. They make me feel dizzy, but they'll have to do.

Exiting the lift, I walk through the casino, peering over the rim of the spectacles. At this time of morning, it seems busy. I don't know much about cruise ships or casinos. Perhaps that's normal. I look sideways and see Bob and Don, working the slot machines again. Neither of them looks my way. In fact, no one does. It's as if I'm invisible, which gives me both a thrill and a new confidence.

I follow the long, curved corridor to the crossroads, where the ominous darkness leads to the old red curtains. I see a man, his face lit by the glow of a telephone. My confidence dissipates, and I hesitate.

I shift on my feet and step backwards.

He looks up from his phone. 'The next talk is about to start,' he calls.

I raise my hand and give him a thumbs up.

'If you hurry, you might get a seat at the front.'

Composing myself, I make my way towards him, tentatively at first.

He's tall and broad with feral, unsettling eyes. 'I just need to check your pass. New rules,' he says, shining a small torch at my face. It lingers for a moment. 'MAGA chick. Smokin' hot,' he purrs.

I'm not sure how to respond to that.

The torch falls to my name badge. He leans forward, a little too close for comfort, and grins. 'Marsha Kowalski. Not a name you'd want if you had a speech impediment.'

Nerves get the better of me and I chuckle. Can't help myself. 'Martha Kowalthki,' I say in what I hope is a convincing mid-American accent. 'That'th funny.' The irony of saying my real name out loud is not lost on me.

He laughs and opens the curtain.

'Go right in,' he says.

I march forward, 'Have a nithe day.'

Relieved, I merge into a crowd flowing in the same direction, like lemmings. Furtively, I scan the faces, praying I'm not recognised. I'm unsure of my plan, so I'm going with the flow for now. We flock into a large conference room with a stage and a giant screen displaying the Midnight Chorus Society 25th Anniversary in huge letters.

The crowd scatters, taking seats as close to the front as possible. I want to remain inconspicuous, so I sit on the edge of the last row. There's a murmur of excitement as more people arrive and fill the auditorium. I spot Karaoke Terence, dressed in a Hawaiian shirt and matching shorts, unsteady on his feet, searching for an empty chair. After my performance, he had wrapped his arm tightly around my waist. I bristle at the memory, but that changes to alarm when he stops beside me. The bitter reek of stale whiskey emanates from him like an invisible cloud of steam. I feel him looking at me, but I daren't meet his gaze. After a moment, he rudely pushes past, mumbling incoherently, and sits further along. Relief sweeps over me. I wasn't recognised.

The audience begins to clap. I look up and see Wilma on the stage with a microphone.

I notice Terence lean forward. 'Fuggin' bitch!' he slurs.

'Hush!' a man says.

Terence gives him the finger.

As the clapping subsides, Wilma speaks. 'Thank you, ladies and gentlemen, and how are you enjoying the 25th Anniversary of the Midnight Chorus Society so far?'

Cheers, whooping, and clapping.

'Fuggin' crap!' Terence cries above the noise.

Wilma hasn't heard him and continues. 'Now, many of you will know we've had some esteemed guests speak at our events over the years. Many are no longer with us. On that note, we will be honouring our departed friends at a special event on our final night before arriving in New York City. Think of it like the Oscars in Memoriam Tribute, but better, and more interesting too . . .'

More cheers and applause.

'. . . So I guess that is a good segue to our next guest . . . not that she's a dead actress or anything like that, oh no . . . She's the Paramour of the Penitentiary, the Concubine of the Coop, the Slammer Sweetheart, please put your hands together and welcome SHEEEEILAAA MOOOORGAAAAN!!!'

My jaw drops.

The audience is standing, and their applause is rapturous.

I stand and clap, too.

The Death Row wife! I feel like I know her. Anyone who has seen or listened to as many true crime podcasts as I have knows about Sheila Morgan. I slide my glasses down and watch as Sheila climbs the stage, all smiles and big glossy hair, a wig like something Cher would wear back in the eighties. She's dressed like eighties Cher too – tight jeans, cowboy boots . . . more a pastiche à la the pound shop. Both her hands are in the air, waving to the adoring crowd. Wilma hands her the microphone.

'Thank you, Wilma, dear.'

Behind her, the screen fades and a new slide appears with what is evidently the title of Sheila's talk:

Sheila Morgan
The Life and Loves of the OG Death Row WAG

'It's so good to be here among y'all. I've been a great admirer of the Society from way back. Some of my dearly departed husbands were loyal members.'

More applause.

'It's such an honour . . . thank you . . . thank you . . . please take the weight off your feet and sit down.'

I notice Terence topple backwards and fall into his seat, much to the disgust of those on either side of him.

'Today, I talk to you from a place of love to tell you my story and the story of my husbands and those almost husbands who were . . . well, "fried", I suppose for want of a better expression, before they could make it to the altar. I will reveal the love, the heartbreak, and the hope we can all find in the most challenging of times.'

Figuratively, I strap myself in because this sort of lecture from 'Slammer Sweetheart' Sheila Morgan is my cup of tea. It's still unclear to me what kind of convention this is. I'm beginning to think it's for true crime aficionados. I scan the audience to figure them out. On the whole, they seem perfectly ordinary, so I'm probably right. On the other side of the auditorium, I spot Victor, his legs crossed. I feel a twist in my tummy. He's listening attentively to Sheila. Am I looking at Buttonface without the mask?

Sheila has been talking for forty minutes about her life as a wife and mother, bringing up the children of serial killers, gangsters, and terrorists. That's a sitcom waiting to be written. 'We're just one big happy family,' she tells us. Now, I don't subscribe to the belief that the apple doesn't fall far from the tree, yet I can't help but wonder if Sheila's choices for who she marries will not impact the stability of her children.

I suddenly feel like I'm being watched and turn to see Terence squinting my way with a curious expression. I sink back into my chair, hiding behind the man next to me.

The talk ends, and it's time for audience questions. One man's hand shoots up. Wilma makes her way to him with a microphone. 'Hi Sheila,' he says.

'Hi honey. How can I help you today?'

'Sheila, if I end up on Death Row, will you marry me?'

The audience laughs. Sheila does too.

'Honey, the answer to that is I DO!'

More cheers and laughter.

'Next question.'

'I have one!' Terence calls.

I notice a hesitation in Wilma. She speaks into the microphone. 'Maybe someone else has a question—'

'No, I have one!' Terence pushes his way down the row and snatches the microphone from Wilma. 'Hey, Sheila.'

'Hello, honey. How are you doing today?'

'I have a joke.'

Wilma tries to take the microphone from him, but he pushes her hand away.

'Knock, Knock.'

Sheila pauses, uncertainty on her face. 'Who's there?'

'Spread,' Terence replies.

'Spread who?'

Terence snorts and thrusts out his hips. 'Spread your legs, there's a mother fuckin' killer in the house.'

Silence falls over the auditorium.

Ouch. I would feel sorry for him but he's a douche and an unfunny one at that.

Terence is howling with laughter despite rising grumbles of disapproval from the audience. 'It's a joke, you guys, come on!'

Wilma takes the microphone from him. 'No more questions,' she says. 'Photo opportunities with Sheila will be $5 a piece in the lobby. Please head there now and form an orderly queue.'

I stand and make my way with the crowd out of the auditorium.

'Hey MAGA!' comes a voice. I feel a hand on my shoulder and turn to see Terence. 'It's you, isn't it?'

Panic sweeps through me, and I charge ahead, quickly pushing through the crowd.

'I know you!' he calls.

I rush past the growing queue to be photographed with Sheila.

'Come back ya little—!'

But I'm fast and already slipping through the curtain, my

heart pounding. I nod my thanks to the guard and walk quickly towards the light, turn right and leg it. What the hell was all that about?

Chapter Twenty-Seven

The Fool

A firm hand grabbed his arm.

'Just what the hell do you think you're playing at?' said Wilma, her voice a growl.

Terence turned to see her lined, round face glowering dangerously at him. He tried to pull his arm away, but her grip was tight. He glanced ahead once more. The karaoke chick was nowhere to be seen. She had vanished into the crowd. 'Fuck it!' he hissed.

His arm was beginning to feel numb. Say what you will about Wilma, but the old broad was as strong as an ox. An ox with the cunningness of a fox and the claws and teeth of a ruthless alley cat who has lived beyond her years. The effects of the booze were beginning to leave him like an exorcised spirit. He was afraid of her. They all were . . . weren't they?

'You and I need to talk,' said Wilma.

He swallowed, his Dutch courage dissipating.

Wilma eased her grip. 'Come with me, Terence,' she said.

Smiling slammer slut Sheila Morgan was being escorted by that insufferable A-hole, the Reverend, to a tall and wide wall poster depicting a dirty prison cell with two bunks pushed together, sprinkled with rose petals. The queue to meet Sheila and take a picture with that tasteless backdrop was impressive. He had to hand it to her. She knew how to profit from other people's murderin'.

He followed Wilma to the reception desk, where Shaky Frank, true to form, was having a midmorning nap. Wilma leant across the desk and squeezed his shoulder. 'Wake up, dear.'

He flinched, as if yanked from a nightmare, glasses slipping from his nose and falling onto his lap. He looked up, his expression like a confused owl's.

Terence suppressed a chuckle.

Wilma fired him a filthy look. Terence smiled and raised his hands in an apologetic gesture.

'I'll get someone to relieve you,' Wilma told Frank.

Frank fumbled his glasses back onto his face.

'What's that?'

'To relieve you, dear. Someone to relieve you.'

'That would be dandy. I could use the bathroom.'

Wilma rolled her eyes. 'Go. I'll watch the desk.'

Triggered at the mention of the bathroom, Terence realised he had an ache in his bladder, which felt like a balloon filled with whiskey, in this instance. Must be 40 per cent at least. 'If you don't mind, I'll join Frank.'

'In a moment,' snapped Wilma.

'Yes, ma'am.'

Frank shuffled from behind the desk with a pained expression and made quick but small steps towards the restroom. Like Terence, there was a desperate man on the verge of pissing his pants. 'Hope you make it, pal!' Terence shifted on his feet and gently rubbed his lower abdomen. 'Shit, I gotta go.'

Wilma stood inches from Terence. It was just the two of them.

The conference attendees focused on the celebrity speaker and her queue of adoring fans.

'What's got into you, Terence?' Wilma asked.

Terence shrugged. 'Don't know what you mean.'

'Is it because you're not featured in this year's line-up?'

He folded his arms. 'I don't care about that.' This was a lie. His ego was bruised.

'Then why are you drunk at the conference?'

'I only had a couple. Ain't nothing wrong with—'

'No, there's not. But you clearly cannot hold your liquor. And you cannot come here in that state and abuse our speakers.'

'It was just a crummy joke, come on!'

'Crummy is one way to describe it.'

'I really need to pee—'

'I can see that.' Swiftly, she grabbed the belt of his shorts with one hand, pushed him against the desk, and with the other hand dug her fingers hard into his bladder.

'No!' he croaked, warm piss trickling down his leg.

She sniffed and recoiled. 'Nasty,' she said.

Trembling with humiliation and anger, he pulled away from her and tried to stem the flow. With his free hand, he clenched his fist and raised it. 'Fuck you, Wilma. Fuck you.'

She smiled slyly.

'You wait until Priscilla hears about this.'

'Priscilla's not in charge. I am.'

'We all know who pays your salary.'

Wilma chuckled darkly. 'The Spider can't bear you, Terence. No one can.'

With a renewed confidence, he inched closer and prodded her with a podgy digit. 'You have no freakin' idea. Priscilla loves me. We have a future together, and I'm telling you, it don't involve you.'

She held his gaze, and he noticed a twitch in her eye. He had planted a seed.

'Clean yourself up. Come back and apologise to Sheila.'

'Fuck you,' he hissed and bolted, colliding with Frank who was returning and awkwardly trying to pull up his trouser zipper. The old man almost toppled over. Terence didn't care, he ran but it seemed pointless now, a failed journey because there was only so long a man could hold on to his diminutive penis to stop a horse-like downpour. 'Fuuuuck!' he cried.

Ten minutes later, with a black cloud over his head, Terence stood, with his shirt tied around his waist to protect his modesty, at the hand dryer in the Men's bathroom, drying his shorts. The door opened. The Reverend stepped inside and looked his way with a wry smile. Terence felt his face reddening.

'Did you have an accident, dear boy?'

Terence felt his hackles rising. 'Did you have an accident, dear boy?' he repeated, mocking his accent. 'My fucking shorts got wet. That's what happened, Jeez!'

The Reverend said nothing. He just smiled, turned and disappeared into a cubicle.

'Good. Fucking flush yourself down the toilet, you piece of shit,' he muttered.

Terence let the dryer finish. He inspected his shorts. To his relief, the damp patch was dry. Bending over, he stepped clumsily into them. His shirt came undone and fell to the floor.

'Some things that are seen cannot be unseen,' came a voice.

Terence yelped and scrambled to pull on his shorts.

The Reverend was standing at a washbasin.

'What the fuck, man?!'

'I don't think I've ever seen such hairy buttocks.'

Terence felt himself shake with anger. 'Buttocks! This ain't the 1940s, pal!'

The Reverend smiled as he washed his hands. Terence belted up his shorts.

As the Reverend was leaving, he stopped at the door and looked back at Terence. 'You should have a bath, dear boy. You smell of urine.'

'Fuck you!' yelled Terence, but the slippery clergyman was gone.

Chapter Twenty-Eight

Martha

I'm with Jacqui and Rudy on stage in the theatre, which has been cleared of the *Murder She Didn't Write* set and replaced with two Art Deco lounge chairs and a large television screen. I'm helping them with final preparations for Jacqui's big interview by Rudy, a career retrospective, on this very stage. They've just finished agreeing on her role in his campy Jessica Fletcher play. Rudy has 'upgraded' her to 'cameo-premium', which essentially means she's on stage for longer and has more lines. Jacqui has surprisingly agreed.

'You'll get top billing,' says Rudy.

'It's been a long time since I treaded the boards.'

'We're expecting a full house.'

'Wonderful,' Jacqui replies.

I'm fiddling with the Bluetooth option on Jacqui's laptop, trying to connect it to the big screen at the rear of the stage. My focus is half on the convention and my narrow escape from that Hawaiian-shirt-clad drunk who almost outed me.

'How're you doing, Martha?' Rudy calls.

I'm totally winging it, but I don't say that. 'Almost there.'

'Did you press the button on the dongle?' Rudy asks.

'What's the dongle?'

'It's the dongle!' he replies, as if I should know what he's talking about. 'It's hanging from the back of the display.'

I sigh and edge my way behind the TV. It's dark, so I take out my phone, switch on the light and sweep the slim beam across the back of the enormous screen. There are many cables and black box-type things that mean nothing to me. After a moment, I see a Bluetooth symbol on one of the boxes.

'I see a Bluetooth button,' I call.

'That might be it.'

'How is that a dongle? It's a button.'

'Button, dongle, tomayto, tomato, potayto, potahto.'

Jacqui laughs. 'You're such a joker.'

Bewildered, I shake my head and press the button. The blue light flashes, and a few moments later, we are in business.

'You got there at last,' Rudy says.

I'm getting a little fed up with his snarkiness.

'Shall we do a dry run?' Rudy suggests.

'I've added a special clip from *LA Dolls* that I want to air tonight,' says Jacqui. 'So make sure Priscilla Hefferman attends.'

'The captain himself will be escorting her.'

Jacqui and Rudy take their seats and go through his list of questions. She gives a quick overview of her answers and cues me to 'roll the tape' at various stages. We spend the rest of the afternoon rehearsing this before Rudy hurries off to run a pool aerobics class.

'Hey, do you want to go shopping?' Jacqui asks, smiling.

'I'm pretty sure they don't cater for thrift shop gals like me on the boat,' I say.

Jacqui arches a brow. 'No, but they have dress, shoe, and jewellery stores.'

'I've seen the window displays. They're all—'

Jacqui dismisses my comment with a wave, grabs her Louis Vuitton bag and heads for the exit. 'Oh, come on. Don't be such a stick in the mud. It'll be fun.'

'. . . out of my price range,' I finish saying, but she doesn't hear. She's rummaging in her bag and pulls out an American Express credit card.

'I take my credit cards like I take my men. Black and strong!' she laughs.

I'm perplexed by Jacqui's jolly mood. 'What's got into you today?' I ask, following her out of the theatre.

'I'm not allowed to be happy, now? What's wrong with you millennials? You're so uptight. Let's go live a little.'

It's a relief to see her happy, especially after the memories of her daughter that I unwittingly triggered.

We take the stairs to the shopping level to help get Jacqui's steps in. On the way down, we're besieged by fans requesting selfies. Jacqui is on cloud nine, smiling and accommodating all who ask. She takes their phones and hands them to me. 'My assistant will take the picture!' she tells them.

I've stopped getting cross at being called her assistant and oblige obediently. At least I haven't been fired. For now, anyway.

The 'shopping mall', as Jacqui insists on calling it, is essentially a row of elegant, Art Deco-styled boutiques accessible from the ship's main lobby, where the concierge desk is located. Stepping onto the gold-coloured carpet and following the path around the stores, I almost forget I'm on a cruise ship.

I see a shop displaying masks for the upcoming Masquerade Ball in the window. 'Let's go there,' I say.

'You're going to the Masquerade Ball?' Jacqui asks.

'I have a date.'

'Oh God, please tell me he's under sixty.'

'He's my age.'

'There's another millennial on the ship – how did that happen?'

'We're everywhere,' I say, as we enter the shop. It's busy with passengers trying on the goods.

'So, who is he?'

'His name's Zach, he's American, and he works in Finance.'

'Is that so?' Jacqui picks up a spooky ivory-coloured Venetian mask, places it over her face and peers at me. 'Have you slept with him yet?'

'You can't ask me that! And no!' I say, my cheeks burning.

Jacqui cackles. 'You want to, don't you?'

I turn away and browse the masks.

'You should seduce him before someone else does.'

I want to point out that, in my estimate, the average age of passengers is sixty-five, but that would be unkind. 'By someone else, you mean who exactly?'

Jacqui grins mischievously. 'You should introduce him to me.'

I hold her gaze. Jacqui is attractive despite being much older. A shudder runs through me, and I wonder if I could be the next Cilla. Would Zach . . .?

Jacqui lets out a raucous laugh. 'Your face! I'm just teasing you.'

'I know that!' I say, although I am relieved.

'But do give him my room number,' she adds, smirking.

I ignore her.

'So, what's your type then?' Jacqui asks.

'I don't have one.'

'Nonsense. Everyone has a type. Describe this Jack.'

'Zach!'

'What is it about him that's got your knickers in a twist?'

I sigh and give in. 'He's unkempt but clean with mousey-blond hair. Tanned skin. He wears loose cotton shirts and looks like he's just rolled out of bed. Bit of a dangerous, preppy-boy vibe. Likes books.'

Jacqui fans herself with the mask. 'Hot, dangerous and bookish. So that's your type. I'm a little on fire myself.'

I start to protest but realise she's right. Every man I've ever fallen for had that same restless energy, that same quiet intensity as Zach. Toby, the journalist who quoted poetry in bars. Josh, the photographer who carried novels in his rucksack. Callum, who vanished to India 'to write'. All of them chasing something, already halfway gone, even when they were with me. Losing them never hurt, because I never really had them. Maybe that was the point.

But then there's Zach. I'm intrigued by him and drawn to him. He knows what it's like to lose someone violently, to have grief twist you into something else. We're two people shaped by loss, orbiting the same unabating darkness.

I pause and make a mental note to use that line in a future story.

'What do you think of this?' Jacqui says.

I pretend not to hear her.

'Martha . . . Martha!'

Rolling my eyes, I turn to face her. 'Should I get this one?' She's wearing an elaborate eye mask with a tall crown of peacock feathers.

'Subtle, even by your standards,' I say, instantly regretting my sarcasm.

'Ouch,' says Jacqui.

'Sorry, I didn't mean that.'

'One of the things I like about you . . . sometimes . . . is your sass,' Jacqui says, handing the mask to the sales assistant. 'I'll take it.'

Relieved she's not offended, I chew my lip and scan the masks.

'See anything yet?' says Jacqui.

They're expensive and for a moment I consider stealing one to save some cash. 'I can't make up my mind.'

The shop is getting crowded as more passengers enter. Jacqui pays the sales assistant. 'My friend here is looking for a mask. Something sophisticated and sexy that screams "Fuck me senseless." Do you have anything like that?'

Everyone in the store is looking at me. My cheeks are on fire.

'We sure do,' says the sales assistant.

Jacqui lifts the bag containing her mask, smiles and winks at me. 'I'll wait outside.'

I settle on a red lace mask, one of the cheapest in the store at £29.99.

I see Jacqui browsing in a store opposite. Mannequins pose in couture by designers I've never heard of, each one elegant and more self-assured than I'll ever be. As I enter the shop, I notice a sign saying that the designs had been curated by the *Jewel of the Atlantic*'s CEO, Priscilla Hefferman, to mark the final voyage of the soon-to-be retired cruise liner. I'm assuming Jacqui hasn't seen it. Otherwise, she wouldn't set foot inside. She pulls a dress from the rack and holds it up in front of a mirror. 'Does this work?' she asks about a long-fitted gown in gold lamé fabric.

'Maybe if you're Kylie Minogue,' I say.

She selects two more and is bowled over by the unique craftsmanship. 'You wouldn't find these in LA.'

I find myself staring at a crimson halter dress.

'Would you like to try it on?' says the sales assistant, a young Spanish woman with a kind smile.

'It's a bit out of my pay scale.'

'Come on!' says Jacqui.

'There's no point.'

Jacqui turns to the sales assistant. 'She'll try it on.'

The sales assistant nods and takes the dress to the changing room. I give in. What harm can it do? Five minutes later, I'm wearing it and not quite believing that the person in the reflection is me.

'Come out and show us!' Jacqui calls.

I step outside. Both Jacqui and the sales assistant wear surprised expressions and say nothing.

'What? Is it awful?' I ask.

They look at each other.

'It's beautiful, no?' says the sales assistant.

'No question,' Jacqui replies. 'How much is it?'

'One thousand, two hundred and fifty dollars.'

'What?!' I reply, suddenly terrified I might tear it and have to pay for it.

'She'll take it,' says Jacqui.

'I can't afford this!'

Jacqui holds up her black Amex. 'I can.'

'You can't buy this dress. It's too much money.'

'Box it up,' she tells the sales assistant.

'Jacqui, no!'

'If you're that uptight about it, I'll deduct it from your salary.'

'You will not!'

'Then I'm buying it. It's a gift. Get over it.'

I don't know what to say. I'm shocked but also delighted.

Jacqui's fishing in her handbag. 'Take this too,' she says, pressing something hard into my hand. She waves a finger at my face. 'This Greta Thunberg back-to-basics look is not working.'

In my hand is a shiny gold lipstick container. Written in deep red lettering is Crimson Lady. I pull open the cap and twist the bottom.

'Paint your lips with that, honey, and doors will open for you,' says Jacqui.

I don't think so. Not wishing to offend, I smile gratefully, thank her and pop it into my bag.

Chapter Twenty-Nine

Martha

I'm sitting on an uncomfortable plastic chair behind the curtain at the side of the stage with Jacqui's laptop, preparing for her interview with Rudy, and anxiously flicking through my notes to ensure I time the slides correctly and play the clips when she cues them in.

So far, so good.

I hear the chatter of the audience as they enter the theatre and take their seats. Peeking from behind the curtain, I see the faces of some familiar passengers. Among them are Bob, Don, Wilma, Bernard, Victor (yikes!), Sheila Morgan (of all people!), and Zach. He catches my eye, waves and mouths 'Good luck.' I smile back and mouth a thank-you. Sitting on the front row priority seats are Priscilla Hefferman and Captain Dexter Perry, both dressed to impress. Priscilla wears a loud zebra-print jumpsuit (courageous), and Perry is dressed in his immaculate Captain's whites.

With everyone seated, a smiling Rudy, dressed in a white polo shirt and a smart navy blazer, takes to the stage. 'Welcome, welcome ladies and gentlemen, and everyone in between . . .' Rudy laughs at his quip and looks to the audience for support, but it falls flat, and he's met with silence. I cringe inside and hope this is not a reflection on what's to come. 'Haha . . . so, thank you all for coming. My name is Rudy Turner. I am your devoted onboard Events Director here on the final ever voyage of the beautiful *Jewel of the Atlantic*.' The audience claps warmly, and some boo at the same time. 'I know, it's sad to see this beautiful lady being retired after thirty years of service.' Enthusiastic clapping and cheers erupt from the audience.

I hear my name being whispered and turn to see Jacqui being escorted up the stage steps by a crew member. Jacqui looks as if she has dressed for a Hollywood red carpet. Her blonde hair is elegantly curled, and she shimmers in a sparkling tiger-print jumpsuit.

'How do I look?' she asks.

'Like you're ready to slay.'

She smiles mischievously. 'Good.'

We turn to look at Rudy.

'And so, it is my great honour and pleasure to welcome the star of your favourite TV shows, including *Return to Hollywood Wives*, *LA Dolls*, and *Lady Detective*. Please welcome the incredible, the fabulous, Jacqui DuLac!'

'Good luck,' I say to Jacqui as she makes her way onto the stage, blowing kisses to the audience who are on their feet, clapping and cheering.

Jacqui and Rudy take their seats on the lounge chairs. From his blazer pocket, Rudy takes out a set of flash cards that he begins fumbling with. 'Haha . . . one moment . . . I thought I had these in order.'

'Take your time,' says Jacqui. 'We have three more days before we hit New York.'

The audience laughs.

'Ah, here we are,' he says, staring down at one of the cards. 'You first became a household name in the 1980s, playing women with very specific, shall we say, "aspirations". Looking back, what was it like to embody those often glamorous, manipulative characters?'

Jacqui smiles demurely, 'Are you implying I was typecast as a gold digger?'

'Haha . . . no, not at all—'

'That patriarchal term was what my characters were called back then. Yes, they were glamorous women, but no more manipulative than the male characters. They were ambitious women, doing whatever they could to succeed and survive. They were fun to play. I had a blast.'

'I bet you did . . . so . . . erm . . . did you ever find yourself judging your characters, or did you embrace their motivations?'

It becomes apparent that Rudy may not have a future interviewing celebrities. Perhaps it's the sycophancy, lack of preparation and fluidity. It's not quite what we had rehearsed, but I put that down to his nerves and being in awe of Jacqui. She, on the other hand, has years of experience and can navigate these situations like a pro. She's steering the conversation while simultaneously opening up to the audience, revealing insights into her turbulent career, love life, and the loss of her beloved daughter.

'My biggest regret about Billie is that I did not spend as much time with her as I should have done. As a single, working mom, I had to put food on the table and pay for a nanny. I was working constantly to give her a better life and then . . . and then . . . she was diagnosed . . .' Jacqui's voice cracks momentarily. I feel a knot in my tummy, but she quickly composes herself and smiles at the audience. 'She was a wonderful person, kind, and loving. Nothing like her mother. I often wondered if I picked up the wrong baby.'

The audience laugh.

'What's next for Jacqui DuLac?'

'I'm writing a book.'

'That's exciting. An autobiography?'

'No, but maybe one day I'll write that. This new book is a crime novel starring . . . guess who?'

'Please tell me it's Cassie?'

'I can neither confirm nor deny, but what the hell. Yes, it's a new Cassie mystery.'

Cheers from the audience.

'Oh my, can you tell us anything about it?'

'I'm not really supposed to talk about it . . .'

'Oh, come on, give us something at least.'

More cheers from the audience. Jacqui is lapping up the attention.

'You guys will get me into so much trouble.'

Rudy addresses the audience: 'What happens on the *Jewel* stays on the *Jewel*, am I right or am I right?'

'You're right!' an audience member calls.

'OK,' says a grinning Jacqui. 'As long as it stays on board this ship. So, the story is set in the present day. Cassie is close to retirement. She has a daughter and lives in a small town in Maine where she is a senior detective. She's investigating a string of murders that lead her to a guest house in . . .' Jacqui looks across at me. 'Martha, what's the name of that town?'

'Kennebunkport.'

Jacqui frowns. 'I can't hear you.'

I say it again, but still, she doesn't hear.

'Come out and meet the nice people.'

Groaning inside, I place the laptop on the chair and make my way hesitantly to the other side of the curtain. I'm not a shy person, but I don't relish suddenly becoming the focus of attention, especially with Zach in the audience. 'This is my assistant, Martha.'

I quickly ponder how unfazed I've become about being called Jacqui's assistant and not her ghostwriter.

I get a modest round of applause and give them a dorky wave back.

Jacqui asks, 'What's the name of that small town in Maine with the old couple who run the guest house?'

'It's called Kennebunkport,' I say, louder this time so that it reaches her ears.

'That's the one. Thank you, Martha.'

I nod and turn to leave. Looking into the audience, my eyes catch Wilma staring at me, with the oddest expression that for some indefinable reason makes my skin crawl. I look away, pick up the laptop and take my seat off stage.

Rudy is drawing to a close after a short round of audience questions. 'We have one final question from Bob Cunningham.' Rudy squints into the audience. 'Where are you, Bob?'

On the way back from our shopping trip, Jacqui had pulled Bob aside and given him some cash. I smile, forgetting the weird look from Wilma. Jacqui is about to slay.

Bob is handed a roving microphone.

'Hi, I'm Bob.'

'Hello, Bob,' says Jacqui.

'What's your question?' says Rudy.

'Ms DuLac, it's been a great pleasure to meet you onboard this fine ship and hear you talk so honestly and eloquently this evening.'

The audience claps and cheers. I catch Priscilla suppressing a yawn.

'Thank you, Bob. That's very kind,' says Jacqui.

'Well, my question is about the miniseries *LA Dolls*, a hot favourite of mine I don't mind telling you.'

Jacqui laughs. 'That was a popular show.'

'There was another actress . . . I forget her name . . . Cilla something.'

'Cilla Ryder.'

'That's her. She was a fox.'

'She sure was. And she knew it.'

I notice Priscilla firing daggers at Jacqui and recall her mentioning that Priscilla had a short career as an actress.

'I don't know what happened to her,' says Bob. 'But I did hear a rumour she went into the adult film industry.'

Priscilla chokes out a cough.

'I wouldn't know about that,' says Jacqui. 'That might have been better suited to her acting ability. Acting was something that didn't come naturally to her, as hard as she may, or may not, have tried.'

The audience laugh. Priscilla clutches the armrests, as if bracing for a crash. 'I played Sabrina Logan, an ambitious, sexy businesswoman who bedded a lot of rich men and slapped many faces. Usually their wives. Cilla played my nemesis, Joanie Summers, the mistress of my billionaire lover, Spencer. It's funny you should ask about her. It just so happens I have a clip of that iconic fight scene.' She turns to look at me. 'Martha, under the *LA Dolls* folder is a file called Sabrina Joanie Fight. Could you play it, please?'

I haven't seen this clip, so I'm not sure what to expect. I find the file and run it, as instructed.

The scene opens on a sunny day by a lily pond with a young Jacqui and an unrecognisable Cilla playing their respective characters, Sabrina and Joanie. They are both dressed expensively and beautifully in shoulder-padded suits, big hair, and full make-up. Sabrina has a smug expression as she marches ahead of Joanie.

'You have no business being here!' says an utterly wooden Joanie.

'Pack your bags and go back to Idaho, you gold-digging little tramp!'

With an almost laughable furious expression, Joanie grabs Sabrina's arm and swings her around. 'You bitch!' She then lifts her hand and slaps Sabrina's face. The screen closes in on Sabrina's shocked face, which quickly changes to an evil grin as she lashes back. The gloves are off, and both women tumble into the pond, slapping, wrestling, and tearing at each other's hair and clothes.

As the screen fades, the audience laughs and cheers once more.

'That wasn't acting,' Jacqui says. 'That fight was real.'

Chapter Thirty

The Fool

Terence Lamb was alone in the diner, eating a bacon double cheeseburger with dirty fries, washed down with a whiskey sour, his third that day. Hot sauce dripped onto his plump fingers. He finished chewing and licked them clean. Last year, at Halloween, when the committee had first sat down to discuss the 25th anniversary convention, Terence had pitched his event. They were all seated around the table at the guest house in Kennebunkport: Wilma, Frank, the Undertaker, the Dentist, the Reverend. Priscilla was on the speaker phone dialling in on a secure line from somewhere in Europe.

'You're up next, Terence, dear,' Wilma said.

'OK, great choice for a venue by the way, which begs the question. Why do serial killers love the ocean?'

Stony faces from the committee. He heard Priscilla sighing and noticed Wilma checking the clock.

'Do tell us,' Wilma urged.

''Cause it's cold, deep, and dark. Just like us!'

Not one smile.

'OK, one more.'

Groans from the table.

'This is for you, amigo,' Terrence said to the Undertaker.

The Undertaker's face regarded him with contempt.

'Knock, knock.'

Silence.

'Ernest, dear, answer him and let's move on.'

The Undertaker sucked his teeth and shook his head. 'Who's there?'

'Murder.'

'Murder who?'

'Murder you, you big freakin' marica!'

Before Terence could double over in laughter, the Undertaker swiftly reached across the table and grabbed his throat with a vice-like grip. Despite not being able to breathe, Terence was still laughing. It took a few moments for the others to extract Ridgewell, calm the situation, and resume business.

'No more jokes. Get on with your pitch!' Priscilla demanded.

'Ja, mein Anführer!'

Across the table, eyes rolled like a Mexican wave.

'Jeez, you guys are a tough audience . . . Right, for the 25th convention, I thought I'd reveal the secrets behind my magic act.'

'This isn't the Magic Circle,' the Reverend said.

'No, but people dig my act.'

'Do they?' Bernard asked.

'Yeah.'

'The people attending our conference are not wannabe magicians.'

'You don't know that.'

'I think we do,' said Wilma, who was usually on his side. 'They come to learn from us, network with peers and have fun too.'

'OK, I could bring my Sawing a Lady in Half equipment and demonstrate how I—'

'No!' they all said in unison.

Terence had flinched and felt his anger rising. 'So, you've all decided you don't want me. That's just freaking peachy!'

'It's not that,' said Wilma. 'You've done the same talk for several years now. We all need to up our game for the 25th anniversary. No exceptions.'

He rubbed his neck and swallowed. 'But—'

Priscilla's voice crackled over the speaker. 'We need a showman to run the karaoke. Terence, you're perfect for that.'

He brightened at that suggestion. 'Sure. I can do it.'

That had been a difficult meeting despite getting the karaoke gig. Clearly, they all hated him. He finished off the sour cocktail and wiped his mouth with the back of his hand. But the truth was, he hated them too. Treacherous fucks!

He settled the bill with the waiter and stood to leave. His head spun, disorienting him for a moment. Maybe he'd get some air before heading back to his room.

Stepping outside, he felt better when the cool evening air hit him. The calm was soon interrupted when people began flooding onto the deck. 'Fuck!' he muttered, angrily. They were talking about how wonderful Jacqui DuLac had been. Walking away from them towards the pool area, he noticed there was a gathering around the pool. There was a lot of flesh on show, mostly his age and older, but hey, beggars can't be choosers. Terence decided a post-dinner swim was precisely what he needed to get out of this eating and drinking slump. First things first, he needed to find his swimming costume.

Back in his room, he rummaged through his suitcase, found his yellow trunks, which had seen better days, and sniffed them. They were a little ripe but would do. Besides, chlorine kills bacteria. Undressing, he pulled the trunks over his thighs and hips, which had seemingly thickened since he'd last worn them.

He stood before the mirror, holding his stomach in. Terence frowned. The trunks were a little too snug and revealing. It was hard to tell his pecker from either of his nuts. They were the same shape and size. Small and bulbous like three marbles squeezed into a medieval pauper's purse.

He spotted a dirty grey sock on the floor. Picking it up, he inserted it into his trunks, shaping it around his precious jewels. The difference was almost miraculous. It was as if he was stacked downstairs. He looked sideways from the left, and then the right. Facing the mirror, he thrust out his hips and growled, 'Come ride this baby, if you dare.'

What a sexy beast!

Maybe the fuckable karaoke girl would be at the pool. Maybe Priscilla, too. He recalled his threesome fantasy and felt a stirring from the muggy depths of his sock and trunks.

A knock on the door shook him from his thoughts.

He answered.

A bellhop dressed in a red uniform with a dumb pillbox hat was standing outside with his hands behind his back. 'Mr Lamb?'

'Who wants to know?'

The bellhop smiled and presented a golden envelope, similar to the one Priscilla had sent. As before, it was perfumed and had his name written with a calligraphy-style pen. Taking it from him, Terence slammed the door and opened the envelope. Inside was a letter and a door key. He was puzzled but also intrigued.

Dear Terence,

I feel I might explode if I don't see you. Can you meet me tonight? Enclosed you'll find a room key. I'll be waiting. I have so much to say to you. I can't contain myself for another moment.

See you soon.
With love.
PH x

Terence pulled on his robe and flip-flops. The room number on the key said 4.104. Room 104 on the fourth floor. Exiting his cabin, he pushed his hair back with his palms and checked his breath. It smelt of burgers, onions and whiskey, but it would do. He hurried up the corridor, counting down the door numbers until he reached Room 4.104.

He knocked on the door before letting himself in.

'Hello,' he said in a sing-song voice.

The room was dark, lit only by the television screen, which was broadcasting an old black-and-white Hitchcock movie. The scene showed Janet Leigh showering in the Bates Motel.

He loved that movie.

There was no sign of his secret admirer. A breeze blew from the half-open balcony doors, lifting the curtain. He could see her outside. She wore a robe and had a towel wrapped around her head. Clean and ready for action, he thought. He slid the door open and took in the fresh, salty air. 'I'm here,' he said.

'I've been expecting you,' she replied. Her voice sounded huskier than usual.

'I was stoked to get your letter.'

She giggled girlishly. Almost coquettishly. Stepping onto the balcony, he stood beside her. She was looking the other way. He looked her up and down and didn't realise just how broad she was. He supposed it was that couture fashion that made her look skinny. He placed a hand on her shoulder.

She turned her head quickly to look his way.

He flinched.

It wasn't Priscilla underneath the head towel, but the face of a mask, a balaclava with eyes and a crooked smile constructed from buttons.

She lifted her arm. In her hand was a knife, which she plunged hard into his chest several times. He could feel the icy steel lodge in his heart and could hear the shrieking stabs of strings from his favourite movie broadcasting on the television at this very moment. What about that, he thought, as he shivered and blinked. Terence opened his mouth to speak, but the masked Priscilla hushed him and eased him to the balcony floor. 'It'll be over soon,' she said, but it wasn't Priscilla's voice. It seemed familiar, but as the life seeped from him, Terence 'The Fool' Lamb could not place it.

'Oh crap,' said Terence, as he shut his eyes forever.

Chapter Thirty-One

Martha

I wake the following morning, having set my alarm for 8 a.m. After yesterday evening's interview and a well-deserved standing ovation, Jacqui had wanted to go back to her suite for a celebratory drink. She was buzzing and ready to party, having sucker-punched Priscilla Hefferman with that scene from *LA Dolls*. I chuckle at the memory and wonder what the wealthy CEO and former 'bit-part actress' thought when she woke up this morning. Anyway, despite being dosed up on caffeine, I told Jacqui I was knackered and faked a yawn. I was running criminally behind on the outline and planned to stay up as long as I could before the breakfast meeting that Jacqui had just sprung on me. As it happened, Rudy was on hand to escort her and celebrate with a quick drink before turning in.

I had stayed up until 4 a.m., at which point I hit a wall, my head spinning with chapters, scenes and arcs for middle-aged Detective Kowalski, her terminally ill daughter, and the plethora of new characters I had plucked from my caffeinated and pleasingly fertile imagination. I feel confident that Jacqui will like what I've done. I've adhered to her brief but also incorporated some modern ideas and diversity that I will fight to maintain.

I shower, get ready, and notice two missed voice messages on my phone that came in while I was in the bathroom. Both from Diane. I stare at her name for a moment, thumb hovering, before pressing play.

'Hi, it's me. I walked past that café we used to go to when you were little. The one with the awful hot chocolate. They've redone it, all graffiti-style, like that what's-his-face who does the protest art. You like him, don't you? Anyway, you wouldn't recognise it now. Hope the training programme's going well. Lots of love.'

Diane still thinks I'm learning about sausage rolls.

I listen to her second message.

'It's me again. I decided to go in. To the café. I'm here now.'

In the background, I can hear voices, cups clinking, the hiss of the coffee machine.

'I never told you this, but your father and I had our first date here. It looks so different, but it's still the same, if you know what I mean . . .'

There's a pause, then a soft sniff.

'I know you blame me for what happened. I blame me too. Oh, my skinny latte's here. I have to go. Call me.'

I stare at the screen, her voice still echoing in my head. For a moment, I don't move. The sound of the café lingers – the clatter of cups, the low hum of other people's lives. I should call her back. I always tell myself I will, but I never know what to say. A knot tightens in my stomach. It'll have to wait.

We're having breakfast at the Seven Dials diner, which surprised me, as Jacqui had recently preferred to meet in private. 'I just fancy a change of scenery,' she told me. As I approach the sliding doors, I hear the familiar clink of cutlery and the hum of chattering voices. I step into the Seven Dials diner and the smell of bacon and toast hits me. The place is buzzing. Couples leaning over coffee, a pair of teenage siblings bickering over who took the last croissant, a man reading the paper like the world outside doesn't exist. No one looks like they know they're on a cruise ship with a murderer. Then again, one of them could be the killer.

I see Jacqui. Hair up, dressed in a simple white blouse and lime-green slacks, she is both glamorous and elegant, enjoying the attention of those lauding her for last night's intimate reveal of her life and career. She's smiling and laughing. I now understand why we're meeting here, rather than in the privacy of her suite.

As I weave my way through, she catches my eye and waves. 'Here's my assistant. We have a breakfast meeting. I must dash,' she tells a table of four people. I pause as I see their faces: Bernard, Wilma, Frank, and some Vicar I don't recognise.

'Hallo Martha,' says Bernard, grinning, as Jacqui makes a beeline for the buffet.

Wilma's face tightens. Frank's head is down, his hands shaking, his concentration on his plate as he unsuccessfully tries to jab a piece of sausage with his fork.

'Hi,' I say.

'Last call for Musical Deckchairs!' a familiar upbeat voice calls out.

I turn to see Rudy, dressed in absurdly tight white shorts and a T-shirt, striding across the diner.

A few passengers glance up from their breakfasts. Rudy grins, catches my eye, and winks.

He stops beside Wilma's table. 'Four slots left,' he says brightly. 'You'll love it,' he tells them. 'Think of it as survival of the spry – a test of balance, reflex, and misplaced confidence.'

Laughter ripples through the room. Rudy tips an imaginary hat.

'What say you, madam, gentlemen?'

'We're busy,' Wilma says, giving him a look that could curdle milk.

'I'm not sure my back is up for the challenge,' Bernard chuckles.

'Love to, but I have a meeting with you know who,' I add.

'No matter,' Rudy says cheerfully. 'We're on the top deck if you change your minds.'

He's joined by two pensioners who shuffle behind him as he heads out. 'Let's warm those limbs up – and may the best knees win!' he calls.

I nod a goodbye at Bernard and leave quickly. The last thing I want is for Frank to recognise me.

I follow Jacqui who is making her way outside, where she has secured a shaded table overlooking the ocean.

'Those people give me the heebie-jeebies,' I say.

Jacqui frowns at me. 'Why? They seem perfectly nice.'

If I tell her that I skipped work to go chasing a killer connected to the Midnight Chorus Society, of which three of those people are members, then I will be in a whole load of shit. 'Just a feeling,' I reply.

Jacqui shakes her head. 'Do you want to drop your bag and get something from the buffet?'

I look back, relieved to see Wilma escort Frank from the restaurant with Bernard and the vicar in tow. 'Yeah. I'm famished.'

'Nothing new there.'

I order myself a flat white, for a change, and an Americano for Jacqui. We head to the buffet, Jacqui smiling and waving at her adoring new fan base. 'Everyone loved the interview,' she says, picking up a tray and a tiny plate.

I scoop bacon, egg, sausages, beans, toast, and a zero-fat

raspberry yoghurt for afters. 'It was a big success,' I tell her, as I take a bite from a slice of cold toast.

'I said to Rudy last night that that was the first time I had ever been so open in a public interview.'

'You did well, considering his interviewing skills were on the amateur side.'

'Oh God, did you think that too? It was bad, but not terrible. I should know. I've had worse interviews on live TV with audience figures in their millions.'

'What time did you guys party to?'

'We didn't. By the time we made the trip back to my suite, I was ready to hit the hay.'

'Did you get any sleep?'

'My body wanted to, but my head was spinning with the glory of revenge.' She cackles and adds, 'A couple of temazepam sorted that out.'

We leave the buffet. Jacqui has a plate of melon and toast and I have enough to feed a third-world country. Jacqui arches a brow at my food. 'Are you sure you have enough? There's a mountain of pastries you missed.'

I ignore her and take my seat.

'I'm in the mood for a mimosa,' says Jacqui. 'Would you like one?'

'It's not even 9 a.m. yet.'

'It's a breakfast cocktail! Besides, we didn't have a celebratory drink last night. You were tired, remember?' She summons a waiter. 'Two mimosas please. With Champagne, not Prosecco.' Jacqui unfolds her napkin and pecks at her food.

'I don't get how you survive on so little.'

'I don't have much of an appetite these days.'

'Oh, are you OK?'

'It's the Ozempic. I should eat more, but don't feel like it.'

'Aren't you supposed to eat a balanced diet on that stuff?'

'You know, sometimes when you're busy working, you just forget.'

It's my turn to arch my brow. 'I'm not saying this is a jolly, but we're on a cruise with delicious, healthy food at our fingertips.'

She points at my plate. 'Like that?'

'There are healthier options.'

She shrugs. 'I'll try.'

The waiter arrives with our mimosas. Jacqui smiles and thanks him. We clink glasses and say 'Cheers' in unison. The cocktail is tart and refreshing.

'Delicious,' says Jacqui. 'So, did you catch Cilla's face last night?'

I grin. 'She was mortified.'

'Believe me, I'll be dining out on that moment FOREVER!'

We laugh and clink glasses once more. I finish up my food. The waiter arrives to clear our plates, but Jacqui has barely touched her breakfast. 'May I take your plate, ma'am?'

She slides it towards him. 'Please. I'm stuffed. Thank you.'

I roll my eyes.

'So, what have you got for me?' Jacqui asks.

I reach for my bag, take out my notes and lay them on the table. It's common knowledge that writers absorb the world around them and use what they see, hear, and smell to enrich their stories and characters. In the case of my proposal for Jacqui's Cassie Kowalski novel, that is undoubtedly true. In the few days that I've been on the ship, I've experienced every emotion from happiness and excitement to terror and anger. I've also met some of the oddest and most interesting people that I've ever encountered. Through osmosis, I've taken all of what I have observed, combined it with Jacqui's wishes, and formulated an outline for the novel.

Glancing at Jacqui, I feel a tingling of nerves and take a moment.

'I'm sensing apprehension. Am I going to like what I hear?'

I swallow. 'At this stage, the story is still malleable. We can adapt depending—'

'Let's get on with it.'

'To recap, we're taking Cassie out of the city to Kennebunkport. It's an old shipbuilding town, a beautiful and thriving community with characteristic colonial-style houses, sandy beaches, a fishing port, and a 168-year-old lighthouse on the nearby Goat Island. As a backdrop to Cassie's life, it will add colour and variety, which could be gold for a possible TV adaptation.'

The waiter arrives, and she orders two more mimosas.

'Not for me,' I say.

The waiter hesitates.

'I'm not drinking alone,' says Jacqui.

I give in and nod at the waiter.

'Two mimosas coming up,' he says.

'Any questions so far?'

'It sounds idyllic, but boring. It's a small town. Where's the threat and the action?'

'Good question. Like everywhere, it has a seedy underbelly. Interestingly, I chose this place because of two passengers on this ship.'

'Oh God, please tell me you haven't been talking to two ancient, town gossips.'

'I haven't spoken to them at all. I know they run a guest house in Kennebunkport and for decades have been fronting the neighbourhood watch scheme.'

Jacqui sighs. I'm losing her.

'Over the past twenty years, men and women have drifted to that part of the world never to be seen again.'

'How do you know that?'

'I saw it in an article online in the town paper from ten years back. The two passengers in question – Wilma and Frank Franklin – were among several people interviewed about the mysterious missing persons.'

'So, what does any of that have to do with Cassie's story?'

'We can incorporate it into the story, make the missing persons victims of a serial killer. This will be Cassie's case.'

That thoughtful expression again as Jacqui considers this. 'OK, tell me more.'

'We open with the murder of a woman, a drug addict, in the back streets of late-night Kennebunkport. The killer tries to take the body to their car but is disturbed by someone passing by. That person calls the cops. Enter Detective Cassie Kowalski, who had to leave the hospital where her pregnant, and recently diagnosed terminally ill daughter sleeps. Cassie's life is upside down, but she is a pro and turns her focus to the victim. Cassie sees a common thread between a recent spate of missing people and the victim. They were either addicts, homeless or both. Could a vigilante killer be cleaning the streets of people they consider unworthy? Cassie and her new partner, Dakota, the thirty-something, whip-smart, sizzling-hot, queer, Native American, are on the case—'

'I hate that expression.'

'Native American?'

'No. Queer. What does it even mean?'

I bite my tongue. The DuLac-asaurus has risen. 'He's . . . from the queer community.'

She frowns at me. 'There are many people who don't accept being pulled into that new categorisation.'

In my head, I hum the *Jurassic Park* theme. It's hardly new, I think. 'How old are these people?'

'Oh, I see! Because they're older, their opinions are irrelevant?'

'That's not what I meant.' But when I think about it, it probably is what I meant.

'One of my oldest friends, Miguel, said to me, no one has the right to call themselves 'queer' if they have not grown up and had that insult spat at them day in and day out. Nowadays, anyone can be queer. You don't even have to be gay, bi, or trans. You can be heterosexual, have rainbow-coloured dreadlocks, and come out as queer and that's that. Membership secured.'

We're getting sidetracked, and I'm eager to move on. I scribble out queer from my notes and write gay in its place. 'He's gay. Happy?'

Jacqui shifts on her chair. 'Whatever. I like the sound of him.' The mimosas arrive. Jacqui takes hers and swiftly necks half. Eyes focused on her drink; she taps the glass rhythmically with an immaculately painted nail. 'Miguel died last year. A short illness and then he was gone.' Her eyes begin to well.

Shit. 'I'm sorry.'

She shakes her head and smiles. 'He had a good life, aside from the early years of abuse, that is. Anyway, maybe I'm not as progressive as I should be.'

I don't know what to say to that.

'Let's carry on,' she says.

'In Cassie's personal life, her daughter returns home with a healthy newborn girl. With the investigation heating up, Cassie is reluctant to leave them and is forced to call on family, including her flaky ex-husband, for whom she still has feelings, to help. This leads to much drama. Cassie's case hits the news. The killer picks up on it and sees an opportunity for a cat-and-mouse game with our crime-fighting duo. And so, the location of the remains of each missing person is revealed, forcing Cassie and Dakota into a race against time to find a killer living in or around the town. What about the locals? Are they who they seem to be? The pastor who knows everyone and their business, the owners of a popular bed and breakfast who are also leaders of the neighbourhood watch scheme, the local friendly dentist, or the woman obsessed with marrying Death Row prisoners, or could it be Cassie's new-in-town, hot partner, Dakota?' I close my notes.

'Is that it?'

'It's a work in progress. I need to figure out the finer details.'

'Who's the killer?'

'I'm working on that.'

'It has to be the bed-and-breakfast, neighbourhood watch couple.'

'Why them?'

'It seems to me that if they're out and about at night, that would be the perfect time to murder waifs and strays and go unnoticed while keeping up the ruse of being good citizens.'

A light pings in my brain, and I smile. 'No one would ever suspect them.'

Chapter Thirty-Two

The Reverend

For more than thirty years, the good Reverend Timothy Garland has been a popular figure in the parishes that had the pleasure of having him as their clergyman. A comforting presence in Christian prayer, the Reverend had done his utmost to be a guiding light and a spiritual anchor. Admired and trusted by his flock, he had remained steadfast in his support for the aged and vulnerable. He had found immense joy in being alone with those in their final moments as they departed this world, sometimes with the assistance of a pillow to the face, or occasionally divine intervention with prescription drugs. It was a fact that he had presided over more funerals in the United Kingdom than any other clergyman. It was the very least he could do for his many, many victims.

In the bathroom of his cabin, the Reverend filled the kettle with water and carried it back to the bedroom where he attached the electric cable and pressed the boil button. Toying with the modest wooden crucifix hanging around his neck, he turned his attention to the photos of old friends and acquaintances Blu-tacked to the wall. Some might call it a murder wall. A crude name, but he supposed it an accurate one. In one picture, smiling back at him was the pale, wrinkled face of Gerald, who passed at eighty-five years old. A widower, estranged from his remaining family, bedridden with crippling osteoporosis, Gerald had been a special man. A little cantankerous, perhaps, and prone to soiling himself, nevertheless, he had enjoyed spending time sitting with him by his bedside, listening to his stories and recollections of his life, over and over and over again, until the time came and the good Reverend could bear it no more. Pinching Gerald's nose, he gently held his mouth closed and recited the Lord's Prayer. Gerald's eyes widened, his body trembled, he tried to resist, but was too weak, and in moments was on his way to the Pearly Gates where St Peter was waiting.

A plume of steam rose from the kettle, the button clicked, and the bubbling waters calmed. Taking a sachet of Earl Grey from the complimentary box of teas, he dropped it into a china cup. He poured the hot water on top, waited a few minutes, stirred and added a little milk. Raising the cup to his mouth, he inhaled the floral aroma and took a sip of the delicious, hot tea.

The photo to the right of Gerald was a portrait of seventy-nine-year-old Margaret, one hand holding a tray piled high with her homemade cream-filled cupcakes at the village fete, the other hand gripping her walking stick. Margaret was a large lady suffering from Type 1 Diabetes, Chronic Obstructive Pulmonary Disease, and had a dodgy ticker to boot. She had been perfect for what he had in mind. A spinster with no close family, Margaret was a popular face in the community. Always jolly and putting others before herself, she would rally around being charitable to everyone, which, in his opinion, made her utterly insufferable. She had latched on to the Reverend from day one, sharing the secrets of her health, or lack thereof, and gossip about the villagers. She liked to eat all the wrong things despite warnings from her doctor. Food, in particular cake and ice cream, was a great comfort to her. 'They'll be the death of me,' she'd often say. Thenceforth, the Reverend was forever plying her with sugary and full-fat foods when she visited him. She had the utmost faith and trust in him and would sometimes eat several cakes or portions of chocolate in one sitting. 'These are so naughty,' she would say, to which he would respond, 'Give us today our daily bread.' They would both giggle and he would encourage her to eat more. To give her credit, she was strong as an ox and lasted longer than he expected. It was three years into his tenure before she eventually clutched her heart and keeled over. They were alone in his living room in the vicarage. He made a trip to the bathroom to spend a penny, returning ten minutes later, waiting some more, and when he was certain she was toast, he picked up the phone and dialled for an ambulance.

A brisk knock on the door interrupted his musings. A flash of fear darkened his mood. Have the authorities caught up with him at last? Shaking the paranoia from his head, he set the teacup on the dressing table, made his way to the door and peered through the peephole. Wilma was standing outside holding a tote bag with the *Jewel of the Atlantic* logo. She knocked a second time, and he opened the door.

She smiled insincerely at him. 'Timothy, do you have a moment?'

He shifted on his feet. This was his room, his sanctuary. He didn't want anyone else here, polluting his private space, not even the cleaners. He was quite capable of cleaning his own room. 'I'm preparing for my presentation.'

'It won't take a moment,' she said, pushing past him.

He gritted his teeth and closed the door.

'I'm sorry to barge in on you, but we are undergoing a crisis that we must not ignore.'

'I understand that, but my talk—'

'Will run on time. I promise I won't keep you.'

On the whole, he and Wilma generally got along. She was a pushy woman, a little too controlling in his opinion, but he did respect her, despite not trusting her. She was a serial killer, after all. It just wouldn't do to trust someone like that. He had been with the Society for almost five years now, the only board member who was not an American citizen. He mostly attended their meetings via Zoom from the vicarage, and as a result, did not feel he had the same kind of relationship with her that the Dentist and the Undertaker had.

She was looking at his wall of photos. 'In the wrong hands, these pictures could incriminate you.'

'They're photos of very dear old friends.'

'Dear old friends that you put in the ground.'

'Not all of them.'

'Oh?'

'Some were burnt and scattered to the wind.'

Wilma noticed his unfinished drink. Lifting it, she held it under her nose and sniffed. He felt himself seethe inside. She might as well have spat into it. As soon as she leaves, that is going down the toilet.

'You Brits love your tea, don't you?'

'What can I do for you, Wilma?'

She took a moment to respond and in that time walked around his room, her eyes scanning, searching.

'Looking for something in particular?' he asked.

'Nothing. Just being nosey.'

'You don't say.'

She peered down at the small, neat pile of papers on his immaculately made bed. 'Today's presentation. I'm looking forward to it.'

'I hope people find it inspiring.'

She regarded him momentarily. 'Timothy, I just wanted to check in since our last discussion and see if you have noticed anything unusual since Ernest's murder?'

'At the conference?'

She nodded.

'I can't say that I have. It's just your common or garden serial killer convention. Nothing unusual about that.'

She pursed her lips and held his gaze. 'His murder has really put the cat among the pigeons. We are in troubled waters.'

'That's a terrible pun.'

She frowned as she thought this over and then chuckled. 'I didn't mean it to be.' Reaching into the tote bag, she rummaged for a moment and took out a red button, which she held up. Two eyes and a smile were daubed onto it. 'Does this mean anything to you?'

'A button?'

'With a smiley face. Have you come across it or anything like it before?'

'I can't say that I have.'

'We found it in Ernest's room.'

'I don't recall him wearing anything other than black.'

'The man who killed him was wearing a mask with a face made from buttons.'

'Yes, they call him Buttonface,' he replied, impatiently.

'But I think this is more than that. I think it's a calling card, a warning.'

'I see.'

'Have you received one?'

'Not that I'm aware. Is that what you were looking for?'

She didn't answer his question. 'I should let you get on.'

'I would appreciate that.'

Wilma made her way to the door, but stopped, inches from

him. Looking into his eyes, she said. 'Did you do it, Timothy?'

He held her gaze, his hackles rising. 'Is that what this is about?'

She searched his face and then patted his shoulder. 'Of course you didn't. I'm sorry to ask. I just needed to be sure.'

He felt his face burning. 'You should go,' he said, opening the door.

'Yes.' And with that Wilma exited the room.

As the door slowly closed behind her, he listened to her footsteps fade, each one echoing like an accusation he couldn't silence. The Reverend stood rigid, his hand hovering over the teacup. He took it to the bathroom, deposited the tea down the sink and ran the hot water tap. He smothered the cup in hand soap and scrubbed it hard until it was clean, muttering curse after curse under his breath.

Chapter Thirty-Three

Martha

Our meeting is finished. Jacqui is on her third mimosa and enjoying the attention of Bob and Don, who have just joined us.

I gather my notes. 'I'll go type this up and work on the detail,' I tell Jacqui.

She nods in approval.

'Don't go on account of us,' says Bob.

'I have a lot of work to do.'

'She's on a tight schedule,' Jacqui adds.

I say my farewells and hear Jacqui ask Bob and Don what they're drinking. It's not even 11 a.m.! I hurry out of the Seven Dials diner and make my way down to level two. I haven't been entirely honest with Jacqui. I'll work on the notes and outline, but not right now. I have a killer to track down, and my sights are set on one particular person. For the next few hours, I'm going to stake out the Midnight Chorus Society conference. But this time, I'm playing it safe and will watch from the casino, where I will indulge in a bit of gambling on the slots and secretly take some pictures. I'm going full-on Veronica Mars.

First stop is the casino's cash booth, where I quickly exchange a twenty-pound note for the equivalent in pound coins, in a plastic cup. Eyeing up the machines, I choose one close to the aisle that will give me the best view of the traffic and perch myself on a stool. I sit in the glow of a Buffalo Gold slot machine, one eye on the game, the other on the traffic going to and from the Hefferman Centre. For the time being, it's flowing in one direction to the conference, which makes me think a talk is about to begin. I feel a slap of FOMO and regret not going undercover again.

I recognise some faces, including the vicar I had seen at breakfast with Wilma. He's in a hurry and is carrying a bunch of papers rolled up under his arm; his face is red as he navigates the throng. I wonder what his story is. Why would a member of the clergy be attending a true crime convention? Interesting. I notice a large, grey-haired man haul himself up from a Blackjack table. Unsteady on his feet, clearly inebriated, he tries to balance himself but fails and stumbles backwards, colliding with the vicar. The startled clergyman drops his papers to the floor and swears angrily. Unusual language for a gentleman of the cloth. He drops to the floor like Thelma from *Scooby Doo* when she loses her glasses, and scrambles to pick up the scattered sheets that are being walked on by people flocking to the conference. The drunk has stumbled away, unaware of the chaos he just created. I notice Bernard stopping beside him. I inch behind the slot machine and peek at the two men exchanging words, but I cannot hear. After a few moments, they proceed to the convention. The crowd is thinning, but minutes pass before I see my prey. With a Bible in hand, wearing the same buttoned-up shirt and braces, Victor strides through the casino. I take out my phone and furtively take a few shots of him. He slows to a stop, a frown forming on his long face.

I freeze.

Is he glancing in my direction?

Gasping, I dart behind the machine out of sight. Has he seen me? My heart begins to thud. I fumble a hand in the cup and pull out a coin, insert it into the machine and set it in motion. The dials start to spin. I take a breath, relax my expression, and smile sweetly so as not to appear nervous in the event he rocks up beside me. I hum the *Jurassic Park* theme tune. It's still in my head.

Moments pass, and he doesn't show.

My mouth is dry. I need peace of mind but can't risk peeking in case he's still standing there. I knock the cup of coins and allow them to spill to the floor. I make a show of being cross with myself and emerge from behind the slot machine to gather them up. I'm on all fours and without looking directly up, I can see that the spot where he stood is vacant. Picking up a coin, I peer up the aisle and see his silhouette disappear through the doors. Relief washes over me. As I gather the remaining coins, I notice a sheet of paper lying against the slot machine next to mine. I pick it up. There are words in bold, like it's the heading of a PowerPoint presentation.

THE AGONY AND THE ECSTASY
Finding the Joy in Assisted Dying
The Reverend Timothy Garland

'I think that might be mine,' comes a voice.

I flinch.

The Reverend is standing inches from me, his hand held out. Where the hell did he appear from?

He smiles benevolently, yet his gaze is piercing and cold, and quite frankly, creepy.

I swallow. 'I dropped my coins . . . and found it here on the floor. I was going to throw it away. I . . . I hate litter, don't you?'

'That won't be necessary,' he says, taking it from me and turning to leave.

'Sounds interesting,' I say.

He turns back and gives me a smile that is off-the-scale insincere. 'It's for a book I'm writing,' he says, scratching his ear.

'You're an author!'

'I am many things.'

'I can see you're a vicar too,' I say with a nervous laugh.

'Very observant of you.'

'Coincidentally, I'm also a writer.' There's something odd about him that makes me uneasy. I don't want to, but I hold out my hand. 'My name's Martha. You must be the Reverend Timothy Garland.'

He doesn't take my hand. 'It would be best not to mention this to anyone. My publishers have an embargo on the title.'

'My lips are sealed. Who's your publisher? Maybe we have the same one? Is it fiction?' I laugh. 'Of course it is. I'd love to hear more about it.'

He steps away. 'I'm late for my appointment.' And with that, he turns and leaves.

I watch him go with a hundred questions in my head. Was he giving a presentation on finding the joy in assisted dying? What does that even mean? Taking out my phone, I try to connect to the Wi-Fi, but I fail because, down here in the depths of the ship, actually pretty much everywhere, the Wi-Fi is like a ghost that isn't sure it wants to haunt you or not. I watch the Reverend hurry through the doors and make a mental note to google him when I get a decent signal.

Chapter Thirty-Four

Wilma

It just seemed too much of a coincidence for Wilma. Last night, Jacqui DuLac, and her assistant, Martha, had mentioned a guest house in Kennebunkport related to a string of murders in the former's upcoming book. Wilma had felt her world collapsing when she heard her hometown mentioned, especially in the context of a guest house. Did Jacqui and her assistant know the truth about her and Frank? Was it their way of sending a message that they were on to them? Had someone from the Society betrayed her? She had not slept a wink and intended to find out. Ms DuLac and her assistant had just found themselves added to her suspect list. For the moment, she had other business.

A long queue was forming outside Conference Room 3 in preparation for the Reverend Timothy Garland's lecture. At 100 feet by 40 feet, this was the smallest space and one she had deliberately booked for the Reverend's event because she didn't think it would be well attended. Judging by the gathering crowd, it was looking like a full house.

This surprised Wilma for two reasons. Firstly, he was relatively new to the Society and unknown in the US, but that was on her. She had not made much of a song and dance about his appointment. She'd gone and recruited him against the wishes of the others because she wanted to expand the Society and open a chapter in Europe where there was more money to be made. Secondly, 'The Agony and the Ecstasy' was too highbrow a title for a conference lecture. It would put people off, she said, arguing with him to change it to something less grand, but he wouldn't hear of it. That had incensed her. But none of that mattered now. She had gone to visit him in his room, little over an hour ago, and had come right out and asked him if he was the masked killer. The question had rattled him. He did not break eye contact with her, yet his left eye had twitched, and his face reddened. Was this a subconscious reaction to guilt, or was it nothing? Time would tell. For now, it was too early to wipe him from the suspect slate.

Of course, there were plenty of other people on the suspect slate. Jeez Louise, to narrow it down, that included everyone attending this conference, killers and wannabes. For that reason, it was time to begin mingling properly with her guests. She would talk to each and every one of them, look them in the eye, make small talk, gently interrogate them before presenting the button and asking if it meant anything to them.

A diminutive young man with thick horn-rimmed glasses and protruding teeth stood at the top of the queue. Dressed in knee-length shorts, a pressed shirt with a dickie bow, it seemed like he was from a different time. Wilma had an idea and approached him. Glancing at his name badge, she held out her hand. 'Are you enjoying the conference, Kent?'

He looked at her hand momentarily with a gormless expression before taking it and giving it a limp shake. His skin was soft and moist. 'Erm . . . I guess.' Wilma relaxed her hand. Kent's face turned to a frown, and he looked down at his palm, where the red button with the smiley face was sitting.

'Oh, silly me!' she said, eyes studying every inch of his expression as if it would somehow reveal his identity as the masked killer.

Shrugging, he extended his hand, 'You can have it back.'

There was nothing she could glean. No shock, or nerves. 'Thank you.' Taking the button from him, she made a mental note to work on this strategy.

The conference room door opened, and Frank popped his head out. His eyes caught Wilma's. There was an urgency to his expression as he beckoned her inside. Wilma excused herself and joined him, closing the door behind her. The Reverend was sitting in the front row, quietly reading through his presentation.

'We have a problem,' said Frank.

Wilma sighed. 'What is it now?'

Frank nodded to the rear of the room. Someone was lying across a row of chairs, huddled under a blanket. Wilma tutted. 'Who in the heck is that?'

'Terence.'

Wilma rolled her eyes. 'Of course it is. Get him out of here before there's any more trouble. Any minute now, those doors will open, and people will stream inside.'

'I already tried that, but he stinks of liquor and he ain't saying or moving for that matter.'

As if on cue, the doors opened and the people rushed to grab the best seats. 'Shoot!' said Wilma. 'Keep an eye on him. I'll introduce the Reverend and think of something.' Wilma made her way to the stage and the wooden lectern. On top was a microphone and a device for operating the large display at the back of the stage. Pointing it at the screen, she pressed the green button and brought it to life. The Reverend's title slide appeared:

'The Agony and the Ecstasy'
Finding the Joy in Assisted Dying
The Reverend Timothy Garland

Wilma turned to face the audience and lifted the mic. Leaning into it, she said: 'Is this on?'

'Speak up, we can't hear you!' someone shouted.

'Ah . . .' Examining the mic, she found the On button and pressed it. 'Can you hear me now?'

'Goddamnit stop shouting,' came that voice again.

The audience laughed.

'Is it too loud?' she said.

'I'm just pulling your leg.'

She looked in the direction of the voice. A thin man older than his years with a handlebar moustache, missing teeth and a scruffy baseball cap. His name was Rooster Calhoun. He was the Woodchipper disposal expert who was taking part in what promised to be a lively debate later that afternoon, titled 'Woodchippers VS Acid Baths – the best way to dispose of a body'.

'Very funny, Rooster.' She shot a glance at Frank, who was gently tapping the sleeping Terence. How on earth could they get him out of here without disturbing the event? The last thing she needed was more complaints from dissatisfied customers. Composing herself, she smiled and looked out at the attendees, eyes scanning their faces, some she recognised and some she didn't. 'Our next speaker is a very special man, a dear friend, and a recently appointed member of the Midnight Chorus Society no less.' She turned and smiled at the Reverend, but he did not smile back. 'What can I say about him. He's British . . . very British . . . he won't mind me saying . . . haha . . . in a way that he drinks tea from a china teacup and he eats cucumber sandwiches.' Wilma giggles at this. No one else does. She feels her mouth drying and now knows how Terence feels when none of his jokes hit the target. 'Anyway, it's an honour to open this talk on finding the joy in assisted dying . . . something I'm sure you'll agree we can all relate to . . .' This gets a laugh, and she feels a bounce in her confidence. 'So, without further ado, please welcome to the stage, our speaker, the Reverend Timothy Garland.'

An eruption of applause saw the Reverend rise from his chair and step up to the stage. 'Break a leg,' she said, handing him the mic. He smiled thinly. Wilma stepped down and made her way down the centre aisle to the rear of the room.

The Reverend's voice reverberated from the speakers. 'Thank you, Wilma, for that inspiring introduction.'

Wilma glanced at Rooster, who gave her an unsettling wink. She frowned and hurried to join Frank. Terence lay across three chairs at the back of room, oddly cocooned in a dark blanket pulled up to his nose, and wearing sunglasses. As the Reverend began his lecture, she began to feel hot and prickly at the Fool for being so out-of-line once again, and at Frank being so . . . darn it . . . useless! 'For Pete's sake, Frank! Couldn't you have tried a little harder?' she hissed.

'What more could I do?'

'Wake him up and ship him out might be a good start!'

'Hush!' came a voice. Wilma looked up to see Kent frowning at her.

Wilma gritted her teeth, pushed past her husband and sat on the chair next to Terence's head. Leaning down, she shook his shoulder and whispered into his ear, 'Terence, wake up!' She wrinkled her nose. He smelt not only of stale whiskey but something else, something sour and coppery too. The odours were starkly familiar. 'Terence?'

Kent was watching, eyes fixed on Terence.

Wilma tugged at the blanket, partially covering Terence's face. It wouldn't come loose and felt like it was stuck to his face. She shook his shoulder, but still no response. 'For Pete's sake, Terence!' she hissed, utterly exasperated. Enough was enough. Reaching for the blanket, she yanked it. She sometimes forgot her own strength because Terence rolled from the chairs and fell to the floor.

Wilma let out a gasp.

Terence stared up at the ceiling with lifeless eyes. His chest was bare and covered in blood and knife wounds. His mouth was wide open. Inside it, resting on his tongue, was a red button with a smiley face daubed on it. Wilma swallowed. 'Okee-dokee,' she said, placing the blanket back over him. Turning to face the stage, she blinked, looked at the Reverend and pretended to listen, but inside she let out an almighty scream.

'Awesome!' said Kent.

Chapter Thirty-Five

Martha

Almost twenty minutes have passed. I'm still at the Buffalo Gold slot machine, one eye on the game and the other keenly watching the traffic traversing to and from the convention. It's been uneventful; presumably, there's a talk, which I suspect is the Reverend Garland's mysterious true crime tale, which I'm intrigued about. To kill time, I'm pumping coins into the slot, and to my surprise, I'm hitting the jackpot every other game.

As my winnings pile up, I notice a group of people emerge from the doors leading to the convention. The talk must be over. That was quick. More stream out in their wake, several huddled together, talking in whispers as if sharing a great secret.

'Martha!'

I jolt at the sound of Jacqui's voice hollering my name across the casino. *Bollocks!* I've been caught bunking off work. I see her with Bob and Don sitting down at a Blackjack table. I scoop up my winnings, deposit them into the plastic cup and head over to her, wondering how I will talk my way out of this one.

Jacqui is examining the two cards of her hand, as I approach. She has a queen and a three of clubs.

'Hey, fancy seeing you here,' I say, brightly.

'I could say the same about you,' she replies without making eye contact and signals to the dealer for a third card.

I laugh nervously, 'Yeah . . . I had this idea for a scene in a casino—'

'And you thought you would come down and do some research.'

'I did. It's been . . . useful.'

'I'm sure it has.'

The dealer deals Jacqui's card. It's an eight of diamonds. She smiles. 'Fortune favours the brave.'

'I should get going.'

'A casino in Maine's small town, Kennebunkport,' says Jacqui.

'Some states are a little strict about gambling,' says Bob.

'That's right, Bob,' Jacqui replies. 'I doubt the same restrictions apply in the United Kingdom.'

'It doesn't have to be local,' I say, winging it. 'It can be anywhere in Maine. The important thing is we inject some money laundering sleaze into the narrative.'

'There are two casinos in Maine,' says Don. 'One in Oxford, the other in Bangor.'

'Right,' I reply enthusiastically, as if I already knew that.

Jacqui looks at me suspiciously. 'Do your homework.'

'I'm on it.'

'I'm looking forward to reading the scene,' Jacqui says. I know she can see through my bullshit. 'What you got in your hand?' she asks, glancing at my cup.

'I won some money . . .'

'Gambling on my time?'

I feel myself bristling. 'Technically, it's the publisher's time, and it is research.'

'Well, let's try and win them some more money, shall we?' Jacqui points at the Blackjack table. 'Let's gamble.'

I smile insincerely and place the cup on the table. 'Be my guest.' I feel two hands grip my arms and tug me from the table. The scent of ashes tickles my nostrils. The air seems to thicken in my throat, like I'd swallowed incense smoke. 'Martha. Martha,' comes the weedy, ethereal voices of the bonkers twins.

We see your hands, we see your face,
We know you do not own your place.
The dealer laughs, the wheel will spin,
But little lambs don't always win.

I snatch my arms from their grip and step back.

'That's enough, ladies,' comes a Southern drawl. Victor is approaching, Bible in hand.

The twins giggle softly and, to my astonishment, begin to coo like pigeons. 'Oh Victor,' they say, pawing and stroking his chest and head. As if things couldn't get any weirder, Victor bares his teeth which include two weird pointy canines. He hisses at them. They howl with laughter and then run away as if expecting to be chased. I watch them go, my mouth open.

'You must introduce me to your friends,' Jacqui says, cackling.

'Sorry about that,' says Victor. 'They can get a little carried away sometimes.'

'Who are they?'

'Tammy and Toya Bickel. They're twins.'

'You don't say.'

Behind me, I hear a familiar, urgent voice. 'Out of my way! Excuse me!' I turn to see a red-faced Wilma navigate through the throng and make her way outside the casino, where she holds up her phone as if trying to catch a signal. I watch her and wonder what has got her into such a state of agitation.

'She ain't happy,' says Victor.

'What's up with her?' I ask,

He doesn't answer. Instead, he asks, 'Are you following me, Martha?'

'What? No, of course not.' I glance back at Jacqui, focused on the game, but judging by the tilt in her head, she is listening in on my exchange with Victor.

'I don't mind if you do.'

'I'm not.'

'It's OK if you like me. I like you.'

I hear a snort of laughter behind me.

'But I don't . . . I mean I do.' I laugh awkwardly.

'I know you do.'

'I should go . . . I have work to do.'

Victor leans across and whispers. 'They found a dead body.'

I blink, not quite believing what he just said. 'Who found a dead body?'

His eyes slide to Wilma. 'She's not having a good day.'

'Who's dead and how did it happen?'

Victor shrugs his shoulders. 'Wasn't me,' he says, holding up his hands as if he's innocent of a crime. 'But it's cool, right?'

I'm not sure what to say to that.

'We should team up, you and me,' he says.

'Why would we do that?' I say, looking at Wilma, who is still trying in vain to get a signal.

'Wilma will sort it out. She always does.'

I look from Victor to Wilma and back to Victor again. 'What does that mean?'

'She takes care of business.'

'Are dead bodies a thing at the Midnight Chorus Society conventions?'

'This is a first.'

'I'm relieved to hear that.'

'Would you like to accompany me to the Masquerade Ball?' Victor asks.

I'm struck by how challenging it is to get information from him, but also how brazenly he comes out with asking me on a date. I ignore his question. Tit for tat and all that. 'Did you know Ernest Ridgewell?' I ask.

'Of course. Everyone knows Ernest.'

He's talking about Ernest in the present tense. 'Have you seen him around lately?'

He thinks this over momentarily, his gaze seemingly focused on thin air. 'Now that you mention it, I don't think I have.'

If he doesn't know Ernest is dead, does Wilma 'the fixer' know?

'Hey, so what about you and me at the Masquerade Ball?'

'Actually, I already have a date.'

His face drops. And in that moment, a swarm of convention attendees engulf us. One, a slight young man with a bow tie and buck teeth, taps Victor's shoulder. I turn and look outside the casino. Wilma has gone. Time for me to go. I follow in pursuit of her. I need to know more about this dead body.

'Martha!' Jacqui calls.

'I'll be right back!' I say.

Wilma picks up her pace, zigzagging through pockets of passengers in the busy lobby. She hurries for the lift, slipping inside before the glass doors close. I take the stairs, two at a time, making sure she doesn't notice me. She gets out at the 11th floor. By the time I get there, I'm gasping for breath and have worked up a sweat. This is Jacqui's level, for VIPs. Who can she be calling on here? I slow my pace as I turn on the staircase and see her dash from the lift and head down the corridor, the same one where Jacqui's suite is located. I keep a safe, measured distance between us. If she stops, turns, and suddenly asks why

I'm following her, I'll tell her I'm here to visit my boss. Wilma turns a corner out of sight. I pass Jacqui's suite. I'm nervous now, and I don't know why. I take out my phone and pretend to be one of those annoying people who stare at their screens while walking. An excuse to cover my guilt should Wilma confront me. I need to calm down. Why on earth would she?

I hear a door being knocked on, and as I turn the corner, I step back and peek at Wilma outside the entrance to the Presidential Suite, according to the sign on the door. This is where the corridor ends. It's a kind of Art Deco mini cul-de-sac, styled with elegant potted plants, black-and-white prints in chrome frames and what looks like an unmanned reception desk. There's only one person on the ship I can think of who is staying here. The door opens, but I can't see who's on the other side. Wilma is talking with urgency. There appears to be an angry exchange before she eventually enters the suite. I wonder what to do. Wait it out or leave? I decide to walk towards the door and hover outside, under the pretence of looking at my phone, listening hard for voices, but I can't hear anything.

But then I hear someone. A man's voice. Approaching the door.

I panic, run to the reception desk and crouch behind it.

The door opens and then closes. I hear footfalls walking away. I wait a moment and then emerge from behind the desk. I hurry back towards the corridor and in the distance see the man walking casually towards the lifts.

I swallow.

It's Zach.

Chapter Thirty-Six

Wilma

Wilma exited the Spider's suite, slamming the door hard like a petulant teenager who had just been chastised by her bitch mother. Her head was beginning to spin to the point of dizziness, and Lord knows, she did not have time for spells like that. She had brought Priscilla up to speed on the Terence situation.

The Spider's jaw had dropped.

And then she lost her poop. 'This is all your fucking fault!' she screamed. 'You and that bunch of bumbling knuckleheads! How could I ever have trusted any of you . . .' She pointed at Wilma with a taloned finger, bared her teeth, her eyes darkening as they looked her up and down. 'Especially you . . . you hick!'

Wilma had flinched.

She had been prepared for a disagreement, but not to be insulted in such an uncouth display of bad manners. Wilma took a breath and remained composed. 'We both stood in Ernest's room and agreed that his murder may not be the last on this ship.'

'So! What's your point?'

'My point? You seem surprised and . . . angry. The latter I understand. However, your reaction is . . . how can I put this delicately . . . not unlike one of those gold-digging tramps you once played on TV.'

It was the Spider's turn to flinch. She had fired the first shot, calling Wilma a 'hick'. And now Wilma had fired back and hit the bullseye.

'You dare!'

Wilma was losing patience. 'This is getting us nowhere. We need to work together and fix this mess!'

The Spider had closed her eyes and breathed heavily through her cosmetically enhanced, dainty nose. 'Where's the body now?'

'It's been moved to an office at the rear of the conference centre.'

Priscilla had moved out of Wilma's earshot and made a call on her cell. Wilma took in the palatial suite. They were in the living room. It had deep club chairs and long, low sofas upholstered in rich blue velvet with yellow piping. Wilma had not been invited to sit. She wasn't important enough. There was a cocktail bar with illuminated shelves, crystal decanters, and etched glass panels. The ceiling was as high as a basketball court with a glittering, grand chandelier in chrome and frosted glass hanging at the centre like an upside-down skyscraper. On the walls, angular, sleek sconces with etched glass radiated a warm amber glow that seemed at odds with the unwelcome coldness of what was the Spider's lair.

The call ended.

'OK. We have a plan. Go to the lobby on the fifth floor. Wait at the reception desk. My contact will meet you there and issue further instructions.'

'Your contact?'

'You heard me.'

'Who is it?'

'You'll find out.'

Wilma felt a prickling on the back of her neck. 'You wouldn't be thinking of betraying me now, would you?'

'You think I'm plotting your downfall?' Priscilla laughed. 'You're doing an impressive job of that already.'

Wilma bunched her hands into fists. She looked across at the crystal decanter and pictured swinging it hard at Priscilla's insufferable face. She smiled politely and turned to leave.

Priscilla, who always had to have the last word, said: 'When this is over, I want you to step down.'

Wilma paused but did not look back. 'This is my Society. I created it and made it what it is.'

'With my money.'

'We'll find another sponsor.'

'No, you won't.'

In her heart, Wilma knew this was true. Nevertheless, she was hopping mad.

Wilma had called the elevator and waited quietly, trying her best not to tremble. She considered that Priscilla was setting her up, that Security would be waiting for her at the reception desk, ready to take her to the brig. But then again, she wouldn't be so careless. Wilma knew a lot about the Spider's history, and if she went down, she would bring the God darn Spider down with her. The elevator's glass doors slid open. Wilma stepped inside, grateful that it was empty and she was alone. As she began the slow descent, she lifted her head and screamed like a banshee. It was visceral, yet it felt good at the same time. The elevator slowed gently and opened its elegant doors on the fifth floor. Wilma held her hands together, stepped outside and made her way through the bustling crowd to the reception desk, ready for whatever came next.

She scanned the faces of her fellow passengers. There was

no one she recognised. She imagined, or hoped, that Frank, Bernard and the Reverend had successfully shifted Terence's foul-smelling body to the back office, so that the convention could continue.

Nearby, a statuesque woman in a sun hat the size of a satellite dish navigated the crowd with the grace of a pick-up truck. Her gaze caught Wilma's and held. Was she the contact?

'Darling!' came a man's voice.

The woman smiled, turned and opened her arms to embrace a much smaller man with a pencil moustache. They chatted to each other, their voices disappearing in the throng.

Ten minutes passed and the crowd was thinning.

She saw a gentleman in a white linen suit explaining to the receptionist in a loud voice that he always had a cabin with a better view than the captain. He was holding a tumbler filled with whiskey, by the look of it. On occasion, he would rub his chin and look across at Wilma curiously. In different circumstances, she would ignore him, yet maybe he was the Spider's contact. She concluded that his persistent bluster at the receptionist suggested he wasn't.

She sighed and watched a pair of newlyweds clutching matching Piña Coladas while having their photo taken on the grand staircase. On the other side of the lobby, a man wearing a tropical print shirt documented every square inch of the space on his phone, narrating in a mock travel-show voice that carried all the way to the elevator. The glass doors opened, and a man stepped out. He scanned the lobby and stopped when he saw Wilma. He held her gaze momentarily before making a call on his mobile phone.

Wilma swallowed.

When the call had finished, he made his way towards her, his expression grim, his eyes never leaving hers.

Wilma glanced around, looking for a weapon: a paperweight, a bottle, a whiskey tumbler, but there was nothing.

'Mrs Franklin, will you come this way, please, ma'am,' said Deputy Gomez.

Chapter Thirty-Seven

Martha

Jacqui had texted me to say she had overheard my conversation with Victor, and she wanted to know just what the hell was going on. You're not the only one, I thought. A hundred questions whirled in my head like kites in a storm. I texted her back and told her I was returning to the casino. I took the stairs rather than waiting for the lift. I wanted time to process my thoughts and think about what my next step would be.

Another body has been found, this time on site at the Midnight Chorus Society conference. Had a second murder been committed, or had someone simply dropped dead? If it was a murder, was Buttonface responsible? He must be. What are the chances of two killers being on this ship? That would be too much of a coincidence. My stomach churns at the thought of him murdering again and getting away with it. That aside, I've now concluded that my dad's killer and this Society are somehow connected. I take my time going down the sweeping staircase and think about my conversation with Victor. He had said of Wilma: 'She takes care of business.' If that's what she does, why were there no cruise ship medics or a doctor at the scene? Shouldn't that have been her top priority, as well as alerting Todd Atkins?

Instead, she made a beeline for Priscilla Hefferman's suite. So, what kind of business is Wilma actually taking care of? And what does it have to do with Priscilla? And finally, what was Zach doing in Priscilla's suite? My heart is racing. These questions feel like pieces of a puzzle that are, for now, beyond my reach. I need answers, and I intend to get them. I'm meeting Zach later for the Masquerade Ball. I'm not sure how I feel about him at the moment. He does have his demons. He's been open and honest about that. But has he been entirely honest with me? I had thought he was travelling alone or at least assumed he was.

I reach the bottom of the stairs, as a small group of passengers enter the lift. Across the lobby, I see Jacqui waving.

'Hold that elevator!' she calls.

I turn and press the button, but I'm too late. The doors have shut, and the glass lift is already rising.

'Sorry,' I say.

'Never mind. We'll take the stairs.'

We start climbing.

'So, Miss Marple, what's going on?'

I know as much as she does about the latest body, but I begin by telling her about Victor.

'He keeps a knife in his Bible! What on earth for?'

'I don't think it's for peeling potatoes. Who knows. Protection?'

'The only thing anyone needs protection from on this ship is tie-dye fashion choices and couples who wear matching pastel polo shirts.'

'There's been one murder already, remember.'

'So you say.'

We're on the fifth floor when I notice the lift coming down. Inside is Wilma, standing with her back to us. 'Look,' I say.

'Who is she?' asks Jacqui.

Before I can respond, Wilma lets out a terrifying and piercing scream, startling us both. We watch open-mouthed as the lift descends and she disappears out of sight.

We turn to look at each other.

I have to come clean. So, I explain everything to Jacqui: what I know about the Midnight Chorus Society, Wilma and the other players in that group: Bernard the dentist, Terence the stinky drunk, and the Reverend Garland. But I leave out the detail about Zach. I need to think more about that before discussing it.

'I know Bernard. We had a drink together,' Jacqui says.

'You went on a date with him?'

'No! I was at the martini bar. He was there too, and he joined me for a nightcap.'

'Did he admire your teeth by any chance?'

'He said they were like pale ivory jewels.'

'He kept staring at my teeth when I was talking to him as if he was sizing them up. Don't you think that's weird?'

Jacqui frowns at me. 'He was very sweet. He'll be at the Masquerade Ball.'

'Will you meet him for a "martini"?'

'We did make tentative plans. I'll ask him about the Society.'

'Good idea.'

I tell her that I followed Wilma from the casino to Priscilla's room. This sparks her interest even more. 'If Wilma runs the Society, and there was a body, why would she go straight to Priscilla and not Security?'

Jacqui is thinking this over. 'She must be involved with the Society.'

'Perhaps she's in charge.'

'There is something odd about this, and it doesn't surprise me that Cilla has her claws in it.'

'Do you think you could talk to her?'

Jacqui snorts. 'After the stunt I pulled on stage? She won't talk to me. She'll be plotting her revenge already.'

'She might get Security to make you walk the plank.'

'I wouldn't put it past her.'

We both chuckle.

'What are you doing now?' Jacqui asks, eyebrows arched.

I'm tempted to go talk to Todd, and tell him what I've discovered, but that would be a waste of time. I have no proof, and I'm not sure he will believe me or take me seriously. 'I'm going to try and finish the outline.'

'Try?'

'I'll do my best.'

Jacqui nods. 'Make sure you do. I will see you later at the Masquerade Ball and expect news of a completed outline.'

I salute her. 'Yes, ma'am.'

She gives me a withering look. 'Don't do that.'

I'm parched by the time I get to my cabin. Grabbing a bottle of water from the fridge, I make my way to the balcony, perching myself on the warm rattan chair. I take two large swallows of the deliciously cold liquid and let my gaze fall to the expansive ocean surface, a calming aqua mirror reflecting the afternoon sun.

My phone pings. A message from Zach. I shift in my seat.

Hey, I'm unable to do dinner this evening. Duty calls. Sorry. I'm still on for the ball. See you at 8? Z x

Duty calls? I feel a twist in my stomach. His connection to Priscilla is bothering me. Why would he not mention it? But then again, why would he? I'm a stranger to him. Maybe they're related, and perhaps he didn't want to name drop. I type a reply.

No worries. I'll be there at eight, masked and ready to party. M x

He sends back a flame emoji, which, despite everything, makes me feel a bit gooey inside.

Chapter Thirty-Eight

Wilma

'Where are we going?' Wilma asked Deputy Gomez.

He did not answer.

Gomez was a stocky man with thick, muscular arms and fists like hams. One strike and she would be out cold, if not dead. She had no doubt he was a killer. She could see it in the hollow of his dark eyes, the lack of warmth, personality, and empathy that she recognised in her society friends and colleagues. Priscilla was not going to have her arrested. She was going to have her murdered and dropped into the ocean this fate has not yet been decided for Terence. She followed Gomez out of the lobby and up a quiet corridor to a black door labelled Crew Only. He opened it with an electronic key and gestured for her to enter.

'Not until you tell me where we are going?'

'Ma'am, please step inside, and we can talk.'

Wilma could take care of herself. She was strong, with years of experience behind her, and could overcome the average man. But Gomez was anything but average. Without a knife or a blunt object of some kind, she was vulnerable.

'You have nothing to be afraid of,' he said, as if reading her thoughts. 'I'm here to help you clean up your mess.'

Wilma was not the most trusting of persons. She studied his face for a trace of deception, but his grave expression gave nothing away. 'You go first,' she said. 'I'll follow.'

'As you wish.'

She kept a safe distance behind him as they descended a set of steel stairs leading to a long, bustling corridor with crew going about their business. Bar staff wheeled trolleys of alcohol, cleaning teams pushed baskets of linen, chefs carried containers of raw meat and fish.

No one gave her a second glance.

In Wilma's estimation, they walked for another five hundred yards or so before Gomez came to a stop at a doorway. 'Wait here,' he said. The deputy opened the door and closed it behind him. From what she could see, it looked like a storeroom. Wilma stood against the wall, head down, arms folded as a stream of cruise staff passed by. Moments later, she heard a squeaking sound from behind the door. Gomez appeared, pushing a wheelchair. 'Not far now. We'll take the staff elevator to the casino.' He went ahead. Wilma realised the squeaking sound was one of the chair's wheels.

'Why is it making that noise?' she asked.

'Probably needs oiling.'

Minutes later, they were inside the boxy steel elevator, travelling down to the second floor.

Gomez reached into his pocket, took out a plastic electronic room key and handed it to Wilma. 'This is the key to room 3.110. It is unoccupied and located on the rear of the third floor. Take this wheelchair and transport the body to the room. Tonight, during the Masquerade Ball, throw the body into the sea.'

'But what if someone sees us?'

'The balcony is at an oblique angle. No one can see in. There is nothing below, only the ocean. I will ensure the cameras are not watching.'

'You're making it sound easy.'

'You'd be surprised.'

'When do we take the body?'

'You and your colleagues have a lot of experience moving corpses. That's for you to figure out. I would suggest you do everything within your power to avoid implicating or embarrassing Mrs Hefferman. Do I make myself clear?'

Wilma simmered and gave a curt nod.

The elevator pinged, and the doors slid open. A slim man dressed in cleaning overalls, carrying a mop and bucket, stood outside. Beyond him, she could see the flashing coloured lights of the casino.

'This lady is coming through,' said Gomez.

The man nodded and stepped aside.

'Have a good day, ma'am,' said Gomez.

Gripping the handles firmly, Wilma pushed the wheelchair out of the elevator and did not look behind her. Hurrying through the casino, she made her way to the conference centre.

She parked the wheelchair outside the office. The door was shut, and she could hear Bernard speaking.

'I think we should let Wilma make that decision,' he said. 'Frank, do you agree?'

'Wil—'

'Of course,' interrupted the Reverend. 'But I suspect the Spider will have other ideas.'

Wilma felt a twitching in her eyes. *That slippery limey son of a . . .* Grasping the door handle, she entered the office, her eyes fixing on the Reverend. 'And what ideas—'

She paused.

Her stomach churned.

The stench . . .

Wilma's hand flew to her nose and mouth. 'Urrgh!' She

wobbled on her feet and steadied herself against the door.

Terence's stiff body was standing upright against the desk, with both arms sticking out, as if he was ready to embrace her. 'The smell!' she squeaked, backing swiftly out of the room, gasping for clean air.

The others followed her out. Frank shut the door behind them.

'Wilma?' said Bernard.

Wilma raised her hand, shook her head and took several breaths. What was wrong with her? She'd smelt dozens of rotting corpses in her career. Maybe it was being on this ship, or perhaps it was the stress of the conference crumbling around her.

'Do you need to sit down, dear?' said Frank.

'For Pete's sake, the smell . . .'

'He's never smelt better in my opinion,' said Bernard.

'True,' added Frank.

Wilma turned to the Reverend, 'What ideas of the Spider were you referring to just now?'

The Reverend blinked and looked to Bernard for support. 'It was just we thought she might want to shut down the conference now that there's been a second murder.'

'Who is "we"?'

'In truth, Timothy,' said Bernard, 'This was all speculation from you.'

'The conference will not be closing,' said Wilma. 'And that is that.'

The Reverend shrugged and pushed his spectacles up his nose.

'I have spoken with the Spider, and she has provided us with a way to dispose of the body. It will take all four of us to make it happen.' Wilma explained about the wheelchair and room 3.110.

'But, as you pointed out, he's a little ripe,' said Bernard.

'I have an idea for that,' she replied.

'What about his rigor mortis?' the Reverend asked.

'Flex your muscles. You and Bernard can break him into the wheelchair. Frank, I need you to go shopping. We need to disguise him so that he doesn't look so . . . corpsy . . . is that a word?'

'I'm sure it must be, dear,' said Frank.

'We'll need to cover his eyes with some dark glasses, maybe a hat, a scarf, and some air freshener. Got that?'

'Glasses, hat, scarf, air freshener.'

'Four things . . . just four things.'

'Got it.'

'Quick as you can. We need to move while the next talk is on.'

As Frank hurried away, Wilma turned to Bernard and the Reverend, 'Let's get him into the wheelchair.'

Wilma stood outside the office keeping guard and occasionally peering inside for a progress update and to hurry them along. It took the best part of a long twenty minutes for the two men using all their strength to bend Terence's knees and back before seating him in the wheelchair. Bernard and the Reverend had removed their jackets and were sweating and out of breath. With the problem of rigor mortis, there was also an added complication. Terence's arms were sticking out as if he were about to take flight.

'What happened to his arms?'

Bernard took a large, creased handkerchief from his pocket, shook it out and wiped his forehead. 'I think, Wilma, Terence is still in there and is trying to make it as difficult for us as he can.'

'I'm back!' came Frank's voice.

Relief surged through Wilma. She turned, gasped, and for a moment didn't recognise her husband. Frank was wearing a large pair of lime-green sunglasses with wipers that swung back and forth. Around his neck were two long feather boas, one purple, the other bright yellow. He was carrying two large shopping bags, one filled with more boas and what looked like party hats. The other bag was from a bakery. 'What the heck, Frank?'

He grinned a stupid smile as his wipers swiped back and forth. 'I have a master plan,' he said.

Ten minutes later, Wilma couldn't quite believe what they were doing, but give Frank his due, he wasn't as dumb as she preferred him to be. They were all wearing cone-shaped, coloured, stripey party hats and feather boas. Terence had two hats on his head, like rabbit ears. Two boas were wrapped around his neck, and he was wearing the wiper sunglasses.

'So, now what?' said Wilma.

Frank had also bought a birthday cake, taken a large scoop of it with his hand and smeared it onto Terence's face. He then licked his fingers. 'We pretend it's his birthday. He's shit-faced—'

'Language!' Wilma admonished.

'Sorry, dear. Terence is three sheets to the wind and sleeping off the whiskey.' Frank had bought a bottle that he had already opened and helped himself to, she noticed. He began pouring it over Terence before splashing it over Wilma, Bernard and the Reverend. Wilma raised her hands to shield off the whiskey, 'Holy mackerel, Frank, will you stop!'

'Give me some of that,' Bernard said, taking the bottle from Frank. 'In for a penny, as they say.'

'Nice cake,' said the Reverend, who had taken a fistful and was shoving it into his mouth.

At that same moment, Frank leant across and smeared Wilma's face with the sweet icing. She shrieked and felt she was losing her mind. 'What's happening?!'

'We're drunk and are simply transporting our inebriated, "unconscious" friend to his cabin so that he may sleep and recover. That's our story.'

Bernard laughed, raised the bottle and smeared his face with cake. 'It's a genius plan,' he said. 'Bravo!'

'What about the air freshener?'

'I couldn't find it. Whiskey seemed like a nice alternative.'

Wilma rolled her eyes. Time was not on their side. Whiskey would have to do.

Flanked by Bernard and Frank, who held down the dead man's open arms, the Reverend gripped the handles and pushed the wheelchair. The squeaking noise seemed more pronounced from the weight of the body. Wilma wondered if it would survive the journey to room 3.110.

Frank began to sing 'Happy Birthday'. Bernard and the Reverend joined in. Wilma hummed along and walked ahead, smiling politely at the stragglers who were running late for the *Meat is Murder* cannibal panel. She saw Kent, standing by the reception desk, face buried in his phone. *Darn it!* Wilma thought. She wanted to tell Frank and the others to be quiet. Maybe they could pass unnoticed by the only other person outside of their group who had seen Terence's dead body.

But it was too late.

Kent peered up from his device with a curious expression. He frowned as he glanced at Terence. Wilma sidestepped into his field of vision and smiled. 'You're missing a fascinating panel discussion, young man.'

Kent shrugged and looked past her for a better view, 'It's not my jam. I'm a pescatarian.' His thin lips parted into a wicked grin. 'Is that—'

Wilma felt her neck flushing red. 'I don't give two hoots what you are! Get into that panel NOW!'

Kent flinched and paled at Wilma's ferocious tone. 'Yes, ma'am. Right away.' He turned and bolted.

'And Kent,' she called after him.

Pausing, he turned to look back at her.

Wilma raised an index finger and made a hushing gesture.

Kent nodded and hurried away.

They exited the conference centre without incident and squeaked their way down the dimly lit, quiet corridor towards the casino. 'The chair is broken,' said the Reverend. 'It's leaning to the right a little too much.'

They stopped several yards before the casino doors and crouched down to examine the right-hand side wheel, which stuck out at an angle more than its left-side equivalent. Bernard shook it. The wheel wobbled.

'Goddarn!' said Wilma.

Bernard pushed it inwards, straightening it. 'Maybe that will do it.'

'Let's hope.'

It was quiet. The only sound was the whirring of Terence's wipers. She looked at him. Behind the ridiculous sunglasses and underneath the smeared cake icing, his face and lips were swollen. She swallowed. 'We need to hurry.'

Huddled around the chair, they stared towards the casino entrance.

'As soon as we get inside, start singing,' said Wilma.

A moment of quiet passed.

'Ready?' said Wilma.

They nodded in unison.

'Go!' said Wilma, hurrying ahead and opening the doors.

The casino was busy as always.

They raised their voices, singing a faux drunken version of

'Happy Birthday' as the Reverend tried his best to push the wheelchair forward.

'Coming through!' Wilma hollered in a jovial voice, channelling Moses parting the Red Sea.

Looking behind her, she saw the Reverend struggling to move the wheelchair. 'Bernard, Frank, help him!' she hissed.

'Is that Terence?' came a man's voice.

Wilma's heart sank.

'Happy Birthday, Terence!' came a second voice.

'Buddy, your face is a bit swollen. Been chewing on a wasp nest?'

It was the two retired policemen that Terence had been playing craps with yesterday.

Wilma's eyes darted from Bernard to the Reverend, and Frank. Their horrified expressions mirrored her own. 'Quickly!' The wheel screeched in protest as Bernard, Frank, and the Reverend tried to push Terence through the casino.

'Hey, wait up!' said one of the men.

Wilma reached for the wheelchair and started pulling it. The others pushed, but it was stiff and wouldn't move.

'Push harder!' she said.

Bernard gave the wheel a sharp kick. It started moving. Relief swamped over her. Letting go of the chair, she resumed her role as Moses. 'Coming through,' she trilled.

Bernard, Frank and the Reverend sang to Terence once more, the wheel's squeaking increasing in pace.

Ahead, she could see the exit. They were almost out. She let out a breath and noticed the squeaking sound had stopped. Behind her, she heard a shuffling noise, peppered with grunting and swearing. She heard the two policeman chuckling. 'Hey, Bob. There's been an accident and our pal, Terence, was driving under the influence. Let's read him his rights.' The two men roared with laughter. Her gaze dropped slowly to the wheelchair. The wheel had come off, and Terence was lying face down on the ground, arms out, knees bent, backside in the air.

The two policemen were hovering beside him. 'Someone had a good time,' the heavy, moustached one said. 'Let's get you up.'

'No!' Wilma cried, startling the two men. 'My husband and our friends will take care of him.' She turned a steely gaze to Frank, Bernard and the Reverend, who seemed like three helpless children. 'Get him out of here!' she hissed through gritted teeth.

'Sure we can't help!' said the heavy cop.

'I'm sure!'

Wilma joined Frank and took Terence's right arm. Bernard and the Reverend took the left, and together they stumbled as swiftly as they could, singing in as cheery a way as their exhausted, spent lungs would allow.

Chapter Thirty-Nine

Martha

With a few hours to kill, and my head full of chaotic theories that generate more questions than I can deal with right now, I take time out and focus on Jacqui's book. I grab my laptop and notes and begin working on the outline. Having been caught red-handed by Jacqui in the casino, I need to magically weave a casino storyline into the plot. I'll figure something out. I can always cut it out later if she doesn't like it. As I start to brainstorm ideas, my encounter with the Reverend Timothy Garland begins to niggle at me. I want to know more about him.

I open Google and start a search.

I find several pictures of church fetes, scenes from village halls, and hospital bedsides in the Images section linked to various Facebook profiles. The Reverend Timothy is smiling benignly with different people from his flock, consisting mainly of middle-aged and older people. I delve deeper, perusing the Facebook profiles, and discover that many of those pictured have passed away from short or sudden illnesses. That in itself is not unusual, but what is remarkable is one common thread: the Reverend was with them in their dying hours. He also, it seems, presided over their burials. I think about the title page of his presentation sheet that I had picked up from the floor this morning: *Finding the Joy in Assisted Dying.* Subconsciously, I had thought it innocuous, perhaps a Christian interpretation of helping a terminally ill person leave this world and go on to the glory of Heaven, or whatever. But then why would the good Reverend be presenting at a true crime convention? Yet, with news of an unnamed body at the conference as well as the murder of Ernest Ridgewell, I can only conclude that the suspiciously secret Midnight Chorus Society conference is not about true crime. What could the alternative be? I have no idea, but I intend to find out.

I grab an early steak and mash dinner at the buffet, accompanied by a bottle of fizzy water to wash it down. No booze, as I want a clear head this evening when I press Zach for info. I see Patty and her douche husband several tables away. With Mr O's attention firmly on his mountain of food, Patty looks across and catches my gaze. I feel for her, for what she witnessed and the gaslighting she's been subjected to by her husband and the *Jewel of the Atlantic* authorities. How alone and frightened she must feel. She gives me a discreet nod. I smile reassuringly at her. Eating swiftly, I leave, feeling more determined than ever to find out the truth about the Midnight Chorus Society and how they are linked to Buttonface.

I shower and blow-dry my hair, fluffing it into shape as best I can. Styling is not my forte, but the result isn't too shabby and will do. I slip carefully into my brand-new, designer red dress, the wonderfully generous gift from Jacqui. The material feels delicate, like soft paper that might tear at any moment, but it is deceptively strong. I stand in front of the mirror and aside from a post-dinner bump in my tummy, which I hope will soon disappear, I almost don't recognise myself. I look taller for some reason. Can an expensive fitted dress do that to you? Maybe it's my hair, which is bigger than usual. That'll be it. I don't have fancy shoes to go with the dress. My Converse trainers are out of the question, so my DMs will have to suffice. I buff them up with a quick polish using a *Jewel of the Atlantic* face cloth from the bathroom and pull them on. I put on my red lace mask and tie the ribbon at the back of my head. I'm in front of the mirror once more. I'm definitely giving off sexy, cocktail-supping, rock chick vibes. That said, my lips are too pale, so I grab the Crimson Lady lipstick from the bathroom. I hesitate before applying, but then think, what the hell.

It's just gone 8.30 p.m. I'm running late as usual. I leave my room and make my way up the corridor, threading my way through couples dressed to the nines in their glad rags with fancy masks. The lifts are crowded, so I take the stairs and emerge on the main deck. The night air is cooler than it has been but is still lovely. Earlier today, the captain had announced a possible change in weather due to an unexpected cold front that could cause the warm air to rise and form towering cumulonimbus clouds along the front. In other words, he added, expect a thunderstorm, a sharp drop in temperature, a significant wind shift, and intense rain.

Oh hurrah!

He also informed us that it could impact the Masquerade Ball, which may be relocated from the upper deck to the Grand Ballroom. Fortunately, the weather has held, and the ball remains on the upper deck. I'm relieved the party is outside but remind myself there is no need to celebrate, considering it is the same spot where Buttonface had sent poor Ernest Ridgewell to his death.

A runway of lights stretches across to the upper deck stairwell. I hear jazz music that evokes the roaring twenties and feel a spring in my step. Looking up, I see some of the crew dressed as flappers dancing in the warm glow of the lamps that crisscross above the heads of the revellers. Someone is watching me as I make my way up. I feel a knot in my tummy. A good knot. Dressed in an expensive fitted tuxedo, wearing a black eye mask with his thick hair combed neatly back, is Zach, giving me Christian Grey vibes. He's standing at a bistro table, holding up a bottle of Champagne and two flutes.

I feel my stomach flutter.

He looks so different.

'For a moment I thought you weren't coming,' he says, smiling.

'It's a lady's prerogative to be fashionably late.'

'You look incredible.'

I feel myself blushing. 'Thank you.'

His smile widens, and I can't peel my eyes away from his sultry lips and gleaming white teeth. Pull yourself together. I need to get over this crush because I have questions.

He hands me a flute of Champagne. 'I'm glad you came.'

'What have I missed?'

'I got here fifteen minutes ago. Nothing so far.'

'So, you were late also?' I say, in a teasing manner.

We clink glasses.

'I had some business to take care of.'

I hold his gaze and think of my conversation with Victor about Wilma. It's not the first time I've heard that expression today. 'How is the world of finance?'

'Soul destroying.'

'Those industry wheels never stop turning.'

'The less said about work, the better. How was your day?'

I shrug, 'It was . . . interesting.'

'Did you make progress on the book?'

'Jacqui and I have been working on the outline. I have to complete it by the time we reach New York or else the publishing deal will fall through.'

'No pressure then.'

The music shifts to a slower rhythm, and we momentarily turn our attention to the party. I try to make out faces behind the masks, but it's tricky, not only because they are masked, but the guests have made an effort with the dressing up. The garish polo shirts, Walmart jeans, faded T-shirts and white socks with sandals have been replaced with smart evening wear. Some of the staff are dressed in Venetian masks, cloaks and hoods, which gives an *Eyes Wide Shut* vibe. I notice Wilma's squat form. She's dressed in a dowdy, heavy green velvet evening gown and is fanning herself with a Venetian mask on a stick. She's watching someone. I follow her gaze and see the brutally thin Priscilla Hefferman texting on her phone. She's wearing a pale lace mask and a long black clingy dress à la Morticia Addams. The captain, dressed in his formal uniform whites with a white eye mask, stands dutifully beside her. Priscilla finishes on her call and focuses her attention our way. She's looking at Zach and then me. I hold her gaze and wonder what she's thinking.

I turn to Zach. He's swaying gently to the music.

Time for me to get to it. 'Hey, have you heard of the Midnight Chorus Society?' I ask.

Leaning in to me, he says, 'The who?'

'The Midnight Chorus Society.'

Refilling our flutes, he frowns and shakes his head. 'Who are they?'

'I'm trying to find out.'

He takes a sip of Champagne and changes the subject, 'This party is something else.'

'Do you know Priscilla Hefferman?' I ask.

He holds my gaze, a puzzled expression on his face.

'Martha!' comes a voice.

I turn to see Jacqui approaching, her mask resembling the

backend of a peacock. She's with Bernard, who is dressed in a dinner suit and a black Venetian mask similar to Wilma's.

'How'd you know it was me?' I say, feigning surprise. 'Must be the dress.'

'Actually, it was the construction worker boots.'

I ignore that comment, gesture to Zach and introduce him.

'Nice to meet you,' she replies, winking at me. 'This is Bernard. He's a dentist and has watched everything I have ever been in. Plus, he loves my teeth.'

'I bet he does,' I say.

'Hallo again, Martha.'

Zach and Bernard shake hands and nod a hello.

'I would love a drink,' says Jacqui.

'Leave it to me,' says Bernard, slipping away.

'Nice to meet you at last,' Jacqui says to Zach. 'Martha can't stop talking about you.'

I feel my face flushing. 'That's not true!'

Zach laughs. 'My mom was a fan of your show,' he says. 'She'd let me stay up and watch it with her sometimes.'

'God, you must have been so young.'

'My dad would be at the bar . . . long story . . . she was alone a lot . . . I wanted to keep her company.'

Peeking through the peacock's feathers, I can see Jacqui's eyes registering that there is more to this brief extract from Zach's childhood. 'That's so sweet,' she says.

Zach says nothing. His moment of reflection seems to have killed the moment. 'Hey, what was your favourite episode?' she asks, brightly.

Zach has no hesitation in answering. 'The one set in the circus. Mom and I loved that episode.'

'The Murder Swing!' I say.

'Everyone loves that episode,' Jacqui says.

'Jacqui did all her own stunts,' I chip in.

'You did?'

Jacqui shrugs as if it's nothing. 'Is your mom here?' she asks.

He hesitates before answering. 'She passed.'

'I'm sorry,' Jacqui says.

'It was a long time ago.'

An awkward silence descends, broken by Bernard, who returns with two martinis. He hands one to Jacqui. 'I'm afraid I must leave you for a short while.'

'Oh?'

'Yes. I have a little something I must take care of.'

'I hope everything is OK,' she says.

'Everything is dandy.' Raising his martini, he clinks Jacqui's glass and knocks back his drink in one swallow.

Jacqui and I exchange a look.

'I will see you all later,' he says.

Zach is checking his phone. I take the opportunity to ask Jacqui privately what she found out from Bernard.

'He laughed and asked how I'd heard of the society. I told him there were Chinese whispers on the ship. He said they were a not-for-profit organisation that meets once a year for networking and talks. Like TED talks, that kind of thing.'

'An organisation that is so private it's practically off grid.'

'I asked about Priscilla Hefferman's involvement. He said she had nothing to do with them, which doesn't surprise me. Cilla would baulk at the idea of being involved with something that does not bring in the dollars.'

I turn to see Bernard make his way across the lighted deck. He's lying. If I wasn't here with Zach, I would follow him, but he'll be back later. I can talk to him then.

Chapter Forty

The Dentist

Bernard exited the Masquerade Ball with a smile on his lips. He had a pleasant buzz from the martini he had just quaffed, and in the company of the enchanting Ms DuLac. She had surprised him when she asked about the Midnight Chorus Society. A 'little birdie' had told her that he was a member. Unfazed, Bernard had been honest about his membership but gave her the stock answer on who the Society were. It was not the first time, nor would it be the last, that curious members of the public would ask him or a colleague questions about the Society. Jacqui had seemed satisfied with his good-natured, seasoned response. If he was not mistaken, she was as charmed by him as he was by her. He was looking forward to returning to the soirée for a dance with her. But, before any of that, he had urgent business to take care of.

It had been a day of drama and dilemmas, navigating Terence Lamb's decaying corpse through several busy public areas of the cruise ship. They had successfully transported the remains through the casino despite a wheel from the wheelchair snapping off, causing the Fool's body to topple over onto the floor. This had brought much unwanted attention from the gambling clientele. Wilma's leadership and quick thinking had spurred

Bernard, the Reverend, and poor old Frank into picking up the corpse under the pretence that they were all intoxicated and were merely helping their unconscious friend to his room. With hardly any breath left for singing, they puffed and panted across the lobby to the elevator, where they made the painfully slow journey upwards to the third floor, crammed into the small space with passengers turning their noses at the Fool's rotting flesh. Bernard would have laughed if he were not so out of breath.

Wilma, on the other hand, was not as insouciant as he was. He had known her for a long time and had never seen her so on edge. It unsettled him, and for good reason. With Ernest and Terence's murders, it was becoming clear that someone was targeting the Society. They all had to be vigilant, she kept reminding them. For someone who had caused so much death in his lifetime, Bernard did not fear his own. His time would come. It was the unavoidable conclusion to everyone's life. Death and taxes, they say. You cannot escape either. The only thing he truly feared was losing his teeth. Not just his own beautiful, small and sharp pearly whites, but his vast collection of jewellery and objets d'art he had created from his victims' extractions: necklaces, bracelets, rings, earrings, tiaras, skull sculptures, lampshades, and small Victorian lady figurines, all constructed from teeth. It was his life's work, and it was more precious to him than his own existence. He hoped that when he was gone, his work would be exhibited in museums and art galleries. That would be his legacy, his gift to the world, and through it all, he would live on.

They had made it without further incident to room 3.110 where they unceremoniously let the corpse fall to the floor. With a hard thud, Terence lay on his back, arms out, dead eyes staring up at the ceiling, the wipers of those ridiculous glasses sweeping back and forth.

The effort of carrying the body had worn them all out, especially Frank, who, to Bernard's surprise, had not collapsed with heart failure. Frank had lain down on the bed to catch his breath. Wilma lay beside him, her expression drawn underneath the dried cake icing.

The Reverend did not stop complaining. He had found the whole situation of his Agony and Ecstasy 'TED Talk' being disrupted as intolerable. 'Even in death, that ignoramus has disrespected me,' he had shrilled. The clergyman kept carping on. Bernard had rolled his eyes and then crouched down beside Terence. He parted his stiff, swollen lips with his fingers and examined his teeth. *Interesting.* He did not much care for the Fool or the Reverend, yet he understood this was a time for unity and harmony. 'My dear Reverend, our poor colleague has been murdered. Perhaps offer up some prayers to your god,' he said, wiping his fingers with a handkerchief.

'I doubt prayers will help that sinner now,' he replied.

Bernard regarded him with a curious expression. 'And what of you? Will prayers save you when your time comes?'

'Unlike the Fool, my work has hastened the departure of the old and infirm from this world to a better one.'

'That's one way to look at it.'

'You're sniping at each other. Stop!' said Wilma.

The Reverend sighed and rubbed his temple. 'I need to lie down. I'm getting one of my heads.'

'Maybe pray the pain away,' said Bernard.

With a plan in place for the evening disposal, they had each left for their own rooms. Wilma had entrusted Bernard with the key. It was his job to lead the charge and ensure the job was done without any hiccups.

Bernard took the stairs down to the third floor and made his way back to room 3.110. He was scheduled to meet Frank and the Reverend in fifteen minutes, but he was early. He had one final appointment with the Fool before saying goodbye forever.

He let himself inside the room and shut the door behind him. Removing the wallet containing his tools from his jacket pocket, he swiftly knelt beside Terence's head and got to work. Using both his thumbs, Bernard pushed up Terence's top lip and examined his teeth for the second time that day. They were a mixed bunch: chipped, uneven, caffeine-stained, riddled with tartar and bits of rotting meat. The molars were mostly gone, cleanly extracted years ago, by the look of it. The incisors and canines were interesting. They were in decent enough shape and could be easily used for something after a spit and polish. Removing the pliers from the wallet, Bernard gripped the front right tooth and, holding down the Fool's forehead, began to pull. Several strenuous minutes passed, sweat formed on Bernard's face, yet the tooth showed no sign of coming out. 'Holy shit.' Bernard gripped the pliers with both hands and tugged furiously so much so that Terence's head pounded on the floor. 'I'm getting too old for this.'

A knock came on the door.

Exasperated but also half relieved, Bernard pulled the duvet from the bed and covered the body. With the stealth of a cat, he made his way to the door and peered through the peephole.

It was only Frank.

Wiping his brow with the back of his hand, Bernard opened the door. 'Come in,' he said, scanning the hallway behind his elderly friend.

'Is everything OK?' Frank asked. 'I heard banging and was worried.'

'Nothing to worry about. I need your help,' said Bernard, removing his dinner jacket.

Frank shut the door behind him.

'Could you please hold Terence's head for me?'

Bernard peeled back the duvet. Frank knelt slowly by the Fool's head and, with trembling hands, gripped his temples. Despite his Parkinson's, he was still strong enough to assume the temporary role of Bernard's dental nurse. It took five minutes to remove three incisors and four canines, leaving a congealed bloody mess in Terence's mouth. Bernard held the grubby teeth in his palm. 'Quite the haul, no?'

'Indeed,' smiled Frank.

'The most useful contribution to the Society from Terence yet.'

Frank chuckled. 'You're not wrong there.'

Bernard's fingers were bloodstained. Tipping the teeth onto the desktop, he removed a large handkerchief from his pocket and wiped at the blood, some of which was too dry to clean off. He then placed the teeth inside the handkerchief, folded it and slipped it into his jacket pocket. 'Thank you, my dear friend.'

There was another knock on the door.

Bernard and Frank exchanged a look.

Frank peered through the peephole. 'It's the limey,' he said, opening the door.

The Reverend entered and frowned at Terence, his mouth open wide in a bloody, toothless, silent scream. 'Oh my God! Have you no shame?'

Bernard shrugged. 'What can I say? I'm a collector.'

The Reverend sighed and shook his head. 'Let's get this over with,' he said, crossing the room and sliding open the balcony door. Damp, cool air filled the room. In the short time that Bernard had been here, the evening had grown darker, the sky bustling with a herd of ominous black clouds.

'I'll take the middle,' said Bernard. 'Reverend, you take the head, and Frank, you take the feet.'

Frank nodded agreeably, crouched down, and looped his arms under the ankles.

'No, I'll take the middle,' said the Reverend, grimacing at the dead man's mouth.

'As you wish.' With everyone in position, Bernard gave the count of three, and they lifted the Fool for one final time. Bernard led them to the balcony, eyes scanning above and around. As Wilma had been instructed, this was a private area. Groaning with the effort, they lifted the corpse to the balcony rail and let it slide over.

They watched as Terence's body plummeted to the choppy dark waters of the Atlantic below.

'Fangs very much for the teeth!' Bernard called.

As the ship sailed away, the Fool's body rolled gracelessly across the surf before vanishing, sinking to its forever watery grave.

Chapter Forty-One

Martha

Zach finishes on the phone and taps it on his chin, lost in his thoughts.

'Everything OK?' I ask.

He turns to me with a half-smile, 'Everything's fine.'

I nod, knowing that it's not.

Pocketing his phone, he says, 'Would you excuse me for one moment?'

'Of course,' I say, a thread of anxiety weaving inside me.

I watch him navigate his way through the revellers and make his way to Priscilla Hefferman.

I hold my breath.

'Does he know Cilla?' Jacqui asks, swiping a glass of Champagne from a waiter's tray.

I look at them, try to read the body language and understand the dynamic. 'I guess so.'

'Good evening, ladies,' comes Todd Atkins's baritone voice.

Jacqui smiles demurely and returns the greeting, like she's a grand dame standing at the edges of the dance floor in an episode of *Bridgerton*. Todd is dressed in a smart, fitted dinner suit, complete with a black bow tie and a simple matching mask.

He puts me in mind of a wealthy villain's bodyguard from a Bond movie. 'Hi,' I say, snatching glances at Zach.

'You both look very well. I trust you're enjoying the party,' he says.

'It's nice to have some glamour,' Jacqui says.

'Indeed,' says Todd.

'Wait,' says Jacqui, 'Didn't you drag Martha kicking and screaming to the brig?'

I roll my eyes.

Todd glances at me with a wry smile. 'Not quite how I would characterise it.'

'She's not easy to deal with. Trust me. I know.'

From underneath my mask, I give Jacqui the iciest of stares.

'Can I get you both something to drink?' he asks.

I hold up my half full glass of bubbles. 'Still working on this.'

'I'm good for the moment,' Jacqui says.

Zach returns with a smile, 'Hey,' he says.

'Hey,' I say back, and finish my Champagne.

'I'll leave y'all to it,' says Todd, moving on to talk to the next guest.

Bernard returns. I notice his fingers are a bit red. 'I'm back,' he says. 'Did you miss me?'

As Jacqui and Bernard reacquaint, Zach and I give them space. 'Your glass is empty,' he says.

'I don't need any more,' I say, placing the glass on the table.

'Security giving you a hard time?'

'He was just saying hello.'

I see Bernard taking a glass of red wine that a cloaked waiter had just passed to him. He takes a sip of it as the music tempo begins to build. I notice something floating in the glass but think nothing of it.

'Why did you ask about Priscilla?' Zach asks, quietly.

Behind the mask, I can't read his expression, but I can see hurt in his eyes that confuses me. 'It's nothing,' I say, but he holds my gaze for a moment, then looks away and takes a large swig from his glass.

'Oh my God, Bernard. Are you OK?' I hear Jacqui cry.

I turn to see Bernard trembling, his face pale and beaded with sweat. His hand closes tightly like a fist over his glass of red, shattering it into shards and spilling the wine over his fingers. In the palm of his other hand, he holds a red button, smeared with wine.

'Someone call 911!' cries Jacqui, taking his elbow.

Bernard clutches his chest, his face turning a dangerous shade of red. Slowly, he turns to look behind him, but stumbles, knees weakening.

I see Wilma pushing her way through the crowd. 'Bernard!' she cries.

'Are any of you a doctor?' I call, but no one hears me above the din.

'I'll go find someone!' says Jacqui, a tremble in her voice.

I nod, feeling her fear, her terror.

Bernard falls backwards. Zach catches him and eases him gently to the floor.

Wilma kneels beside him and places her palm on his head. 'Everything will be fine,' she says.

A crowd begins to gather around us, stifling the air. 'Stand back!' I cry.

I crouch beside Zach, who is loosening Bernard's tie. 'We need a doctor.'

'Jacqui's on it.'

'He's burning up,' says Wilma.

Beneath his mask, I can see Bernard's eyes are wide open, and I am grateful he's wearing it because I have a feeling this is not going to end well. He makes a loud gurgling noise, and seconds later, the trembling stops, and his eyes . . . his eyes . . .

A moment of silence passes.

'He's gone,' says Zach, quietly.

Bernard's arm slides to the floor. Something slips from his hand and clatters across the surface. It's the red button. I lock my gaze on it. My stomach drops. A smiley face has been daubed on it. Picking it up, I stand and shiver, despite the warmth.

'Martha,' says Zach, taking my hand.

'Bernard was looking for someone.' I say, scanning the crowd. 'Just now, while he was choking, he looked back at someone.'

One by one, I pick through the masked revellers and the staff. And then I see him. A cloaked figure navigating his way through the throng. I follow him as he heads towards the stairwell. And then he turns, and in a fleeting moment, I see him, his buttonface mask half concealed under the hood.

A fire rages inside me. 'BUTTONFACE!' I shout.

He hesitates.

And then runs.

'STOP HIM!'

'Martha, what's going on?' says Zach.

'He killed Bernard!' I say, tears filling my eyes. 'And my dad.'

Zach's eyes flare. He turns his gaze to Buttonface with hawk-like precision and then takes off, pushing the gathering crowd out of his way.

Buttonface slides down the stairwell, leaps onto the deck and trips, but rolls and hauls himself up. He's running, cloak flapping in the breeze, but Zach is fast, closing in on him. My heart is in my mouth as I watch Zach leap into the air and tackle him to the floor. They crash into a stack of sun loungers and topple them over. Zach has him in a wrestling hold, his arms wrapped around Buttonface's chest, his legs pinning him down. I fear for him until I see the crew running to help and realise everything will be OK.

Chapter Forty-Two

Martha

The blood thrums in my ears as I hurry down the steps and race back through the runway of lights. Rain is spitting, cooling my hot face. Dressed in his black dinner suit, mask discarded, Todd Atkins overtakes me and barrels ahead, barking out orders to the crew and the dour-faced Deputy Gomez, who has restrained the struggling Buttonface.

I see Zach reach for Buttonface's mask.

'Do not touch that mask!' shouts Todd.

Why the hell not? But it's too late.

I slow down my pace and let the world stand still for a moment as I take him in. He has a slim build, his hair is black, and his eyes are dark and wide with fear. 'Please, no . . . I didn't do nothing . . .' he says with an accent, and broken English. I can't quite believe I'm looking at the man who murdered my dad. My stomach is churning, and I can taste bile. My head begins to spin as I feel a Pandora's box of suppressed emotions burst open inside me: despair, heartbreak . . . love . . . hate, all fuel to a fire that roars through every fibre of my being. 'You killed my dad!' I cry, breathlessly, over and over. Somewhere above my hysteria, I think I hear Zach say my name, but I can't be sure. My head is all over the place. I run at Buttonface, my fists clenched, tears pooling in my eyes, but Zach blocks my path, opening his arms and wrapping them around me. I don't try to resist his warm, comforting grip. 'They have him,' he says.

'Get out of my way!' Priscilla Hefferman's imperious voice cuts through the chuntering of the gathering crowd. 'Mr Atkins, what is the meaning of this?'

'It seems we have a situation,' Todd replies.

'You don't say!' Priscilla replies brusquely. 'Who is this man?'

'His name is Lev Kaplan. He . . . works below deck, ma'am.'

'One of ours!' I hear her mutter obscenities. 'Get him out of here!' she hisses.

'Take him to the brig,' Todd tells his deputy.

'No!' cries Buttonface. 'Please . . . no . . . I do nothing!'

I watch Lev Kaplan, the man who murdered my father, being hauled away. I want to follow and scream at him and then ask him why he did it, but I know they will not let me anywhere near him. That confrontation is for another time.

'Martha, are you OK?' comes Jacqui's voice.

I turn to see her and Rudy fixing me with curious stares. Jacqui is no longer wearing her feather mask. The devoted Rudy is fanning her with it. There are worry creases on her brow, which makes me wonder if she needs a Botox refresh. The truth is, I don't know how I feel other than totally overwhelmed. 'I . . . I think so. . . . I'm not sure.'

'Was that the guy that did Ernest Ridgewell?' Rudy whispers, making a throat-cutting gesture with his free hand.

'He killed my dad, too,' I say.

'I'm so sorry. A serial killer travelling on the *Jewel*. Must be a first,' says Rudy.

I feel an ache in my palm and I realise I'm still squeezing it like a fist. I open it and look at the red button with the twisted smiley face inside.

'Creepy.' says Rudy.

I close my fingers around it, concealing it from sight.

'Mr Turner!' comes Priscilla's voice.

Rudy flinches and jumps to her attention, 'Mrs Hefferman.'

I feel Zach's hold on me loosening.

'A man has been taken ill and has unfortunately passed away. That's our story,' she says. 'Please take those passengers who wish to continue partying out of the rain to the Atlantic Ballroom. The bar tab is on me. I want happy customers, Mr Turner. See to it.'

'Yes, ma'am,' he replies as he begins to shepherd the passengers to the ballroom with the promise of free booze.

'Miss Hammond,' says Todd. 'Could you please come with me. I'd like to ask you some questions.'

'I'm coming too,' says Zach.

'And me!' says Jacqui.

'That won't be necessary. I will look after her,' Todd says.

Jacqui squeezes my arm and winks furtively at me. 'I'll turn in for the night. Contact me if you need anything.'

'Likewise,' says Zach.

I thank them both and tell them I will be in touch later.

I catch Jacqui and Priscilla looking at each other. Priscilla is firing daggers, and Jacqui has a wonderfully smug expression. 'I'd wish you luck cleaning up this mess, but I'm sure you won't need it. You of all people know, money is the salve for all sins, and you have a shitload of both.'

Priscilla's eyes flare, her hands bunch into fists. That hit a nerve. Bravo Jacqui.

The deck is almost clear of passengers. A few crew members are cleaning up nearby, restacking the sun loungers. Todd is talking to Priscilla. On the upper deck, I see the medics covering Bernard's body with a blanket, and feel a pang of sympathy, despite never feeling entirely comfortable in his presence. Descending the stairwell is Wilma, who is looking our way.

I hear Priscilla say to Todd. 'Bernard Koch has been sick for some time.'

'Did you know him well?' I ask her.

She frowns at me, doesn't answer and looks beyond me. 'Here's Wilma. She has known Bernard for years.'

I glance back to see Wilma approach trepidatiously.

'Wilma, dear. Poor Bernard has been unwell, hasn't he?'

A flash of uncertainty crosses Wilma's face. She pauses, looks at Priscilla and then at Todd. 'Yes. I'm afraid so,' she says.

Priscilla is already rewriting the truth about Bernard's death. I'm not going to let her get away with it. 'What was wrong with him?' I ask.

All eyes turn to look at me.

Priscilla smiles icily. 'And you are?'

'Martha Hammond.'

'Miss Hammond claims to have information on the suspect,' says Todd.

'There is no suspect,' says Priscilla.

'Bernard Koch was murdered! Like Ernest Ridgewell, and my dad!'

Her eyes harden. 'Silly girl. Quite the imagination.'

'You need to contact the police,' I tell her.

'What makes you think I haven't?'

'Did you tell them that Ernest Ridgewell was murdered?'

She laughs flippantly. 'Mr Ridgewell took his own life. We have spoken to several of his colleagues, including Wilma. They have confirmed he was a manic depressive and mentally unstable. Isn't that right, Wilma?'

Wilma is looking at me with dark, almost predatory eyes. 'That's correct.'

'You're wrong.' I point in the direction where they took the killer. 'That man is the Buttonface killer, a monicker coined by the press. Original, I know. Thirteen years ago, he murdered my dad. After the welcome party, a witness saw him push Ernest Ridgewell to his death. On my phone, I have a photo of blood from the Upper Deck where he was assaulted. He has just murdered Bernard. He is a serial killer.'

An unsettling silence descends.

'That's quite an accusation,' says Priscilla.

'I can prove it.'

'How?' Todd asks.

I show them the button. 'This was in Bernard's wine, which I suspect was poisoned. It's the killer's calling card. The police found one of these with my dad's body. I wouldn't be surprised if Ernest Ridgewell had one on his person, too.'

I notice a twitch in Wilma's eye.

'Mr Atkins, escort Miss Hammond downstairs and take her statement,' says Priscilla.

'Yes, ma'am.' Todd turns to me. 'Please come with me.'

Priscilla and Wilma turn to leave.

'What about the body at the Midnight Chorus Society convention?' I say.

Both women stop but don't turn round.

'What body?' asks Todd, his face a picture of confusion.

'I've heard enough nonsense, Mr Atkins. Do your job!' says Priscilla.

I seethe as I walk beside him towards the entrance to the staircase and lifts. Priscilla and Wilma are lying. I wonder if there is more to this than protecting Priscilla's empire. I don't know her or Wilma's connection to Buttonface, but I intend to find out.

All of these murders have involved members of the Midnight Chorus Society. But why? I glance back and see them both watching me. I feel the small hairs on the back of my neck rising. Despite my bravado, I get the sense that I have overstepped the mark with these two formidable, dare I say it, dangerous women. To my left, I notice someone dart out of sight behind a stack of sun loungers. As Todd heads to the stairwell, I make out a familiar figure peeking across at me. Jacqui, channelling Cassie Kowalski, is lurking behind the loungers. She has been listening in and has heard everything. 'Call me,' she mouths. I nod and feel relieved that, despite our rocky relationship, she is probably the only friend I have on this ship. As much as I have a massive soft spot for Zach, something tells me to keep my distance. I still don't know what he was doing in Priscilla's suite and what his connection is to her.

Todd removes his dinner jacket and sits me at his desk in his compact, windowless office. My legs are crossed, my arms folded. He rests his thick forearms on the surface and places one hand on top of the other. 'Seems like we're really getting to know one another,' he says, his expression deadpan.

'It's been a blast.'

He arches a brow. 'Miss Hammond, I want you to know I'm on your side.'

'I'm on the side of truth, not the side of protecting your boss's business.'

'My job is to protect and serve the people on this boat. Every one of them. Even those being accused of murder.'

'I want to talk to him.'

He regards me momentarily, a wry smile on his lips. 'You remind me of someone.'

I glance at the key cabinet. The Brig key is missing. 'Deputy Gomez must be helping him settle into his suite. Why don't we go there now? I only need five minutes.'

'I think you know that's not going to happen.'

'He killed my father.'

'How certain are you it was him?'

'He was wearing the same mask.'

'Anyone can wear a mask.'

'It's him . . . it has to be . . .'

'Miss Hammond . . . may I call you Martha?'

'We really are getting to know one another.'

'You've made some serious accusations.'

'Who are the Midnight Chorus Society?'

'I am not at liberty to talk about them.'

I lean forward. 'Why?'

He sighs and folds his arms. 'I'm gonna be straight with you. I don't know anything about them. I am under contract not to ask questions about them. Telling you this could get me fired.'

'Ernest Ridgewell and Bernard, both members of the Society, have been murdered. A third person, as yet unnamed, is dead.'

'How do you know that?'

'A member of the Society told me.'

Todd's brow creases. 'Which member?'

I hesitate before answering. I could get Victor into trouble. Actually, do I care? 'His name is Victor Fryer. Looks like a Mormon, but I suspect he's not. Carries a Bible with a knife inside. Seems nice though, if not a little weird.'

He sighs. 'Martha, I'd like you to return to your room, get some sleep, and let me do my job.'

'When are you going to talk to Lev Kaplan?'

'Not tonight.'

'Tomorrow?'

'Yes.'

'When tomorrow?'

'Martha—'

'Please just tell me,' I plead.

After a moment's hesitation, he says, 'First thing.'

'And you'll let me know what he says?'

He drops his head.

'Please. I've lived with my dad's murder for thirteen years. The fact that his killer is here, in the next room, blows my mind.'

He pauses before answering. 'I will let you know how it goes.'

'And the society. Are you going to investigate them?'

'One step at a time.'

I wasn't sure whether to trust Todd, but I've changed my mind. I do think he's on the right side. Before I exit his office, I ask, 'You said I remind you of someone. Who?'

'My niece. She's the type of person to ask the wrong questions, stick her nose where it shouldn't be, kick a hornet's nest, you get the idea? I love her very much, but she's a handful.'

'I'll take that as a compliment.'

Chapter Forty-Three

Wilma

Wilma sat on the balcony outside her room, wrapped in a cosy blanket, watching the sunrise in the east. The Spider's WhatsApp message had just come through. She'd read it, sighed and placed her phone back on the small table. Blades of sunlight sparkled on the ocean's surface, stabbing at her eyes. She turned away from the glare. She had not slept and had spent the entire night sitting in this exact spot. On his many nighttime trips to the bathroom, Frank had popped his head out to check on her. Wilma had told him she was fine and that he ought to go get some shut-eye but, being stubborn as a mule, he just stood there quietly looking at her. He knew she wasn't fine. He knew the truth about the woman he'd loved for forty years. It had happened around the time of their twentieth anniversary. A spark had ignited between her and Bernard when they first met. Her husband could see it, and Frank, being all docile and obedient, just let it be. And then one day, Wilma and Bernard just fell into each other's arms. It was a simple as that. The love they had shared was brief but passionate, nonetheless. It couldn't last because Wilma believed in marriage, and she was devoted to Frank. Theirs was an unbreakable bond. Yes, Frank might be docile and obedient, but at nighttime when they hunted, he became something wild and untamed. They were two lone alpha wolves, hunting together for life. What they had together was her reason for living.

Yet Bernard's murder had left her broken. She was wallowing in unfamiliar territory, feeling emotions that were alien to her. Was this how people felt when a loved one was taken from them? Wilma had ended the lives of many people in her career, but she had never once thought about how her victims' families and friends must feel. In the quiet calm of the morning, Wilma considered her own emotions. Specifically, whether or not she had any. Happiness was a mystery to her. Happy people seemed to smile a lot and were jolly. Wilma did smile, but it was never an expression of happiness. It was typically an expression of satisfaction, a job well done, such as a successful murder. Wilma couldn't recall the last time she'd been jolly, or even if she ever had been. As a child, she'd been dour, remote and friendless. Her parents had never taken much interest in her. She grew up fending for herself, had learnt independence from a young age and often believed that her parents' neglect had shaped her into the woman she was today. No, emotions were few and far between. Yet this unsettling, deep sadness born from Bernard's horrible death was new to her. That emotion was battling with a familiar adversary. Anger. There was a lot of that in Wilma's life. And right now, she burnt inside with the purest of rages. She wanted revenge, and she would darn well get it.

It was time to go.

Unfurling the blanket, she folded it neatly and placed it on top of the table. She could hear the quiet hum of Frank's snoring, and trod carefully into their bedroom. Slipping out of the velvet gown, she selected a bottle-green blouse, a long grey cardigan and a pair of stretchy jeans from the wardrobe. Five minutes later, dressed and hair combed, Wilma slipped out the door and made her way across the ship to the Spider's lair.

Priscilla's maid, Margery, a five-foot ancient husk of a woman with a low brow and a sour face, answered the Presidential Suite door. 'Madam will receive you in the dining room,' she said before Wilma could open her mouth.

She followed Margery across the expansive suite. The stepped ceiling glowed softly as the first sunbeams caught the brass trim. Walls of rich walnut and ebony warmed beneath the rising light, while frosted glass sconces, unlit and pale, seemed to fade into the glow of day. The garish rug, patterned in sharp zigzags of ivory and jet, appeared alive, like a flat zebra, as the light shifted, echoing the rhythm of the sea beyond the glass. Crystal chandeliers tinkled as they swayed gently with the ship's motion, scattering shards of light across bronze statuettes poised on their pedestals. Wilma had been in awe of this old-world style interior when she first set eyes on it. But now she detested it and yearned to be at home sitting comfortably on the well-worn floral sofa with her slippered feet resting on the braided rug. She missed her hardwood side tables, crocheted doilies, lighthouse prints, and Victorian figurines, made by Bernard. But most of all she missed the nocturnal hunting, albeit she, and Frank more so, were getting too long in the tooth for that kind of physicality.

Priscilla was sitting alone at the head of a long, glossy table, scrolling on her phone with one hand and sipping coffee from a china cup with the other. She did not look up. Margery waited. Wilma seethed, impatient at this pointless display of power play.

Margery coughed politely.

'What is it?' Priscilla asked curtly.

Wilma replied before Margery could answer. 'I'm here as you requested. So, talk,' she said, making her way to where the Spider was sitting. Wilma sat diagonally opposite her. She had the sense that she was approaching the point of no return. What did it matter now that the sacred rule of conference had been broken not once but three times? The truth was they were all up the creek without a paddle. Therefore, if the Spider so much as raised her voice or shot a cuss word her way, Wilma would pluck the knife from the sleeve of her cardigan and swiftly draw the blade across the Spider's skinny, white throat.

Priscilla watched her through thin eyes before waving Margery away.

'Coffee. Black,' said Wilma.

Margery hesitated, eyes shifting to her mistress for approval.

Priscilla nodded, sipped her coffee and returned to her phone.

They sat in silence as Margery returned struggling with a heavy antique silver pot. She poured Wilma's coffee into a cup that matched the Spider's before topping up her mistress's.

'I was thinking about your last husband,' Wilma said. 'He died of a heart attack, brought on by Vesperine, you said.'

Priscilla's jaw tightened. She glared at Margery. 'Leave!' she snapped.

It pleased Wilma to see the Spider rattled.

'What the hell are you playing at mentioning that drug in front of the help?!'

'You call it a drug. Most people would call it a poison.'

'What's your point?'

'Last night I was thinking about our conversation at the funeral of your dearly departed . . .' Wilma tried to recall his name. '. . . You know what, there's been so many I just don't remember his name.'

'Jeffrey.'

'That's him.'

'Vesperine, you said. Colourless, almost tasteless, dissolves instantly. It works well in red wine because the tannic bitterness masks the faint metallic tang. Within minutes, the victim becomes dizzy, flushed, and then collapses as if from sudden heart failure.'

Priscilla laughed mockingly. Wilma's fingers brushed the firm handle of the knife under the wool of her cardigan. 'I smelt the remaining shards from Bernard's glass. There was something not right about them. And then I remembered.'

Priscilla pushed her chair from the table and stood up. 'Your emotions are clouding your judgement.'

Wilma sprung forward, whipped out the knife and held it an inch from the Spider's throat. Priscilla pursed her lips. 'Really? Is this where we are now?'

Wilma stiffened suddenly as the sharp blade of cold steel sank into the soft flesh of her throat. 'Drop the knife, bitch!' said Margery.

Wilma met Priscilla's cold gaze.

'I should do what she says. Margery is not as merciful as I am. Besides, I don't want blood on this rug. It's silk and costs thousands of dollars.'

Margery's bony, claw-like hand groped Wilma's and snatched the knife from her. 'Sit down!' she hissed.

Wilma did as she was told. She glanced at Margery who was holding a Japanese chopper as big as her head. 'She knows about us?' Wilma asked.

'Of course.'

'But when I mentioned the Vesperine?'

'Margery has been by my side for a long time. We've enjoyed disposing of my husbands, haven't we Marge?'

Margery grunted.

Priscilla sat back down. 'For your information, Vesperine is easy to acquire on the Dark Web. I didn't kill Bernard. Why on earth would I? I was actually quite fond of the old bastard.'

'Then who did?'

'As yet, I don't know. But at the centre of this mystery is Jacqui DuLac and that little whore that works for her. We can salvage this monumental fuck-up with their help. So, do you want to hear my plan?'

Wilma hesitated. What choice did she have? 'I'm listening.'

As Priscilla explained her strategy, Wilma smiled for the first time in days. At last, she was beginning to see a light at the end of this voyage of the damned.

Chapter Forty-Four

Martha

I barely slept the whole night, which came as no surprise considering Bernard's murder by Buttonface, AKA cruise employee, Lev Kaplan. The curtains were tightly drawn; the only light was the soft red glow from the bedside digital clock. It was 6:59, but it felt much earlier, like 4:59. My body was a leaden weight as if gravity had doubled down. Pushing myself out of bed, I stretched and thought more about Lev Kaplan. I still had no idea why he had targeted the Midnight Chorus Society. It bugged me that I still didn't know much about them. There was more to them than they wanted us to believe. Whatever that was, I intended to find out. I just needed to get my body and head together.

As I shower, I close my eyes and fantasise about taking over the interrogation of Kaplan, as if I were a kick-ass, no-nonsense undercover detective, like Cassie Kowalski. I imagine I'm dressed in a fitted, navy power suit. Arriving at Todd's office, I thank him for his co-operation and ask his dimwit deputy to fetch me a coffee before unlocking the brig and entering alone, fearless and ready for Buttonface's confession, the easy way or the hard way.

The unmasked killer is chained to a metal table. He watches

me with hooded eyes as I enter. I hold his gaze without blinking. 'It's taken me thirteen years to catch up with you,' I say out loud, rinsing the shampoo from my hair.

Arching his brows, he smiles darkly. His 'Please, I do nothing' innocent act pushed aside because he knows I mean business.

'Why'd you do it?' I ask.

He regards me curiously, a smug smile on his lips. 'But I don't do nothing,' he says, mocking me with that fake accent.

'You murdered my dad,' I say, hearing the faintest of cracks in my voice. 'You ended his life. He had so much to live for.'

'Please—'

I bang my fist on the table and lean in to his face. 'You're going down for a long, long time, mister!'

I hear my phone ringing from the bedroom and wonder if it's Todd, calling with an update. Sliding the shower door open, I grab a towel and pull it around myself to stave off the chill from the air-conditioning. Jacqui's name is on my screen. I swipe to answer. 'Morning.'

'Hey, how are you?' she asks.

'I'm OK.'

'Did you sleep?'

'Not really.'

'That's too bad.'

'Yeah . . . thanks.'

'It's raining outside, so no power walking. I'm going to the gym instead. Do you want to come? You can update me.'

'I'm allergic to gyms. I'll sit this one out.'

'Is that a thing?'

'Yep.'

'OK. Meet me at my suite afterwards. We can go through the outline too. I have some suggestions.'

'OK.'

'9.30 a.m.'

'See you—' Before I can finish, she ends the call. 'Bye . . .' I say, rolling my eyes.

I grab breakfast from the buffet, and as I eat, I keep checking my phone is not on silent and the volume button is turned up. I've done this three times now, desperate as I am not to miss an update from Todd. Sipping my tea, I look around me. The mood is sombre in the restaurant. For good reason. My fellow passengers witnessed a man die last night. They've been fed a lie about a heart attack, of course, but I don't doubt his demise has had an impact on them. If they knew the truth – that a notorious serial killer has been doing his thing during their vacay time – they might flee to their cabins and lock themselves away. Or they might run to the lifeboats and hope he wasn't sitting alongside them. My mind is wandering. It occurs to me that I didn't text Zach last night and feel a twinge of guilt. I was distracted. Who wouldn't be? I did come face to face with the man who killed my dad. That said, he deserved better. Taking out my phone, I compose a text.

Thank you for your White Knight gallantry last night. I'm so, so grateful. My head was all over the place when I got back. Sorry for not reaching out. See you later? M x

The Tannoy bell rings. Captain Perry's voice greets us with a cheery good morning. All I can think about is the murder.

'Ladies and gentlemen, this evening at 9 p.m., we will pass over the waters where the RMS *Titanic* was lost on her maiden voyage in April of 1912. More than 1,500 souls perished there, and the sea has carried their memory ever since. At that time, I will invite you to join me in a brief moment of silence on deck as we honour their courage, their loss, and the reminder that every voyage is both a journey and a fragile gift. I look forward to seeing you all tonight. Have a good day.'

The voices in the restaurant rise to a murmuring hum. I can't determine if it's excitement or terror at the prospect of cruising past the watery grave of 1,500 people honouring one of the most famous, historic tragedies of all time. The captain's announcement has moved me. I had no idea this ceremony was even a thing. It's no secret I was obsessed with the *Titanic* and the lore surrounding it when I saw the movie with my dad all those years ago. I was in love with Jack and Rose's story, although I never quite forgave Rose for not making room for him on that floating door. Despite everything that's been going on, I have every intention of paying my respects and feel a bolt of excitement mixed with awe.

My phone pings with a text from Zach.

I'm the King of the World! It says with two laughing emojis.

I chuckle at Zach's Jack Dawson quote. A second text comes through.

It was my honour. Free at 9 for the Titanic *thing?*

Smiling, I text back: *Paint me like one of your French girls, Zach,* but change my mind, thinking that makes me sound like a gal of 'easy virtue'. I backspace it out and replace it with another movie quote: *I'm flying, Zach!* I send it and follow it up with a second: *Would love to.*

Jacqui is dressed in the ship's monogrammed robe with a towel wrapped around her head like a white turban. She's pulling faces as part of her daily thirty-minute 'Face Gym' routine. As I bring her up to speed I can't help but think of her as a slightly less deranged Norma Desmond waiting for her close-up.

She tries to speak, to ask me something, I think, but what comes out of her mouth mid face-workout is incomprehensible. I gesture to the door, 'Didn't catch any of that. Shall I go look for an interpreter?'

Jacqui thankfully relaxes her face, albeit with a glare. 'I said, I followed them last night after you were dragged off to the slammer for the second time.'

'I wasn't dragged!' I'm not rising to this. 'Who did you follow?'

'Who do you think? Cilla and that creature wearing the repurposed velvet curtains.'

'Wilma?'

'That's her.'

'She's the screamer from the lift.'

'She looked like she was ready to do some screaming last night. I saw them arguing. It was heated but they kept their voices down. I heard a little but not much.' Jacqui left it there and started contorting her face once more.

'What did they say?!'

'They talked about a Terence, whoever that is.'

'You met him before we boarded. Pot-bellied, smells like he sweats cheeseburgers, wears Hawaiian shirts.'

Jacqui curled her lips. 'Oh him. Anyway, apparently, he's "gone".'

'What do you mean "gone"?'

Jacqui shrugs. 'I don't know what that means. He's no longer on the ship is the impression I got.'

'But . . . if there was a medical emergency and he was taken away we would know. There'd be a helicopter or another boat.'

'Who knows. Maybe I was reading too much into it.'

'I don't think so. Another body was discovered at the conference. It must be him.'

'I heard a few other names thrown into the mix.'

'Oh?'

Jacqui levels her gaze at me, her expression serious. 'Yours, and mine.'

I fold my arms. 'That's possibly because I kicked off with Cilla and Wilma.'

'Perhaps. We need to tread carefully. I don't trust Cilla. For years, rumours have circulated about her husbands dying suspiciously. She's ruthless, and it wouldn't surprise me if she had helped them on their way to the promised land.'

This mystery, and everything surrounding the Midnight Chorus Society, was sliding even deeper into a dark pit.

Chapter Forty-Five

Martha

We finished work at lunchtime, at which point Jacqui announced she needed a bout of meat tenderising. And so, she made a call to the Spa and sweet-talked her way into their already packed schedule for hot stones and a massage, before her dinner date with Rudy to discuss her part in tomorrow evening's production of *Murder She Didn't Write*.

I'm back in my room, sitting cross-legged on the bed, staring at my laptop. I'm trying to push away the noise of yesterday's events so that I can concentrate on the outcome of this morning's Detective Cassie Kowalski outline review. Jacqui's suggestions are impressive. She really understands her character and has a clear vision of where she wants to take her, which is not surprising considering she lived and breathed Cassie on the small screen for several years. She did not mince her words when it came to the gambling club scenes that I had clumsily stitched into the plot after she had caught me bunking off work during my Midnight Chorus Society stakeout. Since then, she knew the truth about why I was really there. Yet the uncompromising me kept the scenes in the outline as if to prove the point that I was actually researching and not just spying. She was having none of it. So, the scenes were unceremoniously consigned to the trash. To be honest, I was relieved. They were shoehorned, and they were shit.

It's midafternoon, but you wouldn't know it looking at the sky outside, which is the colour of wet cement. Rain hammers the balcony so hard I half expect it to shatter. I close my laptop and begin pacing, wondering if I should go to Security and find out what was happening with Kaplan.

The knock comes – three sharp raps. Serious. Official. Definitely not room service.

I open the door to find Todd Atkins, looking grim and about as cheerful as a locked safe.

'The rain getting to you?' I ask.

'May I come in?' he says, voice low, steady. Todd Atkins, I decide, could probably deliver a hostage negotiation and a weather report in the same tone.

'Take a pew,' I say.

His mouth opens, he gives me a quizzical look, 'What now?'

Not this again. 'A seat.'

'Right. Thank you, but I can't stay.' He plants himself by the desk, hands behind his back, like a soldier reporting to an invisible general.

I sense bad news. 'I think you're about to ruin my day,' I tell him.

'Kaplan's story checks out.'

My stomach clenches. 'What do you mean his story checks out? How?!'

'He claims he was ordered to wear the mask and deliver the drink to Bernard Koch. Two witnesses verify his story.'

'Who ordered him?'

'Another staff member. They were masked also. Before you

ask, we don't know who it could be, or if it was a member of the crew or someone pretending to be one.'

'What about my dad's murder?'

Todd sighs. 'I checked his passport. He has never been to the US.'

My head spins as I try to process this. I take a pew and sit on the edge of the bed. 'He was set up.'

'It would seem so.'

I hug my chest and look at the floor.

'He's been released, Todd continues, 'but confined to his quarters.'

'So, the killer is still wandering around the ship.'

Todd says nothing to this. I look at him. 'You need to warn the passengers.'

Todd shifts on his feet, 'Mrs Hefferman—'

'You cannot trust her!'

'Martha—'

'She and Wilma Franklin are part of a shady society, whose members are being murdered one by one. They know more than you think they do. You need to talk to them.'

'I spoke to Mrs Franklin and Mrs Hefferman this morning. They strongly disagree with your accusations.'

'Of course they do. Does Mrs Hefferman even care that people have been murdered on her ship?'

'Mrs Hefferman does not believe the deaths of Mr Koch and Mr Ridgewell are foul play.'

'The man who killed my dad is a serial killer. More people are going to die before we reach New York!'

He pauses before replying. 'For what it's worth, I'm keeping an open mind and will investigate further. My advice to you, Martha, is to let me do my job and don't interfere.'

I'm relieved to hear him say that. 'I wouldn't dream of it,' I say.

Todd holds my gaze with an unconvinced expression. He clearly doesn't believe me and is right not to.

It's almost 9 p.m. by the time I arrive on the deck. It's gloomy outside, and nippy. The surface is wet and slippery, but thankfully, the downpour has diminished to a drizzle. A line of flickering candles runs along the deck, lighting a narrow path towards the starboard rail. The small flames fight for life against the sea breeze. A crowd is gathering. Hovering on the perimeter, dressed in a brown suede bomber jacket, is Zach, holding two takeaway cups. He smiles at me. I wave, smile back, and hurry towards him.

'One Americano,' he says, handing me a cup.

'That's so thoughtful. Thank you.'

'How was your day?'

I don't want to dampen the mood with Todd's news about Kaplan, so I affect an upbeat, positive tone and make a typing gesture with my free hand. 'Good. You know me, a slave to my art.' I cringe inside at how wanky that sounded.

'It's so awesome you're a writer. I love books and can't wait to read it.'

'I saw you reading on the train that day.'

'Yeah. I was reading Truman Capote's *In Cold Blood* again.'

'Again?'

'I've read it nine times.'

'Oh wow. I've read it five times. You win.'

His hands cup the mug for warmth. I catch a brief flicker of pain on his face. 'I read it over and over,' he says quietly. 'Not because of the story, but because I wanted to understand how someone gets there. How a person like that thinks. Every line about Perry Smith, I kept seeing my mom's killer in his place. It was like if I could figure out why he did it, I might stop replaying the night she died.'

We say nothing. I look out at the dark stretch of sea beyond the ship.

I feel his gaze on me. 'Did you read it for the same reason?'

'I suppose I did,' I say. 'But I didn't stop there. I went deeper and read every true crime book I could get my hands on and watched every documentary and listened to every podcast. I wanted to know what separates them from us. The ones who cross the line and the ones who don't.' I pause. 'My dad's murder made me curious in a way that never went away. It made me who I am. Understanding them became the only way to understand myself.'

Zach studies me, his expression unreadable. 'And did it help?'

I think about that for a moment. 'It depends on the day,' I say. 'Sometimes it feels like I'm closer to an answer. Other times it feels like I'm staring into the same void they did.'

He nods slowly, eyes distant. 'I can relate. Maybe that's the price of trying to understand monsters,' he says. 'You end up seeing how thin the glass is between you and them.'

The ship hums a low vibration in the silence that follows. Neither of us speaks again. We don't need to. The understanding sits there between us, quiet and heavy, like a shared secret neither of us asked for.

The silence is broken by someone in the crowd: 'Oh look! Here comes the captain,' he says.

I meet Zach's gaze with a warm, reassuring smile, and we turn to see the captain walking down the centre of the deck at a funeral pace with members of his crew. In his hands, he holds a large floral wreath made from white lilies. Beside him is Priscilla Hefferman, dressed head to toe in black with a veil covering her face. A woman next to me takes out her phone and holds it high in the air. I think she's filming but then I hear the *Titanic* movie theme tune in all its haunting glory coming from the device speaker. Zach and I exchange a look. He's stifling laughter as the entourage marches by, some with less than impressed expressions at the unwelcome soundtrack. We watch in silence as they congregate at the starboard, the captain and Priscilla Hefferman in the centre.

Captain Perry begins: 'As you all know, this is the final voyage of our magnificent *Jewel of the Atlantic*. It has been the privilege of my life to be her captain and sail these waters without incident for the past thirty years . . .'

Rudy appears beside the woman next to me and firmly but politely asks her to switch off the music. She pinches her face, switches off the device and glares at him. He glares back, mouths an insincere thank you and steps back. I see him joining Jacqui. Our eyes meet and we nod a hello.

The captain continues. A thin, older woman in a black coat, grey hair pulled into a tight bun, with the look of someone who's just stepped off a Wanted poster, joins the entourage. She's holding a violin. 'This is Margery, Mrs Hefferman's assistant, who will play us a familiar and appropriate hymn for the time. Take it away, Margery, please.'

Priscilla's assistant does not react in any way to the captain's words. She stands there, almost sinister and vacant. No surprise that she works for Priscilla. But then she rests the violin on her shoulder and begins to play.

I swallow.

She plays *Nearer, My God, to Thee,* which was rumoured to have been played by the musicians when the *Titanic* was sinking. I've watched *Titanic* so many times over the years, and this hymn never fails to both move me and make me want to slit my wrists at the same time. I have to hand it to Margery, though. She's knocking it out of the park.

I think of the movie and picture the scenes with the

heartbroken old couple lying on their bed waiting for the water to take them, the mother comforting her children in their room, and the expressions of hopelessness and terror from the people left behind as the lifeboats depart. I swallow, my eyes watering.

Perry continues: 'Ladies and gentlemen, tonight, as the Atlantic stretches endlessly before us, I'd like to call your attention to the waters off the starboard side. Beneath these dark swells lies the resting place of the RMS *Titanic*, claimed by the sea on a cold April night in 1912. Though the ocean keeps her secrets hidden far below, the weight of history is here, moving quietly among the waves. More than fifteen hundred souls were lost in this place, and so we pause to honour their memory.

'May they rest in peace.

'As we continue westward, let us sail on in reverence, carrying with us the reminder that the sea is vast, beautiful, and humbling.'

A tear rolls down my cheek as the captain leans over the starboard and gently drops the wreath below. I feel Zach squeeze my hand. A cool breeze blows across the deck. As the hymn continues in the evening gloom, I notice arms rising on either side of me. One by one people are holding up their phones and switching on the torch light. I take out mine and do the same. And suddenly there's a magical dome of light above us as we sail quietly by. For the first time in days, I feel my faith in humanity returning.

When the ceremony ends, the crowd drifts away in silence, voices low, footsteps hushed, the air fragrant with salt and candle wax. Zach stays beside me as we walk along the deck, the wind flattening his hair.

'That was something,' he says quietly.

'Yeah.' My voice comes out thin. 'I didn't expect it to hit me like that.'

'It was the lights,' he says. 'All those people standing there, together. You could really feel it.'

'It was magical.'

'In the US, we prefer to say "awesome".'

I laugh. 'So awesome.'

We huddle together and laugh again.

At my cabin door, we linger close enough that I can smell the salt on his skin and a trace of whiskey on his breath, mingled with coffee.

'Dutch courage?' I ask, stepping a little closer.

He shrugs, smiling.

'Thanks for walking me,' I say.

'Didn't trust you to make it back alone,' he teases.

'You think I'd get lost?'

'It's a big ship.'

His hand finds my cheek, the caress is tentative, warm. The kiss starts light, careful, then deepens. The world diminishes to a warm heartbeat and the steady hum of the ship.

Then his phone buzzes. Once. Twice. Relentless.

He pulls back with a sigh, forehead resting against mine. 'Work,' he murmurs. 'They never stop calling.'

'Tell them you've scored,' I whisper.

He hesitates, brushes another kiss against my mouth, then steps back. 'I'm sorry.'

A dull ache blooms in my chest. My lips curve into a smile that masks my dismay. 'I understand,' I say, which is a lie.

'Call you tomorrow,' he says retreating.

I take out my key and turn away. The corridor feels suddenly too quiet. I touch my lips, still warm, and stand there a moment longer, listening to his footsteps fade down the hall.

Chapter Forty-Six

Martha

About that faith in humanity. It dissipated the following morning when I found an envelope shoved under my door containing a large red button with a smiley face. I would say *Quelle surprise* but that's one of those annoying clichés Diane churns out at any given opportunity. I know since my public run-in with Priscilla, I've exposed myself. Buttonface knows who I am and I must assume he sees me as a threat, hence the Death button. I squeeze it in my palm as if to crush it. 'I'm not afraid of you,' I say out loud, tossing the button on the dressing table. 'Let's see who gets to who first.' In the meantime, I have other stuff to deal with, plus I still have a faint, stupid ache of disappointment after Zach's unexpected kiss.

It's mid morning. I'm with Jacqui backstage, waiting for her costume fitting, in a theatre dressing room; Rudy has made sure she has her own space, which she negotiated at dinner yesterday evening.

'How was dinner?' I ask her.

She's sitting at a dressing table, leaning forward, lips pulled back, studying her teeth in the reflection of a tall, arched mirror surrounded by lightbulbs.

'Fine. I thought I was a talker. He could talk the hind legs off a donkey, and some. Oh, he gave me some tea on Priscilla,' Jacqui says, smiling wickedly at me in the mirror. 'Apparently, that man, the one they arrested and then let go . . . you know the one,' she says with an apologetic expression for bringing up the fake Buttonface.

'Lev Kaplan.'

'That's him. Apparently, he's one of the illegal immigrants in Priscilla's employ. I can't wait to drop that into the conversation next time we lock horns.'

'Regardless of that, he's innocent of the murders.'

Since Todd had told me Kaplan's story, it felt like the rug had been unceremoniously pulled from under my feet after coming so close to catching my dad's killer. But I had to pull myself together and accept it because deep down I knew he was right. Buttonface is smart. Smarter than we think, and of course, he will use a decoy to throw us off the scent. Fortunately, it didn't work. An innocent man has been freed, and I will continue to hunt for Buttonface.

The door swings open, and Rudy enters. 'Sorry I'm a tad late. Oh, hi Martha.'

'Hi.'

He tilts his head and scrunches his face. 'I heard they let him go. You OK, babe?'

'We were just talking about that,' says Jacqui.

'Oh, sweetie. I can't imagine what you must be going through.'

Jacqui and Rudy begin talking about me, and what's best for me, as if I'm not in the room.

'You should give her the day off,' says Rudy.

'We have a deadline,' she replies.

'A day at the spa would work wonders.'

'She doesn't have the time.'

'An afternoon or a morning?'

I bite my tongue and fold my arms.

'A massage might be nice,' says Jacqui. 'Martha, shall I book you in for some meat tenderising?'

I shake my head. 'I'm fine, thank you.'

'I have a tingler you can borrow,' says Rudy, shaping his fingers into a claw and making a downward stabbing gesture.

'A tingler?'

'Oh, that's a good idea,' says Jacqui. 'You can do it on your break.'

'It's an octopus head massager,' says Rudy. 'Honestly, it's amazing. It's changed my life.'

'Oh . . . I'll pass, thanks.'

'No problem. Oh, by the way, I have some more tea,' he says, smiling at us. 'We have a cast replacement for our vicar, John, who has come down with some kind of virus.'

'Is it George Clooney?' Jacqui asks.

'Sadly, he's not on the ship. No, it's a real-life vicar, the Reverend Timothy Garland.'

Jacqui and I exchange a look. 'Why him?' I ask.

Rudy lowers his voice as if he doesn't want anyone else to hear. 'You didn't learn this from me. Mrs Hefferman had heard about John. She called me personally . . . imagine . . . and asked me to include the reverend in the play.'

'But why him?'

'Well, therein lies a tale. Apparently, some of our older passengers have complained about him. They say he's been sticking his nose in and asking intimate questions about the state of their health. Mrs Hefferman suggested he integrate more with the passengers and start by taking over John's role. It would be good for his reputation, she said.'

Jacqui and I exchange another look.

Rudy shrugs, rubs his hands together and turns to Jacqui, 'Anyway, I have the costumes ready downstairs if you'd like to come this way.'

For me, Rudy's 'tea' on the reverend has cemented Priscilla Hefferman's involvement in the Midnight Chorus Society. She's not only protecting him, she's also protecting the reputation of the Society. I follow Rudy and Jacqui, my mind elsewhere, thinking and planning my next move.

As if this ship could not surprise me any more, Rudy takes us through a network of narrow corridors like a warren.

'What is this place?' I ask.

'A private set of passages. You'd be surprised where they will take you,' he says.

'I read about them,' says Jacqui. 'The rich, movie stars, and politicians could meet their lovers in hidden sitting rooms without fear of being seen on the promenade deck. A steward with the right tip could unlock a door and make sure no one asked questions.'

'That's almost true. Mrs Hefferman's dearly departed husband—'

'Jeffrey Hefferman,' says Jacqui. 'What a douche and an ugly, shrivelled, bitter old man. I often wondered what Priscilla saw in that multi-millionaire.'

Rudy chuckles. 'Yeah, he was a piece of work. She's not much better.' He points to a stairwell. 'That'll take you up to the main deck. It's such a time saver, never mind a solid way to avoid passengers you might not want to bump into.'

We enter a windowless room lined with dark walls and theatre costumes hanging on rails. I recognise some of the eighties outfits from Rudy's dress rehearsal. Rudy takes Jacqui through a curtained area to what looks like a walk-in closet. He lets the curtain close behind him. On the walls, there are shelves with rows of busts with wigs, moustaches, and beards. I stare at them, an idea taking shape.

Jacqui peeks out from behind the curtain, 'Martha, you don't need to hang around. You must have work to do,' she says. 'Rudy and I will sort out my costume.'

'OK,' I say without looking up.

'Performance starts at 7 p.m.'

'I'll be there.'

She disappears behind the curtain, and as their voices fade, I set to work with my nimble fingers, grab what I need and hurry out before either of them sees me.

Chapter Forty-Seven

Martha

I would have preferred to go undercover disguised with a beard, glasses, and a short-haired wig, but showing up as a man at the Midnight Chorus Society conference and flashing my Marsha Kowlaski pass might raise questions. Instead, I'm going full-on goth with a black wig that I have plaited Wednesday Addams style. I'm wearing black lipstick, purple eye shadow, specs and a dark double-breasted suit. It's a little too big for me, but I like this new me and think I might adopt this look. At my last excursion to the Society conference, I clocked several emo types, including the crazy Overlook twins, who I have mercifully not seen much of.

As I walk through the casino, unrecognisable to regulars Bob and Don, which boosts my confidence, I notice the flock of people heading to the conference centre are eccentrically dressed. A man in a pinstripe banker's suit struts past me, his collar stiff with stage blood, swinging a plastic axe like he'd just stepped off Wall Street and into a murder scene. Behind him, two women in matching sequinned gowns that remind me of cosplayers pretending to be the Bickel twins, clutch velvet ribbons that bind their wrists together. They sing softly, voices slipping between nursery rhyme and dirge. A young man in a lab coat squirts red dye from a syringe onto his rubber gloves, laughing as his friends film him. To my right, a woman dressed in a straitjacket and Lecter mask shuffles by. She gives me a little nod, as if we share a fandom. Everywhere I look, killers are dressed for the red carpet. Droogs in bowler hats twirl canes; clowns with sinister smiles and cartoon shoes; women in corsets and butcher's aprons parade cleavers tied with satin bows. It's as if Comic Con has been hijacked by a slasher flick.

The queue for Security is a bottleneck. All bags are being checked, and everyone is being searched. They're obviously taking no chances, and considering the recent murders, they have good reason. Two guards dressed in black man the gap in the old theatrical curtain. One is a thickset female with a red face whom I have never seen before. Her colleague is a tall, willowy man with a gormless expression. Thankfully he's not the same guy I first came across, the 'Martha Kowalthki' joker.

The female security guard eyes me suspiciously as she pats me down, searching for weapons I don't carry. 'Who have you come as?'

I swallow and look her straight in the eye, 'Who do you think?'

'I've no idea. That's why I'm asking.' she replies.

My heart slams like a rabbit's facing a cobra, yet I roll my eyes and affect a stern 'I don't suffer fools' face. 'Wednesday Addams, if you must know.' She regards me with an amused expression that skewers my confidence. 'Of course you are.' The longest of moments passes before she says, 'Go on then. Get yourself inside. Enjoy the carnival.'

The carnival?

I give her a grateful smile and hurry through the musty curtain before she changes her mind.

I don't recognise the conference centre when I step inside. It has been miraculously transformed. Over the double doors, covering the Priscilla Hefferman plaque is a painted arch that glows against the drab beige walls: **DANTE'S CARNIVAL.** The bulbs chase one another in endless loops, buzzing faintly, casting shadows that dance across the ceiling tiles. Above the chatter of the bustling crowd, I hear music. Wheezing organ pipes and overexcited tubas. It's almost dreamlike, or perhaps nightmarish. I'm undecided. Every loop of the melody is just a little too cheerful, like it's trying to convince everyone they are having fun at knifepoint.

The crowd is once more moving like lemmings, as if seduced by the unsettling, hypnotic music. Squeezed in like a sardine, I allow myself to get swallowed up and carried along. Safety in numbers and all that.

I take in the made-over space. Above our heads hangs black, red and purple bunting, which is about as cheerful as a funeral home for dead clowns. On the walls, there are macabre vintage posters depicting bizarre carnival side shows. One is a giant spider with a woman's head. Reminds me of Priscilla. Another contains a laughing, deranged-looking magician dressed in a black suit and a jewelled turban, proudly holding up the bloody saw of the woman he has just sawn in half.

A cracked megaphone of a voice, equal parts circus ringmaster and market stall hustler, bellows across the transformed conference centre. I look in its direction and, speaking of clowns, see one dancing merrily outside a striped tent. He's large and round, his face is painted bone white with thick, cracked crimson lips and large painted yellow eyes. He wears a purple and black shiny romper suit and is without question the stuff of nightmares. 'Welcome to Dante's Carnival. Roll up, roll up. Ladies and gentlemen, boys and girls,' he says, 'Step right this way and see the astounding, the unbelievable, the one and only, Merve the DIY Masochist!'

DIY is a form of masochism in my opinion. I have no interest in seeing someone do home improvements, but at the same time, this act, or performance, or whatever it is, might give me some insight into the Society. I weave my way towards the tent with an enthusiastic throng on either side of me as I lead the charge.

'Step inside now – only a nickel! First show about to begin!' says the clown, blocking the entrance. He looks down at me, his greasepaint grin stretched too wide, as if it had been painted on by trembling hands.

'I don't have a nickel,' I say.

'No nickel!' he cries and laughs with a wheeze and a whistle as if he's about to run out of air. I'm beginning to get the sense that I'm Alice in a twisted Wonderland. He reaches for one of my plaits and strokes it tenderly. I feel my stomach churn. 'No charge for you, pretty daughter of the night,' he says, twirling my hair around his podgy digit. 'Or for any of you children of chaos,' he says to the crowd behind me. 'First show is free!' Stepping aside, he waves his arm with a flourish, gesturing for us to enter. I shudder and hurry away from him.

It's dimly lit inside, with party lights hanging on wire above our heads. There's a raised platform with a spotlight on both ends of a workman's table, centre stage. Facing it are rows of benches enough to seat around twenty people. I find a spot on the aisle at the top row. When the tent is full, the clown closes the flap and skips merrily up the centre aisle and hops onto the stage, which is no mean feat for a man of his size.

'Ladies and gentlemen, boys and girls, prepare to witness the man who fears no nail, no screw, no splinter! The one, the only, Merve the DIY Masochist!'

The spotlights flare yellow, buzzing like angry hornets, as the calliope music lurches into a manic polka.

From the wings comes Merve, wearing a hard hat, overalls dusted with sawdust, tool belt jangling with hammers, spanners, and a suspiciously large staple gun. His grin is wide, his eyes a little too bright. Merve doffs his hard hat with a flourish.

'Afternoon, folks! Who's ready for a little home improvement . . . and a lot of self-destruction?'

The audience whoops and hollers.

Holding up the hammer, he says, 'The Hammer of Honour!'

The crowd lets out an 'Ooh' and an 'Aah'.

Merve takes a seat on the workbench. The clown enters the stage and hands him a thin plank. Placing it on his thigh, he begins tapping nails into wood. With a theatrical gasp, he smacks his thumb instead, holding it up for all to see. The nail bent, his thumb clearly swollen, the audience roar with a mix of laughter and mock horror. Merve seems unfazed. My mouth is open. I close it.

Next comes the Staple Gun. He raises it like a duellist's pistol and aims at his own forearm.

I hold my breath.

He can't be serious. Ka-chunk! He fires a row of staples into his sleeve. He then flexes dramatically, ripping them free one by one. It's a trick, I think, until I see the blood on the sleeve and nails. My mouth dries, but I'm still sceptical. Merve bows. Blood runs from his sleeve onto his hand. The crowd squeals and claps.

The clown walks onto the stage carrying a serving platter with a black cloth on top. I notice a cable running from it to the rear of the stage.

'For my finale, I unveil the Sander of Suffering,' Merve says, pulling the cloth off and revealing an electric power sander strapped with glittering grit. He thanks the clown and switches on the sander. The belt spins. He presses it against a sheet of plywood, sparks flying, then with a wink, presses it against the seat of his trousers. The sander whirrs, his backside smokes, and he leaps three feet in the air, shrieking like a banshee. The tent goes wild with applause, whistles, and cries in delighted disgust. Merve skids to the front of the stage, trousers smouldering, sweat on his brow, and raises his arms triumphantly.

'Remember, folks, don't try any of this at home, but if you do, always wear safety goggles!' He bows, tool belt clattering, as the crowd stamp their feet and chant his name: 'Merve! Merve! Merve!'

At this point, I've had quite enough so I get up and bolt from the tent.

I'm not sure what to make of what I just witnessed. So, he's a masochist. Should I be surprised? That's what the clown promised. That's what we got. I still think it was all just smoke and mirrors as I head deeper into the conference centre and its bizarre indoor carnival.

I freeze.

Walking towards me, two metres away, deep in conversation, eyes alert and watching all around them are Wilma and Priscilla. Furtively, Priscilla hands something to Wilma. It's a small bottle of clear liquid. I have no idea what it is, but I'm certain it's not holy water. To my right is another tent, its flap just about to close. I dart out of sight and duck inside, praying that they did not see me.

Chapter Forty-Eight

Martha

It's hard to believe I'm still on the *Jewel of the Atlantic*, in the middle of the ocean. Inside this tent, it is the polar opposite of the ship's polished chrome and Bakelite Art Deco sensibilities. It also smells of sawdust and lamp oil, with a faint undertone of sweat and boiled sugar that gives me the sense of being in another time, or realm, for that matter. Gas lanterns flicker along the poles, their sooty light turning the stripes of the canvas ceiling into a dizzying whirl of red and cream. Cracked flared speakers on poles and heavy bunting droop overhead, frayed at the edges, stars and stripes faded to the colour of old postcards.

A brass calliope sits in the corner, its pipes bent like organ pipes in a chapel gone rogue, wheezing out haunting music with a manic cheer that sets my teeth on edge. Wooden benches form rough semicircles around a small, raised stage, their slats splintered and carved with initials of past gawkers. Above the din, I hear Priscilla's shrill voice and turn to see her entering the tent. My heart thumps. She hangs by the entrance, arms folded, watching the stage. All the seats are taken. I make my way to the opposite end of the tent and blend in with the people standing on the sidelines.

Onstage, the trappings are half vaudeville, half funeral parlour. Velvet curtains, burgundy and moth-nibbled, frame the platform. A gilt mirror leans against the backdrop, reflecting lantern light in fractured gleams. A tall man, dressed in a long velvet cape with a high collar, stands with his back to the audience.

The crowd presses close, their faces lit in alternating shadow and glow, like a gallery of grotesques caught mid-laugh. The place feels both festive and claustrophobic, like stepping into an old lithograph poster brought awkwardly, unnervingly, to life.

A voice booms from the speakers quietening the hum of the audience. 'Ladies and gentlemen, thrill-seekers and night-creepers!' I can't see who's talking and assume he's behind the scenes like the Wizard of Oz. 'Behold the marvel, the menace, the magnificent mystery of the midway. Prepare your eyes, steady your nerves, for tonight you shall witness the uncanny, the blood-curdling, the positively transfusionary! Presenting the one, the only, the shadow of the Old Dominion, Victor "Vlad" Fryer!'

Victor? It's Victor on stage dressed in that ridiculous cape. The carnival barker continues: 'See how he drinks not wine, not whiskey, but the very lifeblood of his willing prey! And who, you ask, is so bold, so daring, so devoted? None other than the identical, the incomparable Bickel Twins, Tammy and Toya, two sisters of singular taste, who bare their arms to the night and invite the bite!'

What the actual fuck?

'Don't blink, don't flinch, and for heaven's sake, don't faint, for you, my friends, are about to see the most delicious danger this side of the Atlantic Ocean. Please welcome Victor "Vlad" Fryer, the Vampyr of Virginia.'

Cheers and clapping erupt from the audience. I feel disoriented and out of step with everyone else in the tent. I want to laugh, but it catches in my throat. This is obviously a pastiche that I find tasteless and disrespectful to those who were murdered by the real Vampyr of Virginia, a serial killer who drains the blood of his victims and drinks it, according to one survivor who woke from an unconscious state to find a hooded gentleman sucking from her wrist.

Victor turns to face the audience, hamming it up so much I can picture Bela Lugosi spinning in his grave. 'Mortals!' he bellows, his voice slipping somewhere between Transylvanian menace and his Southern drawl. 'Tonight, you shall witness the communion of life essence!' The spotlight swings to stage left, where the Bickel Twins shuffle into view. Pale, identical, and wearing matching black babydoll dresses and white tights, they clasp each other's hands and give the crowd unnervingly slow smiles.

'We volunteer,' they chime in eerie unison, rolling back their sleeves with the casual air of women offering coupons at a checkout. Their arms are heavily scarred with criss crossing knife marks. The audience gasps and claps at the same time.

Two little sisters, pale and sweet,
We bring our blood for Vlad to eat.
One drop, two drops, maybe three –
Save the last little sip for me . . .

Victor bows low, cape nearly tripping him, then rises with theatrical menace.

'Ahhh! My darling doppelgängers of devotion, my radiant rivers of ruby delight! You offer me wrists more precious than diamonds, veins finer than Venetian glass!' Victor turns to the audience. 'Fear not, gentle mortals of the crowd. I do not take what is unwillingly given. These sisters of the sanguine arts come to me freely, joyfully, deliciously!'

One of the twins holds out her hand and opens it, revealing a switchblade. Flicking it open, she swiftly runs the edge across her sister's forearm, and then her own. My stomach turns at the sight of blood seeping from the wound. But surely this is a trick. The twins close their eyes, tilting their heads in exaggerated swoons.

Victor's eyes widen, his lips draw back, revealing his canines. He looks feral as he throws himself at the twin's arms.

'It's ketchup!' someone shouts.

Some in the audience laugh, but most watch on in grim fascination. Someone shouts, 'Drink deep, Vlad!'

The calliope crashes into a triumphant final note, brass blaring like laughter with a head cold. Victor stands and faces the audience, his lips and teeth disturbingly crimson. With a twin on either side of him, he holds their hands and raises their arms in the air. Blood seeps down the sister's arms. The tent erupts, some in thunderous applause, some in scandalised shrieks, and at least one man in hysterical giggles, while another calls, 'Encore!'

My mouth and throat are dry. This was no act. I feel sick and look around the audience, wondering who these people are. I need to get out of here. At the entrance, I notice Priscilla talking with Deputy Gomez. I look for another exit and see a gap behind the stage where Victor and the Bickel sisters have just gone through. Under the cover of the crowd, I navigate my way through them and bolt through the gap and circle around the tent with the aim of leaving the way I came in, but Priscilla has also exited Victor's tent with Gomez and is walking in my direction. Gasping, I turn and, with my head down, walk the opposite way. I pick up my pace, my heart pounding, as I try to rationalise what I just witnessed on the stage. It's just tricks, smoke and mirrors, like Merve the Masochist. Yes, of course it is. Ahead I hear another familiar voice. Wilma. She's walking towards me. I glance up at her and see her frowning my way. Shit! Has she recognised me?

'Wilma!' comes Priscilla's stern voice.

I can still feel Wilma's gaze. To my right is another striped side tent. What choice do I have? I'm sandwiched between her and Priscilla. I turn and dart inside the tent and out of sight. I take a breath and peek outside. Wilma is talking to Priscilla and Gomez. I don't want to risk being recognised, so decide to stay put for the time being. I smell lavender sachets and hot glue.

'Hey there darlin', you're just in time,' trills a woman.

I look behind me and see a gingham-covered table standing in the centre, circled by people with craft supplies: scissors, needles, pastel threads, on their laps. Finally, I think. Something normal.

'Come on inside and take a seat,' she says. Sitting at the head of the table is a plump woman, curls pinned with sequinned barrettes, apron covered in polka dots. She looks like she's stepped straight out of a bake sale. 'Welcome to my little workshop. We're making coin purses today. No experience necessary – only a willingness to stitch with love.'

I glance outside. They're still talking. *Shit!* I smile and take a seat.

'What's your name, honey?' she asks.

'Marsha,' I say, trying to sound American.

Her name, stitched across her apron in pink embroidery, reads: ***Candy Braithwaite***. *Sweet as spun sugar.*

'Candy,' she says, 'But I guess you can see that.'

I force a smile.

She hands me a scrap of leather. At first touch, it feels . . . wrong. Warm. Oily. Not like anything I've ever handled. It has a faint blush and a pinkish undertone you don't get from cows. Or pigs.

'What is this?' I ask.

Candy lifts a finished piece with a flourish. 'All our materials are unethically sourced leather. Gives them such character, don't you think? Every mark tells a story.' She lets out a high-pitched giggle. 'I do such good business on my Etsy Store. It's called Skin Deep Creations. I've been a "Star Seller" five years on the trot.'

I trace my fingers over the purse. And freeze. A tiny patch of stubble catches the light, unmistakable as five-o'clock shadow. My skin crawls.

'Oh yes,' Candy whispers, eyes twinkling like fairy lights. 'Etsy can be so picky about descriptions. But most of my customers don't really mind. Not once they feel how . . . personal it is.'

Around the table, the other crafters looked up, smiling dreamily. Their needles flash. Their hands stroking the 'leather' as if it were alive.

I swallow, set the purse down, very gently, and rub my hand on my trouser leg. Candy leans closer and says, in a voice as sweet as poisoned honey, 'Shall I show you how to do the stitching, dear? The trick is to follow the vein lines. They make the most beautiful seams.'

I shoot up from the table, knocking the chair backwards.

'Now, honey, there's no need to be so squeamish. We all have skin.' She holds out a larger sheet, 'Have a feel of this. It's Italian. Real nice guy, he was too.'

'Lovely class,' I say, my voice wobbling. 'But I've just remembered – I, uh, have to meet my friend.'

Candy looks up from her stitching, needle frozen midair. Her smile never falters, but it deepens like paint cracking over plaster. 'Oh, darling, you can't leave now. You've only just started.'

A ripple passes through the crafters. One by one, they lift their heads from their purses and wallets, eyes glassy, smiles slow and deliberate. Their hands keep moving, needles piercing and pulling, the threads drawing neat, obscene seams.

I edge towards the tent flap. My knees feel unreliable, as though the ground is shifting under me, but I force them forward. One step. Another.

And then someone is there. A woman I hadn't noticed before, thin as wire, with a half-finished wallet dangling from her hand. She stands in the path, swaying slightly, the purse swinging like bait on a hook. 'Stay,' she whispers, her lips not quite matching the word.

My throat dries. Every part of me screams to run, to rip the canvas open with my bare hands if I have to.

I meet Candy's eyes. She tilts her head, and murmurs, 'We don't waste what's given to us, dear. That's our creed.'

I'm in an asylum for the deranged. I push the woman out of the way and bolt out of the tent.

People swarm the conference centre. There's no way I can get out of here fast without attracting attention. I push through the crowd, look back and see Candy standing outside her tent with Deputy Gomez. She's pointing in my direction. I duck down and thread my way through the crowd. I need somewhere to hide. I push my way to the side and see a tall window with thin Venetian blinds and an open door leading into an empty room. This could be my only hope. I make my way towards it, enter and shut the door behind me. Just what kind of convention is this?

Chapter Forty-Nine

Martha

The room is a storage area for conference materials; cardboard boxes, retractable banners, and flyers lie scattered on the floor and on a white desk. I peek through the blinds and see Gomez, an urgency in his stride as he pushes through the throng, grim eyes scanning faces, searching for the goth girl who clearly does not belong. He hurries past. I let out a breath I didn't realise I was holding. I'm safe. For now, at least.

Folding my arms, I pace the room. What the hell have I just witnessed? I feel bile rising in the back of my throat. I look at my palm, the same one that had held Candy's leather. It was human skin. I steady my breathing, fight the urge to puke, and compose myself.

Perching myself on the desk, I try to figure out how I can safely get out of here. I notice a rolled-up banner with a label attached. Written with a Sharpie in block letters is: SHEILA MORGAN. On closer inspection I see it's the Paramour of the Penitentiary's photo-opportunity, prison cell backdrop. I peer into one of the boxes on the desk and see a stack of A4-sized glossy flyers. I take one out. In bold letters at the top it says: **The Midnight Chorus Society 25th Anniversary Conference.**

The flyer is a colourful collage of portrait photos. I recognise Bernard, Wilma, Sheila, Merve and Victor. It's a timetable of talks, debates, live demonstrations, culminating in the final day subtly titled 'Dante's Carnival'. I exhale a breath. Ten points to whoever came up with that.

I scan the page, my eyes skittering over the words.

- **Conference Highlights include:**
    - **Coffins Not Included:** A retrospective on Ernest 'The Undertaker' Ridgewell's career.
    - **Woodchippers or Acid Baths?:** Rooster Calhoun leads the debate.
    - **The Art of the Smile:** Bernard 'The Dentist' Koch unveils his dazzling exhibition of toothsome treasures: jewellery and art lovingly crafted from the smiles of his victims.
    - **The Agony and the Ecstasy:** A lecture from the Revered Garland on finding the joy in assisted dying.
    - **Meat is Murder:** Lionel Bowcott on the challenges of being both a vegan and a cannibal.
- **The Final Day Highlights:**
    - **Dante's Carnival** – a midway of wonder and woe, sins woven together with laughter and screams, including:
    - **Skinning as a Craft**: From Folklore to Etsy with Candy Braithwaite.
    - **The Theatre of Blood:** It's all over in one act with the Vampyr of Virginia himself, Victor 'Vlad' Fryer.

I'm shaking.

The Midnight Chorus Society is an organisation of serial killers. And Buttonface is one of them. I'm still gripping the itinerary when the office door clicks open. Gasping, I dart to the rear of the office, and crouch down behind a row of boxes.

A voice, smooth, commanding, steeped in old-money confidence speaks. 'Zach, darling, enjoying the carnival?' she purrs.

Zach?

A cold tightness seizes my chest. I press myself deeper into the floor, wishing I could melt into it.

'It's an acquired taste. One I don't have.'

'Oh, dear boy. You are so sensitive . . . Close the door . . . we need to talk. As you know we have a predicament, but I have a plan.'

'You always do,' he replies, sardonically.

'First up, I need you to do what I asked.'

'And I told you, I'm not hurting her. She's got nothing to do with this.'

Her laugh is knife sharp. 'Oh, she has everything to do with this. Atkins will be taken care of by Wilma shortly. She will slip one of my concoctions into his meal. He has a severe allergy to shellfish. A few drops and hey presto, he'll be gone. Jacqui DuLac will take the fall for the murders. That bitch humiliated me, and I will make sure she pays for what she did. And as for the girl . . .' A deliberate pause. 'She's a loose end. You'll take care of her.'

I clamp my hand over my mouth. The room seems to shrink, its walls pressing in.

'I said no,' Zach snaps. 'I'm not like you or your cronies!'

'Oh, Zach. You already are. Don't be naive.'

His breath hitches. 'I told you those two men killed my mom. They hurt others. I ended them. I don't regret it. But I won't kill her.'

I stifle a gasp. Zach is a murderer. He's one of them. The man who walked me to my room, who kissed me like I mattered, has killed. The thought rips through me like a knife.

Priscilla's voice shifts, losing the purr and settling into something colder. 'You did what needed doing, and you did it cleanly. But you were clumsy, and killed the wrong people, and then you got caught. I pulled strings and made sure you never saw the inside of a courtroom, didn't I?'

'I will not kill an innocent!'

'But you already have.'

'They were murderers!'

'They were innocent of the crime of killing your mother.'

'Stop twisting things!' he cries, his voice crackling with emotion.

'She's a threat to you, to me, to all of us. You've already proved yourself, my darling. Besides, you owe me so much.'

'I've given you more than enough.'

'I took you under my wing and gave you purpose. You do this, Zach, and I will continue to protect you. You refuse, and everything I cleared goes back on the table. Your little streak of benevolence will look very different in court, will it not?'

'I don't care.'

Silence stretches. I can hear my own breathing, loud and stupid. I don't move. My body wants to bolt, to run, but I sit rigid and terrified.

Priscilla sighs. 'I didn't want to tell you during the conference, but it seems like I have no choice. The people who killed your mother are on board the ship.'

'You're lying.'

'You know them. Quite well, actually.'

'I don't believe you,' he says, but I hear the doubt in his voice.

'Then you have chosen your fate,' Priscilla says, cold as winter. 'And also remember: you did not survive without me. That debt is not erased by sentiment.'

'Who are they?' he asks.

'Take care of the girl and I'll tell you.'

'You'll tell me now!'

'As you wish. It was Wilma and Frank. They laughed as she screamed, apparently. They're such brutes.'

My head spins. I bite my lip hard enough to taste blood.

Zach's voice cracks open, fury spills out. 'You've kept this from me!'

'Oh darling. It was for the best. I couldn't have you causing a scene.'

'Those bastards. I'll kill them. I'll—' He stops, chokes back rage, then spits: 'Fine. I'll do what you want. But after that, they're mine.'

'When we get to New York, you can do whatever you like. Mama's so proud of you . . . ooh, you're so tense . . . let Mama relieve you . . . that's it, good boy.' I hear the rustling of her dress followed by the sound of a zip being unzipped. 'Mama's hungry . . .'

I press my palm to my mouth.

'Stop!' says Zach. I hear his zip being pulled up and the door opening.

'Zach, wait,' says Priscilla, but he's gone and so is she. I'm alone again. I stay wedged in behind the boxes, frozen, the itinerary crumpled in my fist. My crush. My mistake. And now, apparently, my executioner. You're not the only one, I think. Join the queue.

I wait. Ten seconds. Thirty. A full minute, counting heartbeats like drumbeats in my ears. Think. How can I get out of here? I have an idea. I check my phone. It's almost 7.30 p.m. My battery is almost out. Jacqui will be wondering where I am. I call Rudy and pray he answers. It keeps ringing. Oh God, please. Just when I give up hope he picks up.

'Rudy, it's Martha.'

'Martha? Where are you? Jacqui's on stage and I'm due to go on so be quick!'

'I need your help.'

'Can't it wait?'

'No! I'm at the Midnight Chorus Society convention. Rudy, these people, they're all murderers. Serial killers.'

'Have you been drinking?'

'I'm in trouble. They're looking for me. I need to get out of here but I'm afraid they'll be watching the exit.'

'Martha, they're not serial killers. They're just a very strange bunch of people who sing in a choir. Priscilla told me.'

'She's one of them. And so is Zach. He's going to kill me. They're going to kill Todd and frame Jacqui! Please help me.' I can hear the desperation in my voice.

A pause before he answers. 'Where are you?'

'I'm hiding in an office somewhere in the centre of the conference centre.'

'Get out of there and go to the rear of the centre. Top right, you'll see what looks like a storeroom labelled STAFF ONLY. It has a combination lock. The code is 4561. It's not a storeroom. It's an access point to the hidden passages. Go up the stairs and follow the signs to the theatre. Meet me here. Got that?'

'Yeah. Thank you.'

'And—'

My battery dies.

'Shit!'

I uncurl my legs, which are screaming with pins and needles. The itinerary is still balled in my fist. I stuff it into my pocket, as though proof of this nightmare might make it less real. Todd poisoned. Jacqui framed. Me, a loose end to be taken care of. By Zach, of all people. I feel sick, frightened, but angry at the same time.

I step quietly from behind the boxes, each step deliberate, slow. The office smells of Priscilla's perfume – sharp, expensive, poisonous – clinging to the air like a warning. My hand hovers over the door handle, slick with sweat.

If I leave now, I should make it out. Peeking through the blinds I see no sign of Zach, Gomez or Priscilla. The crowd is heavy enough to get lost in.

I press down the handle. It gives.

I slip into the hallway, heart rattling, and pull the door closed behind me. The coloured carnival lights buzz and flash mercilessly overhead.

Run, Martha. Don't think. Just run.

I turn left straight into the path of a carnival usher in a striped jacket. He smiles slyly, showing tobacco teeth. Bernard would not approve.

'Lost, miss?' he asks, voice syrup-thick. His eyes flick to the door I'd come from. 'You're not supposed to be in there.'

My body screams flight. My lips try for charm. 'Just looking for the Ladies' room.'

He tilts his head. That grin doesn't move.

'Ladies' room,' I repeat, flashing the kind of fake smile I usually reserve for relatives asking about my love life. 'Do you mind pointing me in the right direction?'

The usher's grin widens, splitting his face into something closer to a wound than an expression. 'Of course,' he says. 'I'll take you there myself.'

If I let him do that, I'm finished.

'No need,' I say lightly, already edging past him. 'I've got a strong bladder. Probably hold it another hour.'

I circle around him, fast, hoping he'll let me go.

'Miss.'

His voice is sharper now, not sweet but vinegar. Shoes scuff against carpet. He's following.

I quicken my pace, heartbeat hammering. The corridor stretches ahead, lined with double doors stencilled with cheery words – WORKSHOPS, DEMOS, PANELS. Behind each door, the killers' convention churns on, voices rising and falling in gruesome harmony.

'Stop.'

I don't.

The sound of him behind me sharpens – shoes pounding now, not scuffing. I'm running. He's running.

I barrel around a corner, nearly colliding with a poster stand that boasts TONIGHT: THE GREAT DEBATE: Is Strangulation an Art Form? I shove it over behind me. It crashes into the floor, spilling brochures like confetti.

'Security!' the usher bellows.

My lungs burn. My thighs scream. My eyes lock on the STAFF ONLY sign at the top right of the centre, just as Rudy said.

I sprint faster, arms pumping like pistons, braids flying in the air behind me.

I hear more footfalls joining his, men's voices shouting. A chorus now, chasing me through the bellow of the conference centre.

The door looms closer. Ten feet. Five. My hand shoots out. The code what was the code. Think . . . 4 . . . 6 . . . No . . . 4, 5 . . . 4561. That's it. My fingers press it in. The door clicks open.

'Stop her!'

Panic knifes through me, but instinct shoves it aside. I slip inside, slam the door shut and step back to catch my breath. Fists pound the door. They can't get in. I breathe a sigh of relief. Thank you, Rudy. I sprint up the stairs two at a time. There's no time to meet him or Jacqui. I have to save Todd.

Chapter Fifty

Martha

My feet rattle and echo on grating as I race down a corridor with barely enough light to see where I'm going. It's confined and narrow, the walls sweating with condensation. Pipes run overhead like exposed veins, dripping steadily. My palms skim the walls, sticky with grime. Every junction looks the same, ladders, rust, shadow. The floor hums underfoot. It feels less like a cruise ship and more like the metal throat of a submarine that has swallowed me whole. I move fast, half-crouched, following the low whine of machinery and the occasional hiss of steam. It takes forever, or maybe five minutes, I've lost track. The carnival feels a world away and I'm grateful.

Finally, I see a sliver of light slicing through the outline of a door frame. I push through and a bright new world opens out. It's another corridor, bustling with crew in their smart white and cream 1920s uniforms: kitchen staff, porters, waiting staff, cleaners. I get the urge to scream: 'Save yourselves, there are serial killers everywhere!', but I know that would sound ridiculous and they wouldn't believe me. No time to think about any of that. I need to find Todd, that's my priority. He can take over, if he's not already dead that is. I shudder at the thought.

I look up and down the corridor. Being in the hidden passages has disoriented me and I've no idea where I am. I'm getting some odd looks from people as I thread my way through them. A passenger intruding in their space. I get it. I move quickly, avoiding eye contact. It occurs to me the Society will be looking for me. Hopefully my disguise has been strong enough for them to realise it's not me. Therefore, I need to ditch the costume and wig. Ahead I see the Ladies' toilets. Cutting across the flow of people, I enter. It's basic and modern in design, a contrast to the ship's nod to Art Deco glamour and elegance. There's no one inside, thankfully. Swiftly, I pull off my suit jacket, and wig and stuff them into the bin. Looking in the mirror, I can see my hair is all over the place, making me look deranged. Turning on the taps, I run the water and begin splashing my face, using hand soap to clean off the goth make-up. My poor skin. Ten minutes later, I'm back to normal. I make a mental note to moisturise should I survive the day. I comb my hair back with my fingers and satisfied, I dart back into the corridor. I need a quick exit. A woman around my age wearing a receptionist's suit is carrying a steward's uniform with a matching cap. An idea takes shape.

'Hey, I'm lost.'

'Passengers are not allowed here ma'am.'

I laugh, 'Passenger . . . me? If only. I work here. We met boarding the ship, don't you remember? It's me, Martha.'

Uncertain eyes study me. 'I don't remember. You must be thinking of someone else.'

Wow. She's blunt. 'Ha, never mind. I have one of those forgettable faces. Everyone says so.'

She doesn't know what to say to that.

'Anyway, my manager sent me here to get a uniform. Some dude is sick, and he wants me to fill in for him . . . such a douche . . . my manager, not the sick guy . . .'

She shrugs. 'OK.'

'I need a uniform.'

'What kind of uniform?'

'I'll take that one,' I say point to the one she's holding. It's worth a punt.

'I can't give you this one. It belongs to someone else.'

'Of course. Where can I get one?'

She frowns at me. I'm not sure she's buying this story, but she points back the way she came. 'Uniforms are back there. You should know that. Third door on the right.'

'And how do I get out of here?'

Her frown deepens. 'Have you considered going back the way you came?'

Bugger! 'Erm . . . I'd rather not. There's a guy back there. He . . . he's toxic.' I rub my arms in faux distress. 'I just can't.'

'There's a stairwell beyond the uniform room. You should know that too.'

I press my hands in prayer. 'You're a life saver. Truly. Nice to meet you,' I say, walking away. 'Again! Nice to see you again.' I laugh awkwardly and disappear into the crowd.

Third door on the right. I'm inside perusing the uniforms neatly folded on rows of wooden shelves. Who do I want to be today: chef, waitress, cleaner . . . no. I liked the look of the steward's outfit with its double-breasted jacket and flat-top cap. The cap being key to keeping unwanted eyes from recognising me. I'm so channelling undercover Cassie Kowalski.

And so, I'm suited and booted and running up the stairwell. It takes me to the second floor and the opposite end of the casino. I'm relieved to see no sign of cosplaying serial killers, Gomez, Wilma or Priscilla for that matter. I make my way to towards the main stairs. Todd's office is one level up.

'Excuse me. Can I get some help?' comes a voice.

I turn to see a woman, big hair, Armani jumpsuit, exiting the casino, carrying a large stuffed tote bag. 'Can you take these coins to my room?'

I blink and frown, 'I don't think so.'

'Excuse me?'

'I'm busy. Take them yourself.'

'How dare you? Do you know who I am?'

I turn and start walking away. 'No idea.'

'I'm reporting you.'

'Go ahead. My name's Priscilla Hefferman. Have a nice day now.'

I run to the stairs and cautiously make my way to Security. I don't want to bump into Gomez, so I hang back. There's no sign of life, so I make my way to Atkins's office. Through the window I can see he's not there. 'Shit.'

'He's taken the day off.'

I jump and turn to see Todd's assistant, Janie. 'Janie, you made me jump.'

She giggles. 'So, I see.' Her eyebrows arch at my disguise. 'You making a few extra bucks on your trip?'

'A long story.'

'I'm all ears. Can I get you a coff—'

'Where's Todd, Janie?'

'He wasn't feeling well and went to his cabin.'

'Did he say what was wrong with him?'

'He ate something is all he said.'

'Bollocks! Do you have a phone?'

'Of course,' she says, taking out her mobile.

'Can you call him?'

'Deputy Gomez said I shouldn't disturb him.'

'I bet he did. Janie, listen to me. Todd is in danger. He may be dead for all we know.' She gasps. 'Please trust me when I say we need to help him now.'

She nods her head. 'What can I do?'

'Call him.'

She finds him on her Contacts list and dials. It rings but goes straight to voicemail. 'Try again,' I say. Four more tries and still no answer.

'That's not like him,' says Janie, her face pale. 'He keeps his phone by his side twenty-four hours of the day. Part of the job, he says.'

'Where's his cabin?'

'It's number 27. On the second floor, starboard side.'

'I need you to go to the medics and bring a doctor straight away to Todd's cabin.'

'OK.'

'I'll go to Todd's cabin now. Maybe there's something I can do.' I turn to leave.

'Wait!'

Janie lets herself into Todd's office. I follow her inside. On his desktop is a can of pepper spray.

'We need to hurry,' I say, slipping the pepper spray into my pocket. She begins searching his drawers, pulling them open one by one before reaching inside. 'You'll need this,' she says, handing across a room key. 'He always keeps a spare, just in case.'

I hadn't thought about how I would get inside. 'Genius, Thank you!' Something in the drawer blue, white and orange catches my eye. 'What's that?' I ask.

'An EpiPen. He has—'

'Give it to me!'

She hands it over without question.

'How do I use it?'

'It's simple. Blue to the sky, orange to the thigh.'

My stomach clenches. 'OK.'

'See you at Todd's.'

We hurry out together.

'One last thing, Janie. Avoid Deputy Gomez at all costs.'

'Gladly.'

'And Priscilla Hefferman. Don't say anything to her.'

I'm racing down the starboard hallway on the second floor, counting the cabin numbers until I eventually arrive at number 27. I let myself in, and gasp. Dressed in a bathrobe, Todd is sprawled across the bed, skin blotched, lips ballooning, breath rattling like a man drowning on dry land. His hands claw weakly at nothing.

I hold up the EpiPen, my hand shakes. The pen is plastic, stupidly bright like a child's toy. I don't know what I'm doing. I don't have training. But if I freeze, he dies.

Blue to the sky, orange to the thigh.

I rip off the blue safety cap with my teeth, spit it on the floor. My other hand pulls the dressing gown aside, exposing his thigh. I press the orange end against the skin and drive it down, hard. A sharp click. Todd jerks, a gasp tearing out of him. I hold it there, praying, counting too fast in my head. One, two, three – was it supposed to be ten? I don't know. Please let three be enough.

I pull it back, drop it, start massaging his thigh with a trembling hand. I don't even know if I should be doing this, but maybe it will help the medicine flow. 'Come on, Todd. Stay with me.'

His eyes flutter, unfocused. His breath rattles again, still shallow but different. A thread of air, stronger, forcing its way back in.

'Oh God. Is he OK?' Janie has arrived. Behind her is the ship's doctor carrying a medical bag. He perches on the bed, checks Todd's vitals, listens to his chest. Then he looks up and sees the EpiPen in my hand. 'I think you've saved his life.'

My eyes begin to tear up. 'That's good.'

Janie runs to me and throws her arms around me tightly. 'You're a hero.'

'Janie, I need your help again. We get into New York later tonight. Call the police and tell them someone tried to murder Todd. Tell them there are . . .' I need to be careful how I word this or else she'll think I'm mad. 'Three other people have been killed. It's really important you tell them this, and shout, scream, cry if you have to. Just get them to believe you.'

'OK.'

I slip out of her embrace. My work is not done. 'I have to go.'

'But—'

'Say hi to Todd for me.'

I sprint across the ship, lungs burning, weaving through passengers in their best frocks, others in holiday polos, colliding with trays of cocktails and dodging gawkers who glare like I've ruined their vacation. My eyes rake the crowd for Zach's face, or worse, Buttonface. Every shadow feels like a trap, every laugh a warning.

The theatre doors loom ahead. My heart jackhammers. I shove them open and stumble inside, hot with sweat, gulping for breath.

The play is underway. It must be drawing to a close soon. Onstage, I see Rudy stuffed into a wig and cardigan as Jessica Fletcher, looking like a drag queen who's lost a bet. Reverend Garland, playing the vicar, twitches nervously under the lights. I feel my skin crawling.

I see Jacqui standing tall, sharp in her Cassie Kowalski trench coat, every inch the TV detective. Her voice rings out, calm and commanding:

'The murderer is a man.'

She turns to 'Jessica'. 'Do you agree, Mrs Fletcher?'

Rudy dips his head and replies in a falsetto: 'I most certainly do.'

The audience titters. I push down the aisle, breath ragged, willing her to see me, to listen.

Jacqui swivels to the vicar. Her voice cuts like glass. 'Was it really necessary to kill Sister Agatha, Vicar?'

Gasps from the cast. Giggles from the audience.

'You can't prove anything,' he says, his voice weedy.

'Actually, we have a witness that saw everything,' says Jacqui.

'And is willing to testify,' adds Jessica.

The vicar makes a show of bolting.

'Stop right there, mister,' Jacqui commands, raising the stage gun.

He runs.

She fires.

An almighty bang cracks the air. The audience cries out in alarm, the cast jerks back in shock.

The reverend teeters, eyes wide. A red bloom spreads across his back.

Someone screams.

The gun wasn't a prop.

Jacqui stands frozen, gun shaking in her hands, disbelief scrawled across her face.

Deputy Gomez bursts out of nowhere, as if he's been waiting in the wings for this exact cue. He grabs her arm, snaps on the cuffs.

'Jacqui DuLac, you're under arrest.'

Phones blaze like a forest fire, screens glowing, the moment captured from every angle. Photos. Videos. Hashtags already being born.

Jacqui is led away, protesting, her voice drowned by the chaos.

And me? I'm still in the aisle, heart pounding, bile in my throat, watching Priscilla's plan unfold to perfection.

Chapter Fifty-One

Martha

I need to be alone to think. I can't go to my room. I imagine Zach or Buttonface staking it out, wating for my return. What about Jacqui's suite? I don't have a key. But she does and I know where it is. I hide among the exiting audience as Gomez manhandles Jacqui out of the theatre. She is furious, the language coming from her mouth is post watershed on crack. Good for you, Jacqui. Give that 'motherfucker' (one of her many expletives) a lashing with that wicked tongue. Rudy, still dressed as Jessica Fletcher, hurries after them protesting her innocence.

As they pass, I push through the crowd. Onstage, the medics are placing a blanket over the reverend's corpse. I feel nothing for the man. I didn't know him, but I know what he did. Good riddance. I make my way backstage to Jacqui's dressing room. Her handbag is stashed in one of the drawers of her dresser. I take it out and rummage inside. The key is there. Relief washes over me.

I don't want to risk going back through the ship, so I go to the secret passages, head to the stairwell and climb up. I feel the stairwell rocking slightly and steady myself on the rail, we must be going through rough waters.

At the top, I push the door open and gasp at the rain that hits my face like shards of glass. I step outside and almost slip on the wet surface. As I close the door behind me, the ship lurches hard to starboard, the storm gnawing at its hull like some giant beast. Rain hammers against the floor, wind howls, as I hurry towards the entrance to the top floor. I take the stairs down to the seventh floor and force myself down the corridor towards Jacqui's suite. I slip inside Jacqui's rooms, shut the door, and sit in the dark. The curtains whip in the draft, snapping like sails. The air tastes metallic, charged with the storm.

Then the Tannoy crackles, the captain's voice rolls through the ship:

'Ladies and gentlemen, this is the captain. We've run into an unexpected storm, and conditions will be rough for a while. For your safety, I must ask everyone to return to their cabins and remain there until further notice. Thank you for your co-operation.'

For the next few hours, I sit rigid in the armchair, staring at nothing as the ship pitches and groans. Anger churns with fear in my gut. Regardless of the storm, I'm not staying put. Not when Jacqui's been framed, not when Todd's barely breathing.

I'm about to slip out when I hear it – the faint scrape of a key in the lock. My breath snags. I duck low, pressing myself into shadow as the door creaks open.

Deputy Gomez steps in, torch in one hand, something heavier in the other. A weapon. His beam slices across the walls, the sofa, the floor, hunting me. I don't move.

He mutters under his breath, circling slow, deliberate. Then he climbs the stairs to the bedroom, torchlight bobbing.

Now.

I slip from my hiding place and push for the door, careful, careful—

Snap.

The latch clicks back like a gunshot.

'Hey!' shouts Gomez.

I bolt.

The corridor tilts and heaves with the ship's sway as I run, heart clawing at my throat. Behind me, Gomez barrels out, torch swinging. The glint of metal flashes in his hand.

The lift is ahead, but instinct screams no, too easy to trap me. I veer to the stairwell, boots pounding two steps at a time, breath ragged. Terror digs in deep, but anger drives me harder: I refuse to die for Priscilla's twisted satisfaction.

I glance back. Empty. Gomez is gone.

The lift dings. My stomach knots. The doors slide open with a metallic sigh.

He's inside.

Slumped against the wall, his body slack, head bowed. A crimson line carved across his throat. Blood drips steadily pooling on the carpet.

My breath catches. My whole body wants to scream but I clamp it down, shaking, silent.

The keys hang from his belt. The brig. My fingers snatch them before my brain can second-guess. Cold, slick, heavy.

Footsteps.

I whip my head up.

Buttonface. Coming down the stairs, slow and steady, knife dangling from his hand, blade dark with blood.

'Miss,' a voice calls from above, a crew member, calm, oblivious. 'You should be in your room.'

I look up, startled.

When I look back. Buttonface is gone.

The stairs are empty.

The knife, the mask, the man vanished, as if he was never there at all.

*

The brig smells like bleach and loneliness. Fluorescent lights buzz overhead, harsh as interrogation lamps. The Security office is empty. Gomez won't be coming back, but his keys jangle in my hand, slick with sweat.

Through the bars, Jacqui sits hunched on a metal bench, trench coat twisted, face pale and tight with fury. She looks less like Cassie Kowalski and more like a caged animal.

'Martha,' she hisses, springing to her feet.

I jam the key into the lock. It sticks, my hands trembling, then clicks. The bars give way with a groan. She's out in a second, grabbing my arm.

'They set you up,' I say, breathless, urgent. 'The gun wasn't yours. It was Priscilla's plan all along. She wanted you to kill the reverend, take the fall for his death and the others.'

Jacqui's eyes blaze. 'But why not pin it all on Buttonface? He's their monster, isn't he?'

'I don't know,' I admit, shaking my head. 'That's the part I haven't figured out. But right now, it's Priscilla, Wilma, and Frank left standing. Everyone else is . . .' I swallow hard. 'Has been taken care of.'

Jacqui exhales, a sharp, furious sound. 'Then we take care of them.'

I almost laugh, exhausted as I am. 'First, we get somewhere safe. Your suite. We'll lock it down, lay low, figure out a plan. I've got a lot to tell you, Jacqui. More than you're going to want to hear.'

We move, fast and silent, through the corridors. The ship groans under the storm, every wave threatening to throw us off our feet. Shadows stretch long under the flickering lights. Not all people have heeded the captain's warning. Every face we pass could be an enemy; a cleaner, a guest, a guard.

Jacqui keeps her chin high, but I can feel her fury radiating. Me, I've got adrenaline and fear mixed into a cocktail that tastes like iron in my mouth.

We reach her suite without incident, slip inside, and close the door behind us. The storm hammers the glass, drowning the ship in sound. For the first time in hours, I breathe, not easy, not free, but enough.

'Right,' Jacqui says, eyes burning. 'Do not skip on the detail.'

I sink into the armchair, lungs heaving, every nerve still screaming from the chase.

I tell her everything.

Chapter Fifty-Two

Wilma

Wilma Franklin kept a tidy desk. She always had. A tidy desk was a tidy mind, and a tidy mind did not make cockamamie mistakes that landed a gal in handcuffs. The storm outside rattled the hull like a rude caller, but she squared the stack of programmes to a perfect right angle and smoothed the blotter where that beast of a man Gomez, who had been here not twenty minutes back, had left a damp ring. People thought chaos was exciting. Chaos was sloppy. Sloppy got you caught.

Frank snored in the armchair with his shoes off. Eighty-three and still handsome if one looked past the liver spots. Back at home, he kept a boning knife in the magazine rack like other men kept crossword puzzles. Wilma patted his shoulder. 'Rest, honey,' she murmured. 'We'll need our wits about us.'

On her desk sat the letter.

Not a letter so much as a wound in the world: thick paper, hospital white, folded too sharply, the edges cut with something meaner than scissors. Inside, seven words in tidy block print:

Library. 1 a.m. We discuss terms.

Inside was the red button with the smiley face.

Terms. Well now. Wasn't that a peach.

Buttonface had been busy, swatting the board one by one like flies, each death marked by his cunningness and ability to stay one step ahead of them. If she weren't so cross about the resource drain, Wilma would have called it elegant. The head of the Midnight Chorus Society ought not to admire a saboteur, but she did. A talent like that should be recognised.

She slipped the letter back into its envelope and laid it on the blotter, aligning it with the grain. Her hands did not shake. At seventy-six, she harboured no romance about fear. You made the tea. You tidied the room. You sharpened the knife. Then you faced the thing.

It was time to leave. She had an appointment with the Spider.

Frank still slept when Wilma left, his chest rising steady as tidewater. She climbed the service staircase; the ship groaned, the storm chewing at its bones, but she made the climb. The corridors were thin of people, mostly crew skittering by with their heads down as though the weather could see them. Outside, black water heaved under a skin of foam. It looked like someone had whisked Hell. She was not overly concerned about the storm and the unsteadiness of the ship. She was angry, and when she was angry, she became focused. And boy, was she focused.

Margery answered the door with one hand behind her back. Wilma trusted neither her or the Spider, and had her knife primed and ready up her own sleeve. Priscilla Hefferman's voice filled the suite, brassy and brittle as gilt. 'Put it away, Margery. Wilma, come in.'

Wilma did not want to be here, but this was a crisis and by Jiminy they were going fix it.

Priscilla stood at the window looking out at the sea with a glass of something pretentious. 'Sit,' she said, not turning. 'There's been a development.'

'I have one too,' Wilma replied, settling near the light. Always know where your light is.

Priscilla finally looked at her. 'Which is?'

'Yours first.'

'Gomez is dead,' she said.

'That's too bad.'

'You're all heart, Wilma.'

'That fella was dumber than a lobster looking for shade.' She held up the envelope. 'It's from him.'

Priscilla nodded to Margery. Margery, still with her hand behind her back, took it from Wilma, and gave her a shady look.

Priscilla opened it and read the letter. 'He wishes to discuss terms,' she smiled without joy. 'Does he think he's earned a seat? After he butchered half my board? The bold little ghoul.'

'You call him little, but little hooks catch big fish.'

Priscilla paused, eyes studying Wilma. After a moment, she said: 'We'll meet him, naturally. But first, we tidy up the two inconveniences still onboard my ship.'

'Just how do you plan to do that? That girl, she's smart. Was down at the Carnival today sticking her nose in. She's not just another fish in the bucket. She'll bite if you stick your hand in.'

Priscilla's mouth dropped open momentarily, confusion in her eyes. 'What language are you speaking?'

'I'm just warning, is all.'

Priscilla shook her head. 'They're in Jacqui's suite. I'll take care of them personally, as I can't seem to rely on anyone else.' The Spider's eyes slid across the room. Wilma followed her gaze. Priscilla's 'special friend', Zach, was standing quietly, watching Wilma, with a hollow, murderous expression.

'Didn't have the backbone to get rid of that girl, eh?' she said. Sliding his hands into his pockets, he turned casually and walked away. 'That boy oughta learn some manners.'

'Respond to our masked friend,' said Priscilla. 'Text him back and tell him we'll see him at the time he suggested. We'll make him an offer he can't refuse. Meanwhile, I'll pluck our two doves. We cannot go into negotiations with loose feathers floating about. Oh, for Christ's sake! I'm beginning to talk like you!'

Wilma inclined her head. Arguing with arachnids was pointless. 'I'll send the note.'

Chapter Fifty-Three

Martha

Jacqui's suite feels like the last safe house in a world gone feral. She's preparing a martini at the bar. I'm not drinking. I need a clear head. The storm outside drums against the glass like it's got a personal vendetta, and my nerves are shot to ribbons, but I have a mug of Yorkshire tea and there's carpet and curtains and the illusion of control.

But all that changes when Priscilla Hefferman walks in without knocking, holding a bottle of Cristal Champagne.

I shoot up from the sofa, spilling tea on the carpet.

'Oh, don't get up for little old me,' she says.

Jacqui and I exchange a concerned look. Priscilla is alone.

'Do come in, Cilla. Make yourself at home,' says Jacqui through gritted teeth.

'Excuse the intrusion. I didn't think you would let me in, so I thought I'd take advantage of the master key,' she says, holding up a black plastic key with her bony fingers, nails painted a dangerous glossy crimson. She's dripping money and menace, framed by lightning like she's auditioning for *Cruella de Vil: The Musical.* 'Ladies,' she purrs, voice smooth as arsenic. 'You've had such a dreadful evening. I thought you might appreciate . . . my support.'

Jacqui laughs. She's still in costume as Cassie Kowalski, trench coat stiff, chin high, every inch the TV detective who's about to collar the killer. 'The last thing you supported was a facelift, and even that's slipping.'

'How's the serial killing business going?' I ask.

She smiles brightly at me. 'Well, this year has been quite the party.'

'How many husbands have you murdered?' Jacqui asks.

Priscilla blinks as she considers this. 'All of them . . . except Joe, of course. Sweet Joe. The one that got away.'

I notice Jacqui's eyes flash with fury.

Priscilla glides to the bar. 'I have a proposition,' she says, as she begins peeling the foil from the bottle top.

'We're not interested,' Jacqui says.

'We've been in touch with the police,' I say. 'They'll be waiting for you when we dock.'

She wraps her hand around the cork and pops it open. 'Sweetheart, I have contacts in high places. That includes the NYPD. They like the colour of my money.' Priscilla takes three glasses from the rack and with her back to us begins pouring the Cristal.

Jacqui and I look at each other. Does Priscilla, 'The Spider' Hefferman, poisoner of rich husbands really think we're going to drink from one of those glasses?

With two flutes in her hand, she turns and brings them to us. Jacqui and I both take them from her. Priscilla takes her own glass from the bar and joins us.

'Who is Buttonface?' I ask.

'That's the million-dollar question. We don't know.'

'Why is he murdering your stooges?'

'Your guess is as good as mine.'

Jacqui swirls her glass, eyes laser focused on her nemesis.

'How much do you want?' says Priscilla.

'Excuse me?' I say.

'You gotta be kidding me!' says Jacqui.

'Everyone has their price. What's yours?'

'What exactly are you offering?' I ask.

'I'm offering you a large amount of money for your silence.'

'And what would you like us to be silent about?' I ask.

Priscilla takes a sip from her Cristal. 'Do I have to spell it out for you?'

Today I've learnt exactly who Priscilla Hefferman is. The Carnival painting of the large spider with the woman's head, a venomous black widow, gave her away. The poisoner who killed her rich husbands and almost succeeded in killing Todd. Zach's groomer, and lover. I feel sick at the thought. I glance suspiciously at my Champagne and look furtively at Jacqui and shake my head. She nods her understanding. I had briefed her on everything, including Priscilla's modus operandi.

Priscilla raises her glass, 'Bottoms up.' She looks from Jacqui to me and back again. I look at Jacqui, then Priscilla and back to Jacqui. It's a Mexican standoff.

Jacqui sniffs her glass and wrinkles her nose. 'Something's not quite right about this,' she says, handing it back to Priscilla.

Priscilla's smile doesn't falter, but she gently pushes the glass right back. 'It's fine. Drink. I insist.'

'I would much prefer you try and tell me if it's a little sharp,' says Jacqui, handing it back.

Priscilla pushes it back and looks at me. 'Maybe you'd like to try it?'

'Drink it, Cilla!' They level their gaze at each other. It's like watching two professional poker players fight with Champagne.

Finally, Jacqui makes her move. She tosses the drink straight into Priscilla's perfectly powdered face.

Priscilla gasps, shrieks, and retaliates with hers, splashing Jacqui full in the chest.

Jacqui slaps her. A sharp, clean crack that makes me wince.

Priscilla flinches and slaps back, pearls swinging.

Jacqui's eyes flare. 'Just like old times,' she says, once more launching her palm like a missile at Priscilla's face.

It's like I'm watching in slow motion. Priscilla's glass falls to the floor, her mouth is open, the shock of Jacqui's anger reverberating on her plastic face.

And then it's my turn. I fling my drink, no hesitation, no flourish, square at Priscilla's gaping mouth.

Jacqui gasps.

Priscilla blinks and wobbles. Her skin pales. She staggers, clutches at the table, and topples like a Jenga tower.

She's still breathing, shallow and ugly, but she's down.

Silence holds the suite. My heart thumps like it's trying to break out through my ribs.

Then, a ping.

Priscilla's phone, face down on the carpet, glowing with a new message. I stoop before Jacqui can, flipping it over. The name on the screen makes my stomach knot.

Wilma: *Buttonface will be at the library tonight at 1 a.m.*

Thunder growls outside, the storm hammering the ship like it wants to finish the job for us. Over the Tannoy, the captain's velvet voice drones on: 'Passengers are to continue to remain in their cabins for the duration of the storm. Thank you for your understanding.'

'We've got murderers, poisoners, and Buttonface playing librarian,' I say. 'This is going to be one hell of a bedtime story.'

Jacqui's eyes are blazing. 'Then we'd better write the ending ourselves.'

Chapter Fifty-Four

Martha

The medics arrive with their neat cases and clipped voices. Dressed in dark trousers and white polo shirts, they bustle around Priscilla's crumpled body as if she's a fainting, society wife and not the spider at the heart of this nightmare. Jacqui watches them with her arms folded, expression flat as slate. I can't stand the air in the suite anymore.

'We have to warn the captain,' I whisper to Jacqui. 'The ship is full of serial killers. Todd's in hospital. No one's policing the ship.'

'Can we trust him?'

'I don't know. But what choice do we have?'

'We'll make it clear that the cops will be waiting when we dock. Just in case he's one of them.'

'Oh God. I hadn't thought about that.'

'That girl who works for Todd. She did call the cops, didn't she?'

'Janie . . . yeah, I think so.' I realise I don't know the answer to that. 'I hope so.'

'My phone is in my bag back at the theatre. I could go get it.'

'It's too risky. We don't know what Wilma and Priscilla have told the other killers attending the conference. We could be targets.'

'There's no question that you are. Zach and Buttonface already have you in their sights. I don't think you should go. Stay here.'

I take the pepper spray from my pocket and hold it up. 'I'm armed.'

'Just be careful.'

I follow behind the medics who are carrying a groaning Priscilla out on a stretcher. 'You really should be careful about what you drink,' I tell her, but I'm not sure she hears.

I hurry ahead of them, my stomach in knots. Priscilla is down but this is far from over. As Jacqui said, Zach is out for me, as is Buttonface. I keep my hand wrapped firmly around the pepper spray.

The bridge is on deck nine according to the ship map on the wall by the lift. The quickest and safest route would be to go upstairs, out onto the main deck, cross to the bow and enter the stairwell that services the front of the ship. I waste no time and hurry up the stairs and out onto the main deck. The rain is pelting down, prickling my face like needles. Passengers are thankfully locked away, obedient to the captain's wishes. I grip the rail, stumble forward, head down against the spray. The floor is wet and treacherous, but I make it to the entrance without falling to the bow.

I push the door closed and make the descent. The stairwell rattles with every pitch of the ship, the metal handrail slick under my palm. My legs burn by the time I reach deck nine, lungs full of recycled air and sea salt. The crew door at the top is marked AUTHORIZED PERSONNEL ONLY in bold red letters, the kind meant to scare off tourists. The latch, an electronic lock, hums faintly. But luck is with me. An officer bursts out, nearly bowling me over, too busy clutching his headset to notice me slip inside before it slams shut.

And then I'm there.

The bridge.

It's wider than I imagined, a cathedral of steel and glass. Windows stretch across the entire bow, rain lashing against them in sheets, every wave exploding in bursts of white against the black sea. Consoles glow with radar sweeps and warning lights, their hum lost under the storm's roar.

Officers dart from station to station, uniforms soaked through, voices clipped and sharp. 'Port stabiliser at sixty per cent!' 'Adjust heading two degrees to starboard!' The air is thick with urgency, coffee, and sweat.

At the centre, the captain grips the rail, legs spread for balance, eyes locked on the horizon that keeps vanishing into walls of water. He doesn't even glance at me – too busy holding a ship the size of a city steady, in the jaws of a storm.

I wonder for a moment if I don't die at the hands of the Midnight Chorus Society, will the storm finish off the ship and send me to a watery grave? I try not to think about that.

The captain turns and sees me. 'You're not supposed to be here, miss. Back to your cabin.'

'People have been killed,' I shout, but the noise from his colleagues and fury of the storm swallows my words. 'There are serial killers on this ship!'

One of his officers calls for his attention. 'Go back to your room, miss. This is just a storm. We've done this hundreds of times.' He waves me away, too busy fighting the sea to care about my claims. I would probably think the same thing if I rocked up with such an outrageous statement.

But I don't leave.

I keep to the shadows by the bulkhead, the smell of ozone

and oil thick in my nose, eyes flicking to the orange emergency locker mounted on the wall near the starboard exit. Big white stencilled letters: DISTRESS SIGNALS – FOR EMERGENCY USE ONLY.

The lock is just a latch. My pulse hammers so loud I'm sure the officers can hear it.

A man strides past me, headset crackling with voices. Another shouts about the starboard stabilisers. The storm slams us sideways, nearly throwing me off my feet. I press against the wall, pretending to steady myself like just another panicked passenger.

The captain roars, 'Hold her steady!' All eyes are on him.

Now.

I slip to the locker, fingers trembling as I ease the latch open. The metal squeaks. My stomach drops, but no one turns.

The flare gun is bright orange, heavy, sitting in its locker like it's waiting for me. I shove it under my jacket and slip outside. The door to the bridge slams behind me, cutting off the captain's shouts. I half expect a guard to come charging after me, barking about stolen property, but no one does.

The officer with the headset whirls suddenly, eyes scanning the deck. I freeze, the flare gun halfway under my jacket. His gaze skims over me and keeps moving.

When the next wave slams the ship, I stumble and slide across the deck, clutching the flare gun under my coat. No one stops me. No one even notices. My legs are shaking. My heart pounds so hard I think it might set the gun off in my hand.

But it's mine now.

In the event that Janie has not succeeded in calling the cops, this flare gun could be our only hope of alerting the authorities and surviving this nightmare.

I duck out of the deck and into the dry, warmth of the top

floor lobby. When I finally reach Jacqui's suite, I bang twice in our code. She yanks the door open, expression sharp enough to cut glass.

'What the hell is that?' she says, eyeing the bulge under my coat.

'A flare gun. Might be useful.'

She takes it from me and laughs, a short, sharp bark that sounds more like relief than humour. 'Looks like something you'd win at a county fair.'

I collapse onto the sofa, bedraggled, wet, and terrified. We have approximately one and a half hours before we gatecrash the Buttonface party. For now, we wait.

Chapter Fifty-Five

Martha

At 1 a.m., Jacqui and I move through the ship like shadows. She's still wearing her Cassie Kowalski trench coat. She said it helps keep her in character and therefore makes her less jittery about facing death. I could have told her not to come, that this was my fight, but the truth was I needed her. Maybe it was the trench coat, but the Kowalski effect has boosted my confidence too.

The corridors are empty, lights flickering, the whole vessel groaning like it might split in two. Jacqui's carrying the flare gun in a tote bag so as not to arouse suspicion should we encounter crew. Good plan.

The corridor to the library stretches ahead, long and endless, the lights flickering on and off like strobe lamps at some nightmare 1920s jazz club. My stomach's a knot of fury and fear; each step feels like walking straight into a lion's mouth, but my legs don't stop.

The library doors loom tall and heavy, their panes of glass etched with curling Art Deco engravings of sunbursts, chevrons, and stylised waves that catch the light like silver threads. In the flicker of the storm-lit corridor, the designs seem to shift and shimmer, giving the impression of a grand ocean liner trapped forever in its own glittering past.

I glance at Jacqui. 'Wait here.'

She hisses, sharp as a whip: 'Stop, Martha.'

But I'm already moving. My feet drag me across the carpet, pulse booming in my ears.

I push the doors open.

The library is a sanctuary of comfort. The irony is not lost on me. It's opulent in the way only money thinks it can fake warmth. Cosy lamps glow amber, bookshelves gleam like polished mahogany altars, the whole place humming with a fireside hush. Except beyond the massive windows the storm rages, waves slamming against the glass, spray flung like fists. Inside: leather, velvet, the illusion of safety, and on a sofa by the balcony, sitting like predatory owls are Wilma and Frank. Wilma's mouth purses like she's tasting lemons. Frank's hands rest heavy on his knees, and curl into fists.

'Where's Priscilla?' she asks.

'She's feeling unwell. Something she drank, I believe.'

Wilma visibly bristles.

'It's over,' I say, louder now, words riding the thunder outside. 'The society, your carnival, all of it. The police will be waiting when we dock.'

For a moment, silence. Then Frank pushes himself up awkwardly, knife sliding from his jacket, blade catching the lamplight. Wilma follows, her own blade smaller but no less eager.

And then, the bookshelf to my left shifts, and a panel opens, slow, theatrical, and from the shadowed passage behind, Buttonface emerges, dressed in the dark blue overall of maintenance crew. The twisted smile of the mask freezes my heart, the same smile that had watched my dad die under the Huddlestone Arch all those years ago.

He steps forward, silent, inevitable.

And I know this is it.

He looks at Wilma and Frank and then at me before turning back to Wilma. 'Where is the Spider?' His voice is deep, masculine and devoid of warmth. I wouldn't expect anything less.

'Incapacitated,' she replies, looking my way.

Buttonface turns back at me. 'Your doing?'

'You murdered my father,' I say, ignoring his question.

'I have murdered many people.'

'But why?' I ask, my voice cracking.

'Why do people do anything, Martha Hammond? They are compelled.' His voice sharpens, each word hammering: 'Why do gamblers keep betting when they know the house always wins? Why does a drunk reach for another bottle even as it's killing him? Why does a priest kneel to pray when no one's listening? Why does a moth fling itself into the flame?'

Wilma's voice cuts through Buttonface's sermon like a knife through silk. 'We have terms to discuss.'

'We do,' he replies.

She steps forward, her tone brisk, as if she's ordering tea. 'Kill the girl, and we can proceed.'

The air freezes in my lungs.

Buttonface turns his head towards her, birdlike, unnervingly calm. Then back to me. 'You received your button. Time's up, Martha.'

'Why destroy the Society?' My voice scrapes out, thin and raw. The library hums with the storm, thunder rolling against the glass. My heart pounds, but I force the words out. 'Why murder your own?'

Buttonface slides a long knife from his overalls. His voice stays calm, almost polite, which somehow makes it worse.

'My own? That's insulting.'

'You're one of them. Nothing more. Nothing less.'

'I tried to join their ranks thirteen years ago. Knocked on the gilded door, asked for a seat at the table. The Undertaker laughed at me. Said I was small, insignificant. "Reapply when you've got more kills under your belt," he told me, like I was auditioning for an advert. So I went hunting. Found a jogger in Central Park.'

My chest tightens. The air leaves my lungs. 'My. . . my dad.'

He shrugs. 'Sorry. Not sorry.'

Rage burns through me, steadier than fear.

'I went back to them,' he continues. 'They made me beg for a shot at the Killer Pitch. Terence and his pack tore me apart in front of a crowd. They thought I was nothing. Arrogant fools.'

He pulls off the mask.

'They knew me as Hilary,' he says. His lips part in a twisted grin. 'Hilary Rudolph Turner.'

My throat locks. I did not see this twist coming. 'But, you—'

'You thought me the light footed, highly strung Rudy. Another mask I wore.' His voice hardens, cutting sharper than any knife. 'I was angry. But I moved on and honed my craft. And the world noticed. My recognition and reputation grew. I realised I didn't need them. But I kept watching, always watching, and what I saw . . . was absurd.'

He steps closer, the storm light throwing his shadow long across the carpet.

'The Dentist, and his ridiculous obsession with teeth. Carving jewellery like a schoolboy with a craft kit. The Undertaker and his laughable gothic rituals, dressing up corpses like cheap theatre. The Fool, an amateur magician sawing victims in half with a blunt saw and calling it "magic". And of course . . .' he looks towards Wilma, who stiffens. 'The bed-and-breakfast darlings. The pillars of the community. The quiet killers of the weak and the vulnerable.'

Wilma's mouth tightens, but she doesn't speak.

'People in glass houses,' I say.

'Shouldn't throw knives,' says Rudy, raising the glinting blade. 'But some of us are compelled to.'

'So, they humiliated you, and you came back for revenge. A tale as old as time. Don't you think?'

'They were an elite organisation of caricatures. Clowns in bloodstained costumes controlled by the Spider. They had to go.' His voice softens then, almost tender, as if confessing to a lover. 'And I made sure they did.'

My stomach knots. He stares at me, his expression blank. I think I preferred the mask. 'And now you want to be chums with them?'

'I have purged the Society of their leadership team. I will take over.'

I laugh, despite being terrified. 'A power grab. Get you, Ivan the Terrible. So that's what this is about. Why now?' I say, my hand reaching for the pepper spray.

He watches the movement without a flicker of alarm. 'Timing, opportunity, vanity,' he says. 'The twenty-fifth anniversary. A lot of eyes. A perfect thinning of the herd. And perhaps, finally, I can quit this crappy job and be rewarded for my craft.'

'Just kill her and get it over with!' says Wilma.

Lightning crashes outside. Framed in the window, watching everything, is Zach, sopping wet in a white shirt and jeans. Gasping, I lift the spray and press the button, but Rudy has anticipated my clumsy move and grabs my arm. He raises the knife. And suddenly the temperature drops as the storm whirls into the library. I hear thudding footfalls and turn to see Zach hurtling towards us. I'm not a screamer, but at that moment I think I might. I'm frozen. Trapped. I've been foolish.

Two killers who want me dead.

It all happens in the blink of an eye. Zach charges at Rudy, and they tumble to the floor, wrestling, Zach gripping the wrist of Rudy's knife hand. Zach glances my way, his pool-blue eyes full of remorse, 'Get out of here, Martha.'

I blink, confused. He doesn't want me dead?

At that moment, the library doors fly open, and Jacqui enters pointing the flare gun like a pistol. 'Stop, or I'll shoot!' she cries, just like Cassie in *Lady Detective*.

Rudy is on top of Zach, pressing down hard. He has the advantage. I need to help him. A weapon. This is a library. There are no weapons. Only books. I scan the shelves anyway. I see a large leather-bound volume of *Crime and Punishment*. I grab it quickly and run towards Zach and Rudy. My heart sinks, when I see the blood on Zach's shirt, the knife pressed hard into this shoulder. 'Noo!' I cry and slam the heavy book on Rudy's head. He growls in fury, pulls the knife from Zach and stands. Blood drips from the blade. He lunges towards me. I notice Wilma and Frank inching closer to him, circling like hyenas, knives ready. He side-glances Frank. From his pocket, he pulls out another knife and throws it swiftly at the old man. The knife pierces Frank's throat, blood begins to pour out. 'Oh, Frank!' cries Wilma.

I grab another book from the shelf and hold it like a shield.

'Stop!' cries Jacqui, the flare gun quivering in her hands.

But Rudy is not done yet. His jaw set, he raises the knife and lunges at me once more. His mouth is twisted into something halfway between a grin and a snarl. My feet stumble back, the carpet catching me, nowhere left to run.

'Martha!' Jacqui's voice cracks like a whip. 'Get down!'

The sound is nothing like a pistol. It's a hollow, concussive thud followed by a hiss, like the ship itself exhaling. And then I see it. A ball of fire tearing through the air, trailing smoke like a comet.

It slams into Rudy's chest. For a heartbeat, he just stares at it, stunned, as if someone's punched him with the sun. Then the fire blooms.

His scream is unearthly, ripped from deep in his lungs as his clothes ignite, flames racing across his body. He thrashes, arms flailing, crashing into the bookshelves. Volumes tumble like bricks, leather and paper kindling in an instant. The library erupts. Shelves catch fire, varnish blackens, smoke curls thick and fast. The lamps flicker, then vanish in the roar of the flames. The air sears my throat, acrid and choking. Rudy staggers, still shrieking, a human torch clawing at himself, the flames leaping higher with every move. He runs to the balcony and disappears over the edge. Alarms blare overhead, a shrill, ceaseless cry. Somewhere the sprinklers sputter, cough, then die useless against the inferno.

The library becomes a furnace.

Jacqui grabs my arm, her face lit red by the flames, fierce and urgent.

'Move!'

Zach lies sprawled on the floor, blood soaking through his shirt. His eyes flutter open as I drop to my knees beside him.

'Are you OK?'

'I'll live,' he breathes, voice strained but steady.

Jacqui and I haul him up, his weight heavy between us. We drag him away from the fire's glow to the shadows by the wall. He sinks down, grimacing, one hand pressed to his shoulder.

'Why didn't you do it?' I ask. My voice sounds foreign, small but shaking. 'Why didn't you kill me? That's what she wanted, isn't it?'

He can't meet my eyes. His shoulders sag, head bowed.

'I told her what she wanted to hear,' he says quietly. 'I would never have hurt you. Please believe me.'

The alarms don't stop. They echo through every corridor, every stairwell, rattling in my skull. *Evacuate. Evacuate. Evacuate.* The crew herd passengers like sheep, lifejackets already buckled, their voices taut but steady.

By the time Zach, Jacqui and I push out onto the deck, the storm has broken. The sea is still black and restless, but the rain has thinned to a mist, and the sky cracks open just enough to show us salvation. The New York skyline glitters on the horizon, impossibly close, sharp and steady against the night. Searchlights sweep the water. Rescue boats churn white trails towards us. A helicopter beats the air overhead, its floodlight washing the deck in ghostly brilliance.

People press forward, desperate for lifeboats, their orange vests glowing in the artificial light. Crew members shout, counting, guiding, lowering the davits. The smell of smoke from the burning library clings to everything, bitter and acrid even in the fresh air. I see the medics nearby waiting for the inevitable injuries that will come from a panicking crowd. Zach is losing blood. He needs attention.

'We need help!' I shout.

They come towards us, escort him out of the crowd and tend to him.

'Go,' Zach says. 'I'll be fine.'

'But . . .'

He takes my hand and squeezes it. 'I'm sorry.'

I pause and look at him, uncertain how I feel.

Jacqui takes my arm. 'We gotta go.'

I nod and together we climb into the lifeboat, the rope creaking as it swings out over the sea. I look back at Zach. The medics are swift. He's watching me, his hair plastered to his forehead, eyes hollow. For a second, he looks like the boy I trusted, not the man who betrayed me. Beside him is Margery. She slips a blanket around his shoulders, patting him like he's her lost son. He doesn't shake her off. The jewel-encrusted funnel towers above them, flames devouring its gold sheen, stripping it of every trace of splendour.

The lifeboat dips, another wave catching us. And then the deck lifts higher, farther, Zach's figure shrinking as the ropes groan and the sea rises to claim us.

New York glitters ahead. Behind us, the *Jewel of the Atlantic* burns.

Chapter Fifty-Six

Martha

The hotel suite is the kind you only see in glossy magazines. High ceilings, velvet drapes, ridiculous little bowls of fruit no one touches. The kind of place that whispers money, comfort, and anonymity. Except this morning, there's no anonymity.

Jacqui and I are wrecks on the twin sofas, both still smelling faintly of smoke and saltwater, our lives reduced to neat police transcripts. We've spent the night being picked apart in interview rooms, every detail of the Midnight Chorus Society dragged into the light. And it isn't over. More interviews are coming, more faces staring at us over clipboards, more questions asked in cool voices that don't carry the weight of what we've been through.

On the TV, the news anchors are salivating. *Massacre at Sea. Carnival of Death*. Grainy helicopter footage of the *Jewel* burning, the skyline glinting behind it. Every channel has our story. Every headline screams our names.

Wilma Franklin, seventy-six, her lips pressed into the sort of line you see on schoolmistresses when a child has tracked mud through the hall. Frank is gone, but Wilma endures, her wrists cuffed in front of her, two NYPD officers guiding her down the police station steps. Then Priscilla Hefferman, less composed, mascara-streaked, her expensive blouse wrinkled. Even in cuffs she tries to pull her shoulders back, to perform, but it doesn't land. She looks smaller now, diminished, like the pearls around her neck weigh her down instead of lifting her up. The news ticker at the bottom of the screen reads: 'Serial Killer Society Leaders Arrested.'

The screen cuts to a montage: mugshots of the Society's dead serial killers. Ernest 'The Undertaker' Ridgewell, hollow-eyed, dressed in his funereal black suit. Bernard 'The Dentist' Koch, photographed beside one of his grotesque toothy sculptures, his workshop of trophies now bagged as evidence. Terence 'The Fool' Lamb, once a small-time magician and comedian, frozen in a grainy shot that makes him look more like a sad birthday clown than the terror he pretended to be. And finally, Reverend Garland, mentioned by the newscaster with the solemn weight of a eulogy turned inside out: dead now, but remembered for murdering the elderly members of his own flock. The news ticker scrolls their names one by one, a roll call of monsters unmasked, all allegedly killed by the notorious serial killer Buttonface, whose charred body was discovered on the deck of the *Jewel of the Atlantic*.

Jacqui raises her glass of minibar chardonnay in salute. 'Cheers to the Midnight Chorus. Silent at last.'

I can't laugh. Not yet. Watching Wilma's sharp eyes and Priscilla's crumbling poise, hearing their crimes recited to the world, I should feel satisfaction. Instead, it's just noise, the endless chatter of anchors, the press gnawing on the story like marrow.

Jacqui's phone rings. She leaves to take the call in the bedroom.

I channel-hop and stop on a live broadcast outside the police station where Jacqui and I had spent most of the night.

The anchor, a slim woman with blonde hair, tells the same story as every other news channel. I'm about to switch off when the camera cuts to the station steps. Zach emerges, pale but upright, a bandage visible beneath his shirt. Reporters close in. He pauses, glances towards the noise, then looks straight into the lens.

For a second, it feels like he sees me through the screen, through all the chaos and betrayal that hangs between us. A chill runs through me, quick and electric, chased by something I don't want to name. I still feel something for him, though I wish I didn't. What's left now is regret, maybe. Or the ghost of what might have been if neither of us had been broken. The police had asked about him. I was honest and told them he had saved my life. I didn't mention what I'd overheard, the two men he'd killed, or the deal Priscilla made with him. He's already paid his price in scars and nightmares, and I could not destroy what's left of him.

He reaches into his pocket, slips on a pair of dark glasses, and turns away. The reporters follow as he disappears into the crowd.

Jacqui returns.

I switch off the TV.

'They're done,' she says. 'All of them. And we're still here.'

Down in the street, reporters have camped like vultures. Their voices rise whenever a cab door opens, demanding answers, demanding pain. Security guards keep them at bay, but their lenses glint in the morning sun, hungry for a shot of us.

My phone buzzes against the arm of the sofa. I almost don't look. Then I see the name.

Diane.

For a moment, I can't breathe. My thumb hovers. The old anger rises, sharp, familiar. The useless blame I've carried since Dad died. But then I remember Rudy's voice, his knife, the truth.

And I realise how heavy it is, carrying this anger, how much it's cost me.

I swipe.

'Hey,' I say.

'I've just seen the news.' The line is crackling, her voice dips in and out. 'Why didn't you call me?'

'It's been a long night. The police asked a lot of questions.'

'Are you safe? Oh God, Martha, they said there were bodies . . .'

'It's over. I'm fine.'

The line crackles louder. Her words stretch and break apart. 'I was so wor – zzk – ried, I – zzk – kept calling – zzk . . .' Her voice twists into a robotic whine, like a Dalek caught in a storm. Then I hear it. Her crying. Muffled, broken, distorted by static. I press my fingers to my eyes. I'm exhausted, raw, barely holding myself together. The sound should move me, but instead, it grates. I can't do this now. Not like this. 'I have to go. I'll call you later.'

I end the call and let out a heavy sigh.

Jacqui tilts her head, studying me for a beat.

'You hung up on her?'

'The line was bad,' I say, too fast.

She doesn't look convinced. 'I heard her crying. She's hurting.'

I open my mouth, but nothing comes out.

Jacqui leans back, her voice softer now. 'You can't keep punishing her for something neither of you can fix.'

I look away, throat tight. The truth of Jacqui's words landing heavier than I want to admit.

Later that morning, a knock on the door jolts me from a restless snooze. Jacqui groans from her sofa, half-buried in pillows. 'If that's housekeeping, tell them to come back with tequila.'

The knock comes again, crisp and impatient.

Jacqui drags herself up and pulls the door open. Oliver breezes in, grinning like he just won an award for Best Agent in a Crisis. His suit is immaculate, his hair gelled, in his hand a bottle of Champagne clutched like a holy relic.

'Big news,' he announces, pacing straight into the room. 'Correction: huge news. Life-changing news.'

Jacqui drops back onto the sofa. 'Oliver, you're giving me indigestion. Just say it.'

'Book deals,' he says, swiping the screen. 'Multiple publisher auctions. Everyone wants the exclusive. Seven-figure advances. TV networks are circling – morning shows, primetime specials. Netflix already made a call. Film rights on the table. Your story's hot, ladies. You're about to be very, very wealthy.'

Jacqui barks out a laugh, dry and sharp. 'Well, I always did say I'd get my comeback. Just didn't think it would involve lifeboats and body bags.'

Oliver beams, practically vibrating with triumph. 'You're survivors, icons, household names.'

Jacqui shakes her head, incredulous. 'Unbelievable. We nearly died and now people want to binge-watch it.' She glances at me, smirking. 'Guess the critics can't accuse me of hamming this one up.' She laughs and takes the Champagne from Oliver.

Oliver is looking at me thoughtfully. 'You OK?' he mouths.

I give him a half-smile and nod as Jacqui pops the cork.

I lean back and let their voices fade into a low hum. The talk of contracts, cameras, fame – it all feels like it belongs to someone else. Not me. Not the woman who still smells smoke in her hair, who still hears Rudy screaming in the fire.

The window pulls me instead: New York glittering against the morning sky, alive, indifferent, already waiting to swallow the story whole.

Jacqui hands Oliver and me a glass of cold fizz. 'Fine. Let's do the meetings, the interviews, all of it. But right now?' She raises her glass, eyes bright but tired. 'I want bubbles, a burger, and twelve hours of sleep.'

Oliver laughs, promising it all.

I sip the Champagne and look out at the skyline. Survivors. Icons. Household names.

Me? I'm just trying to remember how to breathe.

Epilogue

Martha

Huddlestone Arch looms like something carved out of time itself, a tunnel of colossal boulders locked together without mortar, each stone scarred and weathered but unyielding. I trail my fingers along the cool surface, the rough grooves grounding me, pulling me closer to a man who's been gone too long. In my other hand, the flowers tremble.

Jacqui is beside me, her presence solid, steady. 'Are you sure you want to do this?'

'I have to.'

She nods. 'I'm here if you need me.'

I smile a thank-you and prepare to walk beneath the arch, into the shadowed tunnel.

The murmur of the crowd presses in behind us: reporters, cameras, strangers hungry for a shot of grief. I try to shut them out, to let this place speak louder than their lenses.

And then a voice cuts through. Familiar. Cracked with tears.

'Martha!'

I spin.

Mum is there, her face wet, eyes searching for me through the press. My chest caves. I don't think. I run. And when we crash together, arms wrapped tight, it's like something broken has finally been glued back together.

Her voice comes in broken gasps. 'Martha. Oh, thank God. I thought—' She sobs, messy and unrestrained. 'I thought I'd lost you too.'

The tears burn hot before I know they're there. 'I'm here. I'm OK.' My voice cracks. 'And I'm sorry. I've been . . . I've been cruel. I've blamed you for Dad, for everything, when it wasn't your fault. I just—'

She interrupts, frantic. 'No, no, don't apologise. I should have . . . I should have protected you better. I should have—'

'Mum.' My voice sharpens, steady despite the shaking in my chest. 'Stop. None of this was you. I see that now. I can't . . . I can't lose you too.'

She dips her head. Silence. Then just her weeping, softer now, closer to relief than grief. 'You called me Mum,' she says.

Jacqui joins us and catches my eye. She doesn't say a word, just gives me a nod, wry, approving, like Cassie Kowalski signing off on a case finally solved.

I make my way down to the tunnel.

The air cools as I step beneath the arch. The sound of the world fades until it's only stone, breath, and the trickle of water from the stream. This is where he fell. For years, I thought if I ever stood here, I'd feel peace, or rage, or something that made sense. But all I feel is the weight lifting. The past still hums beneath the surface, but it no longer owns me.

I crouch. The stone is cool under my palm, grounding me, shaking me. I place the flowers on the hard ground, the same place I've seen only in old photos. Cold images then, but now the moment has heat, gravity, truth.

'I love you,' I whisper. 'But I need to let you go.' The words fall into the tunnel and vanish.

Dad's voice used to haunt my dreams, that last day looping over and over. Now it's quieter, as if he's further away, watching, waiting for me to live instead of remember.

The tunnel swallows the light, then returns it in pieces, fractured and golden. I think about Rudy's cold expression, his knife, the sea, Zach. About the moments I thought I was finished. But I wasn't. Oliver once said I was a survivor. I believe him now. And I'm ready for whatever comes next.

Behind me, Jacqui coughs, pretending she isn't crying. Mum's voice drifts, softer now, carried by the wind. I let it fade. This part is mine. I close my eyes, breathe in damp stone and moss. When I stand, the light at the far end of the tunnel seems wider than before. I walk towards it.

Acknowledgements

Thank you to the incredible team at Orion, Charlotte Mursell, Clara Sokhn, Kate Moreton, Kirsty Moore and Niyati Naudiyal for your unwavering support and love for this book.

Thank you to Dan Mogford for the gorgeous cover design.

Thank you to Sam Eades for the support and laughs.

Thank you to my pal, Araminta Hall, for your help digging me out of a hole.

And finally, thank you to my best friend, husband and super-agent David Headley, who championed this story from the get-go and laughed at all the right places.

Credits

David Fennell and Orion Fiction would like to thank everyone at Orion who worked on the publication of *All Killers Aboard*.

Editor
Charlotte Mursell

Copy-editor
Francine Brody

Proofreader
Alex Davis

Editorial Management
Niyati Naudiyal
Clara Sokhn
Jane Hughes
Charlie Panayiotou
Lucy Bilton
Patrice Nelson

Audio
Paul Stark
Louise Richardson
Georgina Cutler-Ross

Contracts
Rachel Monte
Ellie Bowker
Phoebe Miller

Design
Charlotte Abrams-Simpson
Nick Shah
Deborah Francois
Helen Ewing

Photo Shoots & Image Research
Natalie Dawkins

Finance
Nick Gibson
Jasdip Nandra
Sue Baker
Tom Costello

Inventory
Jo Jacobs
Erika Andrejuskinaite

Production
Ruth Sharvell
Katie Horrocks

Marketing
Kirsty Moore

Publicity
Kate Moreton

Sales
Dave Murphy
Victoria Laws
Sammy Luton
Group Sales teams across Digital, Field, International and Non-Trade

Operations
Group Sales Operations team

Rights
Rebecca Folland
Tara Hiatt
Ruth Case-Green
Maddie Stephenson
Ruth Blakemore
Marie Matuschka

RAISING READERS
Books Build Bright Futures

Dear Reader,

We'd love your attention for one more page to tell you about the crisis in children's reading, and what we can all do.

Studies have shown that reading for fun is the **single biggest predictor of a child's future life chances** – more than family circumstance, parents' educational background or income. It improves academic results, mental health, wealth, communication skills, ambition and happiness.[1]

The number of children reading for fun is in rapid decline. Young people have a lot of competition for their time. In 2024, 1 in 10 children and young people in the UK aged 5 to 18 did not own a single book at home.[2]

Hachette works extensively with schools, libraries and literacy charities, but here are some ways we can all raise more readers:

- Reading to children for just 10 minutes a day makes a difference
- Don't give up if children aren't regular readers – there will be books for them!
- Visit bookshops and libraries to get recommendations
- Encourage them to listen to audiobooks
- Support school libraries
- Give books as gifts

There's a lot more information about how to encourage children to read on our website: **www.RaisingReaders.co.uk**

Thank you for reading.

hachette UK

[1] OECD, '21st-Century Readers: Developing Literacy Skills in a Digital World', 2021, https://www.oecd.org/en/publications/21st-century-readers_a83d84cb-en.html

[2] National Literacy Trust, 'Book Ownership in 2024', November 2024, https://literacytrust.org.uk/research-services/research-reports/book-ownership-in-2024